Acclaim for EXTREMELY LOUD AND INCREDIBLY CLOSE

"Inventive and imaginative . . . *Extremely Loud and Incredibly Close* . . . displays the gifts — Foer's energy, imagination, ambition, and humor — that made his first book, *Everything Is Illuminated*, such a success."
— Francine Prose, *People*, Critic's Choice

"Is there a novel that, in a fit of envy, Holden Caulfield, Huck Finn, Harriet the Spy, and Krazy Kat — all of the above — might long to enter? And would feel at home in? Yes! Jonathan Safran Foer's funny, tender, tragic, ingeniously imaginative *Extremely Loud and Incredibly Close* has all the kick and brio of a child's wild vision and a child's wild hurt. Foer's nine-year-old Oskar Schell, confronting the cataclysm of our time, is an American original." — Cynthia Ozick

"Jonathan Safran Foer's second novel is everything one hoped it would be — ambitious, pyrotechnic, riddling, and above all, in its portrait of orphaned Oskar, extremely moving. The powerful emotions generated feel deserved, not borrowed. An exceptional achievement."
— Salman Rushdie

"[*Extremely Loud and Incredibly Close*] contains moments of shattering emotion and stunning virtuosity that attest to Mr. Foer's myriad gifts as a writer." — Michiko Kakutani, *New York Times*

"With humor, wisdom, and exceptionally fine prose, Jonathan Safran Foer has done something both masterful and absolutely necessary: he has written the first great novel about September 11."
— *Atlanta Journal-Constitution*

"Surprisingly consoling . . . What [Foer] has given us is not just a remarkably clever work, but the 9/11 story we need, even if we didn't know it."
— Salon.com

"Funny, and extremely tender, and incredibly brave . . . Maybe this is a novel for young people. By that I mean people who think of the future as exciting . . . I read it in a daze of happiness." — *The Stranger* (Seattle)

"More memorable and psychologically acute than most of the journalism generated by September 11." — Jay McInerney, *Guardian*

EXTREMELY LOUD & INCREDIBLY CLOSE

JONATHAN SAFRAN FOER

For: Kelley 9. 2006

☮ Bran ; John

A MARINER BOOK
Houghton Mifflin Company
BOSTON   NEW YORK

FIRST MARINER BOOKS EDITION 2006

Visit our Web site: www.houghtonmifflinbooks.com.
Also visit www.theprojectmuseum.com.

Library of Congress Cataloging-in-Publication Data

Foer, Jonathan Safran, date.
Extremely loud and incredibly close / Jonathan Safran Foer.
p. cm.
ISBN 0-618-32970-6
I. Title.
PS3606.O38E97 2005
813'.6—dc22   2004065131

ISBN-13: 978-0-618-71165-9 (pbk)
ISBN-10: 0-618-71165-1 (pbk)

Book design by Anne Chalmers
Typeface: Janson Text

Printed in the United States of America
QWT 10 9 8 7 6 5 4 3 2 1

ILLUSTRATIONS

ACKNOWLEDGMENT

A major heartfelt thank you to everyone at Houghton Mifflin.
You have encouraged me to be myself, even when that self would
test a mother's patience. I feel lucky to be part of your family.

For
NICOLE,
my idea of beautiful

EXTREMELY LOUD AND INCREDIBLY CLOSE

WHAT THE?

What about a teakettle? What if the spout opened and closed when the steam came out, so it would become a mouth, and it could whistle pretty melodies, or do Shakespeare, or just crack up with me? I could invent a teakettle that reads in Dad's voice, so I could fall asleep, or maybe a set of kettles that sings the chorus of "Yellow Submarine," which is a song by the Beatles, who I love, because entomology is one of my *raisons d'être*, which is a French expression that I know. Another good thing is that I could train my anus to talk when I farted. If I wanted to be extremely hilarious, I'd train it to say, "Wasn't me!" every time I made an incredibly bad fart. And if I ever made an incredibly bad fart in the Hall of Mirrors, which is in Versailles, which is outside of Paris, which is in France, obviously, my anus would say, *"Ce n'étais pas moi!"*

What about little microphones? What if everyone swallowed them, and they played the sounds of our hearts through little speakers, which could be in the pouches of our overalls? When you skateboarded down the street at night you could hear everyone's heartbeat, and they could hear yours, sort of like sonar. One weird thing is, I wonder if everyone's hearts would start to beat at the same time, like how women who live together have their menstrual periods at the same time, which I know about, but don't really want to know about. That would be so weird, except that the place in the hospital where babies are born would sound like a crystal chandelier in a houseboat, because the babies wouldn't have had time to match up their heartbeats yet. And at the finish line at the end of the New York City Marathon it would sound like war.

And also, there are so many times when you need to make a quick escape, but humans don't have their own wings, or not yet, anyway, so what about a birdseed shirt?

Anyway.

My first jujitsu class was three and a half months ago. Self-defense was something that I was extremely curious about, for obvious reasons, and Mom thought it would be good for me to have a physical activity besides tambourining, so my first jujitsu class was three and a half months ago. There were fourteen kids in the class, and we all had on neat white robes. We practiced bowing, and then we were all sitting down Native American style, and then Sensei Mark asked me to go over to him. "Kick my privates," he told me. That made me feel self-conscious. *"Excusez-moi?"* I told him. He spread his legs and told me, "I want you to kick my privates as hard as you can." He put his hands at his sides, and took a breath in, and closed his eyes, and that's how I knew that actually he meant business. "Jose," I told him, and inside I was thinking, *What the?* He told me, "Go on, guy. Destroy my privates." "Destroy your privates?" With his eyes still closed he cracked up a lot and said, "You couldn't destroy my privates if you tried. That's what's going on here. This is a demonstration of the well-trained body's ability to absorb a direct blow. Now destroy my privates." I told him, "I'm a pacifist," and since most people my age don't know what that means, I turned around and told the others, "I don't think it's right to destroy people's privates. Ever." Sensei Mark said, "Can I ask you something?" I turned back around and told him, "'Can I ask you something?' *is* asking me something." He said, "Do you have dreams of becoming a jujitsu master?" "No," I told him, even though I don't have dreams of running the family jewelry business anymore. He said, "Do you want to know how a jujitsu student becomes a jujitsu master?" "I want to know everything," I told him, but that isn't true anymore either. He told me, "A jujitsu student becomes a jujitsu master by destroying his master's privates." I told him, "That's fascinating." My last jujitsu class was three and a half months ago.

I desperately wish I had my tambourine with me now, because even after everything I'm still wearing heavy boots, and sometimes it helps to play a good beat. My most impressive song that I can play on my tambourine is "The Flight of the Bumblebee," by Nicolai Rimsky-Korsakov, which is also the ring tone I downloaded for the cell phone I got after Dad died. It's pretty amazing that I can play "The Flight of the Bumblebee," because you have to hit incredibly fast in parts, and that's extremely hard for me, because I don't really have wrists yet. Ron offered to buy me a five-piece drum set. Money can't buy me love, obviously, but I asked if it would have Zildjian cymbals. He said, "Whatever you want," and then he took my yo-yo off my desk and started to walk the dog with it. I know he just wanted to be friendly, but it made me incredibly angry. "Yo-yo *moi!*" I told him, grabbing it back. What I really wanted to tell him was "You're not my dad, and you never will be."

Isn't it so weird how the number of dead people is increasing even though the earth stays the same size, so that one day there isn't going to be room to bury anyone anymore? For my ninth birthday last year, Grandma gave me a subscription to *National Geographic*, which she calls "the *National Geographic*." She also gave me a white blazer, because I only wear white clothes, and it's too big to wear so it will last me a long time. She also gave me Grandpa's camera, which I loved for two reasons. I asked why he didn't take it with him when he left her. She said, "Maybe he wanted you to have it." I said, "But I was negative-thirty years old." She said, "Still." Anyway, the fascinating thing was that I read in *National Geographic* that there are more people alive now than have died in all of human history. In other words, if everyone wanted to play Hamlet at once, they couldn't, because there aren't enough skulls!

So what about skyscrapers for dead people that were built down? They could be underneath the skyscrapers for living people that are built up. You could bury people one hundred floors down, and a whole dead world could be underneath the living one. Sometimes I think it would be weird if there were a skyscraper that moved up and down while its elevator stayed in place. So if you wanted to go to the ninety-fifth floor, you'd just press the 95 button and the ninety-fifth floor would come to you. Also, that could be extremely useful, because if you're on the ninety-fifth floor, and a plane hits below you, the building could take you to the ground, and everyone could be safe, even if you left your birdseed shirt at home that day.

I've only been in a limousine twice ever. The first time was terrible, even though the limousine was wonderful. I'm not allowed to watch TV at home, and I'm not allowed to watch TV in limousines either, but it was still neat that there was a TV there. I asked if we could go by school, so Toothpaste and The Minch could see me in a limousine. Mom said that school wasn't on the way, and we couldn't be late to the cemetery. "Why not?" I asked, which I actually thought was a good question, because if you think about it, why not? Even though I'm not anymore, I used to be an atheist, which means I didn't believe in things that couldn't be observed. I believed that once you're dead, you're dead forever, and you don't feel anything, and you don't even dream. It's not that I believe in things that can't be observed now, because I don't. It's that I believe that things are extremely complicated. And anyway, it's not like we were *actually* burying him, anyway.

Even though I was trying hard for it not to, it was annoying me how Grandma kept touching me, so I climbed into the front seat and poked the driver's shoulder until he gave me some attention. "What. Is. Your. Designation." I asked in Stephen Hawking voice. "Say what?" "He wants to know your name," Grandma said from the back seat. He handed me his card.

GERALD THOMPSON
Sunshine Limousine

serving the five boroughs
(212) 570-7249

I handed him my card and told him, "Greetings. Gerald. I. Am. Oskar." He asked me why I was talking like that. I told him, "Oskar's

CPU is a neural-net processor. A learning computer. The more contact he has with humans, the more he learns." Gerald said, "O" and then he said "K." I couldn't tell if he liked me or not, so I told him, "Your sunglasses are one hundred dollars." He said, "One seventy-five." "Do you know a lot of curse words?" "I know a couple." "I'm not allowed to use curse words." "Bummer." "What's 'bummer'?" "It's a bad thing." "Do you know 'shit'?" "That's a curse, isn't it?" "Not if you say 'shiitake.'" "Guess not." "Succotash my Balzac, dipshiitake." Gerald shook his head and cracked up a little, but not in the bad way, which is at me. "I can't even say 'hair pie,'" I told him, "unless I'm talking about an actual pie made out of rabbits. Cool driving gloves." "Thanks." And then I thought of something, so I said it. "*Actually*, if limousines were *extremely* long, they wouldn't *need* drivers. You could just get in the back seat, walk through the limousine, and then get out of the front seat, which would be where you wanted to go. So in this situation, the front seat would be at the cemetery." "And I would be watching the game right now." I patted his shoulder and told him, "When you look up 'hilarious' in the dictionary, there's a picture of you."

In the back seat, Mom was holding something in her purse. I could tell that she was squeezing it, because I could see her arm muscles. Grandma was knitting white mittens, so I knew they were for me, even though it wasn't cold out. I wanted to ask Mom what she was squeezing and why she had to keep it hidden. I remember thinking that even if I were suffering hypothermia, I would never, *ever* put on those mittens.

"Now that I'm thinking about it," I told Gerald, "they could make an *incredibly* long limousine that had its back seat at your mom's VJ and its front seat at your mausoleum, and it would be as long as your life." Gerald said, "Yeah, but if everyone lived like that, no one would ever meet anyone, right?" I said, "So?"

Mom squeezed, and Grandma knitted, and I told Gerald, "I kicked a French chicken in the stomach once," because I wanted to make him crack up, because if I could make him crack up, my boots could be a little lighter. He didn't say anything, probably because he didn't hear me, so I said, "I *said* I kicked a French chicken in the stomach once."

"Huh?" "It said, '*Oeuf*.'" "What is that?" "It's a joke. Do you want to hear another, or have you already had *un oeuf*?" He looked at Grandma in the mirror and said, "What's he saying?" She said, "His grandfather loved animals more than he loved people." I said, "Get it? *Oeuf*?"

I crawled back, because it's dangerous to drive and talk at the same time, especially on the highway, which is what we were on. Grandma started touching me again, which was annoying, even though I didn't want it to be. Mom said, "Honey," and I said, "*Oui*," and she said, "Did you give a copy of our apartment key to the mailman?" I thought it was so weird that she would mention that then, because it didn't have to do with anything, but I think she was looking for something to talk about that wasn't the obvious thing. I said, "The mail*person* is a mail*woman*." She nodded, but not exactly at me, and she asked if I'd given the mailwoman a key. I nodded yes, because I never used to lie to her before everything happened. I didn't have a reason to. "Why did you do that?" she asked. So I told her, "Stan—" And she said, "Who?" And I said, "Stan the doorman. Sometimes he runs around the corner for coffee, and I want to be sure all of my packages get to me, so I thought, if Alicia—" "Who?" "The mailwoman. If she had a key, she could leave things inside our door." "But you can't give a key to a stranger." "Fortunately Alicia isn't a stranger." "We have lots of valuable things in our apartment." "I know. We have really great things." "Sometimes people who seem good end up being not as good as you might have hoped, you know? What if she had stolen your things?" "She wouldn't." "But what if?" "But she wouldn't." "Well, did she give you a key to her apartment?" She was obviously mad at me, but I didn't know why. I hadn't done anything wrong. Or if I had, I didn't know what it was. And I definitely didn't mean to do it.

I moved over to Grandma's side of the limousine and told Mom, "Why would I need a key to her apartment?" She could tell that I was zipping up the sleeping bag of myself, and I could tell that she didn't really love me. I knew the truth, which was that if she could have chosen, it would have been my funeral we were driving to. I looked up at the limousine's sunroof, and I imagined the world before there were ceilings, which made me wonder: Does a cave have no ceiling, or is a cave all ceiling? "Maybe you could check with me next time, OK?" "Don't be mad at me," I said, and I reached over Grandma and opened and closed the door's lock a couple of times. "I'm not mad at you," she said. "Not even a little?" "No." "Do you still love me?" It didn't seem like the perfect time to mention that I had already made copies of the key for the deliverer from Pizza Hut, and the UPS person, and also the nice guys from Greenpeace, so they could leave me articles on manatees and other animals that are going extinct when Stan is getting coffee. "I've never loved you more."

"Mom?" "Yes?" "I have a question." "OK." "What are you squeezing in your purse?" She pulled out her hand and opened it, and it was empty. "Just squeezing," she said.

Even though it was an incredibly sad day, she looked so, so beautiful. I kept trying to figure out a way to tell her that, but all of the ways I thought of were weird and wrong. She was wearing the bracelet that I made for her, and that made me feel like one hundred dollars. I love making jewelry for her, because it makes her happy, and making her happy is another one of my *raisons d'être*.

It isn't anymore, but for a really long time it was my dream to take over the family jewelry business. Dad constantly used to tell me I was too smart for retail. That never made sense to me, because he was smarter than me, so if I was too smart for retail, then he *really* must have been too smart for retail. I told him that. "First of all," he told me, "I'm not smarter than you, I'm more knowledgeable than you, and that's only because I'm older than you. Parents are always more knowledgeable than their children, and children are always smarter than their parents." "Unless the child is a mental retard," I told him. He didn't have anything to say about that. "You said 'first of all,' so what's second of all?" "Second of all, if I'm so smart, then why am I in retail?" "That's true," I said. And then I thought of something: "But wait a minute, it won't be the family jewelry business if no one in the family is running it." He told me, "Sure it will. It'll just be someone else's family." I asked, "Well, what about our family? Will we open a new business?" He said, "We'll open something." I thought about that my second time in a limousine, when the renter and I were on our way to dig up Dad's empty coffin.

A great game that Dad and I would sometimes play on Sundays was Reconnaissance Expedition. Sometimes the Reconnaissance Expeditions were extremely simple, like when he told me to bring back something from every decade in the twentieth century—I was clever and brought back a rock—and sometimes they were incredibly complicated and would go on for a couple of weeks. For the last one we ever did, which never finished, he gave me a map of Central Park. I said, "And?" And he said, "And what?" I said, "What are the clues?" He said, "Who said there had to be clues?" "There are always clues." "That doesn't, in itself, suggest anything." "Not a single clue?" He said, "Unless no clues is a clue." "Is no clues a clue?" He shrugged his shoulders, like he had no idea what I was talking about. I loved that.

I spent all day walking around the park, looking for something that might tell me something, but the problem was that I didn't know what I was looking for. I went up to people and asked if they knew anything that I should know, because sometimes Dad would design Reconnaissance Expeditions so I would have to talk to people. But everyone I went up to was just like, *What the?* I looked for clues around the reservoir. I read every poster on every lamppost and tree. I inspected the descriptions of the animals at the zoo. I even made kite-fliers reel in their kites so I could examine them, although I knew it was improbable. But that's how tricky Dad could be. There was nothing, which would have been unfortunate, unless nothing was a clue. Was nothing a clue?

That night we ordered General Tso's Gluten for dinner and I noticed that Dad was using a fork, even though he was perfect with chopsticks. "Wait a minute!" I said, and stood up. I pointed at his fork. "Is that fork a clue?" He shrugged his shoulders, which to me meant it was a major clue. I thought: *Fork, fork.* I ran to my laboratory and got my metal detector out of its box in the closet. Because I'm not allowed to be in the park alone at night, Grandma went with me. I started at the Eighty-sixth Street entrance and walked in extremely precise lines, like I was one of the Mexican guys who mow the lawn, so I wouldn't miss anything. I knew the insects were loud because it was summer, but I didn't hear them because my earphones covered my ears. It was just me and the metal underground.

Every time the beeps would get close together, I'd tell Grandma to shine the flashlight on the spot. Then I'd put on my white gloves, take the hand shovel from my kit, and dig extremely gently. When I saw something, I used a paintbrush to get rid of the dirt, just like a real archeologist. Even though I only searched a small area of the park that night, I dug up a quarter, and a handful of paper clips, and what I thought was the chain from a lamp that you pull to make the light go on, and a refrigerator magnet for sushi, which I know about, but wish I didn't. I put all of the evidence in a bag and marked on a map where I found it.

When I got home, I examined the evidence in my laboratory under my microscope, one piece at a time: a bent spoon, some screws, a pair of rusty scissors, a toy car, a pen, a key ring, broken glasses for someone with incredibly bad eyes . . .

I brought them to Dad, who was reading the *New York Times* at the kitchen table, marking the mistakes with his red pen. "Here's what I've found," I said, pushing my pussy off the table with the tray of evidence. Dad looked at it and nodded. I asked, "So?" He shrugged his shoulders like he had no idea what I was talking about, and he went back to the paper. "Can't you even tell me if I'm on the right track?" Buckminster purred, and Dad shrugged his shoulders again. "But if you don't tell me anything, how can I ever be right?" He circled something in an article and said, "Another way of looking at it would be, how could you ever be wrong?"

He got up to get a drink of water, and I examined what he'd circled on the page, because that's how tricky he could be. It was in an article about the girl who had disappeared, and how everyone thought the congressman who was humping her had killed her. A few months later they found her body in Rock Creek Park, which is in Washington, D.C., but by then everything was different, and no one cared anymore, except for her parents.

statement, read to the hundreds of
gathered press from a makeshift media center off the back of the family home, Levy's father adamantly restated his confidence that his daughter would be found. "We will not stop looking until we are given a definitive reason to stop looking, namely, Chandra's return." During the brief question and answer period that followed, a reporter from El Pais asked Mr. Levy if by "return" he meant "safe return." Overcome with emotion, Mr. Levy was unable to speak, and his lawyer took the microphone. "We continue to hope and pray for Chandra's safety, and will do everything within

It wasn't a mistake! It was a message to me!

I went back to the park every night for the next three nights. I dug up a hair clip, and a roll of pennies, and a thumbtack, and a coat hanger, and a 9V battery, and a Swiss Army knife, and a tiny picture frame, and a tag for a dog named Turbo, and a square of aluminum foil, and a ring, and a razor, and an extremely old pocket watch that was stopped at 5:37, although I didn't know if it was A.M. or P.M. But I still couldn't figure out what it all meant. The more I found, the less I understood.

I spread the map out on the dining room table, and I held down the corners with cans of V8. The dots from where I'd found things looked like the stars in the universe. I connected them, like an astrologer, and if you squinted your eyes like a Chinese person, it kind of looked like the word "fragile." Fragile. What was fragile? Was Central Park fragile? Was nature fragile? Were the things I found fragile? A thumbtack isn't fragile. Is a bent spoon fragile? I erased, and connected the dots in a different way, to make "door." Fragile? Door? Then I thought of *porte*, which is French for door, obviously. I erased and connected the dots to make "*porte*." I had the revelation that I could connect the dots to make "cyborg," and "platypus," and "boobs," and even "Oskar," if you were extremely Chinese. I could connect them to make almost anything I wanted, which meant I wasn't getting closer to anything. And now I'll never know what I was supposed to find. And that's another reason I can't sleep.

Anyway.

I'm not allowed to watch TV, although I am allowed to rent documentaries that are approved for me, and I can read anything I want. My favorite book is *A Brief History of Time*, even though I haven't actually finished it, because the math is incredibly hard and Mom isn't good at helping me. One of my favorite parts is the beginning of the first chapter, where Stephen Hawking tells about a famous scientist who was giving a lecture about how the earth orbits the sun, and the sun orbits the solar system, and whatever. Then a woman in the back of the room raised her hand and said, "What you have told us is rubbish. The world is really a flat plate supported on the back of a giant tortoise." So the scientist asked her what the tortoise was standing on. And she said, "But it's turtles all the way down!"

I love that story, because it shows how ignorant people can be. And also because I love tortoises.

A few weeks after the worst day, I started writing lots of letters. I don't know why, but it was one of the only things that made my boots lighter. One weird thing is that instead of using normal stamps, I used stamps from my collection, including valuable ones, which sometimes made me wonder if what I was really doing was trying to get rid of things. The first letter I wrote was to Stephen Hawking. I used a stamp of Alexander Graham Bell.

> *Dear Stephen Hawking,*
> *Can I please be your protégé?*
> *Thanks,*
> *Oskar Schell*

I thought he wasn't going to respond, because he was such an amazing person and I was so normal. But then one day I came home from school and Stan handed me an envelope and said, "You've got mail!" in the AOL voice I taught him. I ran up the 105 stairs to our apartment, and ran to my laboratory, and went into my closet, and turned on my flashlight, and opened it. The letter inside was typed, obviously, because Stephen Hawking can't use his hands, because he has amyotrophic lateral sclerosis, which I know about, unfortunately.

*Thank you for your letter. Because of the large
volume of mail I receive, I am unable to write
personal responses. Nevertheless, know that I read
and save every letter, with the hope of one day
being able to give each the proper response it
deserves. Until that day,*
> *Most sincerely,*
> *Stephen Hawking*

I called Mom's cell. "Oskar?" "You picked up before it rang." "Is everything OK?" "I'm gonna need a laminator." "A laminator?" "There's something incredibly wonderful that I want to preserve."

Dad always used to tuck me in, and he'd tell the greatest stories, and we'd read the *New York Times* together, and sometimes he'd whistle "I Am the Walrus," because that was his favorite song, even though he couldn't explain what it meant, which frustrated me. One thing that was so great was how he could find a mistake in every single article we looked at. Sometimes they were grammar mistakes, sometimes they were mistakes with geography or facts, and sometimes the article just didn't tell the whole story. I loved having a dad who was smarter than the *New York Times*, and I loved how my cheek could feel the hairs on his chest through his T-shirt, and how he always smelled like shaving, even at the end of the day. Being with him made my brain quiet. I didn't have to invent a thing.

When Dad was tucking me in that night, the night before the worst day, I asked if the world was a flat plate supported on the back of a giant tortoise. "Excuse me?" "It's just that why does the earth stay in place instead of falling through the universe?" "Is this Oskar I'm tucking in? Has an alien stolen his brain for experimentation?" I said, "We don't believe in aliens." He said, "The earth *does* fall through the universe. You know that, buddy. It's constantly falling toward the sun. That's what it means to orbit." So I said, "Obviously, but why is there gravity?" He said, "What do you mean why is there gravity?" "What's the reason?" "Who said there had to be a reason?" "No one did, exactly." "My question was rhetorical." "What's that mean?" "It means I wasn't asking it for an answer, but to make a point." "What point?"

"That there doesn't have to be a reason." "But if there isn't a reason, then why does the universe exist at all?" "Because of sympathetic conditions." "So then why am I your son?" "Because Mom and I made love, and one of my sperm fertilized one of her eggs." "Excuse me while I regurgitate." "Don't act your age." "Well, what I don't get is why do we exist? I don't mean how, but why." I watched the fireflies of his thoughts orbit his head. He said, "We exist because we exist." "*What the?*" "We could imagine all sorts of universes unlike this one, but this is the one that happened."

I understood what he meant, and I didn't disagree with him, but I didn't agree with him either. Just because you're an atheist, that doesn't mean you wouldn't love for things to have reasons for why they are.

I turned on my shortwave radio, and with Dad's help I was able to pick up someone speaking Greek, which was nice. We couldn't understand what he was saying, but we lay there, looking at the glow-in-the-dark constellations on my ceiling, and listened for a while. "Your grandfather spoke Greek," he said. "You mean he *speaks* Greek," I said. "That's right. He just doesn't speak it here." "Maybe that's him we're listening to." The front page was spread over us like a blanket. There was a picture of a tennis player on his back, who I guess was the winner, but I couldn't really tell if he was happy or sad.

"Dad?" "Yeah?" "Could you tell me a story?" "Sure." "A good one?" "As opposed to all the boring ones I tell." "Right." I tucked my body incredibly close into his, so my nose pushed into his armpit. "And you won't interrupt me?" "I'll try not to." "Because it makes it hard to tell a story." "And it's annoying." "And it's annoying."

The moment before he started was my favorite moment.

"Once upon a time, New York City had a sixth borough." "What's a borough?" "That's what I call an interruption." "I know, but the story won't make any sense to me if I don't know what a borough is." "It's like a neighborhood. Or a collection of neighborhoods." "So if there was once a sixth borough, then what are the five boroughs?" "Manhattan, obviously, Brooklyn, Queens, Staten Island, and the Bronx." "Have I ever been to any of the other boroughs?" "Here we go." "I just want to know." "We went to the Bronx Zoo once, a few years ago. Remember that?" "No." "And we've been to Brooklyn to see the roses at the Botanic Garden." "Have I been to Queens?" "I don't think so." "Have I been to Staten Island?" "No." "Was there *really* a sixth borough?" "I've been trying to tell you." "No more interruptions. I promise."

When the story finished, we turned the radio back on and found someone speaking French. That was especially nice, because it reminded me of the vacation we just came back from, which I wish never ended. After a while, Dad asked me if I was awake. I told him no, because I knew that he didn't like to leave until I had fallen asleep, and I didn't want him to be tired for work in the morning. He kissed my forehead and said good night, and then he was at the door.

"Dad?" "Yeah, buddy?" "Nothing."

The next time I heard his voice was when I came home from school the next day. We were let out early, because of what happened. I wasn't even a little bit panicky, because both Mom and Dad worked in midtown, and Grandma didn't work, obviously, so everyone I loved was safe.

I know that it was 10:22 when I got home, because I look at my watch a lot. The apartment was so empty and so quiet. As I walked to the kitchen, I invented a lever that could be on the front door, which would trigger a huge spoked wheel in the living room to turn against metal teeth that would hang down from the ceiling, so that it would play beautiful music, like maybe "Fixing a Hole" or "I Want to Tell You," and the apartment would be one huge music box.

After I petted Buckminster for a few seconds, to show him I loved him, I checked the phone messages. I didn't have a cell phone yet, and when we were leaving school, Toothpaste told me he'd call to let me know whether I was going to watch him attempt skateboarding tricks in the park, or if we were going to go look at *Playboy* magazines in the drugstore with the aisles where no one can see what you're looking at, which I didn't feel like doing, but still.

Message one. Tuesday, 8:52 A.M. *Is anybody there? Hello? It's Dad. If you're there, pick up. I just tried the office, but no one was picking up. Listen, something's happened. I'm OK. They're telling us to stay where we*

are and wait for the firemen. I'm sure it's fine. I'll give you another call
when I have a better idea of what's going on. Just wanted to let you know
that I'm OK, and not to worry. I'll call again soon.

There were four more messages from him: one at 9:12, one at 9:31, one at 9:46, and one at 10:04. I listened to them, and listened to them again, and then before I had time to figure out what to do, or even what to think or feel, the phone started ringing.

It was 10:26:47.

I looked at the caller ID and saw that it was him.

WHY I'M NOT WHERE YOU ARE
5/21/63

To my unborn child: I haven't always been silent, I used to talk and talk and talk and talk, I couldn't keep my mouth shut, the silence overtook me like a cancer, it was one of my first meals in America, I tried to tell the waiter, "The way you just handed me that knife, that reminds me of—" but I couldn't finish the sentence, her name wouldn't come, I tried again, it wouldn't come, she was locked inside me, how strange, I thought, how frustrating, how pathetic, how sad, I took a pen from my pocket and wrote "Anna" on my napkin, it happened again two days later, and then again the following day, she was the only thing I wanted to talk about, it kept happening, when I didn't have a pen, I'd write "Anna" in the air—backward and right to left—so that the person I was speaking with could see, and when I was on the phone I'd dial the numbers—2, 6, 6, 2—so that the person could hear what I couldn't, myself, say. "And" was the next word I lost, probably because it was so close to her name, what a simple word to say, what a profound word to lose, I had to say "ampersand," which sounded ridiculous, but there it is, "I'd like a coffee ampersand something sweet," nobody would choose to be like that. "Want" was a word I lost early on, which is not to say that I stopped wanting things—I wanted things more—I just stopped being able to express the want, so instead I said "desire," "I desire two rolls," I would tell the baker, but that wasn't quite right, the meaning of my thoughts started to float away from me, like leaves that fall from a tree into a river, I was the tree, the world was the river. I lost "come" one afternoon with the dogs in the park, I lost "fine" as the barber turned me toward the mirror, I lost "shame"—the verb and the noun in the same moment; it was a shame. I lost "carry," I lost the things I carried—"daybook," "pencil," "pocket change," "wallet"—I even lost "loss." After a time, I had only a handful of words left, if someone did something nice for me, I would tell him, "The thing that comes before 'you're welcome,'" if I was hungry, I'd point at my stomach and say, "I am the opposite of full," I'd lost "yes," but I still had "no," so if someone asked me, "Are you Thomas?" I would answer, "Not no," but then I lost "no," I went to a tattoo parlor and had YES written onto the palm of my left hand, and NO onto my right palm, what can I say, it hasn't made life wonderful, it's made life possible, when I rub my hands against each other in the middle of winter I am warming myself with the friction of YES and NO, when I clap my hands I am showing my appreciation through the uniting and parting of YES and NO, I signify "book" by peeling open my clapped hands, every book, for me, is the balance of YES and NO, even this one, my last one, especially this one. Does it break my heart, of course, every moment of every day, into more pieces than my heart was made of, I never thought of myself as quiet, much less silent, I never thought about things at all, everything changed, the distance that wedged itself between me and my happiness wasn't the world, it wasn't the bombs and burning buildings, it was me, my thinking, the cancer of never letting go, is ignorance bliss, I don't know, but it's so painful to think, and tell me, what did thinking ever do for me, to what great place did thinking ever bring me? I think and think and think, I've thought myself out of happiness one million times, but never once into it. "I" was the last word I was able to speak aloud, which is a terrible thing, but there it is, I would walk around the neighborhood saying, "I I I I." "You want a cup of coffee, Thomas?" "I." "And maybe something sweet?" "I." "How about this weather?" "I." "You look upset. Is anything wrong?" I wanted to say, "Of course," I wanted to ask, "Is anything right?" I wanted to pull the thread, unravel the scarf of my silence and start again from the beginning, but instead I said, "I." I know I'm not alone in this disease, you hear the old people in the street and some of them are moaning, "Ay yay yay," but some of them are clinging to their last word, "I," they're saying, because they're desperate, it's not a complaint it's a prayer, and then I lost "I" and my silence was complete. I started carrying blank books like this one around, which I would fill with all the things I couldn't say, that's how it started, if I wanted two rolls of bread from the baker, I would write "I want two rolls" on the next blank page and show it to him, and if I needed help from someone, I'd write "Help," and if something made me want to laugh, I'd write "Ha ha ha!" and instead of singing in the shower I would write out the lyrics of my favorite songs, the ink would turn the water blue or red or green, and the music would run down my legs, at the end of each day I would take the book to bed with me and read through the pages of my life:

I want two rolls

And I wouldn't say no to something sweet

I'm sorry, this is the smallest I've got

Start spreading the news . . .

The regular, please

Thank you, but I'm about to burst

I'm not sure, but it's late

Help

Ha ha ha!

It wasn't unusual for me to run out of blank pages before the end of the day, so should I have to say something to someone on the street or in the bakery or at the bus stop, the best I could do was flip back through the daybook and find the most fitting page to recycle, if someone asked me, "How are you feeling?" it might be that my best response was to point at, "The regular, please," or perhaps, "And I wouldn't say no to something sweet," when my only friend, Mr. Richter, suggested, "What if you tried to make a sculpture again? What's the worst thing that could happen?" I shuffled halfway into the filled book: "I'm not sure, but it's late." I went through hundreds of books, thousands of them, they were all over the apartment, I used them as doorstops and paper-weights, I stacked them if I needed to reach something, I slid them under the legs of wobbly tables, I used them as trivets and coasters, to line the birdcages and to swat insects from whom I begged forgiveness, I never thought of my books as being special, only necessary, I might rip out a page — "I'm sorry, this is the smallest I've got" — to wipe up some mess, or empty a whole day to pack up the emergency light bulbs, I re-member spending an afternoon with Mr. Richter in the Central Park Zoo, I went weighted down with food for the animals, only someone who'd never been an animal would put up a sign saying not to feed them, Mr. Richter told a joke, I tossed hamburger to the lions, he rat-tled the cages with his laughter, the animals went to the corners, we laughed and laughed, together and separately, out loud and silently, we were determined to ignore whatever needed to be ignored, to build a new world from nothing if nothing in our world could be salvaged, it was one of the best days of my life, a day during which I lived my life and didn't think about my life at all. Later that year, when snow started to hide the front steps, when morning became evening as I sat on the sofa, buried under everything I'd lost, I made a fire and used my laugh-ter for kindling: "Ha ha ha!" "Ha ha ha!" "Ha ha ha!" "Ha ha ha!" I was already out of words when I met your mother, that may have been what made our marriage possible, she never had to know me. We met at the Columbian Bakery on Broadway, we'd both come to New York lonely, broken and confused, I was sitting in the corner stirring cream into cof-fee, around and around like a little solar system, the place was half

empty but she slid right up next to me, "You've lost everything," she said, as if we were sharing a secret, "I can see." If I'd been someone else in a different world I'd've done something different, but I was myself, and the world was the world, so I was silent, "It's OK," she whispered, her mouth too close to my ear, "Me too. You can probably see it from across a room. It's not like being Italian. We stick out like sore thumbs. Look at how they look. Maybe they don't know that we've lost everything, but they know something's off." She was the tree and also the river flowing away from the tree, "There are worse things," she said, "worse than being like us. Look, at least we're alive," I could see that she wanted those last words back, but the current was too strong, "And the weather is one hundred dollars, also, don't let me forget to mention," I stirred my coffee. "But I hear it's supposed to get crummy tonight. Or that's what the man on the radio said, anyway," I shrugged, I didn't know what "crummy" meant, "I was gonna go buy some tuna fish at the A&P. I clipped some coupons from the Post this morning. They're five cans for the price of three. What a deal! I don't even like tuna fish. It gives me stomachaches, to be frank. But you can't beat that price," she was trying to make me laugh, but I shrugged my shoulders and stirred my coffee, "I don't know anymore," she said. "The weather is one hundred dollars, and the man on the radio says it's gonna get crummy tonight, so maybe I should go to the park instead, even if I burn easily. And anyway, it's not like I'm gonna eat the tuna fish tonight, right? Or ever, if I'm being frank. It gives me stomachaches, to be perfectly frank. So there's no rush in that department. But the weather, now that won't stick around. Or at least it never has. And I should tell you also that my doctor says getting out is good for me. My eyes are crummy, and he says I don't get out nearly enough, and that if I got out a little more, if I were a little less afraid . . ." She was extending a hand that I didn't know how to take, so I broke its fingers with my silence, she said, "You don't want to talk to me, do you?" I took my daybook out of my knapsack and found the next blank page, the second to last. "I don't speak," I wrote. "I'm sorry." She looked at the piece of paper, then at me, then back at the piece of paper, she covered her eyes with her hands and cried, tears seeped between her fingers and collected in the little webs, she cried and cried and cried, there weren't any napkins nearby, so I ripped the page from the book—"I don't speak. I'm sorry."—and used it to dry her cheeks, my explanation and apology ran down her face like mascara, she took my pen from me and wrote on the next blank page of my daybook, the final one:

Please marry me

I flipped back and pointed at, "Ha ha ha!" She flipped forward and pointed at, "Please marry me." I flipped back and pointed at, "I'm sorry, this is the smallest I've got." She flipped forward and pointed at, "Please marry me." I flipped back and pointed at, "I'm not sure, but it's late." She flipped forward and pointed at, "Please marry me," and this time put her finger on "Please," as if to hold down the page and end the conversation, or as if she were trying to push through the word and into what she really wanted to say. I thought about life, about my life, the embarrassments, the little coincidences, the shadows of alarm clocks on bedside tables. I thought about my small victories and everything I'd seen destroyed, I'd swum through mink coats on my parents' bed while they hosted downstairs, I'd lost the only person I could have spent my only life with, I'd left behind a thousand tons of marble, I could have released sculptures, I could have released myself from the marble of myself. I'd experienced joy, but not nearly enough, could there be enough? The end of suffering does not justify the suffering, and so there is no end to suffering, what a mess I am, I thought, what a fool, how foolish and narrow, how worthless, how pinched and pathetic, how helpless. None of my pets know their own names, what kind of person am I? I lifted her finger like a record needle and flipped back, one page at a time:

Help

GOOGOLPLEX

As for the bracelet Mom wore to the funeral, what I did was I converted Dad's last voice message into Morse code, and I used sky-blue beads for silence, maroon beads for breaks between letters, violet beads for breaks between words, and long and short pieces of string between the beads for long and short beeps, which are actually called blips, I think, or something. Dad would have known. It took me nine hours to make, and I had thought about giving it to Sonny, the homeless person who I sometimes see standing outside the Alliance Française, because he puts me in heavy boots, or maybe to Lindy, the neat old woman who volunteers to give tours at the Museum of Natural History, so I could be something special to her, or even just to someone in a wheelchair. But instead I gave it to Mom. She said it was the best gift she'd ever received. I asked her if it was better than the Edible Tsunami, from when I was interested in edible meteorological events. She said, "Different." I asked her if she was in love with Ron. She said, "Ron is a great person," which was an answer to a question I didn't ask. So I asked again. "True or false: you are in love with Ron." She put her hand with the ring on it in her hair and said, "Oskar, Ron is my *friend*." I was going to ask her if she was humping her friend, and if she had said yes, I would have run away, and if she had said no, I would have asked if they heavy-petted each other, which I know about. I wanted to tell her she shouldn't be playing Scrabble yet. Or looking in the mirror. Or turning the stereo any louder than what you needed just to hear it. It wasn't fair to Dad, and it wasn't fair to me. But I buried it all inside me. I made her other Morse code jewelry with Dad's messages—a necklace, an anklet, some dangly earrings, a tiara—but the bracelet was definitely the most beautiful, probably because it was the last, which made it the most precious. "Mom?" "Yes?" "Nothing."

Even after a year, I still had an extremely difficult time doing certain things, like taking showers, for some reason, and getting into elevators, obviously. There was a lot of stuff that made me panicky, like suspension bridges, germs, airplanes, fireworks, Arab people on the subway (even though I'm not racist), Arab people in restaurants and coffee shops and other public places, scaffolding, sewers and subway grates, bags without owners, shoes, people with mustaches, smoke, knots, tall buildings, turbans. A lot of the time I'd get that feeling like I was in the middle of a huge black ocean, or in deep space, but not in the fascinating way. It's just that everything was incredibly far away from me. It was worst at night. I started inventing things, and then I couldn't stop, like beavers, which I know about. People think they cut down trees so they can build dams, but in reality it's because their teeth never stop growing, and if they didn't constantly file them down by cutting through all of those trees, their teeth would start to grow into their own faces, which would kill them. That's how my brain was.

One night, after what felt like a googolplex inventions, I went to Dad's closet. We used to Greco-Roman wrestle on the floor in there, and tell hilarious jokes, and once we hung a pendulum from the ceiling and put a circle of dominoes on the floor to prove that the earth rotated. But I hadn't gone back in since he died. Mom was with Ron in the living room, listening to music too loud and playing board games. She wasn't missing Dad. I held the doorknob for a while before I turned it.

Even though Dad's coffin was empty, his closet was full. And even after more than a year, it still smelled like shaving. I touched all of his white T-shirts. I touched his fancy watch that he never wore and the extra laces for his sneakers that would never run around the reservoir again. I put my hands into the pockets of all of his jackets (I found a receipt for a cab, a wrapper from a miniature Krackle, and the business card of a diamond supplier). I put my feet into his slippers. I looked at myself in his metal shoehorn. The average person falls asleep in seven minutes, but I couldn't sleep, not after hours, and it made my boots lighter to be around his things, and to touch stuff that he had touched, and to make the hangers hang a little straighter, even though I knew it didn't matter.

His tuxedo was over the chair he used to sit on when he tied his shoes, and I thought, *Weird*. Why wasn't it hung up with his suits? Had he come from a fancy party the night before he died? But then why would he have taken off his tuxedo without hanging it up? Maybe it needed to be cleaned? But I didn't remember a fancy party. I remembered him tucking me in, and us listening to a person speaking Greek on the shortwave radio, and him telling me a story about New York's sixth borough. If I hadn't noticed anything else weird, I wouldn't have thought about the tuxedo again. But I started noticing a lot.

There was a pretty blue vase on the highest shelf. What was a pretty blue vase doing way up there? I couldn't reach it, obviously, so I moved over the chair with the tuxedo still on it, and then I went to my room to get the *Collected Shakespeare* set that Grandma bought for me when she found out that I was going to be Yorick, and I brought those over, four tragedies at a time, until I had a stack that was tall enough. I stood on all of that and it worked for a second. But then I had the tips of my fingers on the vase, and the tragedies started to wobble, and the tuxedo was incredibly distracting, and the next thing was that everything was on the floor, including me, and including the vase, which had shattered. "I didn't do it!" I hollered, but they didn't even hear me, because they were playing music too loud and cracking up too much. I zipped myself all the way into the sleeping bag of myself, not because I was hurt, and not because I had broken something, but because they were cracking up. Even though I knew I shouldn't, I gave myself a bruise.

I started to clean everything up, and that was when I noticed something else weird. In the middle of all of that glass was a little envelope, about the size of a wireless Internet card. *What the?* I opened it up, and inside there was a key. *What the, what the?* It was a weird-looking key, obviously to something extremely important, because it was fatter and shorter than a normal key. I couldn't explain it: a fat and short key, in a little envelope, in a blue vase, on the highest shelf in his closet.

The first thing I did was the logical thing, which was to be very secretive and try the key in all of the locks in the apartment. Even without trying I knew it wasn't for the front door, because it didn't match up with the key that I wear on a string around my neck to let myself in when nobody's home. I tiptoed so I wouldn't be noticed, and I tried the key in the door to the bathroom, and the different bedroom doors, and the drawers in Mom's dresser. I tried it in the desk in the kitchen where Dad used to pay the bills, and in the closet next to the linen closet where I sometimes hid when we played hide and seek, and in Mom's jewelry box. But it wasn't for any of them.

In bed that night I invented a special drain that would be underneath every pillow in New York, and would connect to the reservoir. Whenever people cried themselves to sleep, the tears would all go to the same place, and in the morning the weatherman could report if the water level of the Reservoir of Tears had gone up or down, and you could know if New York was in heavy boots. And when something *really* terrible happened—like a nuclear bomb, or at least a biological weapons attack—an extremely loud siren would go off, telling everyone to get to Central Park to put sandbags around the reservoir.

Anyway.

The next morning I told Mom that I couldn't go to school, because I was too sick. It was the first lie that I had to tell. She put her hand on my forehead and said, "You do feel a bit hot." I said, "I took my temperature and it's one hundred point seven degrees." That was the second lie. She turned around and asked me to zip up the back of her dress, which she could have done herself, but she knew that I loved to do it. She said, "I'll be in and out of meetings all day, but Grandma can come by if you need anything, and I'll call to check on you every hour." I told her, "If I don't answer, I'm probably sleeping or going to the bathroom." She said, "Answer."

Once she left for work, I put on my clothes and went downstairs. Stan was sweeping up in front of the building. I tried to get past him without him noticing, but he noticed. "You don't look sick," he said, brushing a bunch of leaves into the street. I told him, "I feel sick." He asked, "Where's Mr. Feeling Sick going?" I told him, "To the drugstore on Eighty-fourth to get some cough drops." Lie #3. Where I actually went was the locksmith's store, which is Frazer and Sons, on Seventy-ninth.

"Need some more copies?" Walt asked. I gave him a high-five, and I showed him the key that I had found, and asked him what he could tell me about it. "It's for some kind of lockbox," he said, holding it up to his face and looking at it over his glasses. "A safe, I'm guessing. You can tell it's for a lockbox by its build." He showed me a rack that had a ton of keys on it. "See, it's not like any of these. It's much thicker. Harder to break." I touched all the keys that I could reach, and that made me feel OK, for some reason. "But it's not for a fixed safe, I don't think. Nothing too big. Maybe something portable. Could be a safe-deposit box, actually. An old one. Or some kind of fire-retardant cabinet." That made me crack up a little, even though I know there's nothing funny about being a mental retard. "It's an old key," he said. "Could be twenty, thirty years old." "How can you tell?" "Keys are what I know." "You're cool." "And not many lockboxes use keys anymore." "They don't?" "Well, hardly anyone uses keys anymore." "I use keys," I told him, and I showed him my apartment key. "I know you do," he said. "But people like you are a dying breed. It's all electronic these days. Keypads. Thumbprint recognition." "That's so awesome." "I like keys." I thought for a minute, and then I got heavy, heavy boots. "Well, if people like me are a dying breed, then what's going to happen to your business?" "We'll become specialized," he said, "like a typewriter shop. We're useful now, but soon we'll be interesting." "Maybe you need a new business." "I like this business."

I said, "I have a question that I was just wondering." He said, "Shoot." "Shoot?" "Shoot. Go ahead. Ask." "Are you Frazer, or are you Son?" "I'm Grandson, actually. My grandfather started the shop." "*Cool.*" "But I suppose I'm also Son, since my dad ran things when he was alive. I guess I'm Frazer, too, since my son works here during the summers."

I said, "I have another question." "Shoot." "Do you think I could find the company that made this key?" "Anyone could've made it." "Well then, what I want to know is how can I find the lock that it opens?" "I'm afraid I can't help you with that, any more than telling you to try it in every lock you come across. I could always make you a copy, if you'd like." "I could have a googolplex keys." "Googolplex?" "A googol to the googol power." "Googol?" "That's a one with one hundred zeroes after it." He put his hand on my shoulder and said, "You need the lock." I reached up real high and put my hand on his shoulder and said, "Yeah."

As I was leaving he asked, "Shouldn't you be in school?" I thought fast and told him, "It's Dr. Martin Luther King Jr. Day." Lie #4. "I thought that was in January." "It used to be." Lie #5.

When I got back to the apartment, Stan said, "You've got mail!"

> *Dear Osk,*
>   *Hello, lad! Thanks for your glorious letter*
> *and the bulletproof drumsticks, which I hope I'll*
> *never have to use! I have to confess, I've never*
> *thought too much about giving lessons . . .*
>   *I hope you like the enclosed T-shirt, which I*
> *took the liberty of signing for you.*
>   *Your mate,*
>   *Ringo*

I didn't *like* the enclosed T-shirt. I *loved* it! Although unfortunately it wasn't white, so I couldn't wear it.

I laminated Ringo's letter and tacked it to my wall. Then I did some research on the Internet about the locks of New York, and I found out a lot of useful information. For example, there are 319 post offices and 207,352 post office boxes. Each box has a lock, obviously. I also found out that there are about 70,571 hotel rooms, and most rooms have a main lock, a bathroom lock, a closet lock, and a lock to the mini-bar. I didn't know what a mini-bar was, so I called the Plaza Hotel, which I knew was a famous one, and asked. Then I knew what a mini-bar was. There are more than 300,000 cars in New York, which doesn't even count the 12,187 cabs and 4,425 buses. Also, I remembered from when I used to take the subway that the conductors used keys to open and close the doors, so there were those, too. More than 9 million people live in New York (a baby is born in New York every 50 seconds), and everyone has to live somewhere, and most apartments have two locks on the front, and to at least some of the bathrooms, and maybe to some other rooms, and obviously to dressers and jewelry boxes. Also there are offices, and art studios, and storage facilities, and banks with safe-deposit boxes, and gates to yards, and parking lots. I figured that if you included everything—from bicycle locks to roof latches to places for cufflinks—there are probably about 18 locks for every person in New York City, which would mean about 162 million locks, which is a crev*asse*-load of locks.

"Schell residence . . . Hi, Mom . . . A little bit, I guess, but still pretty sick . . . No . . . Uh-huh . . . Uh-huh . . . I guess . . . I think I'll order Indian . . . But still . . . OK. Uh-huh. I will . . . I know . . . I *know* . . . Bye."

I timed myself and it took me 3 seconds to open a lock. Then I figured out that if a baby is born in New York every 50 seconds, and each person has 18 locks, a new lock is created in New York every $2.\overline{777}$ seconds. So even if all I did was open locks, I'd still be falling behind by $.\overline{333}$ locks every second. And that's if I didn't have to travel from one lock to the next, and if I didn't eat, and didn't sleep, which is an OK if, because I didn't actually sleep, anyway. I needed a better plan.

That night, I put on my white gloves, went to the garbage can in Dad's closet, and opened the bag that I'd thrown all of the pieces of the vase into. I was looking for clues that might lead me in a direction. I had to be extremely careful so that I wouldn't contaminate the evidence, or let Mom know what I was doing, or cut and infect myself, and I found the envelope that the key was in. It was then that I noticed something that a good detective would have noticed at the very beginning: the word "Black" was written on the back of the envelope. I was so mad at myself for not noticing it before that I gave myself a little bruise. Dad's handwriting was weird. It looked sloppy, like he was writing in a hurry, or writing down the word while he was on the phone, or just thinking about something else. So what would he have been thinking about?

I Googled around and found out that Black wasn't the name of a company that made lockboxes. I got a little disappointed, because it would have been a logical explanation, which is always the best kind, although fortunately it isn't the only kind. Then I found out that there was a place called Black in every state in the country, and actually in almost every country in the world. In France, for example, there is a place called Noir. So that wasn't very helpful. I did a few other searches, even though I knew they would only hurt me, because I couldn't help it. I printed out some of the pictures I found—a shark attacking a girl, someone walking on a tightrope between the Twin Towers, that actress getting a blowjob from her normal boyfriend, a soldier getting his head cut off in Iraq, the place on the wall where a famous stolen painting used to hang—and I put them in *Stuff That Happened to Me*, my scrapbook of everything that happened to me.

The next morning I told Mom I couldn't go to school again. She asked what was wrong. I told her, "The same thing that's always wrong." "You're sick?" "I'm sad." "About Dad?" "About everything." She sat down on the bed next to me, even though I knew she was in a hurry. "What's everything?" I started counting on my fingers: "The meat and dairy products in our refrigerator, fistfights, car accidents, Larry—" "Who's Larry?" "The homeless guy in front of the Museum of Natural History who always says 'I promise it's for food' after he asks for money." She turned around and I zipped her dress while I kept counting. "How you don't know who Larry is, even though you probably see him all the time, how Buckminster just sleeps and eats and goes to the bathroom and has no *raison d'être*, the short ugly guy with no neck who takes tickets at the IMAX theater, how the sun is going to explode one day, how every birthday I always get at least one thing I already have, poor people who get fat because they eat junk food because it's cheaper . . ." That was when I ran out of fingers, but my list was just getting started, and I wanted it to be long, because I knew she wouldn't leave while I was still going. ". . . domesticated animals, how I *have* a domesticated animal, nightmares, Microsoft Windows, old people who sit around all day because no one remembers to spend time with them and they're embarrassed to ask people to spend time with them, secrets, dial phones, how Chinese waitresses smile even when there's nothing funny or happy, and also how Chinese people own

Mexican restaurants but Mexican people never own Chinese restaurants, mirrors, tape decks, my unpopularity at school, Grandma's coupons, storage facilities, people who don't know what the Internet is, bad handwriting, beautiful songs, how there won't be humans in fifty years—" "Who said there won't be humans in fifty years?" I asked her, "Are you an optimist or a pessimist?" She looked at her watch and said, "I'm *optimistic*." "Then I have some bad news for you, because humans are going to destroy each other as soon as it becomes easy enough to, which will be very soon." "Why do beautiful songs make you sad?" "Because they aren't true." "Never?" "Nothing is beautiful and true." She smiled, but in a way that wasn't just happy, and said, "You sound just like Dad."

"What do you mean I sound just like Dad?" "He used to say things like that." "Like what?" "Oh, like *nothing* is so-and-so. Or *everything* is so-and-so. Or *obviously*." She laughed. "He was always very definitive." "What's 'definitive'?" "It means certain. It comes from 'definite.'" "What's wrong with definitivity?" "Dad sometimes missed the forest for the trees." "What forest?" "Nothing."

"Mom?" "Yes?" "It doesn't make me feel good when you say that something I do reminds you of Dad." "Oh. I'm sorry. Do I do that a lot?" "You do it all the time." "I can see why that wouldn't feel good." "And Grandma always says that things I do remind her of Grandpa. It makes me feel weird, because they're gone. And it also makes me feel unspecial." "That's the last thing that either Grandma or I would want. You know you're the most special thing to us, don't you?" "I guess so." "The *most*."

She petted my head for a while, and her fingers went behind my ear to that place that's almost never touched.

I asked if I could zip her dress up again. She said, "Sure," and turned around. She said, "I think it would be good if you tried to go to school." I said, "I am trying." "Maybe if you just went for first period." "I can't even get out of bed." Lie #6. "And Dr. Fein said I should listen to my feelings. He said I should give myself a break sometimes." That wasn't a lie, exactly, although it wasn't exactly the truth, either. "I just don't want it to become a habit," she said. "It won't," I said. When she put her hand on the covers, she must have felt how puffy they were, because she asked if I had my clothes on in bed. I told her, "I do, and the reason is because I am cold." #7. "I mean, in addition to being hot."

As soon as she left, I got my things together and went downstairs. "You look better than yesterday," Stan said. I told him to mind his own business. He said, "Jeez." I told him, "It's just that I'm feeling worse than yesterday."

I walked over to the art supply store on Ninety-third Street, and I asked the woman at the door if I could speak to the manager, which is something Dad used to do when he had an important question. "What can I do for you?" she asked. "I need the manager," I said. She said, "I know. What can I do for you?" "You're incredibly beautiful," I told her, because she was fat, so I thought it would be an especially nice compliment, and also make her like me again, even though I was sexist. "Thanks," she said. I told her, "You could be a movie star." She shook her head, like, *What the?* "Anyway," I said, and I showed her the envelope, and explained how I had found the key, and how I was trying to find the lock it opened, and how maybe black meant something. I wanted to know what she could tell me about black, since she was probably an expert of color. "Well," she said, "I don't know that I'm an *expert* of anything. But one thing I *can* say is it's sort of interesting that the person wrote the word 'black' in red pen." I asked why that was interesting, because I just thought it was one of the red pens Dad used when he read the *New York Times.* "Come here," she said, and she led me to a display of ten pens. "Look at this." She showed me a pad of paper that was next to the display.

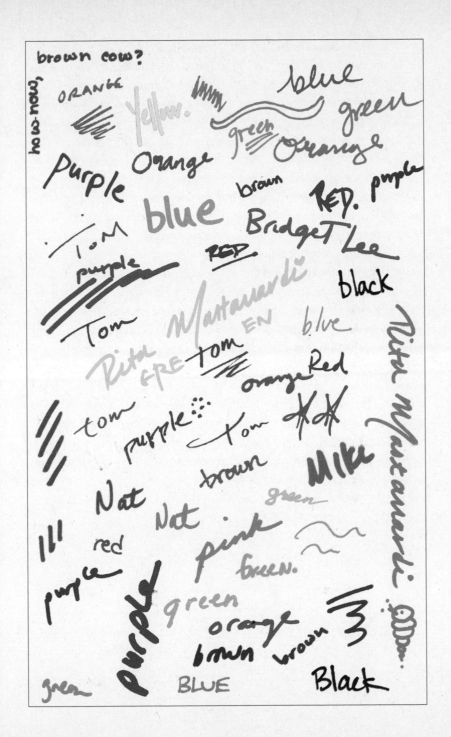

"See," she said, "most people write the name of the color of the pen they're writing with." "Why?" "I don't know why. It's just one of those psychological things, I guess." "Psychological is mental?" "Basically." I thought about it, and I had the revelation that if I was testing out a blue pen, I'd probably write the word "blue." "It's not easy to do what your dad did, writing the name of one color with another color. It doesn't come naturally." "Really?" "This is even harder," she said, and she wrote something on the next piece of paper and told me to read it out loud. She was right, it didn't feel natural at all, because part of me wanted to say the name of the color, and part of me wanted to say what was written. In the end I didn't say anything.

I asked her what she thought it meant. "Well," she said, "I don't know that it *means* anything. But look, when someone tests a pen, usually he either writes the name of the color he's writing with, or his name. So the fact that 'Black' is written in red makes me think that Black is someone's name." "Or *her* name." "And I'll tell you something else." "Yeah?" "The *b* is capitalized. You wouldn't usually capitalize the first letter of a color." "Jose!" "Excuse me?" "Black was written by Black!" "What?" "*Black* was *written* by *Black!* I need to find Black!" She said, "If there's anything else I can help you with, just let me know." "I love you." "Would you mind not shaking the tambourine in the store?"

She walked away, and I stayed there for a bit, trying to catch up with my brain. I flipped back through the pad of paper while I thought about what Stephen Hawking would do next.

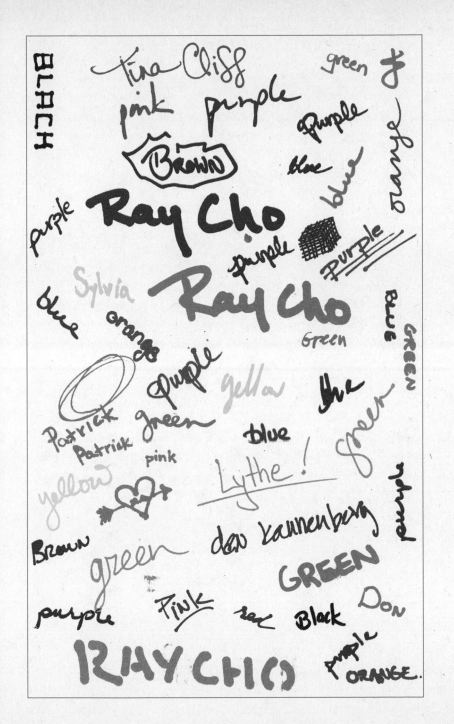

Orange

black

Dave Stanley

PURPLE

red

pink   blue   orange.   black

orange   Dave Stanley

blue

PURPLE   blue

green   blue   green

green   brown   8   Wendy   blue   yellow

pink   Yellow

MARCO   Yellow

Kelly Rica   purple   blue

Sarah   orange

Yellow   orange   GREEN

TARYER   RED   blue   pink

Sarah   blue

Trisha Grand

green

Beth Feiya

Yellow

black

orange

red

John

black

pink

Thomas Schell

purple

Purple   Purple

Jeremy   GREEN

orange

pink

Fred

Maria Souza

brown

BLUE

BLUE

Pink

orange

blue

green   red   GREEN

Purple   John   BROWN   DENNIS
         RED

blue   green   brown

John   green   Nick
       yellow

I ripped the last sheet from the pad and ran to find the manager again. She was helping somebody with paintbrushes, but I thought it wouldn't be rude to interrupt her. "That's my dad!" I told her, putting my finger on his name. "Thomas Schell!" "What a coincidence," she said. I told her, "The only thing is, he didn't buy art supplies." She said, "Maybe he bought art supplies and you didn't know it." "Maybe he just needed a pen." I ran around the rest of the store, from display to display, looking to see if he'd tested any other art supplies. That way I could prove if he had been buying art supplies or just testing out pens to buy a pen.

I couldn't believe what I found.

His name was *everywhere*. He'd tested out markers and oil sticks and colored pencils and chalk and pens and pastels and watercolors. He'd even scratched his name into a piece of moldable plastic, and I found a sculpting knife with yellow on its end, so I knew that was what he did it with. It was as if he was planning on making the biggest art project in history. But I didn't get it: that had to have been more than a year ago.

I found the manager again. "You said if there was anything else you could help me with, that I should just let you know." She said, "Let me finish with this customer, and then you'll have my full attention." I stood there while she finished with the customer. She turned to me. I said, "You said if there was anything else you could help me with, that I should just let you know. Well, I need to see all of the store's receipts." "Why?" "So I can know what day my dad was here and also what he bought." "Why?" "So I can know." "But why?" "Your dad didn't die, so I won't be able to explain it to you." She said, "Your dad died?" I told her yes. I told her, "I bruise easily." She went over to one of the registers, which was actually a computer, and typed something on the screen with her finger. "How do you spell the name again?" "S. C. H. E. L. L." She pressed some more buttons, and made a face, and said, "Nothing." "Nothing?" "Either he didn't buy anything or he paid cash." "Shiitake, hold on." "Excuse me?" "Oskar Schell . . . Hi, Mom . . . Because I'm in the bathroom . . . Because it was in my pocket . . . Uh-huh. Uh-huh. A little, but can I call you back when I'm not going to the bathroom? Like in half an hour? . . . That's personal. . . I guess . . . Uh-huh . . . Uh-*huh* . . . OK, Mom . . . Yuh . . . Bye."

"Well then, I have another question." "You're saying that to me or to the phone?" "You. How long have those pads been by the displays?" "I don't know." "He died more than a year ago. That would be a long time, right?" "They couldn't have been out there that long." "You're sure?" "Pretty sure." "Are you more or less than seventy-five-percent sure?" "More." "Ninety-nine percent?" "Less." "Ninety percent?" "About that." I concentrated for a few seconds. "That's a lot of percent."

I ran home and did some more research, and I found 472 people with the name Black in New York. There were 216 different addresses, because some of the Blacks lived together, obviously. I calculated that if I went to two every Saturday, which seemed possible, plus holidays, minus *Hamlet* rehearsals and other stuff, like mineral and coin conventions, it would take me about three years to go through all of them. But I couldn't survive three years without knowing. I wrote a letter.

> *Cher Marcel,*
>
> *Allô. I am Oskar's mom. I have thought about it a ton, and I have decided that it isn't obvious why Oskar should go to French lessons, so he will no longer be going to go to see you on Sundays like he used to. I want to thank you very much for everything you have taught Oskar, particularly the conditional tense, which is weird. Obviously, there's no need to call me when Oskar doesn't come to his lessons, because I already know, because this was my decision. Also, I will keep sending you checks, because you are a nice guy.*
>
> *Votre ami dévouée,*
> *Mademoiselle Schell*

That was my great plan. I would spend my Saturdays and Sundays finding all of the people named Black and learning what they knew about the key in the vase in Dad's closet. In a year and a half I would know everything. Or at least know that I had to come up with a new plan.

Of course I wanted to talk to Mom that night I decided to go hunting for the lock, but I couldn't. It's not that I thought I would get in trouble for snooping around, or that I was afraid she'd be angry about the vase, or even that I was angry at her for spending so much time laughing with Ron when she should have been adding to the Reservoir of Tears. I can't explain why, but I was sure that she didn't know about the vase, the envelope, or the key. The lock was between me and Dad.

So for those eight months when I went looking around New York, and she would ask where I was going and when I'd be back, I would just say, "I'm going out. I'll be back later." What was so weird, and what I should have tried harder to understand, was that she never asked anything else, not even "Out where?" or "Later when?" even though she was normally so cautious about me, especially since Dad died. (She had bought me the cell phone so we could always find each other, and had told me to take cabs instead of the subway. She had even taken me to the police station to be fingerprinted, which was great.) So why was she suddenly starting to forget about me? Every time I left our apartment to go searching for the lock, I became a little lighter, because I was getting closer to Dad. But I also became a little heavier, because I was getting farther from Mom.

In bed that night, I couldn't stop thinking about the key, and how every $2.\overline{777}$ seconds another lock was born in New York. I pulled *Stuff That Happened to Me* from the space between the bed and the wall, and I flipped through it for a while, wishing that I would finally fall asleep.

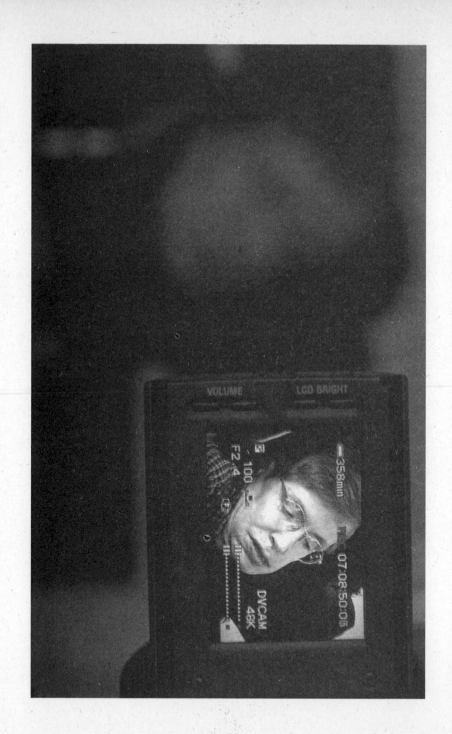

Intrepid Flyer

PAPER AIRPLANE #14

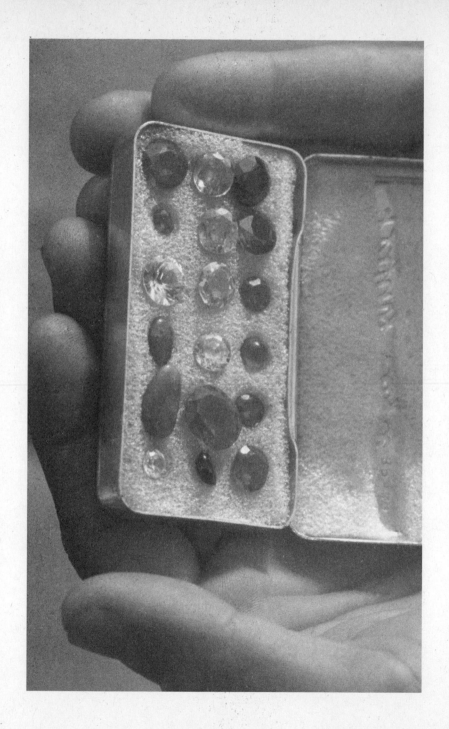

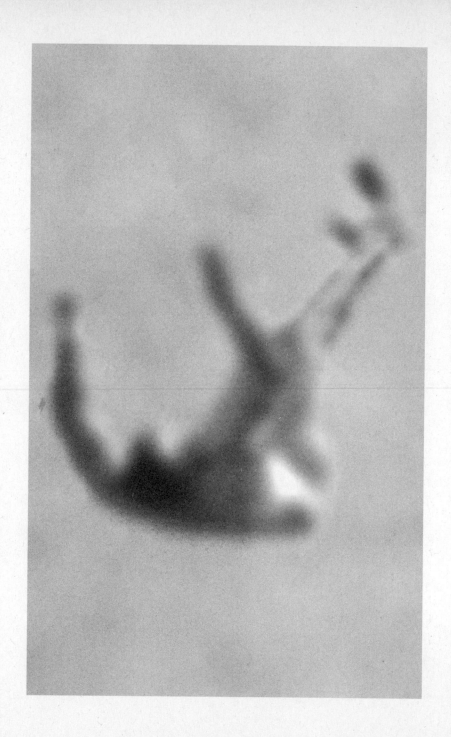

Purple

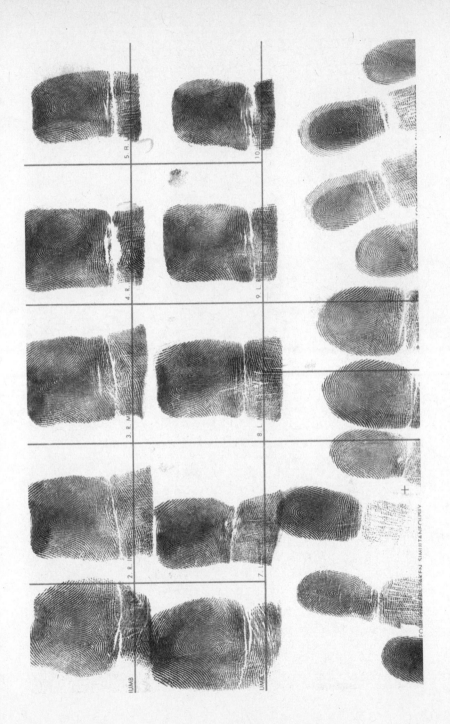

65

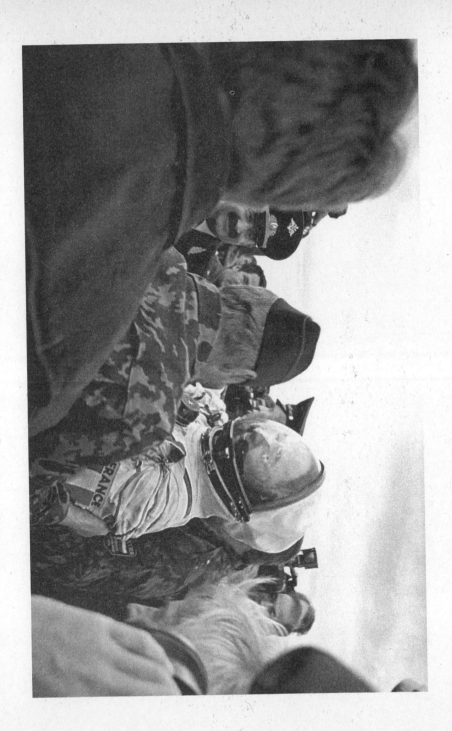

After forever, I got out of bed and went to the closet where I kept the phone. I hadn't taken it out since the worst day. It just wasn't possible.

A lot of the time I think about those four and a half minutes between when I came home and when Dad called. Stan touched my face, which he never did. I took the elevator for the last time. I opened the apartment door, put down my bag, and took off my shoes, like everything was wonderful, because I didn't know that in reality everything was actually horrible, because how could I? I petted Buckminster to show him I loved him. I went to the phone to check the messages, and listened to them one after another.

Message one: 8:52 A.M.
Message two: 9:12 A.M.
Message three: 9:31 A.M.
Message four: 9:46 A.M.
Message five: 10:04 A.M.

I thought about calling Mom. I thought about grabbing my walkie-talkie and paging Grandma. I went back to the first message and listened to them all again. I looked at my watch. It was 10:26:41. I thought about running away and never talking to anyone again. I thought about hiding under my bed. I thought about rushing downtown to see if I could somehow rescue him myself. And then the phone rang. I looked at my watch. It was 10:26:47.

I knew I could never let Mom hear the messages, because protecting her is one of my most important *raisons d'être*, so what I did was I took Dad's emergency money from on top of his dresser, and I went to the Radio Shack on Amsterdam. It was on a TV there that I saw that the first building had fallen. I bought the exact same phone and ran home and recorded our greeting from the first phone onto it. I wrapped up the old phone in the scarf that Grandma was never able to finish because of my privacy, and I put that in a grocery bag, and I put that in a box, and I put that in another box, and I put that under a bunch of stuff in my closet, like my jewelry workbench and albums of foreign currencies.

That night when I decided that finding the lock was my ultimate *raison d'être*—the *raison* that was the master over all other *raisons*—I really needed to hear him.

I was extremely careful not to make any noise as I took the phone out of all of its protections. Even though the volume was way down, so Dad's voice wouldn't wake Mom, he still filled the room, like how a light fills a room even when it's dim.

Message two. 9:12 A.M. *It's me again. Are you there? Hello? Sorry if. It's getting a bit. Smoky. I was hoping you would. Be. Home. I don't know if you've heard about what's happened. But. I. Just wanted you to know that I'm OK. Everything. Is. Fine. When you get this, give Grandma a call. Let her know that I'm OK. I'll call again in a few minutes. Hopefully the firemen will be. Up here by then. I'll call.*

I wrapped the phone back up in the unfinished scarf, and put that back in the bag, and put that back in the box, and that in the other box, and all of that in the closet under lots of junk.

I stared at the fake stars forever.

I invented.

I gave myself a bruise.

I invented.

I got out of bed, went over to the window, and picked up the walkie-talkie. "Grandma? Grandma, do you read me? Grandma? Grandma?" "Oskar?" "I'm OK. Over." "It's late. What's happened? Over." "Did I wake you up? Over." "No. Over." "What were you doing? Over." "I was talking to the renter. Over." "He's still awake? Over." Mom told me not to ask questions about the renter, but a lot of the time I couldn't help it. "Yeah," Grandma said, "but he just left. He had to go run some errands. Over." "But it's 4:12 A.M.? Over."

The renter had been living with Grandma since Dad died, and even though I was at her apartment basically every day, I still hadn't met him. He was constantly running errands, or taking a nap, or in the shower, even when I didn't hear any water. Mom told me, "It probably gets pretty lonely to be Grandma, don't you think?" I told her, "It probably gets pretty lonely to be anyone." "But she doesn't have a mom, or friends like Daniel and Jake, or even a Buckminster." "That's true." "Maybe she needs an imaginary friend." "But I'm real," I said. "Yes, and she loves spending time with you. But you have school to go to, and friends to hang out with, and *Hamlet* rehearsals, and hobby shops—" "Please don't call them hobby shops." "I just mean you can't be around all the time. And maybe she wants a friend her own age." "How do you know her imaginary friend is old?" "I guess I don't."

She said, "There's nothing wrong with someone needing a friend." "Are you actually talking about Ron now?" "No. I'm talking about Grandma." "Except actually you're talking about Ron." "No, Oskar. I'm not. And I don't appreciate that tone." "I wasn't using a tone." "You were using your accusatory tone." "I don't even know what 'accusatory' means, so how could that be my tone?" "You were trying to make me feel badly for having a friend." "No I wasn't." She put her hand with the ring on it in her hair and said, "You know, I actually *was* talking about Grandma, Oskar, but it's true, I need friends, too. What's wrong with that?" I shrugged my shoulders. "Don't you think Dad would want me to have friends?" "I wasn't using a tone."

Grandma lives in the building across the street. We're on the fifth floor and she's on the third, but you can't really tell the difference. Sometimes she'll write notes for me on her window, which I can see through my binoculars, and once Dad and I spent a whole afternoon trying to design a paper airplane that we could throw from our apartment into hers. Stan stood in the street, collecting all of the failed attempts. I remember one of the notes she wrote right after Dad died was "Don't go away."

Grandma leaned her head out the window and put her mouth incredibly close to the walkie-talkie, which made her voice sound fuzzy. "Is everything OK? Over?" "Grandma? Over." "Yes? Over." "Why are matches so short? Over." "What do you mean? Over." "Well, they always seem to run out. Everyone's always rushing at the end, and sometimes even burning their fingers. Over." "I'm not very smart," she said, insulting herself like she always does before she gives an opinion, "but I think the matches are short so they can fit in your pocket. Over." "Yeah," I said, balancing my chin on my hand, and my elbow on the windowsill. "I think that, too. So what if pockets were a lot bigger? Over." "Well, what do I know, but I think the people might have a hard time reaching the bottoms of them if they went much lower. Over." "Right," I said, switching hands, because that one was getting tired, "so what about a portable pocket? Over." "A portable pocket? Over." "Yeah. It would be sort of like a sock, but with a Velcro outside, so you could attach it to anything. It's not quite a bag, because it actually becomes part of what you're wearing, but it's not quite a pocket either, because it's on the outside of your clothes, and also you can remove it, which would have all sorts of advantages, like how you could move things from one outfit to another easily, and how you could carry bigger things around, since you can take the pocket off and reach your arm all the way in. Over." She put her hand against the part of her nightgown that covered her heart and said, "That sounds like one hundred dollars. Over." "A portable pocket would prevent a lot of finger burns from short matches," I said, "but also a lot of dry lips from short ChapSticks. And why are candy bars so short, anyway? I mean, have you ever finished a candy bar and not wanted more? Over." "I can't eat chocolate," she said, "but I understand what you're telling me. Over." "You could have longer combs, so your part could be all the way straight, and bigger mencils—" "Mencils?" "Pencils for men." "Yes, yes." "And bigger mencils that are easier to hold, in case your fingers are fat, like mine, and you could probably even train the birds that save you to take shiitakes in the portable pocket—" "I don't understand." "On your *birdseed shirt.*"

"Oskar? Over." "I'm OK. Over." "What's wrong, darling? Over." "What do you mean what's wrong? Over." "What's wrong? Over." "I miss Dad. Over." "I miss him, too. Over." "I miss him a lot. Over." "So do I. Over." "All the time. Over." "All the time. Over." I couldn't explain to her that I missed him *more*, more than she or anyone else missed him, because I couldn't tell her about what happened with the phone. That secret was a hole in the middle of me that every happy thing fell into. "Did I ever tell you about how Grandpa would stop and pet every animal he saw, even if he was in a rush? Over?" "You've told me a googolplex times. Over." "Oh. And what about how his hands were so rough and red from all of his sculptures that sometimes I joked to him that it was really the sculptures that were sculpting his hands? Over." "That, too. But you can tell me again if you want. Over." She told me again.

An ambulance drove down the street between us, and I imagined who it was carrying, and what had happened to him. Did he break an ankle attempting a hard trick on his skateboard? Or maybe he was dying from third-degree burns on ninety percent of his body? Was there any chance that I knew him? Did anyone see the ambulance and wonder if it was me inside?

What about a device that knew everyone you knew? So when an ambulance went down the street, a big sign on the roof could flash

DON'T WORRY! DON'T WORRY!

if the sick person's device didn't detect the device of someone he knew nearby. And if the device *did* detect the device of someone he knew, the ambulance could flash the name of the person in the ambulance, and either

IT'S NOTHING MAJOR! IT'S NOTHING MAJOR!

or, if it was something major,

IT'S MAJOR! IT'S MAJOR!

And maybe you could rate the people you knew by how much you loved them, so if the device of the person in the ambulance detected the device of the person he loved the most, or the person who loved him the most, and the person in the ambulance was really badly hurt, and might even die, the ambulance could flash

GOODBYE! I LOVE YOU! GOODBYE! I LOVE YOU!

One thing that's nice to think about is someone who was the first person on lots of people's lists, so that when he was dying, and his ambulance went down the streets to the hospital, the whole time it would flash

GOODBYE! I LOVE YOU! GOODBYE! I LOVE YOU!

"Grandma? Over?" "Yes, darling? Over?" "If Grandpa was so great, then why did he leave? Over." She took a little step back so that she disappeared into her apartment. "He didn't want to leave. He had to leave. Over." "But *why* did he have to leave? Over." "I don't know. Over." "Doesn't that make you angry? Over." "That he left? Over." "That you don't know why. Over." "No. Over." "Sad? Over." "Sure. Over." "Hold on," I said, and I ran back to my field kit and grabbed Grandpa's camera. I brought it to the window and took a picture of her window. The flash lit up the street between us.

   10. Walt
    9. Lindy
    8. Alicia

Grandma said, "I hope you never love anything as much as I love you. Over."

    7. Farley
    6. The Minch / Toothpaste (tied)
    5. Stan

I could hear her kissing her fingers and then blowing.

    4. Buckminster
    3. Mom

I blew her a kiss back.

    2. Grandma

"Over and out," one of us said.

    1. Dad

We need much bigger pockets, I thought as I lay in bed, counting off the seven minutes that it takes a normal person to fall asleep. We need enormous pockets, pockets big enough for our families, and our friends, and even the people who aren't on our lists, people we've never met but still want to protect. We need pockets for boroughs and for cities, a pocket that could hold the universe.

Eight minutes thirty-two seconds . . .

But I knew that there couldn't be pockets that enormous. In the end, everyone loses everyone. There was no invention to get around that, and so I felt, that night, like the turtle that everything else in the universe was on top of.

Twenty-one minutes eleven seconds . . .

As for the key, I put it on the string next to my apartment key and wore it like a pendant.

As for me, I was awake for hours and hours. Buckminster curled up next to me, and I conjugated for a while so I wouldn't have to think about things.

> *Je suis*
>
> > *Tu es*
> >
> > > *Il/elle est*
> > >
> > > > *Nous sommes*
> > > >
> > > > > *Vous êtes*
> > > > >
> > > > > > *Ils/elles sont*
> > > > > >
> > > > > > > *Je suis*
> > > > > > >
> > > > > > > > *Tu es*
> > > > > > > >
> > > > > > > > > *Il/elle est*
> > > > > > > > >
> > > > > > > > > > *Nous*

I woke up once in the middle of the night, and Buckminster's paws were on my eyelids. He must have been feeling my nightmares.

MY FEELINGS

12 September 2003
Dear Oskar,
I am writing this to you from the airport.
I have so much to say to you.   I want to begin at the beginning, because that is what you deserve.   I want to tell you everything, without
leaving out a single detail.   But where is the beginning?   And what is
everything?
I am an old woman now, but once I was a girl.   It's true.   I was a girl
like you are a boy.   One of my chores was to bring in the mail.   One
day there was a note addressed to our house.   There was no name on
it.   It was mine as much as anyone's, I thought.   I opened it.   Many
words had been removed from the text by a censor.
14 January 1921
To Whom Shall Receive This Letter:
My name is XXXXXXX XXXXXXXXX, and I am a XXXXXXXX in
Turkish Labor Camp XXXXX, Block XX. I know that I am lucky XX X
XXXXXXX to be alive at all.   I have chosen to write to you without
knowing who you are.   My parents XXXXXXX XXX.   My brothers
and sisters XXXXX XXXX, the main XXXXXX XX XXXXXXXX!
I have written XXX XX XXXXX XXXXXXX every day since I have
been here.   I trade bread for postage, but have not yet received a re-
sponse.   Sometimes it comforts me to think that they do not mail the
letters we write.
XXX XX XXXXXX, or at least XXX XXXXXXXXX?
XX XXXXX X XX throughout XXXXX XX.
XXX XXX XX XXXXX, and XXXXX XX XXXXX XX XXX, without

once XXX XX XXXXXX, XXX XXXXXXXX XXX XXXXX nightmare?

XXX XXX, XX XXXXX XX XXXXX XX!   XXXXX XX XXX XX XXX XX XXXXXX to write a few words to me I would appreciate it more than you ever could know.   Several of the XXXXXX XXXX received mail so I know that XX XX XXXXXXXX.   Please include a picture of yourself as well as your name.   Include everything.

With great hopes,

Sincerely I am,

XXXXXXXX XXXXXXXXX

I took the letter straight to my room.   I put it under my mattress.   I never told my father or mother about it.   For weeks I was awake all night wondering.   Why was this man sent to a Turkish labor camp? Why had the letter come fifteen years after it had been written? Where had it been for those fifteen years?   Why hadn't anyone written back to him?   The others got mail, he said.   Why had he sent a letter to our house?   How did he know the name of my street?   How did he know of Dresden?   Where did he learn German?   What became of him?

I tried to learn as much about the man as I could from the letter.   The words were very simple.   Bread means only bread.   Mail is mail. Great hopes are great hopes are great hopes.   I was left with the handwriting.

So I asked my father, your great-grandfather, whom I considered the best, most kindhearted man I knew, to write a letter to me.   I told him it didn't matter what he wrote about.   Just write, I said.   Write anything.

Darling,

You asked me to write you a letter, so I am writing you a letter.   I do not know why I am writing this letter, or what this letter is supposed to be about, but I am writing it nonetheless, because I love you very much and trust that you have some good purpose for having me write this letter.   I hope that one day you will have the experience of doing something you do not understand for someone you love.

Your father

That letter is the only thing of my father's that I have left.   Not even a picture.

Next I went to the penitentiary.   My uncle was a guard there.   I was able to get the handwriting sample of a murderer.   My uncle asked him to write an appeal for early release.   It was a terrible trick that we played on this man.

To the Prison Board:

My name is Kurt Schluter.   I am Inmate 24922.   I was put here in jail a few years ago.   I don't know how long it's been.   We don't have calendars.   I keep lines on the wall with chalk.   But when it rains, the rain comes through my window when I am sleeping.   And when I wake up the lines are gone.   So I don't know how long it's been.

I murdered my brother.   I beat his head in with a shovel.   Then after I used that shovel to bury him in the yard.   The soil was red.   Weeds came from the grass where his body was.   Sometimes at night I would get on my knees and pull them out, so no one would know.

I did a terrible thing.   I believe in the afterlife.   I know that you can't take anything back.   I wish that my days could be washed away like the chalk lines of my days.

I have tried to become a good person.   I help the other inmates with their chores.   I am patient now.

It might not matter to you, but my brother was having an affair with my wife.   I didn't kill my wife.   I want to go back to her, because I forgive her.

If you release me I will be a good person, quiet, out of the way.

Please consider my appeal.

Kurt Schluter, Inmate 24922

My uncle later told me that the inmate had been in prison for more than forty years.   He had gone in as a young man.   When he wrote the letter to me he was old and broken.   His wife had remarried.   She had children and grandchildren.   Although he never said it, I could tell that my uncle had befriended the inmate.   He had also lost a wife, and was also in a prison.   He never said it, but I heard in his voice that he cared for the inmate.   They guarded each other.   And when I asked my uncle, several years later, what became of the inmate, my uncle told me that he was still there.   He continued to write letters to the board. He continued to blame himself and forgive his wife, not knowing that there was no one on the other end.   My uncle took each letter and promised the inmate that they would be delivered.   But instead he kept them all.   They filled all of the drawers in his dresser.   I remember thinking it's enough to drive someone to kill himself.   I was right.   My uncle, your great-great-uncle, killed himself.   Of course it's possible that the inmate had nothing to do with it.

With those three samples I could make comparisons.   I could at least see that the forced laborer's handwriting was more like my father's than the murderer's.   But I knew that I would need more letters.   As many as I could get.

So I went to my piano teacher.   I always wanted to kiss him, but was afraid he would laugh at me.   I asked him to write a letter.

And then I asked my mother's sister.   She loved dance but hated dancing.

I asked my schoolmate Mary to write a letter to me.   She was funny and full of life.   She liked to run around her empty house without any clothes on, even once she was too old for that.   Nothing embarrassed her.   I admired that so much, because everything embarrassed me, and that hurt me.   She loved to jump on her bed.   She jumped on her bed for so many years that one afternoon, while I watched her jump, the seams burst.   Feathers filled the small room.   Our laughter kept the feathers in the air.   I thought about birds.   Could they fly if there wasn't someone, somewhere, laughing?

I went to my grandmother, your great-great-grandmother, and asked her to write a letter.   She was my mother's mother.   Your father's mother's mother's mother.   I hardly knew her.   I didn't have any interest in knowing her.   I have no need for the past, I thought, like a child.   I did not consider that the past might have a need for me.

What kind of letter? my grandmother asked.

I told her to write whatever she wanted to write.

You want a letter from me? she asked.

I told her yes.

Oh, God bless you, she said.

The letter she gave me was sixty-seven pages long. It was the story of her life. She made my request into her own. Listen to me.

I learned so much. She sang in her youth. She had been to America as a girl. I never knew that. She had fallen in love so many times that she began to suspect she was not falling in love at all, but doing something much more ordinary. I learned that she never learned to swim, and for that reason she always loved rivers and lakes. She asked her father, my great-grandfather, your great-great-great-grandfather, to buy her a dove. Instead he bought her a silk scarf. So she thought of the scarf as a dove. She even convinced herself that it contained flight, but did not fly, because it did not want to show anyone what it really was. That was how much she loved her father.

The letter was destroyed, but its final paragraph is inside of me.

She wrote, I wish I could be a girl again, with the chance to live my life again. I have suffered so much more than I needed to. And the joys I have felt have not always been joyous. I could have lived differently. When I was your age, my grandfather bought me a ruby bracelet. It was too big for me and would slide up and down my arm. It was almost a necklace. He later told me that he had asked the jeweler to make it that way. Its size was supposed to be a symbol of his love. More rubies, more love. But I could not wear it comfortably. I could not wear it at all. So here is the point of everything I have been trying to say. If I were to give a bracelet to you, now, I would measure your wrist twice.

With love,

Your grandmother

I had a letter from everyone I knew. I laid them out on my bedroom floor, and organized them by what they shared. One hundred letters. I was always moving them around, trying to make connections. I wanted to understand.

Seven years later, a childhood friend reappeared at the moment I most needed him. I had been in America for only two months. An agency was supporting me, but soon I would have to support myself. I did not know how to support myself. I read newspapers and magazines all day long. I wanted to learn idioms. I wanted to become a real American.

Chew the fat.   Blow off some steam.   Close but no cigar.   Rings a
bell.   I must have sounded ridiculous.   I only wanted to be natural.
I gave up on that.

I had not seen him since I lost everything.   I had not thought of him.
He and my older sister, Anna, were friends.   I came upon them kissing
one afternoon in the field behind the shed behind our house.   It made
me so excited.   I felt as if I were kissing someone.   I had never kissed
anyone.   I was more excited than if it had been me.   Our house was
small.   Anna and I shared a bed.   That night I told her what I had
seen.   She made me promise never to speak a word about it.   I promised her.

She said, Why should I believe you?

I wanted to tell her, Because what I saw would no longer be mine if I
talked about it.   I said, Because I am your sister.

Thank you.

Can I watch you kiss?

Can you watch us kiss?

You could tell me where you are going to kiss, and I could hide and
watch.

She laughed enough to migrate an entire flock of birds.   That was how
she said yes.

Sometimes it was in the field behind the shed behind our house.
Sometimes it was behind the brick wall in the schoolyard.   It was always behind something.

I wondered if she told him.   I wondered if she could feel me watching
them, if that made it more exciting for her.

Why did I ask to watch?   Why did she agree?

I had gone to him when I was trying to learn more about the forced laborer.   I had gone to everyone.

To Anna's sweet little sister,

Here is the letter you asked for.   I am almost two meters in height.
My eyes are brown.   I have been told that my hands are big.   I want
to be a sculptor, and I want to marry your sister.   Those are my only
dreams.   I could write more, but that is all that matters.

Your friend,

Thomas

I walked into a bakery seven years later and there he was.   He had dogs
at his feet and a bird in a cage beside him.   The seven years were not
seven years.   They were not seven hundred years.   Their length
could not be measured in years, just as an ocean could not explain the
distance we had traveled, just as the dead can never be counted.   I
wanted to run away from him, and I wanted to go right up next to him.
I went right up next to him.
Are you Thomas? I asked.
He shook his head no.
You are, I said.   I know you are.
He shook his head no.
From Dresden.
He opened his right hand, which had NO tattooed on it.
I remember you.   I used to watch you kiss my sister.
He took out a little book and wrote, I don't speak.   I'm sorry.
That made me cry.   He wiped away my tears.   But he did not admit
to being who he was.   He never did.
We spent the afternoon together.   The whole time I wanted to touch
him.   I felt so deeply for this person that I had not seen in so long.
Seven years before, he had been a giant, and now he seemed small.   I
wanted to give him the money that the agency had given me.   I did not
need to tell him my story, but I needed to listen to his.   I wanted to
protect him, which I was sure I could do, even if I could not protect my-
self.
I asked, Did you become a sculptor, like you dreamed?
He showed me his right hand and there was silence.
We had everything to say to each other, but no ways to say it.
He wrote, Are you OK?
I told him, My eyes are crummy.
He wrote, But are you OK?
I told him, That's a very complicated question.
He wrote, That's a very simple answer.
I asked, Are you OK?
He wrote, Some mornings I wake up feeling grateful.
We talked for hours, but we just kept repeating those same things over
and over.

Our cups emptied.

The day emptied.

I was more alone than if I had been alone.   We were about to go in different directions.   We did not know how to do anything else.

It's getting late, I said.

He showed me his left hand, which had YES tattooed on it.

I said, I should probably go home.

He flipped back through his book and pointed at, Are you OK?

I nodded yes.

I started to walk off.   I was going to walk to the Hudson River and keep walking.   I would carry the biggest stone I could bear and let my lungs fill with water.

But then I heard him clapping his hands behind me.

I turned around and he motioned for me to come to him.

I wanted to run away from him, and I wanted to go to him.

I went to him.

He asked if I would pose for him.   He wrote his question in German, and it wasn't until then that I realized he had been writing in English all afternoon, and that I had been speaking English.   Yes, I said in German.   Yes.   We made arrangements for the next day.

His apartment was like a zoo.   There were animals everywhere. Dogs and cats.   A dozen birdcages.   Fish tanks.   Glass boxes with snakes and lizards and insects.   Mice in cages, so the cats wouldn't get them.   Like Noah's ark.   But he kept one corner clean and bright.

He said he was saving the space.

For what?

For sculptures.

I wanted to know from what, or from whom, but I did not ask.

He led me by the hand.   We talked for half an hour about what he wanted to make.   I told him I would do whatever he needed.

We drank coffee.

He wrote that he had not made a sculpture in America.

Why not?

I haven't been able to.

Why not?

We never talked about the past.

He opened the flue, although I didn't know why.

Birds sang in the other room.

I took off my clothes.

I went onto the couch.

He stared at me.   It was the first time I had ever been naked in front of a man.   I wondered if he knew that.

He came over and moved my body like I was a doll.   He put my hands behind my head.   He bent my right leg a little.   I assumed his hands were so rough from all of the sculptures he used to make.   He lowered my chin.   He turned my palms up.   His attention filled the hole in the middle of me.

I went back the next day.   And the next day.   I stopped looking for a job.   All that mattered was him looking at me.   I was prepared to fall apart if it came to that.

Each time it was the same.

He would talk about what he wanted to make.

I would tell him I would do whatever he needed.

We would drink coffee.

We would never talk about the past.

He would open the flue.

The birds would sing in the other room.

I would undress.

He would position me.

He would sculpt me.

Sometimes I would think about those hundred letters laid across my bedroom floor.   If I hadn't collected them, would our house have burned less brightly?

I looked at the sculpture after every session.   He went to feed the animals.   He let me be alone with it, although I never asked him for privacy.   He understood.

After only a few sessions it became clear that he was sculpting Anna. He was trying to remake the girl he knew seven years before.   He looked at me as he sculpted, but he saw her.

The positioning took longer and longer.   He touched more of me.

He moved me around more.   He spent ten full minutes bending and unbending my knee.   He closed and unclosed my hands.

I hope this doesn't embarrass you, he wrote in German in his little book.

No, I said in German.   No.

He folded one of my arms.   He straightened one of my arms.   The next week he touched my hair for what might have been five or fifty minutes.

He wrote, I am looking for an acceptable compromise.

I wanted to know how he lived through that night.

He touched my breasts, easing them apart.

I think this will be good, he wrote.

I wanted to know what will be good.   How will it be good?

He touched me all over.   I can tell you these things because I am not ashamed of them, because I learned from them.   And I trust you to understand me.   You are the only one I trust, Oskar.

The positioning was the sculpting.   He was sculpting me.   He was trying to make me so he could fall in love with me.

He spread my legs.   His palms pressed gently at the insides of my thighs.   My thighs pressed back.   His palms pressed out.

Birds were singing in the other room.

We were looking for an acceptable compromise.

The next week he held the backs of my legs, and the next week he was behind me.   It was the first time I had ever made love.   I wondered if he knew that.   It felt like crying.   I wondered, Why does anyone ever make love?

I looked at the unfinished sculpture of my sister, and the unfinished girl looked back at me.

Why does anyone ever make love?

We walked together to the bakery where we first met.

Together and separately.

We sat at a table.   On the same side, facing the windows.

I did not need to know if he could love me.

I needed to know if he could need me.

I flipped to the next blank page of his little book and wrote, Please marry me.

He looked at his hands.

YES and NO.

Why does anyone ever make love?

He took his pen and wrote on the next and last page, No children.

That was our first rule.

I understand, I told him in English.

We never used German again.

The next day, your grandfather and I were married.

THE ONLY ANIMAL

I read the first chapter of *A Brief History of Time* when Dad was still alive, and I got incredibly heavy boots about how relatively insignificant life is, and how, compared to the universe and compared to time, it didn't even matter if I existed at all. When Dad was tucking me in that night and we were talking about the book, I asked if he could think of a solution to that problem. "Which problem?" "The problem of how relatively insignificant we are." He said, "Well, what would happen if a plane dropped you in the middle of the Sahara Desert and you picked up a single grain of sand with tweezers and moved it one millimeter?" I said, "I'd probably die of dehydration." He said, "I just mean right then, when you moved that single grain of sand. What would that mean?" I said, "I dunno, what?" He said, "Think about it." I thought about it. "I guess I would have moved a grain of sand." "Which would mean?" "Which would mean I moved a grain of sand?" "Which would mean you changed the Sahara." "So?" "*So?* So the Sahara is a vast desert. And it has existed for millions of years. And you changed it!" "That's true!" I said, sitting up. "I changed the Sahara!" "Which means?" he said. "What? Tell me." "Well, I'm not talking about painting the *Mona Lisa* or curing cancer. I'm just talking about moving that one grain of sand one millimeter." "Yeah?" "If you *hadn't* done it, human history would have been one way . . ." "Uh-huh?" "But you *did* do it, *so* . . . ?" I stood on the bed, pointed my fingers at the fake stars, and screamed: "I changed the course of human history!" "That's right." "I changed the universe!" "You did." "I'm God!" "You're an atheist." "I don't exist!" I fell back onto the bed, into his arms, and we cracked up together.

That was kind of how I felt when I decided that I would meet every person in New York with the last name Black. Even if it was relatively insignificant, it was something, and I needed to do something, like sharks, who die if they don't swim, which I know about.

Anyway.

I decided that I would go through the names alphabetically, from Aaron to Zyna, even though it would have been a more efficient method to do it by geographical zones. Another thing I decided was that I would be as secretive about my mission as I could at home, and as honest about it as I could outside home, because that's what was necessary. So if Mom asked me, "Where are you going and when will you be back?" I would tell her, "Out, later." But if one of the Blacks wanted to know something, I would tell everything. My other rules were that I wouldn't be sexist again, or racist, or ageist, or homophobic, or overly wimpy, or discriminatory to handicapped people or mental retards, and also that I wouldn't lie unless I absolutely had to, which I did a lot. I put together a special field kit with some of the things I was going to need, like a Magnum flashlight, ChapStick, some Fig Newtons, plastic bags for important evidence and litter, my cell phone, the script for *Hamlet* (so I could memorize my stage directions while I was going from one place to another, because I didn't have any lines to memorize), a topographical map of New York, iodine pills in case of a dirty bomb, my white gloves, obviously, a couple of boxes of Juicy Juice, a magnifying glass, my *Larousse Pocket Dictionary*, and a bunch of other useful stuff. I was ready to go.

On my way out, Stan said, "What a day!" I said, "Yeah." He asked, "What's on the menu?" I showed him the key. He said, "Lox?" I said, "Hilarious, but I don't eat anything with parents." He shook his head and said, "I couldn't help myself. So what's on the menu?" "Queens and Greenwich Village." "You mean *Gren*-ich Village?" That was my first disappointment of the expedition, because I thought it was pronounced phonetically, which would have been a fascinating clue. "Anyway."

It took me three hours and forty-one minutes to walk to Aaron Black, because public transportation makes me panicky, even though walking over bridges also makes me panicky. Dad used to say that sometimes you have to put your fears in order, and that was one of those times. I walked across Amsterdam Avenue, and Columbus Avenue, and Central Park, and Fifth Avenue, and Madison Avenue, and Park Avenue, and Lexington Avenue, and Third Avenue, and Second Avenue. When I was exactly halfway across the Fifty-ninth Street Bridge, I thought about how a millimeter behind me was Manhattan and a millimeter in front of me was Queens. So what's the name of the parts of New York—exactly halfway through the Midtown Tunnel, exactly halfway over the Brooklyn Bridge, the exact middle of the Staten Island Ferry when it's exactly halfway between Manhattan and Staten Island—that aren't in any borough?

I took a step forward, and it was my first time in Queens.

I walked through Long Island City, Woodside, Elmhurst, and Jackson Heights. I shook my tambourine the whole time, because it helped me remember that even though I was going through different neighborhoods, I was still me. When I finally got to the building, I couldn't figure out where the doorman was. At first I thought maybe he was just getting some coffee, but I waited around for a few minutes and he didn't come. I looked through the door and saw that there was no desk for him. I thought, *Weird.*

I tried my key in the lock, but it didn't go in past the tip. I saw a device with a button for each apartment, so I pressed the button for A. Black's apartment, which was 9E. No one answered. I pressed it again. Nothing. I held down the buzzer for fifteen seconds. Still nothing. I sat down on the ground and wondered if it would be overly wimpy to cry in the lobby of an apartment building in Corona.

"All right, all right," a voice said from the speaker. "Take it easy." I jumped up. "Hello," I said, "my name is Oskar Schell." "What do you want?" His voice sounded mad, but I hadn't done anything wrong. "Did you know Thomas Schell?" "No." "Are you sure?" "Yes." "Do you know anything about a key?" "What do you want?" "I didn't do anything wrong." "What do you want?" "I found a key," I said, "and it was in an envelope with your name on it." "Aaron Black?" "No, just Black." "It's a common name." "I know." "And a color." "Obviously." "Goodbye," the voice said. "But I'm just trying to find out about this key." "Goodbye." "But—" "Goodbye." Disappointment #2.

I sat back down and started to cry in the lobby of an apartment

building in Corona. I wanted to press all of the buttons and scream curse words at everybody who lived in the stupid building. I wanted to give myself bruises. I stood up and pressed 9E again. This time the voice came out immediately. "What. Do. You. Want?" I said, "Thomas Schell was my dad." "And?" "*Was*. Not *is*. He's dead." He didn't say anything, but I knew he was pressing the Talk button because I could hear a beeping in his apartment, and also windows rattling from the same breeze that I was feeling at ground level. He asked, "How old are you?" I said seven, because I wanted him to feel more sorry for me, so he would help me. Lie #34. "My dad's dead," I told him. "Dead?" "He's inanimate." He didn't say anything. I heard more beeping. We just stood there, facing each other, but nine floors apart. Finally he said, "He must have died young." "Yeah." "How old was he?" "Forty." "That's too young." "That's true." "Can I ask how he died?" I didn't want to talk about it, but I remembered the promises I made to myself about my search, so I told him everything. I heard more beeping and wondered if his finger was getting tired. He said, "If you come up, I'll have a look at that key." "I can't go up." "Why not?" "Because you're on the ninth floor and I don't go that high." "Why not?" "It isn't safe." "But it's perfectly safe here." "Until something happens." "You'll be fine." "It's a rule." "I'd come down for you," he said, "but I just can't." "Why not?" "I'm very sick." "But my dad is dead." "I'm hooked up to all sorts of machines. That's why it took me so long to get to the intercom." If I could do it again, I would do it differently. But you can't do it again. I heard the voice saying, "Hello? Hello? Please." I slid my card under the apartment building door and got away from there as fast as I could.

Abby Black lived in #1 in a townhouse on Bedford Street. It took me two hours and twenty-three minutes to walk there, and my hand got exhausted from shaking my tambourine. There was a little sign above the door that said the poet Edna Saint Vincent Millay once lived in the house, and that it was the narrowest house in New York. I wondered if Edna Saint Vincent Millay was a man or a woman. I tried the key, and it went in halfway, but then it stopped. I knocked. No one answered, even though I could hear someone talking inside, and I guessed that #1 meant the first floor, so I knocked again. I was willing to be annoying if that's what was necessary.

A woman opened the door and said, "Can I help you?" She was incredibly beautiful, with a face like Mom's, which seemed like it was smiling even when she wasn't smiling, and huge boobs. I especially liked how her earrings sometimes touched her neck. It made me wish all of a sudden that I'd brought some kind of invention for her, so that she'd have a reason to like me. Even something small and simple, like a phosphorus brooch.

"Hi." "Hello." "Are you Abby Black?" "Yes." "I'm Oskar Schell." "Hello." "Hi." I told her, "I'm sure people tell you this constantly, but if you looked up 'incredibly beautiful' in the dictionary, there would be a picture of you." She cracked up a bit and said, "People never tell me that." "I bet they do." She cracked up a bit more. "They don't." "Then you hang out with the wrong people." "You might be right about that." "Because you're incredibly beautiful."

She opened the door a bit more. I asked, "Did you know Thomas Schell?" "Excuse me?" "Did you know Thomas Schell?" She thought. I wondered why she had to think. "No." "Are you sure?" "Yes." There was something unsure about the way she said she was sure, which made me think that maybe she was keeping some sort of secret from me. So what would that secret be? I handed her the envelope and said, "Does this mean anything to you?" She looked at it for a while. "I don't think so. Should it?" "Only if it does," I told her. "It doesn't," she told me. I didn't believe her.

"Would it be OK if I came in?" I asked. "Now is not really the best time." "Why not?" "I'm in the middle of something." "What kind of something?" "Is that any of your business?" "Is that a rhetorical question?" "Yes." "Do you have a job?" "Yes." "What's your job?" "I am an epidemiologist." "You study diseases." "Yes." "Fascinating." "Listen, I don't know what it is that you need, but if it has to do with that envelope, I'm sure I can't help—" "I'm extremely thirsty," I said, touching my throat, which is the universal sign for thirsty. "There's a deli on the corner." "Actually, I'm diabetic and I need some sugar asap." Lie #35. "Do you mean A.S.A.P.?" "Anyway."

I didn't feel great about lying, and I didn't believe in being able to know what's going to happen before it happens, but for some reason I knew I had to get inside her apartment. In exchange for the lie, I made

a promise to myself that when I got a raise in my allowance, I would donate part of that raise to people who in reality *do* have diabetes. She took a heavy breath, like she was incredibly frustrated, but on the other hand, she didn't ask me to leave. A man's voice called something from inside. "Orange juice?" she asked. "Do you have any coffee?" "Follow me," she said, and she walked into the apartment. "What about non-dairy creamer?"

I got a look around as I followed her, and everything was clean and perfect. There were neat photographs on the walls, including one where you could see an African-American woman's VJ, which made me feel self-conscious. "Where are the sofa cushions?" "It doesn't have cushions." "What is that?" "You mean the painting?" "Your apartment smells good." The man in the other room called again, this time extremely loudly, like he was desperate, but she didn't pay any attention, like she didn't hear it, or didn't care.

I touched a lot of things in her kitchen, because it made me feel OK for some reason. I ran my finger along the top of her microwave, and it turned gray. *"C'est sale,"* I said, showing it to her and cracking up. She became extremely serious. "That's embarrassing," she said. "You should see my laboratory," I said. "I wonder how that could have happened," she said. I said, "Things get dirty." "But I like to keep things clean. A woman comes by every week to clean. I've told her a million times to clean everywhere. I've even pointed that out to her." I asked her why she was getting so upset about such a small thing. She said, "It doesn't feel small to me," and I thought about moving a single grain of sand one millimeter. I took a wet wipe from my field kit and cleaned the microwave.

"Since you're an epidemiologist," I said, "did you know that seventy percent of household dust is actually composed of human epidermal matter?" "No," she said, "I didn't." "I'm an amateur epidemiologist." "There aren't many of those." "Yeah. And I conducted a pretty fascinating experiment once where I told Feliz to save all the dust from our apartment for a year in a garbage bag for me. Then I weighed it. It weighed 112 pounds. Then I figured out that seventy percent of 112 pounds is 78.4 pounds. I weigh 76 pounds, 78 pounds when I'm sopping wet. That doesn't actually prove anything, but it's weird. Where can I put this?" "Here," she said, taking the wet wipe from me. I asked her, "Why are you sad?" "Excuse me?" "You're sad. Why?"

The coffee machine gurgled. She opened a cabinet and took out a mug. "Do you take sugar?" I told her yes, because Dad always took sugar. As soon as she sat down, she got back up and took a bowl of grapes from her refrigerator. She also took out cookies and put them on a plate. "Do you like strawberries?" she asked. "Yes," I told her, "but I'm not hungry." She put out some strawberries. I thought it was weird that there weren't any menus or little magnetic calendars or pictures of kids on her refrigerator. The only thing in the whole kitchen was a photograph of an elephant on the wall next to the phone. "I love that," I told her, and not just because I wanted her to like me. "You love what?" she asked. I pointed at the picture. "Thank you," she said. "I like it, too." "I said I *loved* it." "Yes. I *love* it."

"How much do you know about elephants?" "Not too much." "Not too much a little? Or not too much nothing?" "Hardly anything." "For example, did you know that scientists used to think that elephants had esp?" "Do you mean E.S.P.?" "Anyway, elephants can set up meetings from very faraway locations, and they know where their friends and enemies are going to be, and they can find water without any geological clues. No one could figure out how they do all of those things. So what's actually going on?" "I don't know." "How do they do it?" "It?" "How do they set up meetings if they don't have E.S.P.?" "You're asking me?" "Yes." "I don't know." "Do you want to know?" "Sure." "A lot?" "Sure." "They're making very, very, very, very deep calls, way deeper than what humans can hear. They're talking to each other. Isn't that so awesome?" "It is." I ate a strawberry.

"There's this woman who's spent the last couple of years in the Congo or wherever. She's been making recordings of the calls and putting together an enormous library of them. This past year she started playing them back." "Playing them back?" "To the elephants." "Why?" I loved that she asked why. "As you probably know, elephants have much, much stronger memories than other mammals." "Yes. I think I knew that." "So this woman wanted to see just how good their memories actually are. She'd play the call of an enemy that was recorded a bunch of years earlier—a call they'd heard only once—and they'd get

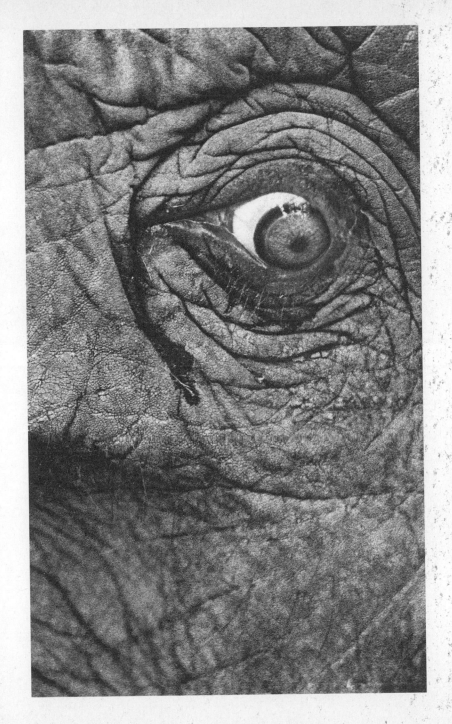

panicky, and sometimes they'd run. They remembered hundreds of calls. Thousands. There might not even be a limit. Isn't that fascinating?" "It is." "Because what's *really* fascinating is that she'd play the call of a dead elephant to its family members." "And?" "They remembered." "What did they do?" "They approached the speaker."

"I wonder what they were feeling." "What do you mean?" "When they heard the calls of their dead, was it with love that they approached the jeep? Or fear? Or anger?" "I don't remember." "Did they charge?" "I don't remember." "Did they cry?" "Only humans can cry tears. Did you know that?" "It looks like the elephant in that photograph is crying." I got extremely close to the picture, and it was true. "It was probably manipulated in Photoshop," I said. "But just in case, can I take a picture of your picture?" She nodded and said, "Didn't I read somewhere that elephants are the only other animals that bury their dead?" "No," I told her as I focused Grandpa's camera, "you didn't. They just gather the bones. Only humans bury their dead." "Elephants couldn't believe in ghosts." That made me crack up a little. "Well, most scientists wouldn't say so." "What would you say?" "I'm just an amateur scientist." "And what would you say?" I took the picture. "I'd say they were confused."

Then she started to cry tears.

I thought, *I'm the one who's supposed to be crying.*

"Don't cry," I told her. "Why not?" she asked. "Because," I told her. "Because what?" she asked. Since I didn't know why she was crying, I couldn't think of a reason. Was she crying about the elephants? Or something else I'd said? Or the desperate person in the other room? Or something that I didn't know about? I told her, "I bruise easily." She said, "I'm sorry." I told her, "I wrote a letter to that scientist who's making those elephant recordings. I asked if I could be her assistant. I told her I could make sure there were always blank tapes ready for recording, and I could boil all the water so it was safe to drink, or even just carry her equipment. Her assistant wrote back to tell me she already had an assistant, obviously, but maybe there would be a project in the future that we could work on together." "That's great. Something to look forward to." "Yeah."

Someone came to the door of the kitchen who I guessed was the man that had been calling from the other room. He just stuck his head in extremely quickly, said something I didn't understand, and walked away. Abby pretended to ignore it, but I didn't. "Who was that?" "My husband." "Does he need something?" "I don't care." "But he's your husband, and I think he needs something." She cried more tears. I went over to her and I put my hand on her shoulder, like Dad used to do with me. I asked her what she was feeling, because that's what he would ask. "You must think this is very unusual," she said. "I think a lot of things are very unusual," I said. She asked, "How old are you?" I told her twelve—lie #59—because I wanted to be old enough for her to love me. "What's a twelve-year-old doing knocking on the doors of strangers?" "I'm trying to find a lock. How old are you?" "Forty-eight." "Jose. You look much younger than that." She cracked up through her crying and said, "Thanks." "What's a forty-eight-year-old doing inviting strangers into her kitchen?" "I don't know." "I'm being annoying," I said. "You're not being annoying," she said, but it's extremely hard to believe someone when they tell you that.

I asked, "Are you sure you didn't know Thomas Schell?" She said, "I didn't know Thomas Schell," but for some reason I *still* didn't believe her. "Maybe you know someone else with the first name Thomas? Or someone else with the last name Schell?" "No." I kept thinking there was something she wasn't telling me. I showed her the little envelope again. "But this is your last name, right?" She looked at the writing, and I could see that she recognized something about it. Or I thought I could see it. But then she said, "I'm sorry. I don't think I can help you." "And what about the key?" "What key?" I realized I hadn't even shown it to her yet. All of that talking—about dust, about elephants—and I hadn't gotten to the whole reason I was there.

I pulled the key out from under my shirt and put it in her hand. Because the string was still around my neck, when she leaned in to look at the key, her face came incredibly close to my face. We were frozen there for a long time. It was like time was stopped. I thought about the falling body.

"I'm sorry," she said. "Why are you sorry?" "I'm sorry I don't know anything about the key." Disappointment #3. "I'm sorry, too."

Our faces were so incredibly close.

97

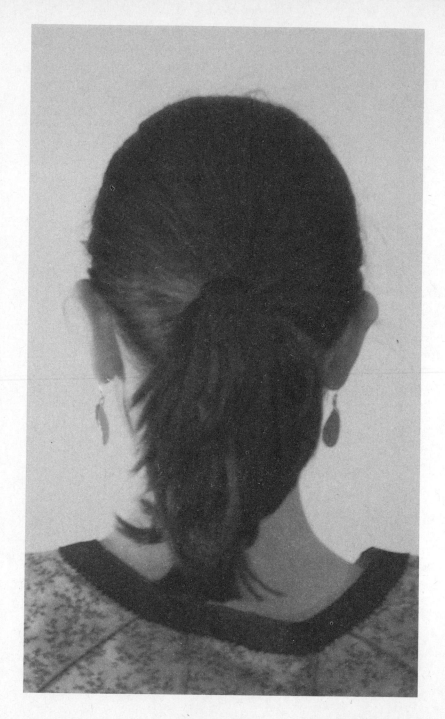

I told her, "The fall play this fall is *Hamlet*, in case you're interested. I'm Yorick. We have a working fountain. If you want to come to opening night, it's twelve weeks from now. It should be pretty great." She said, "I'll try," and I could feel the breath of her words against my face. I asked her, "Could we kiss for a little bit?"

"Excuse me?" she said, although, on the other hand, she didn't pull her head back. "It's just that I like you, and I think I can tell that you like me." She said, "I don't think that's a good idea." Disappointment #4. I asked why not. She said, "Because I'm forty-eight and you're twelve." "So?" "And I'm married." "So?" "And I don't even know you." "Don't you feel like you know me?" She didn't say anything. I told her, "Humans are the only animal that blushes, laughs, has religion, wages war, and kisses with lips. So in a way, the more you kiss with lips, the more human you are." "And the more you wage war?" Then I was the silent one. She said, "You're a sweet, sweet boy." I said, "Young man." "But I don't think it's a good idea." "Does it have to be a good idea?" "I think it does." "Can I at least take a picture of you?" She said, "That would be nice." But when I started focusing Grandpa's camera, she put her hand in front of her face for some reason. I didn't want to force her to explain herself, so I thought of a different picture I could take, which would be more truthful, anyway. "Here's my card," I told her, when the cap was back on the lens, "in case you remember anything about the key or just want to talk."

❧ OSKAR SCHELL ❧

INVENTOR, JEWELRY DESIGNER, JEWELRY FABRI-
CATOR, AMATEUR ENTOMOLOGIST, FRANCOPHILE,
VEGAN, ORIGAMIST, PACIFIST, PERCUSSIONIST,
AMATEUR ASTRONOMER, COMPUTER CONSULTANT,
AMATEUR ARCHEOLOGIST, COLLECTOR OF: *rare coins, butterflies that died natural deaths, miniature cacti, Beatles memorabilia, semiprecious stones, and other things*

E-MAIL: OSKAR_SCHELL@HOTMAIL.COM
HOME PHONE: PRIVATE / CELL PHONE: PRIVATE
FAX MACHINE: I DON'T HAVE A FAX MACHINE YET

· · ·

I went over to Grandma's apartment when I got home, which is what I did basically every afternoon, because Mom worked at the firm on Saturdays and sometimes even Sundays, and she got panicky about me being alone. As I got near Grandma's building, I looked up and didn't see her sitting at her window waiting for me, like she always did. I asked Farley if she was there, and he said he thought so, so I went up the seventy-two stairs.

I rang the doorbell. She didn't answer, so I opened the door, because she always leaves it unlocked, even though I don't think that's safe, because sometimes people who seem good end up being not as good as you might have hoped. As I walked in, she was coming to the door. It looked almost like she had been crying, but I knew that was impossible, because once she told me that she emptied herself of tears when Grandpa left. I told her fresh tears are produced every time you cry. She said, "Anyway." Sometimes I wondered if she cried when no one was looking.

"Oskar!" she said, and lifted me from the ground with one of her hugs. "I'm OK," I said. "Oskar!" she said again, picking me up in another hug. "I'm OK," I said again, and then I asked her where she'd been. "I was in the guest room talking to the renter."

When I was a baby, Grandma would take care of me during the day. Dad told me that she would give me baths in the sink, and trim my fingernails and toenails with her teeth because she was afraid of using clippers. When I was old enough to take baths in the bathtub, and to know I had a penis and a scrotum and everything, I asked her not to sit in the room with me. "Why not?" "Privacy." "Privacy from what? From me?" I didn't want to hurt her feelings, because not hurting her feelings is another of my *raisons d'être*. "Just privacy," I said. She put her hands on her stomach and said, "From *me?*" She agreed to wait outside, but only if I held a ball of yarn, which went under the bathroom door and was connected to the scarf she was knitting. Every few seconds she would give it a tug, and I had to tug back—undoing what she'd just done—so that she could know I was OK.

She was taking care of me when I was four, chasing me around the apartment like she was a monster, and I cut my top lip against the end of our coffee table and had to go to the hospital. Grandma believes in

God, but she doesn't believe in taxis, so I bled on my shirt on the bus. Dad told me it gave her incredibly heavy boots, even though my lip only needed a couple of stitches, and that she kept coming across the street to tell him, "It was all my fault. You should never let him be around me again." The next time I saw her after that, she told me, "You see, I was pretending to be a monster, and I became a monster."

Grandma stayed at our apartment the week after Dad died, while Mom was going around Manhattan putting up posters. We had thousands of thumb wars, and I won every single one, even the ones I was trying to lose. We watched approved documentaries, and cooked vegan cupcakes, and went for lots of walks in the park. One day I wandered away from her and hid. I liked the way it felt to have someone look for me, to hear my name again and again. "Oskar! Oskar!" Maybe I didn't even like it, but I needed it right then.

I followed her around from a safe distance as she started to get incredibly panicky. "Oskar!" She was crying and touching everything, but I wouldn't let her know where I was, because I was sure that the cracking up at the end would make it all OK. I watched her as she walked home, where I knew she would sit on the stoop of our building and wait for Mom to come back. She would have to tell her I had disappeared, and that because she wasn't watching me closely enough, I was gone forever and there would be no more Schells. I ran ahead, down Eighty-second Street and up Eighty-third, and when she came up to the building, I jumped out from behind the door. "But I didn't order a pizza!" I said, cracking up so hard I thought my neck would burst open.

She started to say something, and then she stopped. Stan took her arm and said, "Why don't you sit down, Grandma." She told him, "Don't touch me," in a voice that I'd never heard from her. Then she turned around and went across the street to her apartment. That night, I looked through my binoculars at her window and there was a note that said, "Don't go away."

Ever since that day, whenever we go on walks she makes us play a game like Marco Polo, where she calls my name and I have to call back to let her know that I'm OK.

"Oskar."

"I'm OK."

"Oskar."

"I'm OK."

I'm never exactly sure when we're playing the game and when she's just saying my name, so I always let her know that I'm OK.

A few months after Dad died, Mom and I went to the storage facility in New Jersey where Dad kept the stuff that he didn't use anymore but might use again one day, like when he retired, I guess. We rented a car, and it took us more than two hours to get there, even though it wasn't far away, because Mom kept stopping to go to the bathroom and wash her face. The facility wasn't organized very well, and it was extremely dark, so it took us a long time to find Dad's little room. We got in a fight about his razor, because she said it should go in the "throw it away" pile and I told her it should go in the "save it" pile. She said, "Save it for what?" I said, "It doesn't matter for what." She said, "I don't know why he saved a three-dollar razor in the first place." I said, "It doesn't matter why." She said, "We can't save everything." I said, "So it will be OK if I throw away all of your things and forget about you after you die?" As it was coming out of my mouth, I wished it was going into my mouth. She said she was sorry, which I thought was weird.

One of the things we found were the old two-way radios from when I was a baby. Mom and Dad put one in the crib so they could hear me crying, and sometimes, instead of coming to the crib, Dad would just talk into it, which would help me get to sleep. I asked Mom why he kept those. She said, "Probably for when you have kids." *"What the?"* "That's what Dad was like." I started to realize that a lot of the stuff he'd saved—boxes and boxes of Legos, the set of *How It Works* books, even the empty photo albums—was probably for when I had kids. I don't know why, but for some reason that made me angry.

Anyway, I put new batteries in the two-way radios, and I thought it would be a fun way for me and Grandma to talk. I gave her the baby one, so she wouldn't have to figure out any buttons, and it worked great. When I'd wake up I'd tell her good morning. And before I'd go to bed we'd usually talk. She was always waiting for me on the other end. I don't know how she knew when I'd be there. Maybe she just waited around all day.

"Grandma? Do you read me?" "Oskar?" "I'm OK. Over." "How

did you sleep, darling? Over." "What? I couldn't hear that. Over." "I asked how did you sleep. Over." "Fine," I'll say, looking at her across the street, my chin in my palm, "no bad dreams. Over." "One hundred dollars. Over." We never have all that much to say to each other. She tells me the same stories about Grandpa again and again, like how his hands were rough from making so many sculptures, and how he could talk to animals. "You'll come visit me this afternoon? Over?" "Yeah. I think so. Over." "Please try. Over." "I'll try. Over and out."

Some nights I took the two-way radio into bed with me and rested it on the side of the pillow that Buckminster wasn't on so I could hear what was going on in her bedroom. Sometimes she would wake me up in the middle of the night. It gave me heavy boots that she had nightmares, because I didn't know what she was dreaming about and there was nothing I could do to help her. She hollered, which woke me up, obviously, so my sleep depended on her sleep, and when I told her, "No bad dreams," I was talking about her.

Grandma knitted me white sweaters, white mittens, and white hats. She knew how much I liked dehydrated ice cream, which was one of my very few exceptions to veganism, because it's what astronauts have for dessert, and she went to the Hayden Planetarium and bought it for me. She picked up pretty rocks to give to me, even though she shouldn't have been carrying heavy things, and usually they were just Manhattan schist, anyway. A couple of days after the worst day, when I was on my way to my first appointment with Dr. Fein, I saw Grandma carrying a huge rock across Broadway. It was as big as a baby and must have weighed a ton. But she never gave that one to me, and she never mentioned it.

"Oskar."

"I'm OK."

One afternoon, I mentioned to Grandma that I was considering starting a stamp collection, and the next afternoon she had three albums for me and—"because I love you so much it hurts me, and because I want your wonderful collection to have a wonderful beginning"—a sheet of stamps of Great American Inventors.

"You've got Thomas Edison," she said, pointing at one of the stamps, "and Ben Franklin, Henry Ford, Eli Whitney, Alexander Graham Bell, George Washington Carver, Nikola Tesla, whoever that is, the Wright Brothers, J. Robert Oppenheimer—" "Who's he?" "He invented the bomb." "Which bomb?" "*The* bomb." "He wasn't a Great Inventor!" She said, "Great, not good."

"Grandma?" "Yes, darling?" "It's just that where's the plate block?" "The what?" "The thing on the side of the sheet with the numbers." "With the numbers?" "Yeah." "I got rid of it." "You *what?*" "I got rid of it. Was that wrong?" I felt myself starting to spaz, even though I was trying not to. "Well, it's not worth anything without the plate block!" "What?" "The *plate block!* These stamps. Aren't. *Valuable!*" She looked at me for a few seconds. "Yeah," she said, "I guess I heard of that. So I'll go back to the stamp shop tomorrow and get another sheet. These we can use for the mail." "There's no reason to get another," I told her, wanting to take back the last few things I said and try them again, being nicer this time, being a better grandson, or just a silent one. "There is a reason, Oskar." "I'm OK."

We spent so much time together. I don't think there's anyone that I spent more time with, at least not since Dad died, unless you count Buckminster. But there were a lot of people that I knew better. For example, I didn't know anything about what it was like when she was a kid, or how she met Grandpa, or what their marriage was like, or why he left. If I had to write her life story, all I could say is that her husband could talk to animals, and that I should never love anything as much as she loved me. So here's my question: What were we spending so much time doing if not getting to know each other?

"Did you do anything special today?" she asked that afternoon I started my search for the lock. When I think about everything that happened, from when we buried the coffin to when I dug it up, I always think about how I could have told her the truth then. It wasn't too late to turn around, before I got to the place I couldn't come back from. Even if she wouldn't have understood me, I would have been able to say it. "Yeah," I said. "I put the finishing touches on those scratch-and-sniff earrings for the craft fair. Also I mounted the eastern tiger swallowtail that Stan found dead on the stoop. And I worked on a bunch of letters, because I'd gotten behind on those." "Who are you writing letters to?" she asked, and it still wasn't too late. "Kofi Annan, Siegfried, Roy, Jacques Chirac, E. O. Wilson, Weird Al Yankovic, Bill Gates, Vladimir Putin, and some other people." She asked, "Why don't you write a letter to someone you know?" I started to tell her, "I don't know anyone," but then I heard something. Or I thought I heard something. There was noise in the apartment, like someone walking around. "What is that?" I asked. "My ears aren't a hundred dollars," she said. "But there's someone in the apartment. Maybe it's the renter?" "No," she said, "he went off to a museum earlier." "What museum?" "I don't know what museum. He said he wouldn't be back until late tonight." "But I can hear someone." "No you can't," she said. I said, "I'm ninety-nine percent sure I can." She said, "Maybe it's just your imagination." I was in the place that I couldn't come back from.

Thank you for your letter. Because of the large volume of mail I receive, I am unable to write personal responses. Nevertheless, know that I read and save every letter, with the hope of one day being able to give each the proper response it deserves. Until that day,

> *Most sincerely,*
> *Stephen Hawking*

I stayed up pretty late designing jewelry that night. I designed a Nature Hike Anklet, which leaves a trail of bright yellow dye when you walk, so in case you get lost, you can find your way back. I also designed a set of wedding rings, where each one takes the pulse of the person wearing it and sends a signal to the other ring to flash red with each heartbeat. Also I designed a pretty fascinating bracelet, where you put a rubber band around your favorite book of poems for a year, and then you take it off and wear it.

I don't know why, but as I was working, I couldn't stop thinking about that day Mom and I went to the storage facility in New Jersey. I kept going back to it, like a salmon, which I know about. Mom must have stopped to wash her face ten times. It was so quiet and so dark, and we were the only people there. What drinks were in the Coke machine? What fonts were the signs in? I went through the boxes in my brain. I took out a neat old film projector. What was the last film Dad made? Was I in it? I went through a bunch of the toothbrushes they give you at the dentist, and three baseballs that Dad had caught at games, which he wrote the dates on. What were the dates? My brain opened a box with old atlases (where there were two Germanys and one Yugoslavia) and souvenirs from business trips, like Russian dolls with dolls inside them with dolls inside them with dolls inside them . . . Which of those things had Dad kept for when I had kids?

It was 2:36 A.M. I went to Mom's room. She was sleeping, obviously. I watched the sheets breathe when she breathed, like how Dad used to say that trees inhale when people exhale, because I was too young to understand the truth about biological processes. I could tell that Mom was dreaming, but I didn't want to know what she was dreaming about, because I had enough of my own nightmares, and if she had been dreaming something happy, I would have been angry at her for dreaming something happy. I touched her incredibly gently. She jumped up and said, "What is it?" I said, "It's OK." She grabbed my shoulders and said, "What is it?" The way she was holding me hurt my arms, but I didn't show anything. "Remember when we went to the storage facility in New Jersey?" She let go of me and lay back down. "What?" "Where Dad's stuff is. Remember?" "It's the middle of the night, Oskar." "What was it called?" "*Oskar.*" "It's just that what was the name of the place?" She reached for her glasses on the bedside table, and I would have given all of my collections, and all of the jewelry I'd ever made, and all future birthday and Christmas presents just to hear her say "Black Storage." Or "Blackwell Storage." Or "Blackman." Or even "Midnight Storage." Or "Dark Storage." Or "Rainbow."

She made a weird face, like someone was hurting her, and said, "Store-a-Lot."

I'd lost count of the disappointments.

WHY I'M NOT WHERE YOU ARE
5/21/63

Your mother and I never talk about the past, that's a rule. I go to the door when she's using the bathroom, and she never looks over my shoulder when I'm writing, those are two more rules. I open doors for her but I never touch her back as she passes through, she never lets me watch her cook, she folds my pants but leaves my shirts by the ironing board, I never light candles when she's in the room, but I do blow candles out. It's a rule that we never listen to sad music, we made that rule early on, songs are as sad as the listener, we hardly ever listen to music. I change the sheets every morning to wash away my writing, we never sleep in the same bed twice, we never watch television shows about sick children, she never asks me how my day was, we always eat on the same side of the table, facing the window. So many rules, sometimes I can't remember what's a rule and what isn't, if anything we do is for its own sake, I'm leaving her today, is that the rule we've been organizing ourselves around this whole time, or am I about to break the organizing rule? I used to ride the bus here at the end of every week, to take the magazines and newspapers that people left behind when they got on their planes, your mother reads and reads and reads, she wants English, as much as she can get her hands on, is that a rule? I'd come late Friday afternoon, it used to be that I would go home with a magazine or two and maybe a paper, but she wanted more, more slang, more figures of speech, the bee's knees, the cat's pajamas, horse of a different color, dog-tired, she wanted to talk like she was born here, like she never came from anywhere else, so I started bringing a knapsack, which I would stuff with as much as would fit, it got heavy, my shoulders burned with English, she wanted more English, so I brought a suitcase, I filled it until I could barely zip the zipper, the suitcase sagged with English, my arms burned with English, my hands did, my knuckles, people must have thought I was actually going somewhere, the next morning my back ached with English, I found myself sticking around, spending more time than was necessary, watching the planes bring people and take people away, I started coming twice a week and staying for several hours, when it was time to go home I didn't want to leave, and when I wasn't here, I wanted to be here, now I come every morning before we open the store, and every evening after dinner, so what is it, am I hoping to see someone I know get off one of the planes, am I waiting for a relative who never will come, do I expect Anna? No, that's not it, it's not about my joy, the relief of my burden. I like to see people reunited, maybe that's a silly thing, but what can I say, I like to see people run to each other, I like the kissing and the crying, I like the impatience, the stories that the mouth can't tell fast enough, the ears that aren't big enough, the eyes that can't take in all of the change, I like the hugging, the bringing together, the end of missing someone, I sit on the side with a coffee and write in my daybook, I examine the flight schedules that I've already memorized, I observe, I write, I try not to remember the life that I didn't want to lose but lost and have to remember, being here fills my heart with so much joy, even if the joy isn't mine, and at the end of the day I fill the suitcase with old news. Maybe that was the story I was telling myself when I met your mother, I thought we could run to each other, I thought we could have a beautiful reunion, although we had hardly known each other in Dresden. It didn't work. We've wandered in place, our arms outstretched, but not toward each other, they're marking off distance, everything between us has been a rule to govern our life together, everything a measurement, a marriage of millimeters, of rules, when she gets up to go to the shower, I feed the animals—that's a rule—so she doesn't have to be self-conscious, she finds things to keep herself busy when I undress at night—rule—she goes to the door to make sure it's locked, she double-checks the oven, she tends to her collections in the china cabinet, she checks, again, the curlers that she hasn't used since we met, and when she gets undressed, I've never been so busy in my life. Only a few months into our marriage, we started marking off areas in the apartment as "Nothing Places," in which one could be assured of complete privacy, we agreed that we never would look at the marked-off zones, that they would be nonexistent territories in the apartment in which one could temporarily cease to exist, the first was in the bedroom, by the foot of the bed, we marked it off with red tape on the carpet, and it was just large enough to stand in, it was a good place to disappear, we knew it was there but we never looked at it, it worked so well that we decided to create a Nothing Place in the living room, it seemed necessary, because there are times when one needs to disappear while in the living room, and sometimes one simply wants to disappear, we made this zone slightly larger so that one of us could lie down in it, it was a rule that you never would look at that rectangle of space, it didn't exist, and when you were in it, neither did you, for a while that was enough, but only for a while, we required more rules, on our second anniversary we marked off the entire guest room as a Nothing Place, it seemed like a good idea at the time, sometimes a small patch at the foot of the bed or a rectangle in the living room isn't enough privacy, the side of the door that faced the guest room was Nothing, the side that faced the hallway was Something, the knob that connected them was neither Something nor Nothing. The walls of the hallway were Nothing, even pictures need to disappear, especially pictures, but the hallway itself was Something, the bathtub was Nothing, the bathwater was Something, the hair on our bodies was Nothing, of course, but once it collected around the drain it was Something, we were trying to make our lives easier, trying, with all of our rules, to make life effortless. But a friction began to arise between Nothing and Something, in the morning the Nothing vase cast a Something shadow, like the memory of someone you've lost, what can you say about that, at night the Nothing light from the guest room spilled under the Nothing door and stained the Something hallway, there's nothing to say. It became difficult to navigate from Something to Something without accidentally walking through Nothing, and when Something—a key, a pen, a pocketwatch—was accidentally left in a Nothing Place, it never could be retrieved, that was an unspoken rule, like nearly all of our rules have been. There came a point, a year or two ago, when our apartment was more Nothing than Something, that in itself didn't have to be a problem, it could have been a good thing, it could have saved us. We got worse. I was sitting on the sofa in the second bedroom one afternoon, thinking and thinking and thinking, when I realized I was on a Something island. "How did I get here," I wondered, surrounded by Nothing, "and how can I get back?" The longer your mother and I lived together, the more we took each other's assumptions for granted, the less was said, the more misunderstood, I'd often remember having designated a space as Nothing when she was sure we had agreed that it was Something, our unspoken agreements led to disagreements, to suffering, I started to undress right in front of her, this was just a few months ago, and she said, "Thomas! What are you doing!" and I gestured, "I thought this was Nothing," covering myself with one of my daybooks, and she said, "It's Something!" We took the blueprint of our apartment from the hallway closet and taped it to the inside of the front door, with an orange and a green marker we separated Something from Nothing. "This is Something," we decided. "This is Nothing." "Something." "Something." "Nothing." "Something." "Nothing." "Nothing." "Nothing." Everything was forever fixed, there would be only peace and happiness, it wasn't until last night, our last night together, that the inevitable question finally arose, I told her, "Something," by covering her face with my hands and then lifting them like a marriage veil. "We must be." But I knew, in the most protected part of my heart, the truth.

Excuse me, do you know what time it is?

The beautiful girl didn't know the time, she was in a hurry, she said, "Good luck," I smiled, she hurried off, her skirt catching the air as she ran, sometimes I can hear my bones straining under the weight of all of the lives I'm not living. In this life, I'm sitting in an airport trying to explain myself to my unborn son, I'm filling the pages of this, my last day-book, I'm thinking of a loaf of black bread that I left out one night, the next morning I saw the outline of the mouse that had eaten through it, I cut the loaf into slices and saw the mouse at each moment, I'm thinking of Anna, I would give everything never to think about her again, I can only hold on to the things I want to lose, I'm thinking of the day we met, she accompanied her father to meet my father, they were friends, they had talked about art and literature before the war, but once the war began, they talked only about war, I saw her approaching when she was still far away, I was fifteen, she was seventeen, we sat together on the grass while our fathers spoke inside, how could we have been younger? We talked about nothing in particular, but it felt like we were talking about the most important things, we pulled fistfuls of grass, and I asked her if she liked to read, she said, "No, but there are books that I love, love, love," she said it just like that, three times, "Do you like to dance?" she asked, "Do you like to swim?" I asked, we looked at each other until it felt like everything would burst into flames, "Do you like animals?" "Do you like bad weather?" "Do you like your friends?" I told her about my sculpture, she said, "I'm sure you will be a great artist." "How can you be sure?" "I just am." I told her I already was a great artist, because that's how unsure of myself I was, she said, "I meant famous," I told her that wasn't what mattered to me, she asked what mattered to me, I told her I did it for its own sake, she laughed and said, "You don't understand yourself," I said, "Of course I do," she said, "Of course," I said, "I do!" She said, "There's nothing wrong with not understanding yourself," she saw through the shell of me into the center of me, "Do you like music?" Our fathers came out of the house and stood at the door, one of them asked, "What are we going to do?" I knew that our time together was almost over, I asked her if she liked sports, she asked me if I liked chess, I asked her if she liked fallen trees, she went home with her father, the center of me followed her, but I was left with the shell of me, I needed to see her again, I couldn't explain my need to myself, and that's why it was such a beautiful need, there's nothing wrong with not understanding yourself. The next day, I walked half an hour to her house, fearing someone would see me on the road between our neighborhoods, too much to explain that I couldn't explain, I wore a broad-brimmed hat and kept my head down, I heard the footsteps of those passing me, and I didn't know if they were a man's, woman's, or child's, I felt as if I were walking the rungs of a ladder laid flat, I was too ashamed or embarrassed to make myself known to her, how would I have explained it, was I walking up the ladder or down? I hid behind a mound of earth that had been dug up to make a grave for some old books, literature was the only religion her father practiced, when a book fell on the floor he kissed it, when he was done with a book he tried to give it away to someone who would love it, and if he couldn't find a worthy recipient, he buried it, I looked for her all day but didn't see her, not in the yard, not through a window, I promised myself I would stay until I found her, but as night began to come in, I knew I had to go home, I hated myself for going, why couldn't I be the kind of person who stays? I walked back with my head down, I couldn't stop thinking about her even though I hardly knew her, I didn't know what good would come of going to see her, but I knew that I needed to be near her, it occurred to me, as I walked back to her the next day with my head down, that she might not be thinking of me. The books had been buried, so I hid this time behind a group of trees, I imagined their roots wrapped around books, pulling nourishment from the pages, I imagined rings of letters in their trunks, I waited for hours, I saw your mother in one of the second-floor windows, she was just a girl, she looked back at me, but I didn't see Anna. A leaf fell, it was yellow like paper, I had to go home, and then, the next day, I had to go back to her. I skipped my classes, the walk happened so quickly, my neck strained from hiding my face, my arm brushed the arm of someone passing — a strong, solid arm — and I tried to imagine whom it belonged to, a farmer, a stoneworker, a carpenter, a bricklayer. When I got to her house I hid beneath one of the back windows, a train rattled past in the distance, people coming, people leaving, soldiers, children, the window shook like an eardrum, I waited all day, did she go

on some sort of trip, was she on an errand, was she hiding from me? When I came home my father told me that her father had paid another visit, I asked him why he was out of breath, he said, "Things keep getting worse," I realized that her father and I must have passed each other on the road that morning. "What things?" Was his the strong arm I felt brushing past me? "Everything. The world." Did he see me, or did my hat and lowered head protect me? "Since when?" Perhaps his head was down, too. "Since the beginning." The harder I tried not to think about her, the more I thought about her, the more impossible it became to explain, I went back to her house, I walked the road between our two neighborhoods with my head down, she wasn't there again, I wanted to call her name, but I didn't want her to hear my voice, all of my desire was based on that one brief exchange, held in the palm of our half hour together were one hundred million arguments, and impossible admissions, and silences. I had so much to ask her, "Do you like to lie on your stomach and look for things under the ice?" "Do you like plays?" "Do you like it when you can hear something before you can see it?" I went again the next day, the walk was exhausting, with each step I further convinced myself that she had thought badly of me, or worse, that she hadn't thought of me at all, I walked with my head bowed, my broad-brimmed cap pushed low, when you hide your face from the world, you can't see the world, and that's why, in the middle of my youth, in the middle of Europe, in between our two villages, on the verge of losing everything, I bumped into something and was knocked to the ground. It took me several breaths to gather myself together, at first I thought I'd walked into a tree, but then that tree became a person, who was also recovering on the ground, and then I saw that it was her, and she saw that it was me, "Hello," I said, brushing myself off, "Hello," she said. "This is so funny." "Yes." How could it be explained? "Where are you going?" I asked. "Just for a walk," she said, "and you?" "Just for a walk." We helped each other up, she brushed leaves from my hair, I wanted to touch her hair, "That's not true," I said, not knowing what the next words out of my mouth would be, but wanting them to be mine, wanting, more than I'd ever wanted anything, to express the center of me and be understood. "I was walking to see you." I told her, "I've come to your house each of the last six days. For some reason I needed to see you again." She was silent, I had made a fool of myself, there's nothing wrong with not understanding yourself and she started laughing, laughing harder than I'd ever felt anyone laugh, the laughter brought on tears, and the tears brought on more tears, and then I started laughing, out of the most deep and complete shame, "I was walking to you," I said again, as if to push my nose into my own shit, "because I wanted to see you again," she laughed and laughed, "That explains it," she said when she was able to speak. "It?" "That explains why, each of the last six days, you weren't at your house." We stopped laughing, I took the world into me, rearranged it, and sent it back out as a question: "Do you like me?"

Do you know what time it is?

He told me it's 9:38, he looked so much like me, I could tell that he saw it, too, we shared the smile of recognizing ourselves in each other, how many imposters do I have? Do we all make the same mistakes, or has one of us gotten it right, or even just a bit less wrong, am I the imposter? I just told myself the time, and I'm thinking of your mother, how young and old she is, how she carries around her money in an envelope, how she makes me wear suntan lotion no matter what the weather, how she sneezes and says, "God bless me," God bless her. She's at home now, writing her life story, she's typing while I'm leaving, unaware of the chapters to come. It was my suggestion, and at the time I thought it was a very good one, I thought maybe if she could express herself rather than suffer herself, if she had a way to relieve the burden, she lived for nothing more than living, with nothing to get inspired by, to care for, to call her own, she helped out at the store, then came home and sat in her big chair and stared at her magazines, not at them but through them, she let the dust accumulate on her shoulders. I pulled my old typewriter from the closet and set her up in the guest room with everything she'd need, a card table for a desk, a chair, paper, some glasses, a pitcher of water, a hotplate, some flowers, crackers, it wasn't a proper office but it would do, she said, "But it's a Nothing Place," I wrote, "What better place to write your life story?" She said, "My eyes are crummy," I told her they were good enough, she said, "They barely work," putting her fingers over them, but I knew she was just embarrassed by the attention, she said, "I don't know how to write," I told her there's nothing to know, just let it come out, she put her hands on the typewriter, like a blind person feeling someone's face for the first time, and said, "I've never used one of these before," I told her, "Just press the keys," she said she would try, and though I'd known how to use a typewriter since I was a boy, trying was more than I ever could do. For months it was the same, she would wake up at 4 A.M. and go to the guest room, the animals would follow her, I would come here, I wouldn't see her again until breakfast, and then after work we'd go our separate ways and not see each other until it was time to fall asleep, was I worried about her, putting all of her life into her life story, no, I was so happy for her, I remembered the feeling she was feeling, the exhilaration of building the world anew, I heard from behind the door the sounds of creation, the letters pressing into the paper, the pages being pulled from the machine, everything being, for once, better than it was and as good as it could be, everything full of meaning, and then one morning this spring, after years of working in solitude. She said, "I'd like to show you something." I followed her to the guest room, she pointed in the direction of the card table in the corner, on which the typewriter was wedged between two stacks of paper of about the same height, we walked over together, she touched everything on the table and then handed me the stack on the left, she said, "My Life." "Excuse me?" I asked by shrugging my shoulders, she tapped the page, "My Life," she said again, I riffled the pages, there must have been a thousand of them, I put the stack down, "What is this?" I asked by putting her palms on the tops of my hands and then turning my palms upward, flipping her hands off mine, "My Life," she said, so proudly, "I just made it up to the present moment. Just now. I'm all caught up with myself. The last thing I wrote was 'I'm going to show him what I've written. I hope he loves it.'" I picked up the pages and wandered through them, trying to find the one on which she was born, her first love, when she last saw her parents, and I was looking for Anna, too, I searched and searched, I got a paper cut on my forefinger and bled a little flower onto the page on which I should have seen her kissing somebody, but this was all I saw:

I wanted to cry but I didn't cry, I probably should have cried, I should have drowned us there in the room, ended our suffering, they would have found us floating face-down in two thousand white pages, or buried under the salt of my evaporated tears, I remembered, just then and far too late, that years before I had pulled the ribbon from the machine, it had been an act of revenge against the typewriter and against myself, I'd pulled it into one long thread, unwinding the negative it held—the future homes I had created for Anna, the letters I wrote without response—as if it would protect me from my actual life. But worse—it's unspeakable, write it!—I realized that your mother couldn't see the emptiness, she couldn't see anything. I knew that she'd had difficulty, I'd felt her grasp my arm when we walked, I'd heard her say, "My eyes are crummy," but I thought it was a way to touch me, another figure of speech, why didn't she ask for help, why, instead, did she ask for all of those magazines and papers if she couldn't see them, was that how she asked for help? Was that why she held so tightly to railings, why she wouldn't cook with me watching, or change her clothes with me watching, or open doors? Did she always have something to read in front of her so she wouldn't have to look at anything else? All of the words I'd written to her over all of those years, had I never said anything to her at all? "Wonderful," I told her by rubbing her shoulder in a certain way that we have between us, "it's wonderful." "Go ahead," she said, "Tell me what you think." I put her hand on the side of my face, I tilted my head toward my shoulder, in the context in which she thought our conversation was taking place that meant, "I can't read it here like this. I'll take it to the bedroom, I'll read it slowly, carefully, I'll give your life story what it deserves." But in what I knew to be the context of our conversation it meant, "I have failed you."

Do you know what time it is?

The first time Anna and I made love was behind her father's shed, the previous owner had been a farmer, but Dresden started to overtake the surrounding villages and the farm was divided into nine plots of land, Anna's family owned the largest. The walls of the shed collapsed one autumn afternoon — "a leaf too many," her father joked — and the next day he made new walls of shelves, so that the books themselves would separate inside from outside. (The new, overhanging roof protected the books from rain, but during the winter the pages would freeze together, come spring, they let out a sigh.) He made a little salon of the space, carpets, two small couches, he loved to go out there in the evenings with a glass of whiskey and a pipe, and take down books and look through the wall at the center of the city. He was an intellectual, although he wasn't important, maybe he would have been important if he had lived longer, maybe great books were coiled within him like springs, books that could have separated inside from outside. The day Anna and I made love for the first time, he met me in the yard, he was standing with a disheveled man whose curly hair sprang up in every direction, whose glasses were bent, whose white shirt was stained with the fingerprints of his print-stained hands, "Thomas, please meet my friend Simon Goldberg." I said hello, I didn't know who he was or why I was being introduced to him, I wanted to find Anna, Mr. Goldberg asked me what I did, his voice was handsome and broken, like a cobblestone street, I told him, "I don't do anything," he laughed, "Don't be so modest," Anna's father said. "I want to be a sculptor." Mr. Goldberg took off his glasses, untucked his shirt from his pants, and cleaned his lenses with his shirttail. "You want to be a sculptor?" I said, "I am trying to be a sculptor." He put his glasses back on his face, pulling the wire earpieces behind his ears, and said, "In your case, trying is being." "What do you do?" I asked, in a voice more challenging than I'd wanted. He said, "I don't do anything anymore." Anna's father told him, "Don't be so modest," although he didn't laugh this time, and he told me, "Simon is one of the great minds of our age." "I'm trying," Mr. Goldberg said to me, as if only the two of us existed. "Trying what?" I asked, in a voice more concerned than I'd wanted, he took off his glasses again, "Trying to be." While her father and Mr. Goldberg spoke inside the makeshift salon, whose books separated inside from outside, Anna and I went for a walk over the reeds that lay across the gray-green clay by what once was a stall for horses, and down to where you could see the edge of the water if you knew where and how to look, we got mud halfway up our socks, and juice from the fallen fruit we kicked out of our way, from the top of the property we could see the busy train station, the commotion of the war grew nearer and nearer, soldiers went east through our town, and refugees went west, or stayed there, trains arrived and departed, hundreds of them, we ended where we began, outside the shed that was a salon. "Let's sit down," she said, we lowered ourselves to the ground, our backs against the shelves, we could hear them talking inside and smell the pipe smoke that seeped between the books, Anna started kissing me, "But what if they come out?" I whispered, she touched my ears, which meant their voices would keep us safe. She put her hands all over me, I didn't know what she was doing, I touched every part of her, what was I doing, did we understand something that we couldn't explain? Her father said, "You can stay for as long as you need. You can stay forever." She pulled her shirt over her head, I held her breasts in my hands, it was awkward and it was natural, she pulled my shirt over my head, in the moment I couldn't see, Mr. Goldberg laughed and said, "Forever," I heard him pacing in the small room, I put my hand under her skirt, between her legs, everything felt on the verge of bursting into flames, without any experience I knew what to do, it was exactly as it had been in my dreams, as if all the information had been coiled within me like a spring, everything that was happening had happened before and would happen again, "I don't recognize the world anymore," Anna's father said, Anna rolled onto her back, behind a wall of books through which voices and pipe smoke escaped, "I want to make love," Anna whispered, I knew exactly what to do, night was arriving, trains were departing, I lifted her skirt, Mr. Goldberg said, "I've never recognized it more," and I could hear him breathing on the other side of the books, if he had taken one from the shelf he would have seen everything. But the books protected us. I was in her for only a second before I burst into flames, she whimpered, Mr. Goldberg stomped his foot and let out a cry like a wounded animal, I asked her if she was upset, she shook her head no, I fell onto her, resting my cheek against her chest, and I saw your mother's face in the second-floor window, "Then why are you crying?" I asked, exhausted and experienced, "War!" Mr. Goldberg said, angry and defeated, his voice trembling: "We go on killing each other to no purpose! It is war waged by humanity against humanity, and it will only end when there's no one left to fight!" She said, "It hurt."

Do you know what time it is?

Every morning before breakfast, and before I come here, your mother and I go to the guest room, the animals follow us, I thumb through the blank pages and gesture laughter and gesture tears, if she asks what I'm laughing or crying about, I tap my finger on the page, and if she asks, "Why?" I press her hand against her heart, and then against my heart, or I touch her forefinger to the mirror, or touch it, quickly, against the hot-plate, sometimes I wonder if she knows, I wonder in my Nothingest moments if she's testing me, if she types nonsense all day long, or types nothing at all, just to see what I'll do in response, she wants to know if I love her, that's all anyone wants from anyone else, not love itself but the knowledge that love is there, like new batteries in the flashlight in the emergency kit in the hall closet, "Don't let anyone see it," I told her that morning she first showed it to me, and maybe I was trying to protect her, and maybe I was trying to protect myself, "We'll have it be our secret until it's perfect. We'll work on it together. We'll make it the greatest book anyone has ever written." "You think that's possible?" she asked, outside, leaves fell from the trees, inside, we were letting go of our concern for that kind of truth, "I do," I said by touching her arm, "If we try hard enough." She reached her hands in front of her and found my face, she said, "I'm going to write about this." Ever since that day I've been encouraging her, begging her, to write more, to shovel deeper, "Describe his face," I tell her, running my hand over the empty page, and then, the next morning, "Describe his eyes," and then, holding the page to the window, letting it fill with light, "Describe his irises," and then, "His pupils." She never asks, "Whose?" She never asks, "Why?" Are they my own eyes on those pages? I've seen the left stack double and quadruple, I've heard of asides that have become tangents that have become passages that have become chapters, and I know, because she told me, that what was once the second sentence is now the second-to-last. Just two days ago she said that her life story was happening faster than her life, "What do you mean?" I asked with my hands, "So little happens," she said, "and I'm so good at remembering." "You could write about the store?" "I've described every diamond in the case." "You could write about other people." "My life story is the story of everyone I've ever met." "You could write about your feelings." She asked, "Aren't my life and my feelings the same thing?"

Excuse me, where do you get tickets?

I have so much to tell you, the problem isn't that I'm running out of time, I'm running out of room, this book is filling up, there couldn't be enough pages, I looked around the apartment this morning for one last time and there was writing everywhere, filling the walls and mirrors, I'd rolled up the rugs so I could write on the floors, I'd written on the windows and around the bottles of wine we were given but never drank, I wear only short sleeves, even when it's cold, because my arms are books, too. But there's too much to express. I'm sorry. That's what I've been trying to say to you, I'm sorry for everything. For having said goodbye to Anna when maybe I could have saved her and our idea, or at least died with them. I'm sorry for my inability to let the unimportant things go, for my inability to hold on to the important things. I'm sorry for what I'm about to do to your mother and to you. I'm sorry I'll never get to see your face, and feed you, and tell you bedtime stories. I've tried in my own way to explain myself, but when I think of your mother's life story, I know that I haven't explained a thing, she and I are no different, I've been writing Nothing, too. "The dedication," she said to me this morning, just a few hours ago, when I went to the guest room for the last time, "Read it." I touched my fingers to her eyelids and opened her eyes wide enough to convey every possible meaning, I was about to leave her behind without saying goodbye, to turn my back on a marriage of millimeters and rules, "Do you think it's too much?" she asked, bringing me back to her invisible dedication, I touched her with my right hand, not knowing to whom she had dedicated her life story, "It's not silly, is it?" I touched her with my right hand, and I was missing her already, I wasn't having second thoughts, but I was having thoughts, "It's not vain?" I touched her with my right hand, and for all I knew she'd dedicated it to herself, "Does it mean everything to you?" she asked, this time putting her finger on what wasn't there, I touched her with my left hand, and for all I knew she'd dedicated it to me. I told her that I had to get going. I asked her, with a long series of gestures that would have made no sense to anyone else, if she wanted anything special. "You always get it right," she said. "Some nature magazines?" (I flapped her hands like wings.) "That would be nice." "Maybe something with art in it?"

(I took her hand, like a brush, and painted an imaginary painting in front of us.) "Sure." She walked me to the door, as she always did, "I might not be back before you fall asleep," I told her, putting my open hand on her shoulder and then easing her cheek onto my palm. She said, "But I can't fall asleep without you." I held her hands against my head and nodded that she could, we walked to the door, navigating a Something path. "And what if I can't fall asleep without you?" I held her hands against my head and nodded, "And what if?" I nodded, "Answer me what," she said, I shrugged my shoulders, "Promise me you'll take care," she said, pulling the hood of my coat over my head, "Promise me you'll take extra-special care. I know you look both ways before you cross the street, but I want you to look both ways a second time, because I told you to." I nodded. She asked, "Are you wearing lotion?" With my hands I told her, "It's cold out. You have a cold." She asked, "But are you?" I surprised myself by touching her with my right hand. I could live a lie, but not bring myself to tell that small one. She said, "Hold on," and ran inside the apartment and came back with a bottle of lotion. She squeezed some into her hand, rubbed her hands together, and spread it on the back of my neck, and on the tops of my hands, and between my fingers, and on my nose and forehead and cheeks and chin, everything that was exposed, in the end I was the clay and she was the sculptor, I thought, it's a shame that we have to live, but it's a tragedy that we get to live only one life, because if I'd had two lives, I would have spent one of them with her. I would have stayed in the apartment with her, torn the blueprint from the door, held her on the bed, said, "I want two rolls," sang, "Start spreading the news," laughed, "Ha ha ha!" cried, "Help!" I would have spent that life among the living. We rode the elevator down together and walked to the threshold, she stopped and I kept going. I knew I was about to destroy what she'd been able to rebuild, but I had only one life. I heard her behind me. Because of myself, or despite myself, I turned back, "Don't cry," I told her, by putting her fingers on my face and pushing imaginary tears up my cheeks and back into my eyes, "I know," she said as she wiped the real tears from her cheeks, I stomped my feet, this meant, "I won't go to the airport." "Go to the airport,"

she said, I touched her chest, then pointed her hand out toward the world, then pointed her hand at her chest, "I know," she said, "Of course I know that." I held her hands and pretended we were behind an invisible wall, or behind the imaginary painting, our palms exploring its surface, then, at the risk of saying too much, I held one of her hands over my eyes, and the other over her eyes, "You are too good to me," she said, I put her hands on my head and nodded yes, she laughed, I love it when she laughs, although the truth is I am not in love with her, she said, "I love you," I told her how I felt, this is how I told her: I held her hands out to her sides, I pointed her index fingers toward each other and slowly, very slowly, moved them in, the closer they got, the more slowly I moved them, and then, as they were about to touch, as they were only a dictionary page from touching, pressing on opposite sides of the word "love," I stopped them, I stopped them and held them there. I don't know what she thought, I don't know what she understood, or what she wouldn't allow herself to understand, I turned around and walked away from her, I didn't look back, I won't. I'm telling you all of this because I'll never be your father, and you will always be my child. I want you to know, at least, that it's not out of selfishness that I am leaving, how can I explain that? I can't live, I've tried and I can't. If that sounds simple, it's simple like a mountain is simple. Your mother suffered, too, but she chose to live, and lived, be her son and her husband. I don't expect that you'll ever understand me, much less forgive me, you might not even read these words, if your mother gives them to you at all. It's time to go. I want you to be happy, I want that more than I want happiness for myself, does that sound simple? I'm leaving. I'll rip these pages from this book, take them to the mailbox before I get on the plane, address the envelope to "My Unborn Child," and I'll never write another word again, I am gone, I am no longer here. With love, Your father

I want to buy a ticket to Dresden.

What are you doing here?

You have to go home. You should be in bed.

Let me take you home.

You're being crazy. You're going to catch a cold.

You're going to catch a colder.

~~HEAVY BOOTS~~

HEAVIER BOOTS

Twelve weekends later was the first performance of *Hamlet*, although it was actually an abbreviated modern version, because the real *Hamlet* is too long and confusing, and most of the kids in my class have ADD. For example, the famous "To be or not to be" speech, which I know about from the *Collected Shakespeare* set Grandma bought me, was cut down so that it was just, "To be or not to be, that's the question."

Everyone had to have a part, but there weren't enough real parts, and I didn't go to the auditions because my boots were too heavy to go to school that day, so I got the part of Yorick. At first that made me self-conscious. I suggested to Mrs. Rigley that maybe I could just play tambourine in the orchestra or something. She said, "There is no orchestra." I said, "Still." She told me, "It'll be terrific. You'll wear all black, and the makeup crew will paint your hands and neck black, and the costume crew will create some sort of a papier-mâché skull for you to wear over your head. It'll really give the illusion that you don't have a body." I thought about that for a minute, and then I told her my better idea. "What I'll do is, I'll invent an invisibility suit that has a camera on my back that takes video of everything behind me and plays it on a plasma screen that I'll wear on my front, which will cover everything except my face. It'll look like I'm not there at all." She said, "Nifty." I said, "But is Yorick even a part?" She whispered into my ear, "If anything, I'm afraid you'll steal the show." Then I was excited to be Yorick.

Opening night was pretty great. We had a fog machine, so the cemetery was just like a cemetery in a movie. "Alas, poor Yorick!" Jimmy Snyder said, holding my face, "I knew him, Horatio." I didn't have a plasma screen, because the costumes budget wasn't big enough, but from underneath the skull I could look around without anyone noticing. I saw lots of people I knew, which made me feel special. Mom and Ron and Grandma were there, obviously. Toothpaste was there with Mr. and Mrs. Hamilton, which was nice, and Mr. and Mrs. Minch were there, too, because The Minch was Guildenstern. A lot of the Blacks that I had met in those twelve weekends were there. Abe was there. Ada and Agnes were there. (They were actually sitting next to each other, although they didn't realize it.) I saw Albert and Alice and Allen and Arnold and Barbara and Barry. They must have been half the audience. But what was weird was that they didn't know what they had in common, which was kind of like how I didn't know what the thumbtack, the bent spoon, the square of aluminum foil, and all those other things I dug up in Central Park had to do with each other.

I was incredibly nervous, but I maintained my confidence, and I was extremely subtle. I know, because there was a standing ovation, which made me feel like one hundred dollars.

The second performance was also pretty great. Mom was there, but Ron had to work late. That was OK, though, because I didn't want him there anyway. Grandma was there, obviously. I didn't see any of the Blacks, but I knew that most people go to only one show unless they're your parents, so I didn't feel too bad about that. I tried to give an extra-special performance, and I think I did. "Alas, poor Yorick. I knew him, Horatio; a really funny and excellent guy. I used to ride on his back all the time, and now, it's so awful to think about!"

Only Grandma came the next night. Mom had a late meeting because one of her cases was about to go to trial, and I didn't ask where Ron was because I was embarrassed, and I didn't want him there anyway. As I was standing as still as I could, with Jimmy Snyder's hand under my chin, I wondered, *What's the point of giving an extremely subtle performance if basically no one is watching?*

Grandma didn't come backstage to say hi before the performance the next night, or bye after, but I saw that she was there. Through the eye sockets I could see her standing in the back of the gym, underneath the basketball hoop. Her makeup was absorbing the lighting in a fascinating way, which made her look almost ultraviolet. "Alas, poor Yorick." I was as still as I could be, and the whole time I was thinking, *What trial is more important than the greatest play in history?*

The next performance was only Grandma again. She cried at all the wrong times and cracked up at all the wrong times. She applauded when the audience found out the news that Ophelia drowned, which is supposed to be bad news, and she booed when Hamlet scored his first point in the duel against Laertes at the end, which is good, for obvious reasons.

"This is where his lips were that I used to kiss a lot. Where are your jokes now, your games, your songs?"

Backstage, before closing night, Jimmy Snyder imitated Grandma to the rest of the cast and crew. I guess I hadn't realized how loud she was. I had gotten so angry at myself for noticing her, but I was wrong, it was her fault. Everyone noticed. Jimmy did her exactly right—the way she swatted her left hand at something funny, like there was a fly in front of her face. The way she tilted her head, like she was concentrating incredibly hard on something, and how she sneezed and told herself, "God bless me." And how she cried and said, "That's sad," so everyone could hear it.

I sat there while he made all the kids crack up. Even Mrs. Rigley cracked up, and so did her husband, who played the piano during the set changes. I didn't mention that she was my grandma, and I didn't tell him to stop. Outside, I was cracking up too. Inside, I was wishing that she were tucked away in a portable pocket, or that she'd also had an invisibility suit. I wished the two of us could go somewhere far away, like the Sixth Borough.

She was there again that night, in the back row, although only the first three rows were taken. I watched her from under the skull. She had her hand pressed against her ultraviolet heart, and I could hear her saying, "That's sad. That's so sad." I thought about the unfinished scarf, and the rock she carried across Broadway, and how she had lived so much life but still needed imaginary friends, and the one thousand thumb wars.

MARGIE CARSON. Hey, Hamlet, where's Polonius?

JIMMY SNYDER. At supper.

MARGIE CARSON. At supper! Where?

JIMMY SNYDER. Not where he eats, but where he's eaten.

MARGIE CARSON. Wow!

JIMMY SNYDER. A king can end up going through the guts of a beggar.

I felt, that night, on that stage, under that skull, incredibly close to everything in the universe, but also extremely alone. I wondered, for the first time in my life, if life was worth all the work it took to live. What *exactly* made it worth it? What's so horrible about being dead forever, and not feeling anything, and not even dreaming? What's so great about feeling and dreaming?

Jimmy put his hand under my face. "This is where his lips were that I used to kiss a lot. Where are your jokes now, your games, your songs?"

Maybe it was because of everything that had happened in those twelve weeks. Or maybe it was because I felt so close and alone that night. I just couldn't be dead any longer.

ME. Alas, poor Hamlet [*I take* JIMMY SNYDER's *face into my hand*]; I knew him, Horatio.

JIMMY SNYDER. But Yorick . . . you're only . . . a skull.

ME. So what? I don't care. Screw you.

JIMMY SNYDER. [*whispers*] This is not in the play. [*He looks for help from* MRS. RIGLEY, *who is in the front row, flipping through the script. She draws circles in the air with her right hand, which is the universal sign for "improvise."*]

ME. I knew him, Horatio; a jerk of infinite stupidity, a most excellent masturbator in the second-floor boys' bathroom—I have proof. Also, he's dyslexic.

JIMMY SNYDER. [*Can't think of anything to say*]

ME. Where be your gibes now, your gambols, your songs?

JIMMY SNYDER. What are you *talking* about?

ME. [*Raises hand to scoreboard*] Succotash my cocker spaniel, you fudging crevasse-hole dipshiitake!

JIMMY SNYDER. Huh?

ME. You are guilty of having abused those less strong than you: of making the lives of nerds like me and Toothpaste and The Minch almost impossible, of imitating mental retards, of prank-calling people who get almost no phone calls anyway, of terrorizing domesticated animals and old people — who, by the way, are smarter and more knowledgeable than you — of making fun of me just because I have a pussy . . . And I've seen you litter, too.

JIMMY SNYDER. I never prank-called any retards.

ME. You were adopted.

JIMMY SNYDER. [*Searches audience for his parents*]

ME. And nobody loves you.

JIMMY SNYDER. [*His eyes fill with tears*]

ME. And you have amyotrophic lateral sclerosis.

JIMMY SNYDER. Huh?

ME. On behalf of the dead . . . [*I pull the skull off my head. Even though it's made of papier-mâché it's really hard. I smash it against* JIMMY SNYDER*'s head, and I smash it again. He falls to the ground, because he is unconscious, and I can't believe how strong I actually am. I smash his head again with all my force and blood starts to come out of his nose and ears. But I still don't feel any sympathy for him. I want him to bleed, because he deserves it. And nothing else makes any sense.* DAD *doesn't make sense.* MOM *doesn't make sense.* THE AUDIENCE *doesn't make sense. The folding chairs and fog-machine fog don't make sense. Shakespeare doesn't make sense. The stars that I know are on the other side of the gym ceiling don't make sense. The only thing that makes any sense right then is my smashing* JIMMY SNYDER*'s face. His blood. I knock a bunch of his teeth into his mouth, and I think they go down his throat. There is blood everywhere, covering everything. I keep smashing the skull against his skull, which is also* RON*'s skull (for letting* MOM *get on with life) and* MOM*'s skull (for getting on with life) and* DAD*'s skull (for dying) and* GRANDMA*'s skull (for embarrassing me so much) and* DR. FEIN*'s skull (for asking if any good could come out of* DAD*'s death) and the skulls of everyone else I know.* THE AUDIENCE *is applauding, all of them, because I am making so much sense. They are giving me a standing ovation as I hit him again and again. I hear them call*]

THE AUDIENCE. Thank you! Thank you, Oskar! We love you so much! We'll protect you!

It would have been great.

I looked out across the audience from underneath the skull, with Jimmy's hand under my chin. "Alas, poor Yorick." I saw Abe Black, and he saw me. I knew that we were sharing something with our eyes, but I didn't know what, and I didn't know if it mattered.

It was twelve weekends earlier that I'd gone to visit Abe Black in Coney Island. I'm very idealistic, but I knew I couldn't walk that far, so I took a cab. Even before we were out of Manhattan, I realized that the $7.68 in my wallet wasn't going to be enough. I don't know if you'd count it as a lie or not that I didn't say anything. It's just that I knew I had to get there, and there was no alternative. When the cab driver pulled over in front of the building, the meter said $76.50. I said, "Mr. Mahaltra, are you an optimist or a pessimist?" He said, "What?" I said, "Because unfortunately I only have seven dollars and sixty-eight cents." "Seven dollars?" "And sixty-eight cents." "This is not happening." "Unfortunately, it is. But if you give me your address, I promise I'll send you the rest." He put his head down on the steering wheel. I asked if he was OK. He said, "Keep your seven dollars and sixty-eight cents." I said, "I promise I'll send you the money. I promise." He handed me his card, which was actually the card of a dentist, but he had written his address on the other side. Then he said something in some other language that wasn't French. "Are you mad at me?"

Obviously I'm incredibly panicky about roller coasters, but Abe convinced me to ride one with him. "It would be a shame to die without riding the Cyclone," he told me. "It would be a shame to die," I told him. "Yeah," he said, "but with the Cyclone you can choose." We sat in the front car, and Abe lifted his hands in the air on the downhill parts. I kept wondering if what I was feeling was at all like falling.

In my head, I tried to calculate all of the forces that kept the car on the tracks and me in the car. There was gravity, obviously. And centrifugal force. And momentum. And the friction between the wheels and the tracks. And wind resistance, I think, or something. Dad used to teach me physics with crayons on paper tablecloths while we waited for our pancakes. He would have been able to explain everything.

The ocean smelled weird, and so did the food they were selling on

the boardwalk, like funnel cakes and cotton candy and hot dogs. It was an almost perfect day, except that Abe didn't know anything about the key or about Dad. He said he was driving into Manhattan and could give me a ride if I wanted one. I told him, "I don't get in cars with strangers, and how did you know I was going to Manhattan?" He said, "We're not strangers, and I don't know how I knew." "Do you have an SUV?" "No." "Good. Do you have a gas-electric hybrid car?" "No." "Bad."

While we were in the car I told him all about how I was going to meet everyone in New York with the last name Black. He said, "I can relate, in my own way, because I had a dog run away once. She was the best dog in the world. I couldn't have loved her more or treated her better. She didn't want to run away. She just got confused, and followed one thing and then another." "But my dad didn't run away," I said. "He was killed in a terrorist attack." Abe said, "I was thinking of *you*." He went up with me to the door of Ada Black's apartment, even though I told him I could do it myself. "I'll feel better knowing you made it here safely," he said, which sounded like Mom.

Ada Black owned two Picasso paintings. She didn't know anything about the key, so the paintings meant nothing to me, even if I knew they were famous. She said I could have a seat on the couch if I wanted to, but I told her I didn't believe in leather, so I stood. Her apartment was the most amazing apartment I'd ever been in. The floors were like marble chessboards, and the ceilings were like cakes. Everything seemed like it belonged in a museum, so I took some pictures with Grandpa's camera. "This might be a rude question, but are you the richest person in the world?" She touched a lampshade and said, "I'm the 467th-richest person in the world."

I asked her how it made her feel to know that there were homeless people and millionaires living in the same city. She said, "I give a lot to charity, if that's what you're getting at." I told her that I wasn't getting at anything, and that I just wanted to know how she felt. "I feel fine," she said, and she asked me if I wanted something to drink. I asked her for a coffee, and she asked someone in another room for a coffee, and then I asked her if she thought that maybe no one should have more than a certain amount of money until everyone had that amount of money. That was an idea Dad had once suggested to me. She said, "The Upper West Side isn't free, you know." I asked her how she knew that I lived on the Upper West Side. "Do you have things that you don't need?" "Not really." "You collect coins?" "How did you know I collect coins?" "Lots of young people collect coins." I told her, "I need them." "Do you need them as much as a homeless person needs food?" The conversation was beginning to make me feel self-conscious. She said, "Do you have more things that you need, or more that you don't need?" I said, "It depends on what it means to need."

She said, "Believe it or not, I used to be idealistic." I asked her what "idealistic" meant. "It means you live by what you think is right." "You don't do that anymore?" "There are questions I don't ask anymore." An African-American woman brought me coffee on a silver tray. I told her, "Your uniform is incredibly beautiful." She looked at Ada. "Really," I said. "I think light blue is a very, very beautiful color on you." She was still looking at Ada, who said, "Thanks, Gail." As she walked back to the kitchen I told her, "Gail is a beautiful name."

When it was just the two of us again, Ada told me, "Oskar, I think you made Gail feel quite uncomfortable." "What do you mean?" "I could tell that she felt embarrassed." "I was just trying to be nice." "You might have tried too hard." "How can you try too hard to be nice?" "You were being condescending." "What's that?" "You were talking to her like she was a child." "No I wasn't." "There's no shame in being a maid. She does a serious job, and I pay her well." I said, "I was just trying to be nice." And then I wondered, *Did I tell her my name was Oskar?*

We sat there for a while. She stared out the window, like she was waiting for something to happen in Central Park. I asked, "Would it be OK if I snooped around your apartment?" She laughed and said, "Finally someone says what he's thinking." I looked around a bit, and there were so many rooms that I wondered if the apartment's inside was bigger than its outside. But I didn't find any clues. When I came back she asked if I wanted a finger sandwich, which freaked me out, but I was very polite and just said, "Jose." "Pardon?" "Jose." "I'm sorry. I don't understand what that means." "Jose. As in, 'No way . . .'" She said, "I know what I am." I nodded my head, even though I didn't know what she was talking about or what it had to do with anything. "Even if I don't like what I am, I know what I am. My children like what they are, but they don't know what they are. So tell me which is worse." "What are the options again?" She cracked up and said, "I like you."

I showed her the key, but she had never seen it, and couldn't tell me anything about it.

Even though I told her I didn't need any help, she made the doorman promise to put me in a cab. I told her I couldn't afford a cab. She said, "I can." I gave her my card. She said, "Good luck," and put her hands on my cheeks, and kissed the top of my head.

That was Saturday, and it was depressing.

> *Dear Oskar Schell,*
>
> *Thank you for your contribution to the American Diabetes Foundation. Every dollar — or, in your case, fifty cents — counts.*
>
> *I have enclosed some additional literature about the Foundation, including our mission statement, a brochure featuring past activities and successes, as well as some information about our future goals, both short- and long-term.*
>
> *Thank you, once more, for contributing to this urgent cause. You are saving lives.*
>
> *With gratitude,*
> *Patricia Roxbury*
> *President, New York Chapter*

This might be hard to believe, but the next Black lived in our building, just one floor above us. If it weren't my life, I wouldn't have believed it. I went to the lobby and asked Stan what he knew about the person who lived in 6A. He said, "Never seen anyone go in or come out. Just a lot of deliveries and a lot of trash." "*Cool.*" He leaned down and whispered, "Haunted." I whispered back, "I don't believe in the paranormal." He said, "Ghosts don't care if you believe in them," and even though I was an atheist, I knew he wasn't right.

I walked back up the steps, this time past our floor and to the sixth. There was a mat in front of the door which said Welcome in twelve different languages. That didn't seem like something a ghost would put in front of his apartment. I tried the key in the lock, but it didn't work, so I rang the buzzer, which was exactly where our buzzer was. I heard some noise inside, and maybe even some creepy music, but I was brave and just stood there.

After an incredibly long time the door opened. "Can I help you!" an old man asked, but he asked it extremely loudly, so it was more like a scream. "Yes, hello," I said. "I live downstairs in 5A. May I please ask you a few questions?" "Hello, young man!" he said, and he was kind of weird-looking, because he had on a red beret, like a French person, and an eye patch, like a pirate. He said, "I'm Mr. Black!" I said, "I know." He turned around and started walking into his apartment. I guessed I was supposed to follow him, so I did.

Another thing that was weird was that his apartment looked exactly like our apartment. The floors were the same, the windowsills were the same, even the tiles on the fireplace were the same color green. But his apartment was also incredibly different, because it was filled with different stuff. Tons of stuff. Stuff everywhere. Also, there was a huge column right in the middle of the dining room. It was as big as two refrigerators, and it made it impossible for the room to have a table or anything else in it, like ours did. "What's that for?" I asked, but he didn't hear me. There were a bunch of dolls and other things on the mantel, and the floors were filled with little rugs. "I got those in Iceland!" he said, pointing at the seashells on the windowsill. He pointed at a sword on the wall and said, "I got that in Japan!" I asked him if it was a samurai sword. He said, "It's a replica!" I said, "*Cool.*"

He led me to the kitchen table, which was where our kitchen table was, and he sat down and slapped his hand against his knee. "Well!" he said, so loudly that I wanted to cover my ears. "I've had a pretty amazing life!" I thought it was weird that he said that, because I didn't ask him about his life. I didn't even tell him why I was there. "I was born on January 1, 1900! I lived every day of the twentieth century!" "Really?" "My mother altered my birth certificate so I could fight in the First

World War! That was the only lie she ever told! I was engaged to Fitzgerald's sister!" "Who's Fitzgerald?" "Francis Scott Key Fitzgerald, my boy! A Great Author! A Great Author!" "Oops." "I used to sit on her porch and talk to her father while she powdered her nose upstairs! Her father and I had the most lively conversations! He was a Great Man, like Winston Churchill was a Great Man!" I decided that it would be better to Google Winston Churchill when I got home, instead of mentioning that I didn't know who he was. "One day, she came downstairs and was ready to go! I told her to hold on for a minute, because her father and I were right smack in the middle of a terrific conversation, and you can't interrupt a terrific conversation, right!" "I don't know." "Later that night, as I was dropping her off on that same porch, she said, 'Sometimes I wonder if you like my father more than me!' I inherited that damn honesty from my mother, and it caught up with me again! I told her, 'I do!' Well, that was the last time I told her 'I do,' if you know what I mean!" "I don't." "I blew it! Boy, did I blow it!" He started cracking up extremely loudly, and he slapped his knee. I said, "That's hilarious," because it must have been for him to crack up so much. "Hilarious!" he said. "It is! I never heard from her again! Oh, well! So many people enter and leave your life! Hundreds of thousands of people! You have to keep the door open so they can come in! But it also means you have to let them go!"

He put a teakettle on the stove.

"You're wise," I told him. "I've had enough time to get wise! See this!" he hollered, and he flipped up his eye patch. "That's from Nazi shrapnel! I was a war correspondent and ended up attaching myself to a British tank corps going up the Rhine! We were ambushed one afternoon, toward the end of '44! I bled my eye all over the page I was writing on, but those sons of bitches couldn't stop me! I finished my sentence!" "What was the sentence?" "Ah, who can remember! The point is I wasn't going to let those bastard Krauts stop my pen! It's mightier than the sword, you know! And the MG34!" "Could you please put the patch back?" "See that!" he said, pointing at the kitchen floor, but I couldn't stop thinking about his eye. "There's oak under those rugs! Quarter-sawn oak! I should know, I laid it myself!" "Jose," I said, and I wasn't just saying it to be nice. I was keeping a list in my head of things I could do to be more like him. "My wife and I renovated this kitchen ourselves! With these hands!" He showed me his hands. They looked like the hands on the skeleton in the Rainier Scientific catalogue that Ron offered to buy for me, except they had skin, blotchy skin, and I didn't want gifts from Ron. "Where's your wife now?" The teakettle started to whistle.

"Oh," he said, "she died twenty-four years ago! Long time ago! Yesterday, in my life!" "Oops." "It's OK!" "You don't feel bad that I asked about her? You can tell me if you do." "No!" he said. "Thinking about her is the next best thing!" He poured two cups of tea. "Do you have any coffee?" I asked. "Coffee!" "It stunts my growth, and I'm afraid of death." He slapped the table and said, "My boy, I have some coffee from Honduras that's got your name on it!" "But you don't even know my name."

We sat around for a while and he told me more about his amazing life. As far as he knew, which seemed pretty far, he was the only person still alive who had fought in both of the world wars. He'd been to Australia, and Kenya, and Pakistan, and Panama. I asked him, "If you had to guess, how many countries would you guess you've been to?" He said, "I wouldn't have to guess! One hundred twelve!" "Are there even that many countries?" He told me, "There are more places you haven't heard of than you've heard of!" I loved that. He had reported almost every war of the twentieth century, like the Spanish Civil War, and the genocide in East Timor, and bad stuff that happened in Africa. I hadn't heard of any of them, so I tried to remember them so I could Google them when I got home. The list in my head was getting incredibly long: Francis Scott Key Fitzgerald, powdering her nose, Churchill, Mustang convertible, Walter Cronkite, necking, the Bay of Pigs, LP, Datsun, Kent State, lard, Ayatollah Khomeini, Polaroid, apartheid, drive-in, favela, Trotsky, the Berlin Wall, Tito, *Gone With the Wind*, Frank Lloyd Wright, hula hoop, Technicolor, the Spanish Civil War, Grace Kelly, East Timor, slide rule, a bunch of places in Africa whose names I tried to remember but had already forgotten. It was getting hard to keep all the things I didn't know inside me.

His apartment was filled with the stuff he'd collected during the

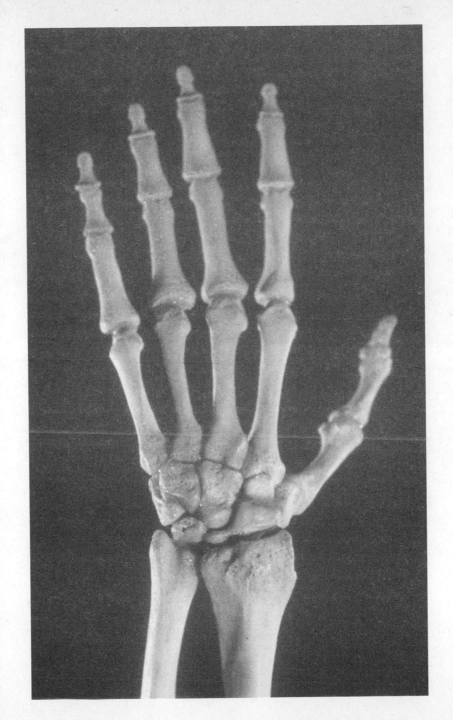

wars of his life, and I took pictures of them with Grandpa's camera. There were books in foreign languages, and little statues, and scrolls with pretty paintings, and Coke cans from around the world, and a bunch of rocks on his fireplace mantel, although all of them were common. One fascinating thing was that each rock had a little piece of paper next to it that said where the rock came from, and when it came from, like, "Normandy, 6/19/44," "Hwach'on Dam, 4/09/51," and "Dallas, 11/22/63." That was so fascinating, but one weird thing was that there were lots of bullets on the mantel, too, and they didn't have little pieces of paper next to them. I asked him how he knew which was which. "A bullet's a bullet's a bullet!" he said. "But isn't a rock a rock?" I asked. He said, "Of course not!" I thought I understood him, but I wasn't positive, so I pointed at the roses in the vase on the table. "Is a rose a rose?" "No! A rose is not a rose is not a rose!" And then for some reason I started thinking about "Something in the Way She Moves," so I asked, "Is a love song a love song?" He said, "Yes!" I thought for a second. "Is love love?" He said, "No!" He had a wall of masks from every country he'd been to, like Armenia and Chile and Ethiopia. "It's not a horrible world," he told me, putting a Cambodian mask on his face, "but it's filled with a lot of horrible people!"

I had another cup of coffee, and then I knew it was time to get to the point, so I took the key off my neck and gave it to him. "Do you know what this opens?" "Don't think so!" he hollered. "Maybe you knew my dad?" "Who was your dad!" "His name was Thomas Schell. He lived in 5A until he died." "No," he said, "that name doesn't ring a bell!" I asked if he was one-hundred-percent sure." He said, "I've lived long enough to know I'm not one-hundred-percent anything!" and he got up, walked past the column in the dining room, and went over to the coat closet, which was tucked under the stairs. That was when I had the revelation that his apartment wasn't just like ours, because his had an upstairs. He opened the closet, and there was a library card catalogue inside. *"Cool."*

He said, "This is my biographical index!" "Your what?" "I started it when I was just beginning to write! I'd create a card for everyone I thought I might need to reference one day! There's a card for everyone I ever wrote about! And cards for people I talked to in the course of writing my pieces! And cards for people I read books about! And cards for people in the footnotes of those books! In the mornings, when I'd read the papers, I would make cards for everyone that seemed biographically significant! I still do it!" "Why don't you just use the Internet?" "I don't have a computer!" That made me start to feel dizzy.

"How many cards do you have?" "I've never counted! There must be tens of thousands by this point! Maybe hundreds of thousands!" "What do you write on them?" "I write the name of the person and a one-word biography!" "Just *one* word?" "Everyone gets boiled down to one word!" "And that's helpful?" "It's hugely helpful! I read an article about Latin American currencies this morning! It referred to the work of someone named Manuel Escobar! So I came and looked up Escobar! Sure enough, he was in here! Manuel Escobar: unionist!" "But he's also probably a husband, or dad, or Beatles fan, or jogger, or who knows what else." "Sure! You could write a book about Manuel Escobar! And that would leave things out, too! You could write ten books! You could never stop writing!"

He slid out drawers from the cabinet and pulled cards from the drawers, one after another.

"Henry Kissinger: war!

"Ornette Coleman: music!

"Che Guevara: war!

"Jeff Bezos: money!

"Philip Guston: art!

"Mahatma Gandhi: war!"

"But he was a pacifist," I said.

"Right! War!

"Arthur Ashe: tennis!

"Tom Cruise: money!

"Elie Wiesel: war!

"Arnold Schwarzenegger: war!

"Martha Stewart: money!

"Rem Koolhaas: architecture!

"Ariel Sharon: war!

"Mick Jagger: money!

"Yasir Arafat: war!

"Susan Sontag: thought!

"Wolfgang Puck: money!

"Pope John Paul II: war!"

I asked if he had a card for Stephen Hawking.

"Of course!" he said, and slid out a drawer, and pulled out a card.

```
┌─────────────────────────────────────────┐
│                                         │
│                                         │
│                                         │
│      STEPHEN HAWKING: ASTROPHYSICS      │
│                                         │
│                                         │
│                                         │
└─────────────────────────────────────────┘
```

"Do you have a card for yourself?"

He slid out a drawer.

```
┌─────────────────────────────────────────┐
│                                         │
│                                         │
│            A. R. BLACK: ~~WAR~~         │
│                     HUSBAND             │
│                                         │
│                                         │
└─────────────────────────────────────────┘
```

"So do you have a card for my dad?" "Thomas Schell, right!" "Right." He went to the S drawer and pulled it halfway out. His fingers ran through the cards like the fingers of someone much younger than

103. "Sorry! Nothing!" "Could you double-check?" His fingers ran through the cards again. He shook his head. "Sorry!" "Well, what if a card is filed in the wrong place?" "Then we've got a problem!" "Could it be?" "It happens occasionally! Marilyn Monroe was lost in the index for more than a decade! I kept checking under Norma Jean Baker, thinking I was smart, but completely forgetting that she was born Norma Jean Mortenson!" "Who's Norma Jean Mortenson?" "Marilyn Monroe!" "Who's Marilyn Monroe?" "Sex!"

"Do you have a card for Mohammed Atta?" "Atta! That one rings a bell! Lemme see!" He opened the A drawer. I told him, "Mohammed is the most common name on earth." He pulled out a card and said, "Bingo!"

MOHAMMED ATTA: WAR

I sat down on the floor. He asked what was wrong. "It's just that why would you have one for him and not one for my dad?" "What do you mean!" "It isn't fair." "What isn't fair!" "My dad was good. Mohammed Atta was evil." "So!" "So my dad deserves to be in there." "What makes you think it's good to be in here!" "Because it means you're biographically significant." "And why is that good!" "I want to be significant." "Nine out of ten significant people have to do with money or war!"

But still, it gave me heavy, heavy boots. Dad wasn't a Great Man, not like Winston Churchill, whoever he was. Dad was just someone who ran a family jewelry business. Just an ordinary dad. But I wished so much, then, that he *had* been Great. I wished he'd been famous, famous like a movie star, which is what he deserved. I wished Mr. Black had written about him, and risked his life to tell the world about him, and had reminders of him around his apartment.

I started thinking: if Dad were boiled down to one word, what would that word be? Jeweler? Atheist? Is copyeditor one word?

"You're looking for something!" Mr. Black asked. "This key used to belong to my dad," I said, pulling it out from under my shirt again, "and I want to know what it opens." He shrugged his shoulders and hollered, "I'd want to know, too!" Then we were silent for a while.

I thought I was going to cry, but I didn't want to cry in front of him, so I asked where the bathroom was. He pointed to the top of the stairs. As I walked up, I held the railing tight and started inventing things in my head: air bags for skyscrapers, solar-powered limousines that never had to stop moving, a frictionless, perpetual yo-yo. The bathroom smelled like an old person, and some of the tiles that were supposed to be on the wall were on the floor. There was a photograph of a woman tucked in the corner of the mirror above the sink. She was sitting at the kitchen table that we were just sitting at, and she was wearing an enormous hat, even though she was inside, obviously. That's how I knew that she was special. One of her hands was on a teacup. Her smile was incredibly beautiful. I wondered if her palm was sweating condensation when the picture was taken. I wondered if Mr. Black took the picture.

Before I went back down, I snooped around a little bit. I was impressed by how much life Mr. Black had lived, and how much he wanted to have his life around him. I tried the key in all of the doors, even though he said he didn't recognize it. It's not that I didn't trust him, because I did. It's that at the end of my search I wanted to be able to say: I don't know how I could have tried harder. One door was to a closet, which didn't have anything really interesting in it, just a bunch of coats. Behind another door was a room filled with boxes. I took the lids off a couple of them, and they were filled with newspapers. The newspapers in some of the boxes were yellow, and some were almost like leaves.

I looked in another room, which must have been his bedroom. There was the most amazing bed I've ever seen, because it was made out of tree parts. The legs were stumps, the ends were logs, and there was a ceiling of branches. Also there were all sorts of fascinating metal things glued to it, like coins, pins, and a button that said ROOSEVELT.

"That used to be a tree in the park!" Mr. Black said from behind me, which scared me so much that my hands started shaking. I asked, "Are you mad at me for snooping?" but he must not have heard me, because he kept talking. "By the reservoir. She tripped on its roots once! That was back when I was courting her! She fell down and cut her hand! A little cut, but I never forgot it! That was so long ago!" "But yesterday in your life, right?" "Yesterday! Today! Five minutes ago! Now!" He aimed his eyes at the ground. "She always begged me to give the reporting a break! She wanted me at home!" He shook his head and said, "But there were things I needed, too!" He looked at the floor, then back at me. I asked, "So what did you do?" "For most of our marriage I treated her as though she didn't matter! I came home only between wars, and left her alone for months at a time! There was always war!" "Did you know that in the last 3,500 years there have been only 230 years of peace throughout the civilized world?" He said, "You tell me which 230 years and I'll believe you!" "I don't know which, but I know it's true." "And where's this civilized world you're referring to!"

I asked him what happened to make him stop reporting war. He said, "I realized that what I wanted was to stay in one place with one person!" "So you came home for good?" "I chose her over war! And the first thing I did when I came back, even before I went home, was to go to the park and cut down that tree! It was the middle of the night! I thought someone would try to stop me, but no one did! I brought the pieces home with me! I made that tree into this bed! It was the bed we shared for the last years we had together! I wish I'd understood myself better earlier!" I asked, "Which was your last war?" He said, "Cutting down that tree was my last war!" I asked him who won, which I thought was a nice question, because it would let him say that he won, and feel proud. He said, "The ax won! It's always that way!"

He went up to the bed and put his finger on the head of a nail. "See these!" I try to be a perceptive person who follows the scientific method and is observant, but I hadn't noticed before that the whole bed was completely covered in nails. "I've hammered a nail into the bed every morning since she died! It's the first thing I do after waking! Eight thousand six hundred twenty-nine nails!" I asked him why, which I thought was another nice question, because it would let him tell me about how much he loved her. He said, "I don't know!" I said, "But if you don't know, then why do you do it?" "I suppose it helps! Keeps me going! I know it's nonsense!" "I don't think it's nonsense." "Nails aren't light! One is! A handful are! But they add up!" I told him, "The average human body contains enough iron to make a one-inch nail." He said, "The bed got heavy! I could hear the floor straining, like it was in pain! Sometimes I'd wake up in the middle of the night afraid that everything would go crashing to the apartment below!" "You couldn't sleep because of me." "So I built that column downstairs! Do you know about the library at Indiana University!" "No," I said, but I was still thinking about the column. "It's sinking a little more than an inch a year, because when they built it, they didn't take into account the weight of all of the books! I wrote a piece about it! I didn't make the connection then, but now I'm thinking of Debussy's *Sunken Cathedral,* one of the most beautiful pieces of music ever written! I haven't heard it in years and years! Do you want to feel something!" "OK," I said, because even though I didn't know him, I felt like I knew him. "Open your hand!" he said, so I did. He reached into his pocket and took out a paper clip. He pressed it into my hand and said, "Make a fist around it!" So I did. "Now extend your hand!" I extended my hand. "Now open your hand!" The paper clip flew to the bed.

It was only then that I observed that the key was reaching toward the bed. Because it was relatively heavy, the effect was small. The string pulled incredibly gently at the back of my neck, while the key floated just a tiny bit off my chest. I thought about all the metal buried in Central Park. Was it being pulled, even if just a little, to the bed? Mr. Black closed his hand around the floating key and said, "I haven't left the apartment in twenty-four years!" "What do you mean?" "Sadly, my boy, I mean exactly what I said! I haven't left the apartment in twenty-four years! My feet haven't touched the ground!" "Why not?" "There hasn't been any reason to!" "What about stuff you need?" "What does someone like me need that he can still get!" "Food. Books. Stuff." "I call in an order for food, and they bring it to me! I call the bookstore for books, the video store for movies! Pens, stationery, cleaning supplies, medicine! I even order my clothes over the phone!

See this!" he said, and he showed me his muscle, which went down instead of up. "I was flyweight champion for nine days!" I asked, "Which nine days?" He said, "Don't you believe me!" I said, "Of course I do." "The world is a big place," he said, "but so is the inside of an apartment! So's this!" he said, pointing at his head. "But you used to travel so much. You had so many experiences. Don't you miss the world?" "I do! Very much!"

My boots were so heavy that I was glad there was a column underneath us. How could such a lonely person have been living so close to me my whole life? If I had known, I would have gone up to keep him company. Or I would have made some jewelry for him. Or told him hilarious jokes. Or given him a private tambourine concert.

It made me start to wonder if there were other people so lonely so close. I thought about "Eleanor Rigby." It's true, where do they all come from? And where do they all belong?

What if the water that came out of the shower was treated with a chemical that responded to a combination of things, like your heartbeat, and your body temperature, and your brain waves, so that your skin changed color according to your mood? If you were extremely excited your skin would turn green, and if you were angry you'd turn red, obviously, and if you felt like shiitake you'd turn brown, and if you were blue you'd turn blue.

Everyone could know what everyone else felt, and we could be more careful with each other, because you'd never want to tell a person whose skin was purple that you're angry at her for being late, just like you would want to pat a pink person on the back and tell him, "Congratulations!"

Another reason it would be a good invention is that there are so many times when you know you're feeling a lot of something, but you don't know what the something is. *Am I frustrated? Am I actually just panicky?* And that confusion changes your mood, it becomes your mood, and you become a confused, gray person. But with the special water, you could look at your orange hands and think, *I'm happy! That whole time I was actually happy! What a relief!*

Mr. Black said, "I once went to report on a village in Russia, a community of artists who were forced to flee the cities! I'd heard that paintings hung everywhere! I heard you couldn't see the walls through all of the paintings! They'd painted the ceilings, the plates, the windows, the lampshades! Was it an act of rebellion! An act of expression! Were the paintings good, or was that beside the point! I needed to see it for myself, and I needed to tell the world about it! I used to live for reporting like that! Stalin found out about the community and sent his thugs in, just a few days before I got there, to break all of their arms! That was worse than killing them! It was a horrible sight, Oskar: their arms in crude splints, straight in front of them like zombies! They couldn't feed themselves, because they couldn't get their hands to their mouths! So you know what they did!" "They starved?" "They fed each other! That's the difference between heaven and hell! In hell we starve! In heaven we feed each other!" "I don't believe in the afterlife." "Neither do I, but I believe in the story!"

And then, all of a sudden, I thought of something. Something enormous. Something wonderful. "Do you want to help me?" "Excuse me!" "With the key." "Help you!" "You could go around with me." "You want my help!" "Yes." "Well, I don't need anyone's charity!" "Jose," I told him. "You're obviously very smart and knowledgeable, and you know a ton of things that I don't know, and also it's good just to have company, so please say yes." He closed his eyes and became quiet. I couldn't tell if he was thinking about what we were talking about, or thinking about something else, or if maybe he'd fallen asleep, which I know that old people, like Grandma, sometimes do, because they can't help it. "You don't have to make a decision right now," I said, because I didn't want him to feel forced. I told him about the 162 million locks, and how the search would probably take a long time, it might even take the full one and a half years, so if he wanted to think about it for a while that would be OK, he could just come downstairs and tell me his answer whenever. He kept thinking. "Take as long as you want," I said. He kept thinking. I asked him, "Do you have a decision?"

He didn't say anything.

"What do you think, Mr. Black?"

Nothing.

"Mr. Black?"

I tapped him on the shoulder and he looked up suddenly. "Hello?"

He smiled, like I do when Mom finds out about something I did that I shouldn't have done.

"I've been reading your lips!" "What?" He pointed at his hearing aids, which I hadn't noticed before, even though I was trying as hard as I could to notice everything. "I turned them off a long time ago!" "You turned them off?" "A long, long time ago!" "On purpose?" "I thought I'd save the batteries!" "For what?" He shrugged his shoulders. "But don't you want to hear things?" He shrugged his shoulders again, in a way so I couldn't tell if he was saying yes or no. And then I thought of something else. Something beautiful. Something true. "Do you want me to turn them on for you?"

He looked at me and through me at the same time, like I was a stained-glass window. I asked again, moving my lips slowly and carefully so I could be sure he understood me: "Do. You. Want. Me. To. Turn. Them. On. For. You?" He kept looking at me. I asked again. He said, "I don't know how to say yes!" I told him, "You don't have to."

I went behind him and saw a tiny dial on the back of each of his hearing aids.

"Do it slowly!" he said, almost like he was begging me. "It's been a long, long time!"

I went back around to his front so he could see my lips, and I promised him I would be as gentle as I could. Then I went back behind him and turned the dials extremely slowly, a few millimeters at a time. Nothing happened. I turned them a few more millimeters. And then just a few more. I went around to the front of him. He shrugged, and so did I. I went back around behind him and turned them up just a tiny bit more, until they stopped. I went back in front of him. He shrugged. Maybe the hearing aids didn't work anymore, or maybe the batteries had died of old age, or maybe he'd gone completely deaf since he turned them off, which was possible. We looked at each other.

Then, out of nowhere, a flock of birds flew by the window, extremely fast and incredibly close. Maybe twenty of them. Maybe more. But they also seemed like just one bird, because somehow they all knew

exactly what to do. Mr. Black grabbed at his ears and made a bunch of weird sounds. He started crying—not out of happiness, I could tell, but not out of sadness, either.

"Are you OK?" I whispered.

The sound of my voice made him cry more, and he nodded his head yes.

I asked him if he wanted me to make some more noise.

He nodded yes, which shook more tears down his cheeks.

I went to the bed and rattled it, so that a bunch of the pins and paper clips fell off.

He cried more tears.

"Do you want me to turn them off?" I asked, but he wasn't paying attention to me anymore. He was walking around the room, sticking his ears up to anything that made any noise, including very quiet things, like pipes.

I wanted to stay there watching him hear the world, but it was getting late, and I had a *Hamlet* rehearsal at 4:30, and it was an extremely important rehearsal, because it was the first one with lighting effects. I told Mr. Black that I would pick him up the next Saturday at 7:00, and we would start then. I told him, "I'm not even through with the A's." He said, "OK," and the sound of his own voice made him cry the most.

Message three. 9:31 A.M. *Hello? Hello? Hello?*

When Mom tucked me in that night, she could tell that something was on my mind, and asked if I wanted to talk. I did, but not to her, so I said, "No offense, but no." "Are you sure?" "*Très fatigué,*" I said, waving my hand. "Do you want me to read something to you?" "It's OK." "We could go through the *New York Times* for mistakes?" "No, thank you." "All right," she said, "all right." She gave me a kiss and turned off the light, and then, as she was about to go, I said, "Mom?" and she said, "Yes?" and I said, "Do you promise not to bury me when I die?"

She came back over and put her hand on my cheek and said, "You're not going to die." I told her, "I am." She said, "You're not going to die any time soon. You have a long, long life ahead of you." I told her,

"As you know, I'm extremely brave, but I can't spend eternity in a small underground place. I just can't. Do you love me?" "Of course I love you." "Then put me in one of those mausoleum-thingies." "A mausoleum?" "Like I read about." "Do we have to talk about this?" "Yes." "Now?" "Yes." "Why?" "Because what if I die tomorrow?" "You're not going to die tomorrow." "Dad didn't think he was going to die the next day." "That's not going to happen to you." "It wasn't going to happen to him." "Oskar." "I'm sorry, but I just can't be buried." "Don't you want to be with Dad and me?" "Dad isn't even there!" "Excuse me?" "His body was destroyed." "Don't talk like that." "Talk like what? It's the truth. I don't understand why everyone pretends he's there." "Take it easy, Oskar." "It's just an empty box." "It's more than an empty box." "Why would I want to spend eternity next to an empty box?"

Mom said, "His spirit is there," and that made me *really* angry. I told her, "Dad didn't have a spirit! He had cells!" "His memory is there." "His memory is here," I said, pointing at my head. "Dad had a spirit," she said, like she was rewinding a bit in our conversation. I told her, "He had cells, and now they're on rooftops, and in the river, and in the lungs of millions of people around New York, who breathe him every time they speak!" "You shouldn't say things like that." "But it's the *truth!* Why can't I say the *truth!*" "You're getting out of control." "Just because Dad died, it doesn't mean you can be illogical, Mom." "Yes it does." "No it doesn't." "Get a hold of yourself, Oskar." "Fuck you!" "Excuse me!" "Sorry. I mean, screw you." "You need a time-out!" "I need a mausoleum!" "Oskar!" "Don't lie to me!" "Who's lying?" "Where were you!" "Where was I when?" "That day!" "What day?" "*The* day!" "What do you mean?" "Where were you!" "I was at work." "Why weren't you at home?" "Because I have to go to work." "Why didn't you pick me up from school like the other moms?" "Oskar, I came home as soon as I could. It takes longer for me to get home than for you to. I thought it would be better to meet you at the apartment than make you wait at school for me to get to you." "But you should have been home when I got home." "I wish I had been, but it wasn't possible." "You should have made it possible." "I can't make the impossible possible." "You should have." She said, "I got home as quickly as I could." And then she started crying.

The ax was winning.

I put my cheek against her. "I don't need anything fancy, Mom. Just something above ground." She took a deep breath, put her arm around me, and said, "That might be possible." I tried to think of some way to be hilarious, because I thought that maybe if I was hilarious, she wouldn't be mad at me anymore and I could be safe again. "With a little elbow room." "What?" "I'm gonna need a little elbow room." She smiled and said, "OK." I sniffled again, because I could tell that it was working. "And a bidet." "Absolutely. One bidet coming up." "And some electrical fencing." "Electrical fencing?" "So that grave robbers won't try to steal all of my jewels." "Jewels?" "Yeah," I said, "I'm gonna need some jewels, too."

We cracked up together, which was necessary, because she loved me again. I pulled my feelings book from under my pillow, flipped to the current page, and downgraded from DESPERATE to MEDIOCRE. "Hey, that's great!" Mom said, looking over my shoulder. "No," I said, "it's mediocre. And please don't snoop." She rubbed my chest, which was nice, although I had to turn a little so she wouldn't feel that I still had my key on, and that there were two keys.

"Mom?" "Yes." "Nothing."

"What is it, baby?" "Well it's just that wouldn't it be great if mattresses had spaces for your arm, so that when you rolled onto your side, you could fit just right?" "That would be nice." "And good for your back, probably, because it would let your spine be straight, which I know is important." "That is important." "Also, it would make snuggling easier. You know how that arm constantly gets in the way?" "I do." "And making snuggling easier is important." "Very."

~~MEDIOCRE~~
OPTIMISTIC, BUT REALISTIC

"I miss Dad." "So do I." "Do you?" "Of course I do." "But do you *really?*" "How could you ask that?" "It's just that you don't act like you miss him very much." "What are you talking about?" "I think you know what I'm talking about." "I don't." "I hear you laughing." "You hear me laughing?" "In the living room. With Ron." "You think because I laugh every now and then I don't miss Dad?" I rolled onto my side, away from her.

~~OPTIMISTIC, BUT REALISTIC~~
EXTREMELY DEPRESSED

She said, "I cry a lot, too, you know." "I don't see you cry a lot." "Maybe that's because I don't want you to see me cry a lot." "Why not?" "Because that isn't fair to either of us." "Yes it is." "I want us to move on." "How much do you cry?" "How much?" "A spoonful? A cup? A bathtub? If you added it up." "It doesn't work like that." "Like what?"

She said, "I'm trying to find ways to be happy. Laughing makes me happy." I said, "I'm not trying to find ways to be happy, and I won't." She said, "Well, you should." "Why?" "Because Dad would want you to be happy." "Dad would want me to remember him." "Why can't you remember him *and* be happy?" "Why are you in love with Ron?" "What?" "You're obviously in love with him, so what I want to know is, why? What's so great about him?" "Oskar, did it ever occur to you that things might be more complicated than they seem?" "That occurs to me all the time." "Ron is my *friend*." "So then promise me you won't ever fall in love again." "Oskar, Ron is going through a lot, too. We help each other. We're *friends*." "Promise me you won't fall in love." "Why would you ask me to promise that?" "Either promise me you'll never fall in love again, or I'm going to stop loving you." "You're not being fair." "I don't have to be fair! I'm your son!" She let out an enormous breath and said, "You remind me so much of Dad." And then I said something that I wasn't planning on saying, and didn't even want to say. As it came out of my mouth, I was ashamed that it was mixed with any of Dad's cells that I might have inhaled when we went to visit Ground Zero. "If I could have chosen, I would have chosen you!"

She looked at me for a second, then stood up and walked out of the room. I wish she'd slammed the door, but she didn't. She closed it carefully, like she always did. I could hear that she didn't walk away.

~~EXTREMELY DEPRESSED~~
INCREDIBLY ALONE

"Mom?"
Nothing.

I got out of bed and went to the door.

"I take it back."

She didn't say anything, but I could hear her breathing. I put my hand on the doorknob, because I thought maybe her hand was on the doorknob on the other side.

"I said I take it back."

"You can't take something like that back."

"Can you apologize for something like that?"

Nothing.

"Do you accept my apology?"

"I don't know."

"How can you not know?"

"Oskar, I *don't know*."

"Are you mad at me?"

Nothing.

"Mom?"

"Yes."

"Are you still mad at me?"

"No."

"Are you sure?"

"I was never mad at you."

"What were you?"

"Hurt."

~~INCREDIBLY ALONE~~

I GUESS I FELL ASLEEP ON THE FLOOR.
WHEN I WOKE UP, MOM WAS PULLING MY
SHIRT OFF TO HELP ME GET INTO MY PJS,
WHICH MEANS SHE MUST HAVE SEEN ALL
OF MY BRUISES. I COUNTED THEM LAST
NIGHT IN THE MIRROR AND THERE WERE
FORTY-ONE. SOME OF THEM HAVE
GOTTEN BIG, BUT MOST OF THEM ARE
SMALL. I DON'T PUT THEM THERE FOR
HER, BUT STILL I WANT HER TO ASK ME

HOW I GOT THEM (EVEN THOUGH SHE
PROBABLY KNOWS), AND TO FEEL SORRY
FOR ME (BECAUSE SHE SHOULD REALIZE
HOW HARD THINGS ARE FOR ME), AND TO
FEEL TERRIBLE (BECAUSE AT LEAST SOME
OF IT IS HER FAULT), AND TO PROMISE ME
THAT SHE WON'T DIE AND LEAVE ME
ALONE. BUT SHE DIDN'T SAY ANYTHING.
I COULDN'T EVEN SEE THE LOOK IN HER
EYES WHEN SHE SAW THE BRUISES,
BECAUSE MY SHIRT WAS OVER MY HEAD,
COVERING MY FACE LIKE A POCKET, OR A
SKULL.

MY FEELINGS

They are announcing flights over the speakers.   We are not listening.
They do not matter to us, because we are not going anywhere.
I miss you already, Oskar.   I missed you even when I was with you.
That's been my problem.   I miss what I already have, and I surround
myself with things that are missing.
Every time I put in a new page, I look at your grandfather.   I am so relieved to see his face.   It makes me feel safe.   His shoulders are
pinched.   His spine is curved.   In Dresden he was a giant.   I'm glad
that his hands are still rough.   The sculptures never left them.
I didn't notice until now that he is still wearing his wedding ring.   I
wonder if he put it on when he came back or if he wore it all those years.
Before I came here I locked up the apartment.   I turned off the lights
and made sure none of the faucets leaked.   It's hard to say goodbye to
the place you've lived.   It can be as hard as saying goodbye to a person.
We moved in after we were married.   It had more room than his apartment.   We needed it.   We needed room for all of the animals, and we
needed room between us.   Your grandfather bought the most expen-
sive insurance policy.   A man from the company came over to take pictures.   If anything happened, they would be able to rebuild the apartment again exactly as it was.   He took a roll of film.   He took a
picture of the floor, a picture of the fireplace, a picture of the bathtub.
I never confused what I had with what I was.   When the man left, your
grandfather took out his own camera and started taking more pictures.
What are you doing? I asked him.
Better safe than sorry, he wrote.   At the time I thought he was right,
but I am not sure anymore.

He took pictures of everything. Of the undersides of the shelves in the closet. Of the backs of the mirrors. Even the broken things. The things you would not want to remember. He could have rebuilt the apartment by taping together the pictures.

And the doorknobs. He took a picture of every doorknob in the apartment. Every one. As if the world and its future depended on each doorknob. As if we would be thinking about doorknobs should we ever actually need to use the pictures of them.

I don't know why that hurt me so much.

I told him, They are not even nice doorknobs.

He wrote, But they are our doorknobs.

I was his too.

He never took pictures of me, and we didn't buy life insurance.

He kept one set of the pictures in his dresser. He taped another set into his daybooks, so they'd always be with him, in case something happened at home.

Our marriage was not unhappy, Oskar. He knew how to make me laugh. And sometimes I made him laugh. We had to make rules, but who doesn't. There is nothing wrong with compromising. Even if you compromise almost everything.

He got a job at a jewelry store, because he knew the machines. He worked so hard that they made him assistant manager, and then manager. He did not care about jewelry. He hated it. He used to say jewelry is the opposite of sculpture.

But it was a living, and he promised me that was OK.

We got our own store in a neighborhood that was next to a bad neighborhood. It was open from eleven in the morning until six at night. But there was always work to be done.

We spent our lives making livings.

Sometimes he would go to the airport after work. I asked him to get me papers and magazines. At first this was because I wanted to learn American expressions. But I gave up on that. I still asked him to go. I knew that he needed my permission to go. It was not out of kindness that I sent him.

We tried so hard. We were always trying to help each other. But not because we were helpless.   He needed to get things for me, just as I needed to get things for him.   It gave us purpose.   Sometimes I would ask him for something that I did not even want, just to let him get it for me.   We spent our days trying to help each other help each other.   I would get his slippers.   He would make my tea.   I would turn up the heat so he could turn up the air conditioner so I could turn up the heat.   His hands didn't lose their roughness.

It was Halloween.   Our first in the apartment.   The doorbell rang. Your grandfather was at the airport.   I opened the door and a child was standing there in a white sheet with holes cut out for her eyes.   Trick or treat! she said.   I took a step back.

Who is that?

I'm a ghost!

What are you wearing that for?

It's Halloween!

I don't know what that means.

Kids dress up and knock on doors, and you give them candy.

I don't have any candy.

It's Hal-lo-ween!

I told her to wait.   I went to the bedroom.   I took an envelope from underneath the mattress.   Our savings.   Our living.   I took out two one-hundred-dollar bills and put them in a different envelope, which I gave to the ghost.

I was paying her to go away.

I closed the door and turned off the lights so no more children would ring our bell.

The animals must have understood, because they surrounded me and pressed into me.   I did not say anything when your grandfather came home that night.   I thanked him for the papers and magazines.   I went to the guest room and pretended to write.   I hit the space bar again and again and again.   My life story was spaces.

The days passed one at a time.   And sometimes less than one at a time. We looked at each other and drew maps in our heads.   I told him my eyes were crummy, because I wanted him to pay attention to me.   We made safe places in the apartment where you could go and not exist.

I would have done anything for him.   Maybe that was my sickness.
We made love in nothing places and turned the lights off.   It felt like
crying.   We could not look at each other.   It always had to be from
behind.   Like that first time.   And I knew that he wasn't thinking of
me.
He squeezed my sides so hard, and pushed so hard.   Like he was try-
ing to push through me to somewhere else.
Why does anyone ever make love?
A year passed.   Another year.   Another year.   Another.
We made livings.
I never forgot about the ghost.
I needed a child.
What does it mean to need a child?
One morning I awoke and understood the hole in the middle of me.
I realized that I could compromise my life, but not life after me.
I couldn't explain it.   The need came before explanations.
It was not out of weakness that I made it happen, but it was not out of
strength either.   It was out of need.   I needed a child.
I tried to hide it from him.   I tried to wait to tell him until it was too
late to do anything about it.   It was the ultimate secret.   Life.   I kept
it safe inside me.   I took it around.   Like the apartment was inside his
books.   I wore loose shirts.   I sat with pillows on my lap.   I was
naked only in nothing places.
But I could not keep it a secret forever.
We were lying in bed in the darkness.   I did not know how to say it.   I
knew, but I could not say it.   I took one of his daybooks from the bed-
side table.
The apartment had never been darker.
I turned on the lamp.
It became bright around us.
The apartment became darker.
I wrote, I am pregnant.
I handed it to him.   He read it.
He took the pen and wrote, How could that have happened?
I wrote, I made it happen.

He wrote, But we had a rule.

The next page was a doorknob.

I turned the page and wrote, I broke the rule.

He sat up in bed.   I don't know how much time passed.

He wrote, Everything will be OK.

I told him OK wasn't enough.

Everything will be ~~OK~~ perfect.

I told him there was nothing left for a lie to protect.

Everything will be ~~OK perfect.~~

I started to cry.

It was the first time I had ever cried in front of him.   It felt like making love.

I asked him something I had needed to know since we made that first nothing place years before.

What are we?   Something or nothing?

He covered my face with his hands and lifted them off.

I did not know what that meant.

The next morning I woke up with a terrible cold.

I did not know if the baby was making me sick or if your grandfather was.

When I said goodbye to him, before he left for the airport, I lifted his suitcase and it felt heavy.

That was how I knew he was leaving me.

I wondered if I should stop him.   If I should wrestle him to the ground and force him to love me.   I wanted to hold his shoulders down and shout into his face.

I followed him there.

I watched him all morning.   I did not know how to talk to him.   I watched him write in his book.   I watched him ask people what time it was, although each person just pointed at the big yellow clock on the wall.

It was so strange to see him from a distance.   So small.   I cared for him in the world as I could not care for him in the apartment.   I wanted to protect him from all of the terrible things that no one deserves.

I got very close to him.   Just behind him.   I watched him write, It's a
shame that we have to live, but it's a tragedy that we get to live only one
life.   I stepped back.   I could not be that close.   Not even then.
From behind a column I watched him write more, and ask for the time,
and rub his rough hands against his knees.   Yes and No.
I watched him get in the line to buy tickets.
I wondered, When am I going to stop him from leaving?
I didn't know how to ask him or tell him or beg him.
When he got to the front of the line I went up to him.
I touched his shoulder.
I can see, I said.   What a stupid thing to say.   My eyes are crummy,
but I can see.
What are you doing here? he wrote with his hands.
I felt suddenly shy.   I was not used to shy.   I was used to shame.
Shyness is when you turn your head away from something you want.
Shame is when you turn your head away from something you do not
want.
I know you are leaving, I said.
You have to go home, he wrote.   You should be in bed.
OK, I said.   I did not know how to say what I needed to say.
Let me take you home.
No.   I do not want to go home.
He wrote, You're being crazy.   You're going to catch a cold.
I already have a cold.
You are going to catch a colder.
I could not believe he was making a joke.   And I could not believe I
laughed.
The laughter sent my thoughts to our kitchen table, where we would
laugh and laugh.   That table was where we were close to each other.
It was instead of our bed.   Everything in our apartment got confused.
We would eat on the coffee table in the living room instead of at the
dining room table.   We wanted to be near the window.   We filled the
body of the grandfather clock with his empty daybooks, as if they were
time itself.   We put his filled daybooks in the bathtub of the second
bathroom, because we never used it.   I sleepwalk when I sleep at all.

Once I turned on the shower.   Some of the books floated, and some stayed where they were.   When I awoke the next morning I saw what I had done.   The water was gray with all of his days.

I am not being crazy, I told him.

You have to go home.

I got tired, I told him.   Not worn out, but worn through.   Like one of those wives who wakes up one morning and says I can't bake any more bread.

You never baked bread, he wrote, and we were still joking.

Then it's like I woke up and baked bread, I said, and we were joking even then.   I wondered will there come a time when we won't be joking?   And what would that look like?   And how would that feel?

When I was a girl, my life was music that was always getting louder. Everything moved me.   A dog following a stranger.   That made me feel so much.   A calendar that showed the wrong month.   I could have cried over it.   I did.   Where the smoke from a chimney ended. How an overturned bottle rested at the edge of a table.

I spent my life learning to feel less.

Every day I felt less.

Is that growing old?   Or is it something worse?

You cannot protect yourself from sadness without protecting yourself from happiness.

He hid his face in the covers of his daybook, as if the covers were his hands.   He cried.   For whom was he crying?

For Anna?

For his parents?

For me?

For himself?

I pulled the book from him.   It was wet with tears running down the pages, as if the book itself were crying.   He hid his face in his hands. Let me see you cry, I told him.

I do not want to hurt you, he said by shaking his head left to right.

It hurts me when you do not want to hurt me, I told him.   Let me see you cry.

He lowered his hands.   On one cheek it said YES backward.   On one

cheek it said NO backward.   He was still looking down.   Now the
tears did not run down his cheeks, but fell from his eyes to the ground.
Let me see you cry, I said.   I did not feel that he owed it to me.   And
I did not feel that I owed it to him.   We owed it to each other, which is
something different.
He raised his head and looked at me.
I am not angry with you, I told him.
You must be.
I am the one who broke the rule.
But I am the one who made the rule you couldn't live with.
My thoughts are wandering, Oskar.   They are going to Dresden, to
my mother's pearls, damp with the sweat of her neck.   My thoughts
are going up the sleeve of my father's overcoat.   His arm was so thick
and strong.   I was sure it would protect me for as long as I lived.   And
it did.   Even after I lost him.   The memory of his arm wraps around
me as his arm used to.   Each day has been chained to the previous one.
But the weeks have had wings.   Anyone who believes that a second is
faster than a decade did not live my life.
Why are you leaving me?
He wrote, I do not know how to live.
I do not know either, but I am trying.
I do not know how to try.
There were things I wanted to tell him.   But I knew they would hurt
him.   So I buried them, and let them hurt me.
I put my hand on him.   Touching him was always so important to me.
It was something I lived for.   I never could explain why.   Little, noth-
ing touches.   My fingers against his shoulder.   The outsides of our
thighs touching as we squeezed together on the bus.   I couldn't explain it, but I needed it.   Sometimes I imagined stitching all of our little touches together.   How many hundreds of thousands of fingers
brushing against each other does it take to make love?   Why does anyone ever make love?
My thoughts are going to my childhood, Oskar.   To when I was a girl.
I am sitting here thinking about fistfuls of pebbles, and the first time I
noticed hairs under my arms.

My thoughts are around my mother's neck.   Her pearls.

When I first liked the smell of perfume, and how Anna and I would lie in the darkness of our bedroom, in the warmth of our bed.

I told her one night what I had seen behind the shed behind our house. She made me promise never to speak a word about it.   I promised her.

Can I watch you kiss?

Can you watch us kiss?

You could tell me where you are going to kiss, and I could hide and watch.

She laughed, which was how she said yes.

We woke up in the middle of the night.   I do not know who woke up first.   Or if we woke up at the same time.

What does it feel like? I asked her.

What does what feel like?

To kiss.

She laughed.

It feels wet, she said.

I laughed.

It feels wet and warm and very strange at first.

I laughed.

Like this, she said, and she grabbed the sides of my face and pulled me into her.

I had never felt so in love in my life, and I have not felt so in love since.

We were innocent.

How could anything be more innocent than the two of us kissing in that bed?

How could anything less deserve to be destroyed?

I told him, I will try harder if you will stay.

OK, he wrote.

Just please do not leave me.

OK.

We never have to mention this.

OK.

I am thinking about shoes, for some reason.   How many pairs I have worn in my life.   And how many times my feet have slipped into and out of them.   And how I put them at the foot of the bed, pointing away from the bed.

My thoughts are going down a chimney and burning.

Footsteps above.   Frying onions.   Clinking crystal.

We were not rich, but there was nothing we wanted.   From my bedroom window I watched the world.   And I was safe from the world.

I watched my father fall apart.   The nearer the war came, the farther he went.   Was that the only way he knew to protect us?   He spent hours in his shed every night.   Sometimes he would sleep in there.   On the floor.

He wanted to save the world.   That's what he was like.   But he wouldn't put our family in danger.   That's what he was like.   He must have weighed my life against a life he might have been able to save.   Or ten.   Or one hundred.   He must have decided that my life weighed more than one hundred lives.

His hair turned gray that winter.   I thought it was snow.   He promised us that everything would be OK.   I was a child, but I knew that everything would not be OK.   That did not make my father a liar.   It made him my father.

It was the morning of the bombing that I decided to write back to the forced laborer.   I do not know why I waited for so long, or what made me want to write to him then.

He had asked me to include a photograph of myself.   I did not have any photographs of myself that I liked.   I understand, now, the tragedy of my childhood.   It wasn't the bombing.   It was that I never once liked a photograph of myself.   I couldn't.

I decided I would go to a photographer the next day and have a picture taken.

That night I tried on all of my outfits in front of the mirror.   I felt like an ugly movie star.   I asked my mother to teach me about makeup.   She didn't ask why.

She showed me how to rouge my cheeks.   And how to paint my eyes.   She had never touched my face so much.   There had never been an excuse to.

My forehead.   My chin.   My temples.   My neck.   Why was she crying?

I left the unfinished letter on my desk.

The paper helped our house burn.

I should have sent it off with an ugly photograph.

I should have sent off everything.

The airport was filled with people coming and going.   But it was only
your grandfather and me.

I took his daybook and searched its pages.   I pointed at, How frustrating, how pathetic, how sad.

He searched through the book and pointed at, The way you just handed
me that knife.

I pointed at, If I'd been someone else in a different world I'd've done
something different.

He pointed at, Sometimes one simply wants to disappear.

I pointed at, There's nothing wrong with not understanding yourself.

He pointed at, How sad.

I pointed at, And I wouldn't say no to something sweet.

He pointed at, Cried and cried and cried.

I pointed at, Don't cry.

He pointed at, Broken and confused.

I pointed at, So sad.

He pointed at, Broken and confused.

I pointed at, Something.

He pointed at, Nothing.

I pointed at, Something.

Nobody pointed at, I love you.

There was no way around it.   We could not climb over it, or walk until
we found its edge.

I regret that it takes a life to learn how to live, Oskar.   Because if I were
able to live my life again, I would do things differently.

I would change my life.

I would kiss my piano teacher, even if he laughed at me.

I would jump with Mary on the bed, even if I made a fool of myself.

I would send out ugly photographs, thousands of them.

What are we going to do? he wrote.

It's up to you, I said.

He wrote, I want to go home.

What is home to you?

Home is the place with the most rules.

I understood him.

And we will have to make more rules, I said.

To make it more of a home.

Yes.

OK.

We went straight to the jewelry store.   He left the suitcase in the back room.   We sold a pair of emerald earrings that day.   And a diamond engagement ring.   And a gold bracelet for a little girl.   And a watch for someone on his way to Brazil.

That night we held each other in bed.   He kissed me all over.   I believed him.   I was not stupid.   I was his wife.

The next morning he went to the airport.   I didn't dare feel his suitcase.

I waited for him to come home.

Hours passed.   And minutes.

I didn't open the store at 11:00.

I waited by the window.   I still believed in him.

I didn't eat lunch.

Seconds passed.

The afternoon left.   The evening came.

I didn't eat dinner.

Years were passing through the spaces between moments.

Your father kicked in my belly.

What was he trying to tell me?

I brought the birdcages to the windows.

I opened the windows, and opened the birdcages.

I poured the fish down the drain.

I took the dogs and cats downstairs and removed their collars.

I released the insects onto the street.

And the reptiles.

And the mice.
I told them, Go.
All of you.
Go.
And they went.
And they didn't come back.

HAPPINESS, HAPPINESS

INTERVIEWER. Can you describe the events of that morning?

TOMOYASU. I left home with my daughter, Masako. She was on her way to work. I was going to see a friend. An air-raid warning was issued. I told Masako I was going home. She said, "I'm going to the office." I did chores and waited for the warning to be lifted.

I folded the bedding. I rearranged the closet. I cleaned the windows with a wet rag. There was a flash. My first thought was that it was the flash from a camera. That sounds so ridiculous now. It pierced my eyes. My mind went blank. The glass from the windows was shattering all around me. It sounded like when my mother used to hush me to be quiet.

When I became conscious again, I realized I wasn't standing. I had been thrown into a different room. The rag was still in my hand, but it was no longer wet. My only thought was to find my daughter. I looked outside the window and saw one of my neighbors standing almost naked. His skin was peeling off all over his body. It was hanging from his fingertips. I asked him what had happened. He was too exhausted to reply. He was looking in every direction, I can only assume for his family. I thought, *I must go. I must go and find Masako.*

I put my shoes on and took my air-raid hood with me. I made my way to the train station. So many people were marching toward me, away from the city. I smelled something similar to grilled squid. I must have been in shock, because the people looked like squid washing up on the shore.

I saw a young girl coming toward me. Her skin was melting down her. It was like wax. She was muttering, "Mother. Water. Mother.

Water." I thought she might be Masako. But she wasn't. I didn't give her any water. I am sorry that I didn't. But I was trying to find my Masako.

I ran all the way to Hiroshima Station. It was full of people. Some of them were dead. Many of them were lying on the ground. They were calling for their mothers and asking for water. I went to Tokiwa Bridge. I had to cross the bridge to get to my daughter's office.

INTERVIEWER. Did you see the mushroom cloud?

TOMOYASU. No, I didn't see the cloud.

INTERVIEWER. You didn't see the mushroom cloud?

TOMOYASU. I didn't see the mushroom cloud. I was trying to find Masako.

INTERVIEWER. But the cloud spread over the city?

TOMOYASU. I was trying to find her. They told me I couldn't go beyond the bridge. I thought she might be back home, so I turned around. I was at the Nikitsu Shrine when the black rain started falling from the sky. I wondered what it was.

INTERVIEWER. Can you describe the black rain?

TOMOYASU. I waited for her in the house. I opened the windows, even though there was no glass. I stayed awake all night waiting. But she didn't come back. About 6:30 the next morning, Mr. Ishido came around. His daughter was working at the same office as my daughter. He called out asking for Masako's house. I ran outside. I called, "It's here, over here!" Mr. Ishido came up to me. He said, "Quick! Get some clothes and go for her. She is at the bank of the Ota River."

I ran as fast as I could. Faster than I was able to run. When I reached the Tokiwa Bridge, there were soldiers lying on the ground. Around Hiroshima Station, I saw more people lying dead. There were more on the morning of the seventh than on the sixth. When I reached the riverbank, I couldn't tell who was who. I kept looking for Masako. I heard someone crying, "Mother!" I recognized her voice. I found her in horrible condition. And she still appears in my dreams that way. She said, "It took you so long."

I apologized to her. I told her, "I came as fast as I could."

It was just the two of us. I didn't know what to do. I was not a nurse. There were maggots in her wounds and a sticky yellow liquid. I tried to clean her up. But her skin was peeling off. The maggots were coming out all over. I couldn't wipe them off, or I would wipe off her skin and muscle. I had to pick them out. She asked me what I was doing. I told her, "Oh, Masako. It's nothing." She nodded. Nine hours later, she died.

INTERVIEWER. You were holding her in your arms all that time?

TOMOYASU. Yes, I held her in my arms. She said, "I don't want to die." I told her, "You're not going to die." She said, "I promise I won't die before we get home." But she was in pain and she kept crying, "Mother."

INTERVIEWER. It must be hard to talk about these things.

TOMOYASU. When I heard that your organization was recording testimonies, I knew I had to come. She died in my arms, saying, "I don't want to die." That is what death is like. It doesn't matter what uniforms the soldiers are wearing. It doesn't matter how good the weapons are. I thought if everyone could see what I saw, we would never have war anymore.

I pressed Stop on the boom box, because the interview was over. The girls were crying, and the boys were making funny barfing noises.

"Well," Mr. Keegan said, wiping his forehead with a handkerchief as he stood up from his chair, "Oskar has certainly given us a lot to think about." I said, "I'm not done." He said, "That seemed pretty complete to me." I explained, "Because the radiant heat traveled in straight lines from the explosion, scientists were able to determine the direction toward the hypocenter from a number of different points, by observing the shadows cast by intervening objects. The shadows gave an indication of the height of the burst of the bomb, and the diameter of the ball of fire at the instant it was exerting the maximum charring effect. Isn't that fascinating?"

Jimmy Snyder raised his hand. I called on him. He asked, "Why are you so weird?" I asked if his question was rhetorical. Mr. Keegan told him to go to Principal Bundy's office. Some of the kids cracked up. I knew they were cracking up in the bad way, which is at me, but I tried to maintain my confidence.

"Another interesting feature that has to do with the explosion was the relationship between the degree of burning and color, because dark colors absorb light, obviously. For example, a famous chess match between two grand masters was going on that morning on a life-size board in one of the big city parks. The bomb destroyed everything: the spectators in the seats, the people who were filming the match, their black cameras, the timing clocks, even the grand masters. All that was left were white pieces on white square islands."

As he walked out of the room, Jimmy said, "Hey, Oskar, who's Buckminster?" I told him, "Richard Buckminster Fuller was a scientist, philosopher, and inventor who is most famous for designing the geodesic dome, whose most famous version is the Buckyball. He died in 1983, I think." Jimmy said, "I mean *your* Buckminster."

I didn't know why he was asking, because I'd brought Buckminster to school for a demonstration only a couple of weeks before, and dropped him from the roof to show how cats reach terminal velocity by making themselves into little parachutes, and that cats actually have a better chance of surviving a fall from the twentieth floor than the eighth floor, because it takes them about eight floors to realize what's going on, and relax and correct themselves. I said, "Buckminster is my pussy."

Jimmy pointed at me and said, "Ha ha!" The kids cracked up in the bad way. I didn't get what was so hilarious. Mr. Keegan got angry and said, "Jimmy!" Jimmy said, "What? What did I do?" I could tell that inside, Mr. Keegan was cracking up, too.

"What I was saying was, they found a piece of paper, about half a kilometer from the hypocenter, and the letters, which they call characters, were neatly burned out. I became extremely curious about what that would look like, so first I tried to cut out letters on my own, but my hands weren't good enough to do it, so I did some research, and I found a printer on Spring Street who specializes in die-cutting, and he said he could do it for two hundred fifty dollars. I asked him if that included tax. He said no, but I still thought it was worth the money, so I took my mom's credit card, and anyway, here it is." I held up the sheet of paper, with the first page of *A Brief History of Time* in Japanese, which I got the translation of from Amazon.co.jp. I looked at the class through the story of the turtles.

That was Wednesday.

I spent Thursday's recess in the library, reading the new issue of

American Drummer, which Librarian Higgins orders especially for me. It was boring. I went to the science lab, to see if Mr. Powers would do some experiments with me. He said he actually had plans to eat lunch with some other teachers, and he couldn't let me be in the lab alone. So I made some jewelry in the art studio, which you are allowed to be in alone.

Friday, Jimmy Snyder called me from across the playground, and then he came up to me with a bunch of his friends. He said, "Hey, Oskar, would you rather have a handjob or a blowjob from Emma Watson?" I told him I didn't know who Emma Watson was. Matt Colber said, "Hermione, retard." I said, "Who's Hermione? And I'm not mentally retarded." Dave Mallon said, "In *Harry Potter*, fag boy." Steve Wicker said, "She has sweet tits now." Jake Riley said, "Handjob or blowjob?" I said, "I've never even met her."

I know a lot about birds and bees, but I don't know very much about the birds and the bees. Everything I do know I had to teach myself on the Internet, because I don't have anyone to ask. For example, I know that you give someone a blowjob by putting your penis in their mouth. I also know that dick is penis, and that cock is penis, too. And monster cock, obviously. I know that VJs get wet when a woman is having sex, although I don't know what they get wet *with*. I know that VJ is cunt, and also ass. I know what dildos are, I think, but I don't know what cum is, exactly. I know that anal sex is humping in the anus, but I wish I didn't.

Jimmy Snyder pushed my shoulder and said, "Say your mom's a whore." I said, "Your mom's a whore." He said, "Say *your* mom's a whore." I said, "*Your* mom's a whore." "Say 'My' 'mom' 'is a whore.' " "Your mom is a whore." Matt and Dave and Steve and Jake were cracking up, but Jimmy was getting really, really angry. He raised a fist and said, "Prepare to die." I looked around for a teacher, but I didn't see any. "My mom's a whore," I said. I went inside and read a few more sentences of *A Brief History of Time*. Then I broke a mechanical pencil. When I came home, Stan said, "You've got mail!"

I counted off seven minutes that night, and then fourteen minutes, and then thirty. I knew I'd never be able to fall asleep, because I was so excited that the next day I'd be able to search for the lock. I started inventing like a beaver. I thought about how in one hundred years every name in the 2003 Yellow Pages will be for someone who's dead, and how once when I was at The Minch's I saw a TV show where someone ripped a phone book in half with his hands. I thought about how I wouldn't want someone to rip a 2003 Yellow Pages in half in one hundred years, because even though everyone will be dead, it still felt like it should make a difference. So I invented a Black Box Yellow Pages, which is a phone book that's made out of the material that they make the black boxes on airplanes out of. I still couldn't sleep.

I invented a postage stamp where the back tastes like crème brûlée. I still couldn't sleep.

What if you trained Seeing Eye dogs to be bomb-sniffing dogs, so that they'd be Sniffing Eye Seeing Bomb dogs? That way, blind people could get paid for being led around, and could be contributing members of our society, and we'd all be safer, too. I was getting further and further from sleep.

When I woke up it was Saturday.

I went upstairs to pick up Mr. Black, and he was waiting in front of his door, snapping his fingers next to his ear. "What's this?" he asked when I handed him the present I made for him. I shrugged my shoulders, just like Dad used to. "What am I supposed to do with it?" I told him, "Open it, obviously." But I couldn't keep my happiness in, and before he got the paper off the box I said, "It's a necklace I made for you with a compass pendant so you can know where you are in relation to the bed!" He kept opening it and said, "How nice of you!" "Yeah," I said, taking the box from him because I could open it faster. "It probably won't work outside your apartment, because the magnetic field of the bed gets smaller the farther you get from it, but still." I handed him the necklace and he put it on. It said that the bed was north.

"So where to?" he asked. "The Bronx," I said. "The IRT?" "The what?" "The IRT train." "There isn't an IRT train, and I don't take public transportation." "Why not?" "It's an obvious target." "So how do you plan on us getting there?" "We'll walk." "That's got to be about twenty miles from here," he said. "And have you seen me walk?" "That's true." "Let's take the IRT." "There is no IRT." "Whatever there is, let's take it."

On our way out, I said, "Stan, this is Mr. Black. Mr. Black, this is Stan." Mr. Black stuck out his hand, and Stan shook it. I told Stan, "Mr. Black lives in 6A." Stan took his hand back, but I don't think Mr. Black was offended.

Almost the whole ride to the Bronx was underground, which made me incredibly panicky, but once we got to the poor parts, it went aboveground, which I preferred. A lot of the buildings in the Bronx were empty, which I could tell because they didn't have windows, and you could see right through them, even at high speeds. We got off the train and went down to the street. Mr. Black had me hold his hand as we looked for the address. I asked him if he was racist. He said poverty made him nervous, not people. Just as a joke I asked him if he was gay. He said, "I suppose so." "Really?" I asked, but I didn't take back my hand, because I'm not homophobic.

The building's buzzer was broken, so the door was held open with a brick. Agnes Black's apartment was on the third floor, and there was no elevator. Mr. Black said he'd wait for me, because the stairs at the subway were enough stairs for him for one day. So I went up alone. The floor of the hallway was sticky, and for some reason all of the peepholes had black paint over them. Someone was singing from behind one of the doors, and I heard TVs behind a bunch of others. I tried my key in Agnes's lock, but it didn't work, so I knocked.

A little woman answered who was in a wheelchair. She was Mexican, I think. Or Brazilian, or something. "Excuse me, is your name

Agnes Black?" She said, "No espeaka Inglesh." "What?" "No espeaka Inglesh." "I'm sorry," I said, "but I don't understand you. Could you please repeat yourself and enunciate a little bit better." "No espeaka Inglesh," she said. I pointed a finger in the air, which is the universal sign for hold on, and then I called down to Mr. Black from the stairwell, "I don't think she speaks English!" "Well, what does she speak?" "What do you speak?" I asked her, and then I realized how dumb my question was, so I tried a different approach: "*Parlez-vous français?*" "*Español,*" she said. "*Español,*" I hollered down. "Terrific!" he hollered back. "I picked up a little *Español* along the way!" So I brought her wheelchair to the stairwell, and they hollered to each other, which was kind of weird, because their voices were traveling back and forth but they couldn't see each other's faces. They cracked up together, and their laughter ran up and down the stairs. Then Mr. Black hollered, "Oskar!" And I hollered, "That's my name, don't wear it out!" And he hollered, "Come on down!"

When I got back to the lobby, Mr. Black explained that the person we were looking for had been a waitress at Windows on the World. "*What the?*" "The woman I just spoke with, Feliz, didn't know her personally. She was told about her when she moved in." "Really?" "I wouldn't make that up." We went out to the street and started walking. A car drove by that was playing music extremely loudly, and it vibrated my heart. I looked up, and there were strings connecting a lot of the windows with clothes hanging on them. I asked Mr. Black if that's what people meant when they said "clotheslines." He said, "That's what they mean." I said, "That's what I thought." We walked some more. Kids were kicking rocks in the street and cracking up in the good way. Mr. Black picked up one of the rocks and put it in his pocket. He looked at the street sign, and then at his watch. A couple of old men were sitting in chairs in front of a store. They were smoking cigars and watching the world like it was TV.

"That's so weird to think about," I said. "What is?" "That she worked there. Maybe she knew my dad. Or not knew him, but maybe she served him that morning. He was there, in the restaurant. He had a meeting. Maybe she refilled his coffee or something." "It's possible."

"Maybe they died together." I know he didn't know what to say to that, because of course they died together. The real question was *how* they died together, like whether they were on different ends of the restaurant, or next to each other, or something else. Maybe they had gone up to the roof together. You saw in some of the pictures that people jumped together and held hands. So maybe they did that. Or maybe they just talked to each other until the building fell. What would they have talked about? They were obviously so different. Maybe he told her about me. I wonder what he told her. I couldn't tell how it made me feel to think of him holding someone's hand.

"Did she have any kids?" I asked. "I don't know." "Ask her." "Ask who?" "Let's go back and ask the woman who's living there now. I bet she knows if Agnes had any kids." He didn't ask me why that question was important, or tell me she already told us everything she knew. We walked back three blocks, and I went up the stairs and brought her wheelchair back to the stairwell, and they talked up and down the stairs for a while. Then Mr. Black hollered, "She didn't!" But I wondered if he was lying to me, because even though I don't speak Spanish, I could hear that she said a lot more than just no.

As we were walking back to the subway, I had a revelation, and then I got angry. "Wait a minute," I said. "What were you cracking up about before?" "Before?" "When you were talking to that woman the first time, you were cracking up. Both of you." "I don't know," he said. "You don't know?" "I don't remember." "Try to remember." He thought for a minute. "I can't remember." Lie #77.

We bought some tamales that a woman was selling by the subway from a huge pot in a grocery cart. Normally I don't like food that isn't individually wrapped or prepared by Mom, but we sat on the curb and ate our tamales. Mr. Black said, "If anything, I'm invigorated." "What's 'invigorated'?" "Energized. Refreshed." "I'm invigorated, too." He put his arm around me and said, "Good." "These are vegan, right?" I shook my tambourine as we walked up the stairs to the subway, and held my breath when the train went underground.

Albert Black came from Montana. He wanted to be an actor, but he didn't want to go to California, because it was too close to home, and the whole point of being an actor was to be someone else.

Alice Black was incredibly nervous, because she lived in a building that was supposed to be for industrial purposes, so people weren't supposed to live there. Before she opened the door, she made us promise that we weren't from the Housing Authority. I said, "I suggest you take a look at us through the peephole." She did, and then she said, "Oh, you," which I thought was weird, and she let us in. Her hands were covered with charcoal, and I saw drawings everywhere, and they were all of the same man. "Are you forty?" "I'm twenty-one." "I'm nine." "I'm one hundred and three." I asked her if she was the one who made the drawings. "Yes." "All of them?" "Yes." I didn't ask who the man in the drawings was, because I was afraid the answer would give me heavy boots. You wouldn't draw someone that much unless you loved him and missed him. I told her, "You're extremely beautiful." "Thanks." "Can we kiss?" Mr. Black stuck his elbow in my side and asked her, "Do you know anything about this key?"

> *Dear Oskar Schell,*
>
> *I am responding on behalf of Dr. Kaley, who is currently in the Congo on a research expedition. She asked that I pass on her appreciation for your enthusiasm about her work with elephants. Given that I am already her assistant — and budget limitations being what they are, as I'm sure you've experienced — she isn't now able to take on anyone else. But she did want me to tell you that should your interest and availability remain, there might be a project next fall in Sudan that she will need help with. (The grant proposals are just now going through.)*
>
> *Please forward us your résumé, including previous research experience, graduate and postgraduate transcripts, and two letters of recommendation.*
>
> *Best,*
> *Gary Franklin*

Allen Black lived on the Lower East Side and was a doorman for a building on Central Park South, which was where we found him. He said he hated being a doorman, because he had been an engineer in Russia, and now his brain was dying. He showed us a little portable TV that he kept in his pocket. "It plays DVDs," he said, "and if I had an e-mail account, I could check it on this, too." I told him I could set up an e-mail account for him if he wanted. He said, "Yeah?" I took his device, which I wasn't familiar with, but figured out pretty quickly, and set everything up. I said, "What do you want for a user name?" I suggested "Allen," or "AllenBlack," or a nickname. "Or 'Engineer.' That could be cool." He put his finger on his mustache and thought about it. I asked if he had any kids. He said, "A son. Soon he's going to be taller than me. Taller and smarter. He'll be a great doctor. A brain surgeon. Or lawyer for the Supreme Court." "Well, you could make it your son's name, although I guess that might be confusing." He said, "Doorman." "What?" "Make it 'Doorman.'" "You can make it anything you want." "Doorman." I made it "Doorman215," because there were already 214 doormen. As we were leaving, he said, "Good luck, Oskar." I said, "How did you know my name was Oskar?" Mr. Black said, "You told him." When I got home that afternoon I sent him an e-mail: "It's too bad you didn't know anything about the key, but it was still nice to meet you."

> Dear Oskar,
>   While you certainly express yourself like an intelligent young man, without ever having met you, and knowing nothing of your experience with scientific research, I'd have a hard time writing a recommendation.
>   Thanks for the kind words about my work, and best of luck with your explorations, scientific and otherwise.
>   Most sincerely,
>   Jane Goodall

Arnold Black got right to the point: "I just can't help. Sorry." I said, "But we haven't even told you what we need help with." He started getting teary and he said, "I'm sorry," and closed the door. Mr. Black said, "Onward ho." I nodded, and inside I thought, *Weird*.

> *Thank you for your letter. Because of the large volume of mail I receive, I am unable to write personal responses. Nevertheless, know that I read and save every letter, with the hope of one day being able to give each the proper response it deserves. Until that day,*
> > *Most sincerely,*
> > *Stephen Hawking*

The week was incredibly boring, except for when I remembered the key. Even though I knew that there were 161,999,999 locks in New York that it didn't open, I still felt like it opened everything. Sometimes I liked to touch it just to know that it was there, like the pepper spray I kept in my pocket. Or the opposite of that. I adjusted the string so the keys—one to the apartment, one to I-didn't-know-what—rested against my heart, which was nice, except the only thing was that it felt too cold sometimes, so I put a Band-Aid on that part of my chest, and the keys rested on that.

Monday was boring.

On Tuesday afternoon I had to go to Dr. Fein. I didn't understand why I needed help, because it seemed to me that you *should* wear heavy boots when your dad dies, and if you *aren't* wearing heavy boots, *then* you need help. But I went anyway, because the raise in my allowance depended on it.

"Hey, buddy." "Actually, I'm not your buddy." "Right. Well. It's great weather today, don't you think? If you want, we could go outside and toss a ball." "Yes to thinking it's great weather. No to wanting to toss a ball." "You sure?" "Sports aren't fascinating." "What do you find fascinating?" "What kind of answer are you looking for?" "What makes you think I'm looking for something?" "What makes you think I'm a huge moron?" "I don't think you're a huge moron. I don't think you're any kind of moron." "Thanks." "Why do you think you're here, Oskar?" "I'm here, Dr. Fein, because it upsets my mom that I'm having an impossible time with my life." "Should it upset her?" "Not really. Life is impossible." "When you say that you're having an impossible time, what do you mean?" "I'm constantly emotional." "Are you emotional right now?" "I'm extremely emotional right now." "What emotions are you feeling?" "All of them." "Like . . ." "Right now I'm feeling sadness, happiness, anger, love, guilt, joy, shame, and a little bit of humor, because part of my brain is remembering something hilarious that Toothpaste once did that I can't talk about." "Sounds like you're feeling an awful lot." "He put Ex-Lax in the *pain au chocolat* we sold at the French Club bake sale." "That *is* funny." "I'm feeling everything." "This emotionalness of yours, does it affect your daily life?" "Well, to answer your question, I don't think that's a real word you used. Emotionalness. But I understand what you were trying to say, and yes. I end up crying a lot, usually in private. It's extremely hard for me to go to school. I also can't sleep over at friends' apartments, because I get panicky about being away from Mom. I'm not very good with people." "What do you think is going on?" "I feel too much. That's what's going on." "Do you think one can feel too much? Or just feel in the wrong ways?" "My insides don't match up with my outsides." "Do anyone's insides and outsides match up?" "I don't know. I'm only me." "Maybe that's what a person's personality is: the difference between the inside and outside." "But it's worse for me." "I wonder if everyone thinks it's worse for him." "Probably. But it really is worse for me."

He sat back in his chair and put his pen on his desk. "Can I ask you a personal question?" "It's a free country." "Have you noticed any tiny hairs on your scrotum?" "Scrotum." "The scrotum is the pouch at the base of your penis that holds your testicles." "My nuts." "That's right." "Fascinating." "Go ahead and take a second to think about it. I can turn around." "I don't need to think. I don't have tiny hairs on my scrotum." He wrote something on a piece of paper. "Dr. Fein?" "Howard." "You told me to tell you when I feel self-conscious." "Yes." "I feel self-conscious." "I'm sorry. I know it was a very personal question. I only asked because sometimes, when our bodies change, we experience dramatic changes in our emotional lives. I was wondering if perhaps some of what you've been experiencing is due to changes in your body." "It isn't. It's because my dad died the most horrible death that anyone ever could invent."

He looked at me and I looked at him. I promised myself that I wouldn't be the first to look away. But, as usual, I was.

"What would you say to a little game?" "Is it a brain teaser?" "Not really." "I like brain teasers." "So do I. But this isn't a brain teaser." "Bummer." "I'm going to say a word and I want you to tell me the first thing that comes to mind. You can say a word, a person's name, or even a sound. Whatever. There are no right or wrong answers here. No rules. Should we give it a try?" I said, "Shoot." He said, "Family." I said, "Family." He said, "I'm sorry. I don't think I explained this well. I'll say a word, and you tell me the first thing you think of." I said, "You said 'family' and I thought of family." He said, "But let's try not to use the same word. OK?" "OK. I mean, yeah." "Family." "Heavy petting." "Heavy petting?" "It's when a man rubs a woman's VJ with his fingers. Right?" "Yes, that's right. OK. There are no wrong answers. How about safety?" "How about it?" "OK." "Yeah." "Bellybutton." "Bellybutton?" "Bellybutton." "I can't think of anything but bellybutton." "Give it a try. Bellybutton." "Bellybutton doesn't make me think of anything." "Dig deep." "In my bellybutton?" "In your brain, Oskar." "Uh." "Bellybutton. Bellybutton." "Stomach anus?" "Good." "Bad." "No, I meant, 'Good. You did good.'" "I did *well*." "Well." "Water." "Celebrate." "Ruff, ruff." "Was that a bark?" "Anyway." "OK. Great." "Yeah." "Dirty." "Bellybutton." "Uncomfortable." "Extremely." "Yellow." "The color of a yellow person's bellybutton." "Let's see if we can keep it to one word, though, OK?" "For a game with no rules, this game has a lot of rules." "Hurt." "Realistic." "Cucumber." "Formica." "Formica?" "Cucumber?" "Home." "Where the stuff is." "Emergency." "Dad." "Is your father the cause of the emergency, or the solution to it?" "Both." "Happiness." "Happiness. Oops. Sorry." "Happiness." "I don't know." "Try. Happiness." "Dunno." "Happiness. Dig." I shrugged my shoulders. "Happiness, happiness." "Dr. Fein?" "Howard." "Howard?" "Yes?" "I'm feeling self-conscious."

We spent the rest of the forty-five minutes talking, although I didn't have anything to say to him. I didn't want to be there. I didn't want to be anywhere that wasn't looking for the lock. When it was almost time for Mom to come in, Dr. Fein said he wanted us to make a plan for how the next week could be better than the last one. He said,

"Why don't you tell me some things you think you can do, things to keep in mind. And then next week we'll talk about how successful you were." "I'll try to go to school." "Good. Really good. What else?" "Maybe I'll try to be more patient with morons." "Good. And what else?" "I don't know, maybe I'll try not to ruin things by getting so emotional." "Anything else?" "I'll try to be nicer to my mom." "And?" "Isn't that enough?" "It is. It's more than enough. And now let me ask you, how do you think you're going to accomplish those things you mentioned?" "I'm gonna bury my feelings deep inside me." "What do you mean, bury your feelings?" "No matter how much I feel, I'm not going to let it out. If I have to cry, I'm gonna cry on the inside. If I have to bleed, I'll bruise. If my heart starts going crazy, I'm not gonna tell everyone in the world about it. It doesn't help anything. It just makes everyone's life worse." "But if you're burying your feelings deep inside you, you won't really be *you*, will you?" "So?" "Can I ask you one last question?" "Was that it?" "Do you think any good can come from your father's death?" "Do I think any *good* can come from my father's death?" "Yes. Do you think *any* good can come from your father's death?" I kicked over my chair, threw his papers across the floor, and hollered, "No! Of course not, you fucking asshole!"

That was what I wanted to do. Instead I just shrugged my shoulders.

I went out to tell Mom it was her turn. She asked me how it went. I said, "OK." She said, "Your magazines are in my bag. And a juice box." I said, "Thanks." She bent down and kissed me.

When she went in, I very quietly took the stethoscope from my field kit, got on my knees, and pressed the whatever-the-end-is-called against the door. The bulb? Dad would have known. I couldn't hear a lot, and sometimes I wasn't sure if no one was talking or if I just wasn't hearing what they were saying.

expect too much too quickly
I know
                    you?
What   *me?*

you doing?

I'm not the point.

Until you're feeling   *to be impossible for Oskar to*

But until he's feeling   *it's*   *to feel OK.*

don't know.   *a problem.*
        you?
I don't
     don't know?

               hours and hours to explain.

         you try to start?
Start   *easy*   *do you*   *happy?*

What's funny?

       used to be   *someone*   *me a question, and I could say yes,*
or   *but*   *believe in short answers anymore.*

Maybe   *the wrong questions. Maybe*   *to remind*
there are simple things.

What's simple?
How many fingers   *holding up?*
It's not that simple

I want to talk   *that's not going to be easy.*

     you ever considered

What?

    what it sounds like.   *even a hospital, in the way*
we usually think   *safe environment.*

    home is a safe environment.

Who the hell do you think you are?

I'm sorry.
        to be sorry for. You're angry.
    it's not you that   *angry*
Who are you angry at?

    good for children to be around   *going through the same process.*

Oskar isn't   *other children.*   *even like being around kids his*
own age.

    a good thing?

Oskar is Oskar, and no one   *that's a wonderful*
thing.

I'm worried that   *to himself.*

I can't believe we're talking about this.

    talk about everything,   *realize there was*
no reason to talk

danger to himself?

I'm concerned about.　　　*indications of a child*

absolutely no way　　　*hospitalize my son.*

We were quiet on the car ride home. I turned on the radio and found a station playing "Hey Jude." It was true, I didn't want to make it bad. I wanted to take the sad song and make it better. It's just that I didn't know how.

After dinner, I went up to my room. I took the box out of the closet, and the box out of the box, and the bag, and the unfinished scarf, and the phone.

> Message four. 9:46 A.M. *It's Dad. Thomas Schell. It's Thomas Schell. Hello? Can you hear me? Are you there? Pick up. Please! Pick up. I'm underneath a table. Hello? Sorry. I have a wet napkin wrapped around my face. Hello? No. Try the other. Hello? Sorry. People are getting crazy. There's a helicopter circling around, and. I think we're going to go up onto the roof. They say there's going to be some. Sort of evacuation — I don't know, try that one — they say there's going to be some sort of evacuation from up there, which makes sense if. The helicopters can get close enough. It makes sense. Please pick up. I don't know. Yeah, that one. Are you there? Try that one.*

Why didn't he say goodbye?
I gave myself a bruise.
Why didn't he say "I love you"?
Wednesday was boring.
Thursday was boring.
Friday was also boring, except that it was Friday, which meant it was almost Saturday, which meant I was that much closer to the lock, which was happiness.

WHY I'M NOT WHERE YOU ARE
4/12/78

To my child: I'm writing this from where your mother's father's shed used to stand, the shed is no longer here, no carpets cover no floors, no windows in no walls, everything has been replaced. This is a library now, that would have made your grandfather happy, as if all of his buried books were seeds, from each book came one hundred. I'm sitting at the end of a long table surrounded by encyclopedias, sometimes I take one down and read about other people's lives, kings, actreses, assassins, judges, anthropologists, tennis champions, tycoons, politicians, just because you haven't received any letters from me don't think I haven't written any. Every day I write a letter to you. Sometimes I think if I could tell you what happened to me that night, I could leave that night behind me, maybe I could come home to you, but that night has no beginning or end, it started before I was born and it's still happening. I'm writing in Dresden, and your mother is writing in the Nothing guest room, or I assume she is, I hope she is, sometimes my hand starts to burn and I am convinced we are writing the same word at the same moment. Anna gave me the typewriter your mother used to write her life story on. She gave it to me only a few weeks before the bombings, I thanked her, she said, "Why are you thanking me? It's a gift for me." "A gift for you?" "You never write to me." "But I'm with you." "So?" "You write to someone you can't be with." "You never sculpt me, but at least you could write to me." It's the tragedy of loving, you can't love anything more than something you miss. I told her, "You never write to me." She said, "You've never given me a typewriter." I started to invent future homes for us, I'd type through the night and give them to her the next day. I imagined dozens of homes, some were magical (a clock tower with a stopped clock in a city where time stood still), some were mundane (a bourgois estate in the country with rose gardens and peacocks), each felt possible and perfect, I wonder if your mother ever saw them. "Dear Anna, We will live in a home built at the top of the world's tallest ladder." "Dear Anna, We will live in a cave in a hillside in Turkey." "Dear Anna, We will live in a home with no walls, so that everywhere we go will be our home." I wasn't trying to invent better and better homes, but to show her that homes didn't matter, we could live in any home, in any city, in any country, in any century, and be happy, as if the world were just what we lived in. The night before I lost everything, I typed our last future home: "Dear Anna, We will live in a series of homes, which will climb the alps, and we'll never sleep in the same one twice. Each morning after breakfast, we'll sled down to the next home. And when we open its front door, the previous home will be destroyed and rebuilt as a new home. When we get to the bottom, we'll take a lift to the top and start again at the beginning." I went to bring it to her the next day, on my way to your mothers house, I heard a noise from the shed, from where I'm now writing this to you, I suspected it was Simon Goldberg. I knew that Anna's father had been hiding him, I had heard them talking in there some nights when Anna and I tiptoed into the fields, they were always whispering, I had seen his charcoal stained shirt on their clothesline. I didn't want to make myself known, so I quietly slid a book from the wall. Anna's father, your grandfather, was sitting in his chair with his face in his hands, he was my hero. When I think back on that moment, I never see him with his face in his hands, I won't let myself see him that way, I see the book in my hands, it was an illustrated edition of Ovid's Metamorphosis. I used to look for the edition in the States, as if by finding it I could slide it back in the shed's wall, block the image of my hero's face in his hands, stop my life and history at that moment, I asked after it in every bookshop in New York, but I never was able to find it, light poured into the room through the hole in the wall, your grandfather lifted his head, he came to the shelf and we looked at each other through the missing Metamorphosis, I asked him if something was wrong, he didn't say anything, I could see only a sliver of his face, the spine of a book of his face, we looked at each other until it felt like everything would burst into flames, it was the silence of my life, I found Anna in her room, "Hi." "Hi." "I just saw your father." "In the shed?" "He seems upset." "He doesn't want to be part of it anymore." I told her, "It will all be over soon." "How do you know?" "Everyone says so." "Everyone has always been wrong." "It will be over, and life will go back to how it was." She said, "Don't be a child." "Don't turn away from me." She wouldn't look at me. I asked, "What's happened?" I'd never seen her cry before. I told her, "Don't cry." She said, "Don't touch me." I asked, "What is it?" She said, "Will you please shut up!" We sat on her bed in silence. The silence pressed down on us like a hand. I said, "Whatever it is—" She said, "I'm pregnant." I can't write what we said to each other then. Before I left, she said, "Please be over joyed." I told her I was, of course I was, I kissed her, I kissed her stomach, that was the last time I ever saw her. At 9:30 that night, the air-raid sirens sounded, everyone went to the shelters, but no one hurried, we were use to the alarms, we assumed they were false, why would anyone want to bomb Dresden? The families on our street turned off the lights in their houses and filed into the shelter, I waited on the steps, I was thinking of Anna. It was silent and still and I couldn't see my own hands in the darkness. One hundred planes flew overhead, massive, heavy planes, pushing through the night like one hundred whales through water, they dropped clusters of red flares to light up the blackness for whatever was to come next, I was alone on the street, the red flares fell around me, thousands of them, I knew that something unimaginable was about to happen, I was thinking of Anna, I was overjoyed. I ran downstairs four steps at a time, they saw the look on my face, before I had time to say anything—what would I have said?—we heard a horrible noise, rapid, approaching explosions, like an applauding audience running toward us, then they were atop us, we were thrown to the corners, our cellar filled with fire and smoke, more powerful explosions, the walls lifted from the floor and separated just long enough to let light flood in before banging back to the ground, orange and blue explosions, violet and white, I later read that the first bombing lasted less than half an hour, but it felt like days and weeks, like the world was going to end, the bombing stopped as matter of factly as it

had began, "Are you OK?" "Are you OK?" "Are you OK?" We ran out
of the cellar, which was flooded with yellow-gray smoke, we didn't recognize anything, I had been on the stoop just half an hour before, and
now there was no stoop in front of no house on no street, only fire in
every direction, all that remained of our house was a patch of the facade
that stubbornly held up the front door, a horse on fire galloped past,
there were burning vehicles and carts with burning refugies, people
were screaming, I told my parents I had to go find Anna, my mother
told me to stay with them, I said I would meet them back at our front
door, my father begged me to stay, I grabbed the doorknob and it took
the skin off my hand, I saw the muscles of my palm, red and pulsing,
why did I grab it with my other hand? My father shouted at me, it was
the first time he had ever shouted at me, I can't write what he shouted,
I told them I would meet them back at our door, he struck me across the
face, it was the first time he had ever struck me, that was the last time I
saw my parents. On my way to Anna's house, the second raid began, I
threw myself into the nearest cellar, it was hit, it filled with pink smoke
and gold flames, so I fled into the next cellar, it caught fire, I ran from
cellar to cellar as each previous cellar was destroyed, burning monkeys
screamed from the trees, birds with their wings on fire sang from the
telephone wires over which desperate calls traveled, I found another
shelter, it was filled to the walls, brown smoke pressed down from the
ceiling like a hand, it became more and more difficult to breathe, my
lungs were trying to pull the room in through my mouth, there was a
silver explosion, all of us tried to leave the cellar at once, dead and dying
people were trampled, I walked over an old man, I walked over children, everyone was losing everyone, the bombs were like a waterfall, I
ran through the streets, from cellar to cellar, and saw terrible things:
legs and necks, I saw a woman whose blond hair and green dress were
on fire, running with a silent baby in her arms, I saw humans melted
into thick pools of liquid, three or four feet deep in places, I saw bodies
crackling like embers, laughing, and the remains of masses of people
who had tried to escape the firestorm by jumping head first into the
lakes and ponds, the parts of their bodies that were submerged in the
water were still intact, while the parts that protruded above water were

charred beyond recognition, the bombs kept falling, purple, orange and white, I kept running, my hands kept bleeding, through the sounds of collapsing buildings I heard the roar of that baby's silence. I passed the zoo, the cages had been ripped open, everything was everywhere, dazed animals cried in pain and confusion, one of the keepers was calling out for help, he was a strong man, his eyes had been burnt closed, he grabbed my arm and asked me if I knew how to fire a gun, I told him I had to get to someone, he handed me his rifle and said, "You've got to find the carnivores," I told him I wasn't a good shot, I told him I didn't know which were carnivores and which weren't, he said, "Shoot everything," I don't know how many animals I killed, I killed an elephant, it had been thrown twenty yards from its cage, I pressed the rifle to the back of its head and wondered, as I squeezed the trigger, Is it necessary to kill this animal? I killed an ape that was perched on the stump of a fallen tree, pulling its hair as it surveyed the destruction, I killed two lions, they were standing side by side facing west, were they related, were they friends, mates, can lions love? I killed a cub that was climbing atop a massive dead bear, was it climbing atop its parent? I killed a camel with twelve bullets, I suspected it wasn't a carnivore, but I was killing everything, everything had to be killed, a rhinoceros was banging its head against a rock, again and again, as if to put itself out of its suffering, or to make itself suffer, I fired at it, it kept banging its head, I fired again, it banged harder, I walked up to it and pressed the gun between its eyes, I killed it, I killed a zebra, I killed a giraffe, I turned the water of the sea lion's tank red, an ape approached me, it was the ape I had shot before, I'd thought I'd killed it, it walked up to me slowly, its hands covering its ears, what did it want from me, I screamed, "What do you want from me?" I shot it again, where I thought its heart was, it looked at me, in its eyes I was sure I saw some form of understanding, but I didn't see forgiveness, I tried to shoot the vultures, but I wasn't a good enough shot, later I saw vultures fattening themselves on the human carnage, and I blamed myself for everything. The second bombing halted as suddenly and totally as it had began, with burnt hair, with black arms and black fingers, I walked, dazed, to the base of the Loschwitz Bridge, I submerged my black hands in the black water, and saw my reflection, I was terrified of my own image, my blood-matted hair, my split and bleeding lips, my red, pulsing palms, which, even as I write this, thirty-five years later, don't look like they should be at the ends of my arms. I remember losing my balance, I remember a single thought in my head: *Keep thinking.* As long as I am thinking, I am alive, but at some point I stopped thinking, the next thing I remember is feeling terribly cold, I realized I was lying on the ground, the pain was complete, it let me know I hadn't died, I started moving my legs and arms, my movements must have been noticed by one of the soldiers that had been put into action all over the city, looking for survivors, I later learned that there had been more than 220 bodies taken from the foot of the bridge, and 4 came back to life, I was one of them. They loaded us onto trucks and took us out of Dresden, I looked out from the flaps of canvas that covered the sides of the truck, the buildings were burning, the trees burning, the asphalt, I saw and heard humans trapped, I smelled them, standing in the moltin, burning streets like living torches, screaming for help that was impossible to give, the air itself was burning, the truck had to make a number of detours to get beyond the chaos, planes bore down on us once more, we were pulled off the truck and placed under it, the planes dove, more machine guns, more bombs, yellow, red, green, blue, brown, I lost consciousness again, when I awoke I was in a white hospital bed, I couldn't move my arms or legs, I wondered if I had lost them, but I couldn't summon the energy to look for myself, hours passed, or days, when I finally looked down, I saw that I was strapped to the bed, a nurse was standing beside me, I asked, "Why have you done this to me?" She told me I had been trying to hurt myself, I asked her to free me, she said she couldn't, she said I would hurt myself, I begged her to free me, I told her I wouldn't hurt myself, I promised, she apologized and touched me, doctors operated on me, they gave me injections and bandaged my body, but it was her touch that saved my life. In the days and weeks after my release, I looked for my parents and for Anna and for you. Everyone was looking for everyone in the rubble of every building, but all of the searching was in vain, I found our old house, the door was still stubbornly standing, a few of our belongings survived, the typewriter survived, I carried it in my arms like a baby, before I was evacuated I wrote on the door that I was alive, and the address of the refugee camp in Oschatz, I waited for a letter, but no letter ever came. Because there were so many bodies, and because so many of the bodies had been destroyed there was never a list of the dead, thousands of people were left to suffer hope. When I had thought I was dying at the base of the Loschwitz Bridge, there was a single thought in my head: *Keep thinking.* Thinking would keep me alive. But now I am alive, and thinking is killing me. I think and think and think. I can't stop thinking about that night, the clusters of red flares, the sky that was like black water, and how only hours before I lost everything, I had everything. Your aunt had told me she was pregnant, I was overjoyed, I should have known not to trust it, one hundred years of joy can be erased in one second, I kissed her belly, even though there was nothing yet to kiss, I told her, "I love our baby." That made her laugh, I hadn't heard her laugh like that since the day we walked into each other halfway between our houses, she said, "You love an idea." I told her, "I love our idea." That was the point, we were having an idea together. She asked, "Are you afraid?" "Afraid of what?" She said, "Life is scarier than death." I took the future home from my pocket and gave it to her, I kissed her, I kissed her stomach, that was the last time I ever saw her, I was at the end of the path when I heard her father. He came out of the shed. "I almost forgot!" he called to me. "There's a letter here for you. It was delivered yesterday. I almost forgot." He ran into the house and came back out with an envelope. "I almost forgot," he said, his eyes were red, his knuckles were white, I later learned that he survived the bombing and then killed himself. Did your mother tell you that? Does she know it herself? He handed a letter to me. It was from Simon Goldberg. The letter had been posted from Westerbork transit camp in Holland, that's where the Jews from our region were sent, from there they went either to work or to their deaths. "Dear Thomas Schell, It was a pleasure meeting you, however briefly. For reasons that need not be explained, you made a strong impression on me. It is my great hope that our paths, however long and winding, will cross again. Until that day, I wish the best for you in these difficult times. Yours most sincerely, Simon Goldberg." I put the letter back in the envelope and the envelope in my pocket, where the future home had been, I heard your grandfather's voice as I walked away, he was still at the door, "I almost forgot." When your mother found me in the bakery on Broadway, I wanted to tell her everything, maybe if I'd been able to, we could have lived differently, maybe I'd be there with you now instead of here. Maybe if I had said, "I lost a baby," if I'd said, "I'm so afraid of losing something I love that I refuse to love anything," maybe that would have made the impossible possible. Maybe, but I couldn't do it, I had buried too much too deeply inside me. And here I am, instead of there. I'm sitting in this library, thousands of miles from my life, writing another letter I know I won't be able to send, no matter how hard I try and how much I want to. How did that boy making love behind that shed become this man writing this letter at this table?

I love you,
Your father

THE SIXTH BOROUGH

"Once upon a time, New York City had a sixth borough." "What's a borough?" "That's what I call an interruption." "I know, but the story won't make any sense to me if I don't know what a borough is." "It's like a neighborhood. Or a collection of neighborhoods." "So if there was once a sixth borough, then what are the five boroughs?" "Manhattan, obviously, Brooklyn, Queens, Staten Island, and the Bronx." "Have I ever been to any of the other boroughs?" "Here we go." "I just want to know." "We went to the Bronx Zoo once, a few years ago. Remember that?" "No." "And we've been to Brooklyn to see the roses at the Botanic Garden." "Have I been to Queens?" "I don't think so." "Have I been to Staten Island?" "No." "Was there *really* a sixth borough?" "I've been trying to tell you." "No more interruptions. I promise."

"Well, you won't read about it in any of the history books, because there's nothing—save for the circumstantial evidence in Central Park —to prove that it was there at all. Which makes its existence very easy to dismiss. But even though most people will say they have no time for or reason to believe in the Sixth Borough, and *don't* believe in the Sixth Borough, they will still use the word 'believe.'

"The Sixth Borough was also an island, separated from Manhattan by a thin body of water whose narrowest crossing happened to equal the world's long jump record, such that exactly one person on earth could go from Manhattan to the Sixth Borough without getting wet. A huge party was made of the yearly leap. Bagels were strung from island to island on special spaghetti, samosas were bowled at baguettes, Greek salads were thrown like confetti. The children of New York captured fireflies in glass jars, which they floated between the boroughs. The bugs would slowly asphyxiate—" "Asphyxiate?" "Suffocate." "Why

217

didn't they just punch holes into the lids?" "The fireflies would flicker rapidly for their last few minutes of life. If it was timed right, the river shimmered as the jumper crossed it." "*Cool.*"

"When the time finally came, the long jumper would begin his approach from the East River. He would run the entire width of Manhattan, as New Yorkers rooted him on from opposite sides of the street, from the windows of their apartments and offices, and from the branches of trees. Second Avenue, Third Avenue, Lexington, Park, Madison, Fifth Avenue, Columbus, Amsterdam, Broadway, Seventh, Eighth, Ninth, Tenth . . . And when he leapt, New Yorkers cheered from the banks of both Manhattan and the Sixth Borough, cheering the jumper on and cheering each other on. For those few moments that the jumper was in the air, every New Yorker felt capable of flight.

"Or maybe 'suspension' is a better word. Because what was so inspiring about the leap was not how the jumper got from one borough to the other, but how he stayed between them for so long." "That's true."

"One year—many, many years ago—the end of the jumper's big toe skimmed the surface of the river, causing a little ripple. People gasped as the ripple traveled out from the Sixth Borough back toward Manhattan, knocking the jars of fireflies against one another like wind chimes.

" 'You must have gotten a bad start!' a Manhattan councilman hollered from across the water.

"The jumper shook his head, more confused than ashamed.

" 'You had the wind in your face,' a Sixth Borough councilman suggested, offering a towel for the jumper's foot.

"The jumper shook his head.

" 'Perhaps he ate too much for lunch,' said one onlooker to another.

" 'Or maybe he's past his prime,' said another, who'd brought his kids to watch the leap.

" 'I bet his heart wasn't in it,' said another. 'You just can't expect to jump that far without some serious feeling.'

" 'No,' the jumper said to all of the speculation. 'None of that's right. I jumped just fine.'

"The revelation—" "Revelation?" "Realization." "Oh yeah." "It traveled across the onlookers like the ripple caused by the toe, and when the mayor of New York City spoke it aloud, everyone sighed in agreement: 'The Sixth Borough is moving.'" "*Moving!*"

"A millimeter at a time, the Sixth Borough receded from New York. One year, the long jumper's entire foot got wet, and after a number of years, his shin, and after many, many years—so many years that no one could remember what it was like to celebrate without anxiety—the jumper had to reach out his arms and grab at the Sixth Borough fully extended, and then he couldn't touch it at all. The eight bridges between Manhattan and the Sixth Borough strained and finally crumbled, one at a time, into the water. The tunnels were pulled too thin to hold anything at all.

"The phone and electrical lines snapped, requiring Sixth Boroughers to revert to old-fashioned technologies, most of which resembled children's toys: they used magnifying glasses to reheat their carryout; they folded important documents into paper airplanes and threw them from one office building into another; those fireflies in glass jars, which had once been used merely for decorative purposes during the festivals of the leap, were now found in every room of every home, taking the place of artificial light.

"The very same engineers who dealt with the Leaning Tower of Pisa . . . which was where?" "*Italy!*" "Right. They were brought over to assess the situation.

"'It wants to go,' they said.

"'Well, what can you say about that?' the mayor of New York asked.

"To which they replied: 'There's nothing to say about that.'

"Of course they tried to save it. Although 'save' might not be the right word, as it did seem to want to go. Maybe 'detain' is the right word. Chains were moored to the banks of the islands, but the links soon snapped. Concrete pilings were poured around the perimeter of the Sixth Borough, but they, too, failed. Harnesses failed, magnets failed, even prayer failed.

"Young friends, whose string-and-tin-can phone extended from island to island, had to pay out more and more string, as if letting kites go higher and higher.

"'It's getting almost impossible to hear you,' said the young girl from her bedroom in Manhattan as she squinted through a pair of her father's binoculars, trying to find her friend's window.

"'I'll holler if I have to,' said her friend from his bedroom in the Sixth Borough, aiming last birthday's telescope at her apartment.

"The string between them grew incredibly long, so long it had to be extended with many other strings tied together: his yo-yo string, the pull from her talking doll, the twine that had fastened his father's diary, the waxy string that had kept her grandmother's pearls around her neck and off the floor, the thread that had separated his great-uncle's childhood quilt from a pile of rags. Contained within everything they shared with one another were the yo-yo, the doll, the diary, the necklace, and the quilt. They had more and more to tell each other, and less and less string.

"The boy asked the girl to say 'I love you' into her can, giving her no further explanation.

"And she didn't ask for any, or say 'That's silly,' or 'We're too young for love,' or even suggest that she was saying 'I love you' because he asked her to. Instead she said, 'I love you.' The words traveled the yo-yo, the doll, the diary, the necklace, the quilt, the clothesline, the birthday present, the harp, the tea bag, the tennis racket, the hem of the skirt he one day should have pulled from her body." "*Grody!*" "The boy covered his can with a lid, removed it from the string, and put her love for him on a shelf in his closet. Of course, he never could open the can, because then he would lose its contents. It was enough just to know it was there.

"Some, like that boy's family, wouldn't leave the Sixth Borough. Some said, 'Why should we? It's the rest of the world that's moving. Our borough is fixed. Let them leave Manhattan.' How can you prove someone like that wrong? And who would want to?" "I wouldn't." "Neither would I. For most Sixth Boroughers, though, there was no question of refusing to accept the obvious, just as there was no underlying stubbornness, or principle, or bravery. They just didn't want to go.

They liked their lives and didn't want to change. So they floated away, one millimeter at a time.

"All of which brings us to Central Park. Central Park didn't used to be where it is now." "You just mean in the story, right?"

"It used to rest squarely in the center of the Sixth Borough. It was the joy of the borough, its heart. But once it was clear that the Sixth Borough was receding for good, that it couldn't be saved or detained, it was decided, by New York City referendum, to salvage the park." "Referendum?" "Vote." "And?" "And it was unanimous. Even the most stubborn Sixth Boroughers acknowledged what must be done.

"Enormous hooks were driven through the easternmost grounds, and the park was pulled by the people of New York, like a rug across a floor, from the Sixth Borough into Manhattan.

"Children were allowed to lie down on the park as it was being moved. This was considered a concession, although no one knew why a concession was necessary, or why it was to children that this concession must be made. The biggest fireworks show in history lit the skies of New York City that night, and the Philharmonic played its heart out.

"The children of New York lay on their backs, body to body, filling every inch of the park, as if it had been designed for them and that moment. The fireworks sprinkled down, dissolving in the air just before they reached the ground, and the children were pulled, one millimeter and one second at a time, into Manhattan and adulthood. By the time the park found its current resting place, every single one of the children had fallen asleep, and the park was a mosaic of their dreams. Some hollered out, some smiled unconsciously, some were perfectly still."

"Dad?" "Yes?" "I know there wasn't really a sixth borough. I mean, objectively." "Are you an optimist or a pessimist?" "I can't remember. Which?" "Do you know what those words mean?" "Not really." "An optimist is positive and hopeful. A pessimist is negative and cynical." "I'm an optimist." "Well, that's good, because there's no irrefutable evidence. There's nothing that could convince someone who doesn't want to be convinced. But there is an abundance of clues that would give the wanting believer something to hold on to." "Like what?" "Like the peculiar fossil record of Central Park. Like the incongruous pH of the reservoir. Like the placement of certain tanks at the zoo, which correspond to the holes left by the gigantic hooks that pulled the park from borough to borough." "Jose."

"There is a tree—just twenty-four paces due east of the entrance to the merry-go-round—into whose trunk are carved two names. There is no record of them in the phone books or censuses. They are absent from all hospital and tax and voting documentation. There is no evidence whatsoever of their existence, other than the proclamation on the tree. Here's a fact you might find fascinating: no less than five percent of the names carved into the trees of Central Park are of unknown origin." "That *is* fascinating."

"As all of the Sixth Borough's documents floated away with the Sixth Borough, we will never be able to prove that those names belonged to residents of the Sixth Borough, and were carved when Central Park still resided there, instead of in Manhattan. Some people believe they are made-up names and, to take the doubt a step further, that the gestures of love were made-up gestures. Others believe other things." "What do you believe?"

"Well, it's hard for anyone, even the most pessimistic of pessimists, to spend more than a few minutes in Central Park without feeling that he or she is experiencing some tense in addition to the present, right?" "I *guess.*" "Maybe we're just missing things we've lost, or hoping for what we want to come. Or maybe it's the residue of the dreams from that night the park was moved. Maybe we miss what those children had lost, and hope for what they hoped for."

"And what about the Sixth Borough?" "What do you mean?" "What happened to it?" "Well, there's a gigantic hole in the middle of it where Central Park used to be. As the island moves across the planet, it acts like a frame, displaying what lies beneath it." "Where is it now?" "Antarctica." "Really?"

"The sidewalks are covered in ice, the stained glass of the public library is straining under the weight of the snow. There are frozen fountains in frozen neighborhood parks, where frozen children are frozen at the peaks of their swings—the frozen ropes holding them in flight. Livery horses—" "What's that?" "The horses that pull the carriages in the park." "They're inhumane." "They're frozen mid-trot. Flea-market vendors are frozen mid-haggle. Middle-aged women are frozen in the middle of their lives. The gavels of frozen judges are frozen between guilt and innocence. On the ground are the crystals of the frozen first breaths of babies, and those of the last gasps of the dying. On a frozen shelf, in a closet frozen shut, is a can with a voice in it."

"Dad?" "Yeah?" "This isn't an interruption, but are you done?" "The end." "That story was really awesome." "I'm glad you think so." "*Awesome.*

"Dad?" "Yeah?" "I just thought of something. Do you think any of those things I dug up in Central Park were actually from the Sixth Borough?"

He shrugged his shoulders, which I loved.

"Dad?" "Yeah, buddy?" "Nothing."

MY FEELINGS

I was in the guest room when it happened.   I was watching the televi-
sion and knitting you a white scarf.   The news was on.   Time was
passing like a hand waving from a train that I wanted to be on.   You'd
only just left for school, and I was already waiting for you.   I hope you
never think about anything as much as I think about you.
I remember they were interviewing the father of a missing girl.
I remember his eyebrows.   I remember his sadly cleanly shaven face.
Do you still believe that she will be found alive?
I do.
Sometimes I was looking at the television.
Sometimes I was looking at my hands knitting your scarf.
Sometimes out the window at your window.
Are there any new leads in the case?
Not to my knowledge.
But you continue to believe.
Yes.
What would it take for you to give up?
Why was it necessary to torture him?
He touched his forehead and said, It would take a body.
The woman asking the questions touched her ear.
She said, I am sorry.   One second.
She said, Something has happened in New York.
The father of the missing girl touched his chest and looked past the
camera.   At his wife?   At someone he didn't know?   At something
he wanted to see?
Maybe it sounds strange, but I didn't feel anything when they showed

the burning building.   I wasn't even surprised.   I kept knitting for you, and I kept thinking about the father of the missing girl.   He kept believing.

Smoke kept pouring from a hole in the building.

Black smoke.

I remember the worst storm of my childhood.   From my window I saw the books pulled from my father's shelves.   They flew.   A tree that was older than any person tipped away from our house.   But it could have been the other way.

When the second plane hit, the woman who was giving the news started to scream.

A ball of fire rolled out of the building and up.

One million pieces of paper filled the sky.   They stayed there, like a ring around the building.   Like the rings of Saturn.   The rings of coffee staining my father's desk.   The ring Thomas told me he didn't need.   I told him he wasn't the only one who needed.

The next morning my father had us carve our names into the stump of the tree that fell away from our house.   We were giving thanks.

Your mother called.

Are you watching the news?

Yes.

Have you heard from Thomas?

No.

I haven't heard from him either. I'm worried.

Why are you worried?

I told you.   I haven't heard from him.

But he's at the store.

He had a meeting in that building and I haven't heard from him.

I turned my head and thought I would vomit.

I dropped the phone, ran to the toilet, and vomited.

I wouldn't ruin the rug.   That's who I am.

I called your mother back.

She told me you were at home.   She had just spoken to you.

I told her I would go over and watch you.

Don't let him see the news.

OK.

If he asks anything, just let him know that it will be OK.

I told her, It will be OK.

She said, The subways are a mess.   I'm going to walk home.   I should be there in an hour.

She said, I love you.

She had been married to your father for twelve years.   I had known her for fifteen years.   It was the first time she told me she loved me.

That was when I knew that she knew.

I ran across the street.

The doorman said you'd gone up ten minutes before.

He asked if I was all right.

I nodded.

What happened to your arm?

I looked at my arm.   It was bleeding through my shirt.   Had I fallen and not noticed?   Had I been scratching it?   That was when I knew that I knew.

No one answered the door when I rang, so I used my key.

I called to you.

Oskar!

You were silent, but I knew you were there.   I could feel you.

Oskar!

I looked in the coat closet.   I looked behind the sofa.   A Scrabble board was on the coffee table.   Words were running into each other.

I went to your room.   It was empty.   I looked in your closet.   You weren't there.   I went to your parents' room.   I knew you were some-where.   I looked in your father's closet.   I touched the tuxedo that was over his chair.   I put my hands in its pockets.   He had his father's hands.   Your grandfather's hands.   Will you have those hands?   The pockets reminded me.

I went back to your room and lay down on your bed.

I couldn't see the stars on your ceiling because the lights were on.

I thought about the walls of the house I grew up in.   My fingerprints.

When the walls collapsed, my fingerprints collapsed.

I heard you breathing beneath me.

Oskar?

I got on the ground.   On my hands and knees.

Is there room for two under there?

No.

Are you sure?

Positive.

Would it be all right if I tried?

I guess.

I could only barely squeeze myself under the bed.

We lay there on our backs.   There wasn't enough room to turn to face

each other.   None of the light could reach us.

How was school?

It was OK.

You got there on time?

I was early.

So you waited outside?

Yeah.

What did you do?

I read.

What?

What what?

What did you read?

A Brief History of Time.

Is it any good?

That's not really a question you can ask about it.

And your walk home?

It was OK.

It's beautiful weather.

Yeah.

I can't remember more beautiful weather than this.

That's true.

It's a shame to be inside.

I guess so.

But here we are.

I wanted to turn to face you, but I couldn't.   I moved my hand to touch

your hand.

They let you out of school?

Practically immediately.

Do you know what happened?

Yeah.

Have you heard from Mom or Dad?

Mom.

What did she say?

She said everything was fine and she would be home soon.

Dad will be home soon, too.   Once he can close up the store.

Yeah.

You pressed your palms into the bed like you were trying to lift it off us.

I wanted to tell you something, but I didn't know what.   I just knew there was something I needed to tell you.

Do you want to show me your stamps?

No thank you.

Or we could do some thumb wars.

Maybe later.

Are you hungry?

No.

Do you want to just wait here for Mom and Dad to come home?

I guess so.

Do you want me to wait here with you?

It's OK.

Are you sure?

Positive.

Can I please, Oskar?

OK.

Sometimes I felt like the space was collapsing onto us.   Someone was on the bed.   Mary jumping.   Your father sleeping.   Anna kissing me. I felt buried.   Anna holding the sides of my face.   My father pinching my cheeks.   Everything on top of me.

When your mother came home, she gave you such a fierce hug.   I wanted to protect you from her.

She asked if your father had called.

No.

Are there any messages on the phone?

No.

You asked her if your father was in the building for a meeting.

She told you no.

You tried to find her eyes, and that was when I knew that you knew.

She called the police.   It was busy.   She called again.   It was busy.

She kept calling.   When it wasn't busy, she asked to speak to someone.

There was no one to speak to.

You went to the bathroom.   I told her to control herself.   At least in front of you.

She called the newspapers.   They didn't know anything.

She called the fire department.

No one knew anything.

All afternoon I knitted that scarf for you.   It grew longer and longer.

Your mother closed the windows, but we could still smell the smoke.

She asked me if I thought we should make posters.

I said it might be a good idea.

That made her cry, because she had been depending on me.

The scarf grew longer and longer.

She used the picture from your vacation.   From only two weeks before.   It was you and your father.   When I saw it, I told her she shouldn't use a picture that had your face in it.   She said she wasn't going to use the whole picture.   Only your father's face.

I told her, Still, it isn't a good idea.

She said, There are more important things to worry about.

Just use a different picture.

Let it go, Mom.

She had never called me Mom.

There are so many pictures to choose from.

Mind your own business.

This is my business.

We were not angry at each other.

I don't know how much you understood, but probably you understood everything.

She took the posters downtown that afternoon.   She filled a rolling suitcase with them.   I thought of your grandfather.   I wondered where he was at that moment.   I didn't know if I wanted him to be suffering.

She took a stapler.   And a box of staples.   And tape.   I think of those things now.   The paper, the stapler, the staples, the tape.   It makes me sick.   Physical things.   Forty years of loving someone becomes staples and tape.
It was just the two of us.   You and me.
We played games in the living room.   You made jewelry.   The scarf grew longer and longer.   We went for a walk in the park.   We didn't talk about what was on top of us.   What was pinning us down like a ceiling.   When you fell asleep with your head on my lap, I turned on the television.
I lowered the volume until it was silent.
The same pictures over and over.
Planes going into buildings.
Bodies falling.
People waving shirts out of high windows.
Planes going into buildings.
Bodies falling.
Planes going into buildings.
People covered in gray dust.
Bodies falling.
Buildings falling.
Planes going into buildings.
Planes going into buildings.
Buildings falling.
People waving shirts out of high windows.
Bodies falling.
Planes going into buildings.
Sometimes I felt your eyelids flickering.   Were you awake?   Or dreaming?
Your mother came home late that night.   The suitcase was empty.
She hugged you until you said, You're hurting me.
She called everyone your father knew, and everyone who might know something.   She told them, I'm sorry to wake you.   I wanted to shout into her ear, Don't be sorry!
She kept touching her eyes, although there were no tears.
They thought there would be thousands of injured people.   Uncon-

scious people.   People without memories.   They thought there would be thousands of bodies.   They were going to put them in an ice-skating rink.

Remember when we went skating a few months ago and I turned around, because I told you that watching people skate gave me a headache?   I saw rows of bodies under the ice.

Your mother told me I could go home.

I told her I didn't want to.

She said, Have something to eat.   Try to sleep.

I won't be able to eat or sleep.

She said, I need to sleep.

I told her I loved her.

That made her cry, because she had been depending on me.

I went back across the street.

Planes going into buildings.

Bodies falling.

Planes going into buildings.

Buildings falling.

Planes going into buildings.

Planes going into buildings.

Planes going into buildings.

When I no longer had to be strong in front of you, I became very weak. I brought myself to the ground, which was where I belonged.   I hit the floor with my fists.   I wanted to break my hands, but when it hurt too much, I stopped.   I was too selfish to break my hands for my only child.

Bodies falling.

Staples and tape.

I didn't feel empty.   I wished I'd felt empty.

People waving shirts out of high windows.

I wanted to be empty like an overturned pitcher.   But I was full like a stone.

Planes going into buildings.

I had to go to the bathroom.   I didn't want to get up.   I wanted to lie in my own waste, which is what I deserved.   I wanted to be a pig in my own filth.   But I got up and went to the bathroom.   That's who I am.

Bodies falling.

Buildings falling.

The rings of the tree that fell away from our house.

I wanted so much for it to be me under the rubble.   Even for a minute.

A second.   It was as simple as wanting to take his place.   And it was more complicated than that.

The television was the only light.

Planes going into buildings.

Planes going into buildings.

I thought it would feel different.   But even then I was me.

Oskar, I'm remembering you onstage in front of all of those strangers.

I wanted to say to them, He's mine.   I wanted to stand up and shout, That beautiful person is mine!   Mine!

When I was watching you, I was so proud and so sad.

Alas.   His lips.   Your songs.

When I looked at you, my life made sense.   Even the bad things made sense.   They were necessary to make you possible.

Alas.   Your songs.

My parents' lives made sense.

My grandparents'.

Even Anna's life.

But I knew the truth, and that's why I was so sad.

Every moment before this one depends on this one.

Everything in the history of the world can be proven wrong in one moment.

Your mother wanted to have a funeral, even though there was no body. What could anyone say?

We all rode in the limousine together.   I could not stop touching you. I could not touch you enough.   I needed more hands.   You made jokes with the driver, but I could see that inside you were suffering. Making him laugh was how you suffered.   When we got to the grave and they lowered the empty coffin, you let out a noise like an animal.   I had never heard anything like it.   You were a wounded animal.   The noise is still in my ears.   It was what I had spent forty years looking for, what I wanted my life and life story to be.   Your mother took you to

the side and held you.   They shoveled dirt into your father's grave.
Onto my son's empty coffin.   There was nothing there.
All of my sounds were locked inside me.
The limousine took us home.
Everyone was silent.
When we got to my building, you walked me to the front door.
The doorman said there was a letter for me.
I told him I'd look at it tomorrow or the next day.
The doorman said the person had just dropped it off.
I said, Tomorrow.
The doorman said, He seemed desperate.
I asked you to read it for me.   I said, My eyes are crummy.
You opened it.
I'm sorry, you said.
Why are you sorry?
No, that's what it says.
I took it from you and looked at it.
When your grandfather left me forty years ago, I erased all of his writing.   I washed the words from the mirrors and the floors.   I painted over the walls.   I cleaned the shower curtains.   I even refinished the floors.   It took me as long as I had known him to get rid of all of his words.   Like turning an hourglass over.
I thought he had to look for what he was looking for, and realize it no longer existed, or never existed.   I thought he would write.   Or send money.   Or ask for pictures of the baby, if not me.
For forty years not a word.
Only empty envelopes.
And then, on the day of my son's funeral, two words.
I'm sorry.
He had come back.

ALIVE AND ALONE

We had been searching together for six and a half months when Mr. Black told me he was finished, and then I was all alone again, and I hadn't accomplished anything, and my boots were the heaviest they'd ever been in my life. I couldn't talk to Mom, obviously, and even though Toothpaste and The Minch were my best friends, I couldn't talk to them either. Grandpa could talk to animals, but I couldn't, so Buckminster wasn't going to be helpful. I didn't respect Dr. Fein, and it would have taken too long to explain to Stan everything that needed to be explained just to get to the beginning of the story, and I didn't believe in talking to dead people.

Farley didn't know if Grandma was home, because his shift had just started. He asked if something was wrong. I told him, "I need her." "You want I should buzz up?" "It's OK." As I ran up the seventy-two stairs, I thought, *And anyway, he was an incredibly old guy who slowed me down and didn't know anything useful.* I was breathing hard when I rang her bell. *I'm glad he said he was finished. I don't know why I invited him to come along with me in the first place.* She didn't answer, so I rang again. *Why isn't she waiting by the door? I'm the only thing that matters to her.*

I let myself in.

"Grandma? Hello? Grandma?"

I figured maybe she went to the store or something, so I sat on the sofa and waited. Maybe she went to the park for a walk to help her digest, which I know she sometimes did, even though it made me feel weird. Or maybe she was getting some dehydrated ice cream for me, or dropping something off at the post office. But who would she send letters to?

Even though I didn't want to, I started inventing.

She'd been hit by a cab while she was crossing Broadway, and the cab zoomed away, and everybody looked at her from the sidewalk, but no one helped her, because everyone was afraid to do CPR the wrong way.

She'd fallen from a ladder at the library and cracked her skull. She was bleeding to death there because it was in a section of books that no one ever looked at.

She was unconscious at the bottom of the swimming pool at the Y. Kids were swimming thirteen feet above her.

I tried to think about other things. I tried to invent optimistic inventions. But the pessimistic ones were extremely loud.

She'd had a heart attack.

Someone had pushed her onto the tracks.

She'd been raped and murdered.

I started looking around her apartment for her.

"Grandma?"

What I needed to hear was "I'm OK," but what I heard was nothing.

I looked in the dining room and the kitchen. I opened the door to the pantry, just in case, but there was only food. I looked in the coat closet and the bathroom. I opened the door of the second bedroom, where Dad used to sleep and dream when he was my age.

It was my first time being in Grandma's apartment without her, and it felt incredibly weird, like looking at her clothes without her in them, which I did when I went to her bedroom and looked in her closet. I opened the top drawer of the dresser, even though I knew she wouldn't be in there, obviously. So why did I do it?

It was filled with envelopes. Hundreds of them. They were tied together in bundles. I opened the next drawer down, and it was also filled with envelopes. So was the drawer underneath it. All of them were.

I saw from the postmarks that the envelopes were organized chronologically, which means by date, and mailed from Dresden, Germany, which is where she came from. There was one for every day, from May 31, 1963, to the worst day. Some were addressed "To my unborn child." Some were addressed "To my child."

What the?

I knew I probably shouldn't have, because they didn't belong to me, but I opened one of them.

It was sent on February 6, 1972. "To my child." It was empty.

I opened another, from another stack. November 22, 1986. "To my child." Also empty.

June 14, 1963. "To my unborn child." Empty.

April 2, 1979. Empty.

I found the day I was born. Empty.

What I needed to know was, where did she put all of the letters?

I heard a sound from one of the other rooms. I quickly closed the drawers, so Grandma wouldn't know I had been snooping around, and tiptoed to the front door, because I was afraid that maybe what I had heard was a burglar. I heard the sound again, and this time I could tell that it was coming from the guest room.

I thought, *The renter!*

I thought, *He's real!*

I'd never loved Grandma more than I loved her right then.

I turned around, tiptoed to the guest room door, and pressed my ear against it. I didn't hear anything. But when I got down on my knees, I saw that the light in the room was on. I stood up.

"Grandma?" I whispered. "Are you in there?"

Nothing.

"Grandma?"

I heard an extremely tiny sound. I got down on my knees again, and this time I saw that the light was off.

"Is someone in there? I'm eight years old and I'm looking for my grandma because I need her desperately."

Footsteps came to the door, but I could only barely hear them because they were extremely gentle and because of the carpet. The footsteps stopped. I could hear breathing, but I knew it wasn't Grandma's, because it was heavier and slower. Something touched the door. A hand? Two hands?

"Hello?"

The doorknob turned.

"If you're a burglar, please don't murder me."

The door opened.

A man stood there without saying anything, and it was obvious he wasn't a burglar. He was incredibly old and had a face like the opposite of Mom's, because it seemed like it was frowning even when it wasn't frowning. He was wearing a white short-sleeve shirt, so you could see his elbows were hairy, and he had a gap between his two front teeth, like Dad had.

"Are you the renter?"

He concentrated for a second, and then he closed the door.

"Hello?"

I heard him moving stuff around in the room, and then he came back and opened the door again. He was holding a little book. He opened it to the first page, which was blank. "I don't speak," he wrote, "I'm sorry."

"Who are you?" He went to the next page and wrote, "My name is Thomas." "That was my dad's name. It's pretty common. He died." On the next page he wrote, "I'm sorry." I told him, "You didn't kill my dad." On the next page there was a picture of a doorknob, for some reason, so he went to the page after that and wrote, "I'm still sorry." I told him, "Thanks." He flipped back a couple of pages and pointed at "I'm sorry."

We stood there. He was in the room. I was in the hall. The door was open, but it felt like there was an invisible door between us, because I didn't know what to say to him, and he didn't know what to write to me. I told him, "I'm Oskar," and I gave him my card. "Do you know where my grandma is?" He wrote, "She went out." "Where?" He shrugged his shoulders, just like Dad used to. "Do you know when she'll be back?" He shrugged his shoulders. "I need her."

He was on one kind of carpet, I was on another. The line where they came together reminded me of a place that wasn't in any borough.

"If you want to come in," he wrote, "we could wait for her together." I asked him if he was a stranger. He asked me what I meant. I told him, "I wouldn't go in with a stranger." He didn't write anything, like he didn't know if he was a stranger or not. "Are you older than seventy?" He showed me his left hand, which had YES tattooed on it. "Do you have a criminal record?" He showed me his right hand, which had

NO. "What other languages do you speak?" He wrote, "German. Greek. Latin." *"Parlez-vous français?"* He opened and closed his left hand, which I think meant *un peu.*

I went in.

There was writing on the walls, writing everywhere, like, "I wanted so much to have a life," and "Even just once, even for a second." I hoped, for his sake, that Grandma never saw it. He put down the book and picked up another one, for some reason.

"For how long have you been living here?" I asked. He wrote, "How long did your grandmother tell you I've been living here?" "Well," I said, "since Dad died, I guess, so about two years." He opened his left hand. "Where were you before that?" "Where did your grandmother tell you I was before that?" "She didn't." "I wasn't here." I thought that was a weird answer, but I was getting used to weird answers.

He wrote, "Do you want something to eat?" I told him no. I didn't like how much he was looking at me, because it made me feel incredibly self-conscious, but there was nothing I could say. "Do you want something to drink?"

"What's your story?" I asked. "What's my story?" "Yeah, what's your story?" He wrote, "I don't know what my story is." "How can you not know what your story is?" He shrugged his shoulders, just like Dad used to. "Where were you born?" He shrugged his shoulders. "How can you not know where you were born!" He shrugged his shoulders. "Where did you grow up?" He shrugged his shoulders. "OK. Do you have any brothers or sisters?" He shrugged his shoulders. "What's your job? And if you're retired, what *was* your job?" He shrugged his shoulders. I tried to think of something I could ask him that he couldn't not know the answer to. "Are you a human being?" He flipped back and pointed at "I'm sorry."

I'd never needed Grandma more than I needed her right then.

I asked the renter, "Can I tell you my story?"

He opened his left hand.

So I put my story into it.

I pretended he was Grandma, and I started at the very beginning.

I told him about the tuxedo on the chair, and how I had broken the vase, and found the key, and the locksmith, and the envelope, and the art supply store. I told him about the voice of Aaron Black, and how I was so incredibly close to kissing Abby Black. She didn't say she didn't want to, just that it wasn't a good idea. I told him about Abe Black in Coney Island, and Ada Black with the two Picasso paintings, and the birds that flew by Mr. Black's window. Their wings were the first thing he'd heard in more than twenty years. Then there was Bernie Black, who had a view of Gramercy Park, but not a key to it, which he said was worse than looking at a brick wall. Chelsea Black had a tan line around her ring finger, because she got divorced right after she got back from her honeymoon, and Don Black was also an animal-rights activist, and Eugene Black also had a coin collection. Fo Black lived on Canal Street, which used to be a real canal. He didn't speak very good English, because he hadn't left Chinatown since he came from Taiwan, because there was no reason for him to. The whole time I talked to him I imagined water on the other side of the window, like we were in an aquarium. He offered me a cup of tea, but I didn't feel like it, but I drank it anyway, to be polite. I asked him did he really love New York or was he just wearing the shirt. He smiled, like he was nervous. I could tell he didn't understand, which made me feel guilty for speaking English, for some reason. I pointed at his shirt. "Do? You? Really? Love? New York?" He said, "New York?" I said, "Your. Shirt." He looked at his shirt. I pointed at the N and said "New," and the Y and said "York." He looked confused, or embarrassed, or surprised, or maybe even mad. I couldn't tell what he was feeling, because I couldn't speak the language of his feelings. "I not know was New York. In Chinese, *ny* mean 'you.' Thought was 'I love you.'" It was then that I noticed the "I♥NY" poster on the wall, and the "I♥NY" flag over the door, and the "I♥NY" dishtowels, and the "I♥NY" lunchbox on the kitchen table. I asked him, "Well, then why do you love everybody so much?"

Georgia Black, in Staten Island, had turned her living room into a museum of her husband's life. She had pictures of him from when he was a kid, and his first pair of shoes, and his old report cards, which weren't as good as mine, but anyway. "Y'all're the first visitors in more than a year," she said, and she showed us a neat gold medal in a velvet box. "He was a naval officer, and I loved being a naval wife. Every few years we'd have to travel to some exotic place. I never did get a chance to put down many roots, but it was thrilling. We spent two years in the Philippines." "*Cool*," I said, and Mr. Black started singing a song in some weird language, which I guess was Philippinish. She showed us her wedding album, one picture at a time, and said, "Wasn't I slim and beautiful?" I told her, "You were." Mr. Black said, "And you are." She said, "Aren't you two the sweetest?" I said, "Yeah."

"This is the three-wood that he hit his hole in one with. He was real proud of that. For weeks it was all I'd hear about. That's the airplane ticket from our trip to Maui, Hawaii. I'm not too vain to tell you it was our thirtieth anniversary. Thirty years. We were going to renew our vows. Just like in a romance novel. His carry-on bag was filled with flowers, bless his heart. He wanted to surprise me with them on the plane, but I was looking at the x-ray screen as his bag went through, and don't you know there was a dark black bouquet. It was like the shadows of flowers. What a lucky girl I am." She used a cloth to wipe away our fingerprints.

It had taken us four hours to get to her house. Two of those were because Mr. Black had to convince me to get on the Staten Island Ferry. In addition to the fact that it was an obvious potential target, there had also been a ferry accident pretty recently, and in *Stuff That Happened to Me* I had pictures of people who had lost their arms and legs. Also, I don't like bodies of water. Or boats, particularly. Mr. Black asked me how I would feel in bed that night if I didn't get on the ferry. I told him, "Heavy boots, probably." "And how will you feel if you did?" "Like one hundred dollars." "So?" "So what about while I'm *on* the ferry? What if it sinks? What if someone pushes me off? What if it's hit with a shoulder-fired missile? There won't be a tonight tonight." He said, "In which case you won't feel anything anyway." I thought about that.

"This is an evaluation from his commanding officer," Georgia said, tapping the case. "It's exemplary. This is the tie he wore to his mother's funeral, may she rest in peace. She was such a nice woman. Nicer than most. And this here is a picture of his childhood home. That was before I knew him, of course." She tapped every case and then wiped away her own fingerprints, kind of like a Möbius strip. "These are his varsity let-

CNN
FERRY DEATHS
STATEN ISLAND FERRY HITS PIER
FALL OF SADDAM HUSSEIN IS 'GOOD RIDDANCE,' PRES BUSH
NEW YORK

ters. This is his cigarette case from when he used to smoke. Here's his Purple Heart."

I started to get heavy boots, for obvious reasons, like where were all of *her* things? Where were *her* shoes and *her* diploma? Where were the shadows of *her* flowers? I made a decision that I wouldn't ask about the key, because I wanted her to believe that we had come to see her museum, and I think Mr. Black had the same idea. I decided to myself that if we went through the whole list and still hadn't found anything, then maybe, if we had no choice, we could come back and ask her some questions. "These are his baby shoes."

But then I started to wonder: she said we were the first visitors in a little more than a year. Dad had died a little more than a year ago. Was *he* the visitor before us?

"Hello, everyone," a man said from the door. He was holding two mugs, which steam was coming out of, and his hair was wet. "Oh, you're awake!" Georgia said, taking the mug that said "Georgia" on it. She gave him a big kiss, and I was like, *What in the what the?* "Here he is," she said. "Here who is?" Mr. Black asked. "My husband," she said, almost like he was another exhibit in his life. The four of us stood there smiling at one another, and then the man said, "Well, I suppose you'd like to see my museum now." I told him, "We just did. It was really great." He said, "No, Oskar, that's *her* museum. Mine's in the other room."

> *Thank you for your letter. Because of the large volume of mail I receive, I am unable to write personal responses. Nevertheless, know that I read and save every letter, with the hope of one day being able to give each the proper response it deserves. Until that day,*
> *Most sincerely,*
> *Stephen Hawking*

The week passed quickly. Iris Black. Jeremy Black. Kyle Black. Lori Black . . . Mark Black was crying when he opened the door and saw us, because he had been waiting for someone to come back to him, so every time someone knocked on the door, he couldn't stop himself from hoping it might be that person, even though he knew he shouldn't hope.

Nancy Black's roommate told us Nancy was at work at the coffee store on Nineteenth Street, so we went there, and I explained to her that coffee actually has more caffeine than espresso, even though a lot of people don't think so, because the water is in contact with the grounds for a much longer time with coffee. She told me she didn't know that. "If he says it, it's true," Mr. Black said, patting my head. I told her, "Also, did you know that if you yell for nine years, you'll produce enough sound energy to heat one cup of coffee?" She said, "I didn't." I said, "Which is why they should put a *coffee store* next to the *Cyclone* at Coney *Island!* Get it?" That made me crack up, but only me. She asked if we were going to order anything. I told her, "Iced coffee, please." She asked, "What size?" I said, "Vente, and could you please use coffee ice cubes so it doesn't get all watery when the ice cubes melt?" She told me they didn't have coffee ice cubes. I said, "*Exactly.*" Mr. Black said, "I'm going to get right to the point," and then he did. I went to the bathroom and gave myself a bruise.

Ray Black was in prison, so we weren't able to talk to him. I did some research on the Internet and found out that he was in prison because he murdered two kids after he raped them. There were also pictures of the dead kids, and even though I knew it would only hurt me to look at them, I did. I printed them out and put them in *Stuff That Happened to Me*, right after the picture of Jean-Pierre Haigneré, the French astronaut who had to be carried from his spacecraft after returning from the Mir space station, because gravity isn't only what makes us fall, it's what makes our muscles strong. I wrote a letter to Ray Black in prison, but I never got a response. Inside, I hoped he didn't have anything to do with the key, although I couldn't help inventing that it was for his jail cell.

The address for Ruth Black was on the eighty-sixth floor of the Empire State Building, which I thought was incredibly weird, and so did Mr. Black, because neither of us knew that people actually lived there. I told Mr. Black that I was panicky, and he said it was OK to be panicky. I told him I felt like I couldn't do it, and he said it was OK to feel like I couldn't do it. I told him it was the thing that I was most afraid of. He said he could understand why. I wanted him to disagree with me, but he wouldn't, so I had no way to argue. I told him I would wait for him in the lobby, and he said, "Fine." "OK, OK," I said, "I'll go."

As the elevator takes you up, you hear information about the building, which was pretty fascinating, and I normally would have taken some notes, but I needed all of my concentration for being brave. I squeezed Mr. Black's hand, and I couldn't stop inventing: the elevator cables snapping, the elevator falling, a trampoline at the bottom, us shooting back up, the roof opening like a cereal box, us flying toward parts of the universe that not even Stephen Hawking was sure about . . .

When the elevator door opened, we got out on the observation deck. We didn't know who to look for, so we just looked around for a while. Even though I knew the view was incredibly beautiful, my brain started misbehaving, and the whole time I was imagining a plane coming at the building, just below us. I didn't want to, but I couldn't stop. I imagined the last second, when I would see the pilot's face, who would be a terrorist. I imagined us looking each other in the eyes when the nose of the plane was one millimeter from the building.

I hate you, my eyes would tell him.

I hate you, his eyes would tell me.

Then there would be an enormous explosion, and the building would sway, almost like it was going to fall over, which I know is what it felt like from descriptions I've read on the Internet, although I wish I hadn't read them. Then there would be smoke coming up at me and people screaming all around me. I read one description of someone who made it down eighty-five flights of stairs, which must have been about two thousand stairs, and he said that people were screaming "Help!" and "I don't want to die!" and one man who owned a company was screaming "Mommy!"

It would be getting so hot that my skin would start to get blisters. It would feel so good to get away from the heat, but on the other hand, when I hit the sidewalk I would die, obviously. Which would I choose? Would I jump or would I burn? I guess I would jump, because then I wouldn't have to feel pain. On the other hand, maybe I would burn, because then I'd at least have a chance to somehow escape, and even if I couldn't, feeling pain is still better than not feeling, isn't it?

I remembered my cell phone.

I still had a few seconds.

Who should I call?

What should I say?

I thought about all of the things that everyone ever says to each other, and how everyone is going to die, whether it's in a millisecond, or days, or months, or 76.5 years, if you were just born. Everything that's born has to die, which means our lives are like skyscrapers. The smoke rises at different speeds, but they're all on fire, and we're all trapped.

You can see the most beautiful things from the observation deck of the Empire State Building. I read somewhere that people on the street are supposed to look like ants, but that's not true. They look like little people. And the cars look like little cars. And even the buildings look little. It's like New York is a miniature replica of New York, which is nice, because you can see what it's really like, instead of how it feels when you're in the middle of it. It's extremely lonely up there, and you feel far away from everything. Also it's scary, because there are so many ways to die. But it feels safe, too, because you're surrounded by so many people. I kept one hand touching the wall as I walked carefully around to each of the views. I saw all of the locks I'd tried to open, and the 161,999,831 that I hadn't yet.

I got down on my knees and crawled to one of the binocular machines. I held it tightly as I pulled myself up, and I took a quarter from the change dispenser on my belt. When the metal lids opened, I could see things that were far away incredibly close, like the Woolworth Building, and Union Square, and the gigantic hole where the World Trade Center was. I looked into the window of an office building that I guessed was about ten blocks away. It took me a few seconds to figure out the focus, but then I could see a man sitting at his desk, writing something. What was he writing? He didn't look at all like Dad, but he reminded me of Dad. I pressed my face closer, and my nose got smooshed against the cold metal. He was left-handed like Dad. Did he

have a gap between his front teeth like Dad? I wanted to know what he was thinking. Who did he miss? What was he sorry for? My lips touched the metal, like a kiss.

I found Mr. Black, who was looking at Central Park. I told him I was ready to go down. "But what about Ruth?" "We can come back another day." "But we're already here." "I don't feel like it." "It'll just take a few—" "I want to go home." He could probably tell that I was about to cry. "OK," he said, "let's go home."

We got at the end of the line for the elevator.

I looked at everyone and wondered where they came from, and who they missed, and what they were sorry for.

There was a fat woman with a fat kid, and a Japanese guy with two cameras, and a girl with crutches whose cast was signed by lots of people. I had a weird feeling that if I examined it I would find Dad's writing. Maybe he would have written "Get better soon." Or just his name. An old woman was standing a few feet away, staring back at me, which made me self-conscious. She was holding a clipboard, although I couldn't see what was on it, and she was dressed old-fashioned. I promised myself I wouldn't be the first to look away, but I was. I pulled on Mr. Black's sleeve and told him to look at her. "You know what," he whispered. "What?" "I bet you she's the one." For some reason, I knew he was right. Although no part of me wondered if maybe we were looking for different things.

"Should we go up to her?" "Probably." "How?" "I don't know." "Go say hello." "You can't just go say hello." "Tell her the time." "But she didn't ask the time." "Ask her the time." "You do it." "*You* do it." We were so busy arguing about how to go up to her that we didn't even realize that she had come up to us. "I see that you're thinking about leaving," she said, "but could I interest you in a very special tour of this very special building?" "What's your name?" I asked. She said, "Ruth." Mr. Black said, "We'd love a tour."

She smiled, took a huge breath in, and then started walking while she talked. "Construction on the Empire State Building began in March of 1930, on the site of the old Waldorf-Astoria Hotel, at 350 Fifth Avenue at Thirty-fourth Street. It was completed one year and forty-five days later—seven million man-hours of work, including Sundays and holidays. Everything about the building was designed to expedite its construction—prefabricated materials were used as much as possible—and as a result, work progressed at a rate of about four and a half stories each week. The entire framework took less than half a year to complete." That was less time than how long I'd been searching for the lock.

She took a breath.

"Designed by the architectural firm of Shreve, Lamb, and Harmon Associates, the original plan called for eighty-six stories, but a 150-foot mooring mast for zeppelins was added. Today the mast is used for TV and radio broadcasts. The cost of the building, including the land that it rests on, was $40,948,900. The cost of the building itself was $24,718,000, less than half of the estimated cost of $50,000,000, due to deflated labor and materials costs during the Great Depression." I asked, "What was the Great Depression?" Mr. Black said, "I'll tell you later."

"At 1,250 feet, the Empire State Building was the tallest building in the world until the completion of the first tower of the World Trade Center in 1972. When the building was opened, they had such a hard time finding tenants to rent space within it that New Yorkers began calling it the Empty State Building." That made me crack up. "It was this observatory that saved the building from going into bankruptcy." Mr. Black patted the wall, like he was proud of the observatory.

"The Empire State Building is supported by 60,000 tons of steel. It has approximately 6,500 windows and 10,000,000 bricks, weighing in the neighborhood of 365,000 tons." "That's a heavy neighborhood," I said. "More than 500,000 square feet of marble and Indiana limestone encase this skyscraper. Inside, there is marble from France, Italy, Germany, and Belgium. In fact, New York's most famous building is made with materials from just about everywhere but New York, in much the same way that the city itself was made great by immigrants." "Very true," Mr. Black said, nodding his head.

"The Empire State Building has been the location of dozens of movies, the reception site of foreign dignitaries, and even had a World

War Two bomber crash into the seventy-ninth floor in 1945." I concentrated on happy, safe things, like the zipper on the back of Mom's dress, and how Dad needed a drink of water whenever he whistled for too long. "An elevator fell to the bottom. You'll be relieved to know that the passenger was saved by the emergency brakes." Mr. Black gave my hand a squeeze. "And speaking of elevators, there are seventy of them in the building, including the six freight elevators. They travel at speeds from 600 to 1,400 feet per minute. Or, if you so choose, you can walk the 1,860 steps from the street level to the top." I asked if you could also take the stairs down.

"On a clear day like this, you can see for eighty miles—well into Connecticut. Since the observatory opened to the public in 1931, almost 110 million visitors have enjoyed the breathtaking vision of the city beneath them. Each year, over 3.5 million people are whisked to the eighty-sixth floor to be where Cary Grant waited in vain for Deborah Kerr in *An Affair to Remember,* where Tom Hanks and Meg Ryan had their fateful meeting in the movie *Sleepless in Seattle.* Also, the observatory is handicap accessible."

She stopped and put her hand on her heart.

"All in all, the feeling and spirit of New York City is embodied in the Empire State Building. From the people who fell in love here, to the ones who have returned with their children and grandchildren, everyone recognizes the building not only as an awe inspiring landmark which offers one of the most spectacular views on earth, but an unequaled symbol of American ingenuity."

She bowed. We clapped.

"Do you young men have another minute?" "We have a lot of minutes," Mr. Black said. "Because that was the end of the official tour, but there are a couple of things I really love about this building, and I only share them with people I suspect will care." I told her, "We'll care incredibly much."

"The dirigible mooring mast, now the base of the TV tower, was part of the original construction of the building. One attempt to moor a privately owned blimp was successful. But during another attempt, in September 1931, a navy blimp was almost upended, and nearly swept away the celebrities attending the historic affair, while the water ballast drenched pedestrians several blocks away. The mooring mast idea was ultimately abandoned, although it was very romantic." She started walking again, and we followed her, but I wondered if she would have kept talking even if we hadn't followed her. I couldn't tell if she was doing what she was doing for us, or for herself, or for some completely other reason.

"During the spring and autumn bird-migration season, the lights that illuminate the tower are turned off on foggy nights so they won't confuse birds, causing them to fly into the building." I told her, "Ten thousand birds die every year from smashing into windows," because I'd accidentally found that fact when I was doing some research about the windows in the Twin Towers. "That's a lot of birds," Mr. Black said. "And a lot of windows," Ruth said. I told them, "Yeah, so I invented a device that would detect when a bird is incredibly close to a building, and that would trigger an extremely loud birdcall from another skyscraper, and they'd be drawn to that. They'd bounce from one to another." "Like pinball," Mr. Black said. "What's pinball?" I asked. "But the birds would never leave Manhattan," Ruth said. "Which would be great," I told her, "because then your birdseed shirt would be reliable." "Would it be all right if I mentioned the ten thousand birds in my future tours?" I told her they didn't belong to me.

"A natural lightning rod, the Empire State Building is struck up to five hundred times each year. The outdoor observation deck is closed during thunderstorms, but the inside viewing areas remain open. Static electricity buildup is so mammoth on top of the building that, under the right conditions, if you stick your hand through the observatory fence, St. Elmo's fire will stream from your fingertips." "St. Elmo's fire is *sooo* awesome!" "Lovers who kiss up here may find their lips crackling with electric sparks." Mr. Black said, "That's my favorite part." She said, "Mine, too." I said, "Mine's the St. Elmo's fire." "The Empire State Building is located at latitude 40 degrees, 44 minutes, 53.977 seconds north; longitude 73 degrees, 59 minutes, 10.812 seconds west. Thank you."

"That was delightful," Mr. Black said. "Thank you," she said. I asked her how she knew all of that stuff. She said, "I know about this building because I love this building." That gave me heavy boots, because it reminded me of the lock that I still hadn't found, and how until I found it, I didn't love Dad enough. "What is it about this building?" Mr. Black asked. She said, "If I had an answer, it wouldn't really be love, would it?" "You're a terrific lady," he said, and then he asked where her family was from. "I was born in Ireland. My family came when I was a young girl." "Your parents?" "My parents were Irish." "And your grandparents?" "Irish." "That's marvelous news," Mr. Black said. "Why?" she asked, which was a question I was also wondering. "Because my family has nothing to do with Ireland. We came over on the Mayflower." I said, "*Cool.*" Ruth said, "I'm not sure I understand." Mr. Black said, "We're not related." "Why would we be related?" "Because we have the same last name." Inside I thought, *But technically she never actually said her last name was Black. And even if it actually was Black, why wasn't she asking how he knew her last name?* Mr. Black took off his beret and got down onto one of his knees, which took him a long time. "At the risk of being too forthright, I was hoping I might have the pleasure of your company one afternoon. I will be disappointed, but in no way offended, if you decline." She turned her face away. "I'm sorry," he said, "I shouldn't have." She said, "I stay up here."

Mr. Black said, "*What the?*" "I stay up here." "Always?" "Yes." "For how long?" "Oh. A long time. Years." Mr. Black said, "Jose!" I asked her how. "What do you mean how?" "Where do you sleep?" "On nice nights, I'll sleep out here. But when it gets chilly, which is most nights up this high, I have a bed in one of the storage rooms." "What do you eat?" "There are two snack bars up here. And sometimes one of the young men will bring me food, if I have a taste for something different. As you know, New York offers so many different eating experiences."

I asked if they knew she was up there. "Who's *they?*" "I don't know, the people who own the building or whatever." "The building has been owned by a number of different people since I moved up here." "What about the workers?" "The workers come and go. The new ones see I'm here and assume I'm supposed to be here." "No one has told you to leave?" "Never."

"Why don't you go down?" Mr. Black asked. She said, "I'm more comfortable here." "How could you be more comfortable here?" "It's hard to explain." "How did it start?" "My husband was a door-to-door salesman." "And?" "This was in the old days. He was always selling something or other. He loved the next thing that would change life. And he was always coming up with wonderful, crazy ideas. A bit like you," she said to me, which gave me heavy boots, because why couldn't I remind people of me? "One day he found a spotlight in an army surplus store. This was right after the war and you could find just about anything. He hooked it up to a car battery and fixed all of that to the crate he rolled around. He told me to go up to the observation deck of the Empire State Building, and as he walked around New York, he'd occasionally shine the light up at me so I could see where he was."

"It worked?" "Not during the day it didn't. It had to get quite dark before I could see the light, but once I could, it was amazing. It was as if all of the lights in New York were turned off except for his. That was how clearly I could see it." I asked her if she was exaggerating. She said, "I'm understating." Mr. Black said, "Maybe you're telling it exactly as it was."

"I remember that first night. I came up here and everyone was looking all over, pointing at the things to see. There are so many spectacular things to see. But only I had something pointing back at me." "Some*one*," I said. "Yes, something that was someone. I felt like a queen. Isn't that funny? Isn't it silly?" I shook my head no. She said, "I felt just like a queen. When the light went off, I knew his day was over, and I'd go down and meet him at home. When he died, I came back up here. It's silly." "No," I said. "It isn't." "I wasn't looking for him. I'm not a girl. But it gave me the same feeling that I'd had when it was daytime and I was looking for his light. I knew it was there, I just couldn't see it." Mr. Black took a step toward her.

"I couldn't bear to go home," she said. I asked why not, even though I was afraid I was going to learn something I didn't want to know. She said, "Because I knew he wouldn't be there." Mr. Black told her thank you, but she wasn't done. "I curled up in a corner that night, that corner over there, and fell asleep. Maybe I wanted the guards to notice me. I don't know. When I woke up in the middle of the night, I

was all alone. It was cold. I was scared. I walked to the railing. Right there. I'd never felt more alone. It was as if the building had become much taller. Or the city had become much darker. But I'd never felt more alive, either. I'd never felt more alive or alone."

"I wouldn't make you go down," Mr. Black said. "We could spend the afternoon up here." "I'm awkward," she said. "So am I," Mr. Black said. "I'm not very good company. I just told you everything I know." "I'm terrible company," Mr. Black said, although that wasn't true. "Ask him," he said, pointing at me. "It's true," I said, "he sucks." "You can tell me about this building all afternoon. That would be marvelous. That's how I want to spend my time." "I don't even have any lipstick." "Neither do I." She let out a laugh, and then she put her hand over her mouth, like she was angry at herself for forgetting her sadness.

It was already 2:32 P.M. when I finished walking the 1,860 stairs down to the lobby, and I was exhausted, and Mr. Black seemed exhausted, too, so we went straight home. When we got to Mr. Black's door—this was just a few minutes ago—I was already making plans for next weekend, because we had to go to Far Rockaway, and Boerum Hill, and Long Island City, and if we had time also to Dumbo, but he interrupted me and said, "Listen. Oskar?" "That's my name, don't wear it out." "I think I'm finished." "Finished with what?" "I hope you understand." He stuck out his hand for a shake. "Finished with what?" "I've loved being with you. I've loved every second of it. You got me back into the world. That's the greatest thing anyone could have done for me. But now I think I'm finished. I hope you understand." His hand was still open, waiting for my hand.

I told him, "I don't understand."

I kicked his door and told him, "You're breaking your promise."

I pushed him and shouted, "It isn't fair!"

I got on my tiptoes and put my mouth next to his ear and shouted, "Fuck you!"

No. I shook his hand . . .

"And then I came straight here, and now I don't know what to do."

As I had been telling the renter the story, he kept nodding his head and looking at my face. He stared at me so hard that I wondered if he wasn't listening to me at all, or if he was trying to hear something incredibly quiet underneath what I was saying, sort of like a metal detector, but for truth instead of metal.

I told him, "I've been searching for more than six months, and I don't know a single thing that I didn't know six months ago. And actually I have negative knowledge, because I skipped all of those French classes with Marcel. Also I've had to tell a googolplex lies, which doesn't make me feel good about myself, *and* I've bothered a lot of people who I've probably ruined my chances of ever being real friends with, *and* I miss my dad more now than when I started, even though the whole *point* was to *stop* missing him."

I told him, "It's starting to hurt too much."

He wrote, "What is?"

Then I did something that surprised even me. I said, "Hold on," and I ran down the 72 stairs, across the street, right past Stan, even though he was saying "You've got mail!" and up the 105 stairs. The apartment was empty. I wanted to hear beautiful music. I wanted Dad's whistling, and the scratching sound of his red pen, and the pendulum swinging in his closet, and him tying his shoelaces. I went to my room and got the phone. I ran back down the 105 stairs, past Stan, who was still saying "You've got mail!," back up the 72 stairs, and into Grandma's apartment. I went to the guest room. The renter was standing in exactly the same position, like I'd never left, or never been there at all. I took the phone out of the scarf that Grandma was never able to finish, plugged it in, and played those first five messages for him. He didn't show anything on his face. He just looked at me. Not even at me, but into me, like his detector sensed some enormous truth deep inside me.

"No one else has ever heard that," I said.

"What about your mother?" he wrote.

"Especially not her."

He crossed his arms and held his hands in his armpits, which for him was like putting his hands over his mouth. I said, "Not even Grandma," and his hands started shaking, like birds trapped under a tablecloth. Finally he let them go. He wrote, "Maybe he saw what happened and ran in to save somebody." "He would have. That's what he was like." "He was a good person?" "He was the best person. But he was in the building for a meeting. And also he said he went up to the roof, so he must have been above where the plane hit, which means he didn't run in to save anyone." "Maybe he just said he was going to the roof." "Why would he do that?"

"What kind of meeting was it?" "He runs the family jewelry business. He has meetings all the time." "The family jewelry business?" "My grandpa started it." "Who's your grandpa?" "I don't know. He left my grandma before I was born. She says he could talk to animals and make a sculpture that was more real than the real thing." "What do you think?" "I don't think anyone can talk to animals. Except to dolphins, maybe. Or sign language to chimps." "What do you think about your grandpa?" "I don't think about him."

He pressed Play and listened to the messages again, and again I pressed Stop after the fifth was finished.

He wrote, "He sounds calm in the last message." I told him, "I read something in *National Geographic* about how, when an animal thinks it's going to die, it gets panicky and starts to act crazy. But when it *knows* it's going to die, it gets very, very calm." "Maybe he didn't want you to worry." Maybe. Maybe he didn't say he loved me *because* he loved me. But that wasn't a good enough explanation. I said, "I need to know how he died."

He flipped back and pointed at, "Why?"

"So I can stop inventing how he died. I'm always inventing."

He flipped back and pointed at, "I'm sorry."

"I found a bunch of videos on the Internet of bodies falling. They were on a Portuguese site, where there was all sorts of stuff they weren't showing here, even though it happened here. Whenever I want to try to learn about how Dad died, I have to go to a translator program and find out how to say things in different languages, like 'September,' which is 'Wrzesień,' or 'people jumping from burning buildings,' which is 'Menschen, die aus brennenden Gebäuden springen.' Then I Google those words. It makes me incredibly angry that people all over the world can know things that I can't, because it happened *here*, and happened to *me*, so shouldn't it be *mine?*

"I printed out the frames from the Portuguese videos and examined them extremely closely. There's one body that could be him. It's dressed like he was, and when I magnify it until the pixels are so big that it stops looking like a person, sometimes I can see glasses. Or I think I can. But I know I probably can't. It's just me wanting it to be him."

"You want him to have jumped?"

"I want to stop inventing. If I could know how he died, exactly how he died, I wouldn't have to invent him dying inside an elevator that was stuck between floors, which happened to some people, and I wouldn't have to imagine him trying to crawl down the outside of the building, which I saw a video of one person doing on a Polish site, or trying to use a tablecloth as a parachute, like some of the people who were in Windows on the World actually did. There were so many different ways to die, and I just need to know which was his."

He held out his hands like he wanted me to take them. "Are those tattoos?" He closed his right hand. I flipped back and pointed at "Why?" He took back his hands and wrote, "It's made things easier. Instead of writing yes and no all the time, I can show my hands." "But why just YES and NO?" "I only have two hands." "What about 'I'll think about it,' and 'probably,' and 'it's possible'?" He closed his eyes and concentrated for a few seconds. Then he shrugged his shoulders, just like Dad used to.

"Have you always been silent?" He opened his right hand. "Then why don't you talk?" He wrote, "I can't." "Why not?" He pointed at, "I can't." "Are your vocal cords broken or something?" "Something is broken." "When was the last time you talked?" "A long, long time ago." "What was the last word you said?" He flipped back and pointed at "I." "*I* was the last word you said?" He opened his left hand. "Does that even count as a word?" He shrugged his shoulders. "Do you try to talk?" "I know what will happen." "What?" He flipped back and pointed at, "I can't."

"Try." "Now?" "Try to say something." He shrugged his shoulders. I said, "Please."

He opened his mouth and put his fingers on his throat. They fluttered, like Mr. Black's fingers looking for a one-word biography, but no sound came out, not even an ugly sound, or breath.

I asked him, "What were you trying to say?" He flipped back and pointed at, "I'm sorry." I said, "It's OK." I said, "Maybe your vocal cords actually are broken. You should go to a specialist." I asked him, "What were you trying to say?" He pointed at, "I'm sorry."

I asked, "Can I take a picture of your hands?"

He put his hands on his lap, face-up, like a book.

YES and NO.

I focused Grandpa's camera.

He kept his hands extremely still.

I took the picture.

I told him, "I'm going to go home now." He picked up his book and wrote, "What about your grandma?" "Tell her I'll talk to her tomorrow."

As I was halfway across the street, I heard clapping behind me, almost like the birds' wings outside Mr. Black's window. I turned around and the renter was standing at the building's door. He put his hand on his throat and opened his mouth, like he was trying to speak again.

I called back to him, "What are you trying to say?"

He wrote something in his book and held it up, but I couldn't see it, so I ran back over. It said, "Please don't tell your grandmother that we met." I told him, "I won't if you won't," and I didn't even wonder the obvious thing, which was why would *he* want to keep it a secret? He wrote, "If you ever need me for anything, just throw pebbles at the guest room window. I'll come down and meet you under the streetlamp." I said, "Thanks." Although inside what I was thinking was, *Why would I ever need you?*

All I wanted was to fall asleep that night, but all I could do was invent.

What about frozen planes, which could be safe from heat-seeking missiles?

What about subway turnstiles that were also radiation detectors?

What about incredibly long ambulances that connected every building to a hospital?

What about parachutes in fanny packs?

What about guns with sensors in the handles that could detect if you were angry, and if you were, they wouldn't fire, even if you were a police officer?

What about Kevlar overalls?

What about skyscrapers made with moving parts, so they could rearrange themselves when they had to, and even open holes in their middles for planes to fly through?

What about . . .

What about . . .

What about . . .

And then a thought came into my brain that wasn't like the other thoughts. It was closer to me, and louder. I didn't know where it came from, or what it meant, or if I loved it or hated it. It opened up like a fist, or a flower.

What about digging up Dad's empty coffin?

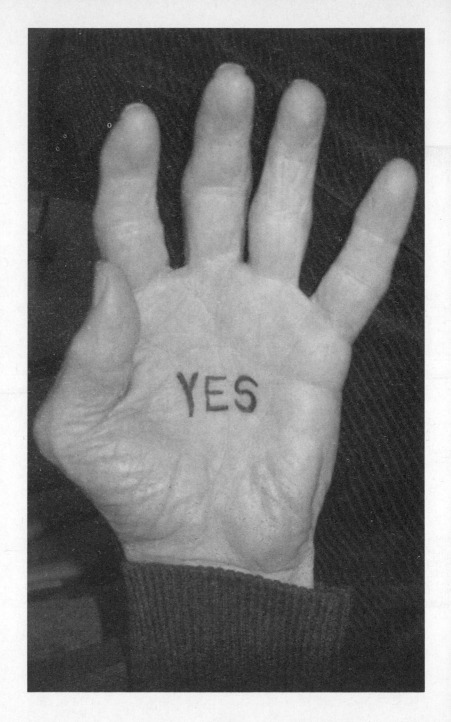

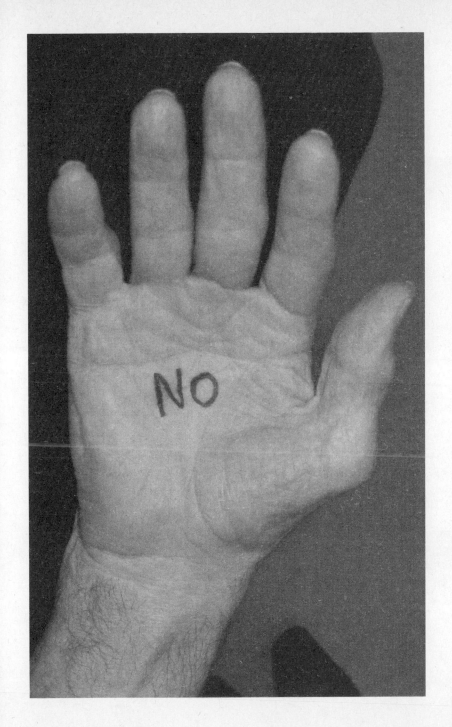

WHY I'M NOT WHERE YOU ARE
9/11/03

I don't speak, I'm sorry.

My name is Thomas.

I'm sorry.

I'm still sorry.

To my child: I wrote my last letter on the day you died, and I assumed I'd never write another word to you, I've been so wrong about so much that I've assumed, why am I surprised to feel the pen in my hand tonight? I'm writing as I wait to meet Oskar, in a little less than an hour, I'll close this book and find him under the streetlight, we'll be on our way to the cemetery, to you, your father and your son, this is how it happened. I gave a note to your mother's doorman almost two years ago. I watched from across the street as the limousine pulled up, she got out, she touched the door, she'd changed so much but I still knew her, her hands had changed but the way she touched was the same, she went into the building with a boy, I couldn't see if the doorman gave her my note, I couldn't see her reaction, the boy came out and went into the building across the street. I watched her that night as she stood with her palms against the window, I left another note with the doorman, "Do you want to see me again, or should I go away?" The next morning there was a note written on the window, "Don't go away," which meant something, but it didn't mean "I want to see you again." I gathered a handful of pebbles and tossed them at her window, nothing happened, I tossed some more, but she didn't come to the window, I wrote a note in my daybook—"Do you want to see me again?"—I ripped it out and gave it to the doorman, the next morning I went back, I didn't want to make her life any harder than it was, but I didn't want to give up either, there was a note on the window, "I don't want to want to see you again," which meant something, but it didn't mean yes. I gathered pebbles from the street and threw them at her window, hoping she would hear me and know what I meant, I waited, she didn't come to the window, I wrote a note—"What should I do?"—and gave it to the doorman, he said, "I'll make sure she gets it," I couldn't say, "Thank you." The next morning I went back, there was a note on her window, the first note, "Don't go away," I gathered pebbles, I threw them, they tapped like fingers against the glass, I wrote a note, "Yes or no?" for how long could it go on? The next day I found a market on Broadway and bought an apple, if she didn't want me I would leave, I didn't know where I would go, but I would turn around and walk away, there was no note on her window, so I threw the apple, anticipating the glass that would rain down on me, I wasn't afraid of the shards, the apple went through her window and into her apartment, the doorman was standing in front of the building, he said, "You're lucky that was open, pal," but I knew I wasn't lucky, he handed me a key. I rode the elevator up, the door was open, the smell brought back to me what for forty years I had struggled not to remember but couldn't forget. I put the key in my pocket, "Only the guest room!" she called from our bedroom, the room in which we used to sleep and dream and make love. That was how we began our second life together . . . When I got off the plane, after eleven hours of travel and forty years away, the man took my passport and asked me the purpose of my visit, I wrote in my daybook, "To mourn," and then, "To ~~mourn~~ try to live," he gave me a look and asked if I would consider that business or pleasure, I wrote, "Neither." "For how long do you plan to mourn and try to live?" I wrote, "For the rest of my life." "So you're going to stay?" "For as long as I can." "Are we talking about a weekend or a year?" I didn't write anything. The man said, "Next." I watched the bags go around the carousel, each one held a person's belongings, I saw babies going around and around, possible lives, I followed the arrows for those with nothing to declare, and that made me want to laugh, but I was silent. One of the guards asked me to come to the side, "That's a lot of suitcases for someone with nothing to declare," he said, I nodded, knowing that people with nothing to declare carry the most, I opened the suitcases for him, "That's a lot of paper," he said, I showed him my left palm, "I mean, that's a whole lot of paper." I wrote, "They're letters to my son. I wasn't able to send them to him while he was alive. Now he's dead. I don't speak. I'm sorry." The guard looked at the other guard and they shared a smile, I don't mind if smiles come at my expense, I'm a small price to pay, they let me through, not because they believed me but because they didn't want to try to understand me, I found a pay phone and called your mother, that was as far as my plan went, I assumed so much, that she was still alive, that she was in the same apartment I'd left forty years before, I assumed she would come pick me up and everything would begin to make sense, we would mourn and try to live, the phone rang and rang, we would forgive ourselves, it rang, a woman answered, "Hello?" I knew it was her, the voice had changed but the breath was the same, the spaces between the words were the same, I pressed "4, 3, 5, 5, 6," she said, "Hello?" I asked, "4, 7, 4, 8, 7, 3, 2, 5, 5, 9, 9, 6, 8?" She said, "Your phone isn't one hundred dollars. Hello?" I wanted to reach my hand through the mouthpiece, down the line, and into her room, I wanted to reach YES, I asked, "4, 7, 4, 8, 7, 3, 2, 5, 5, 9, 9, 6, 8?" She said, "Hello?" I told her, "4, 3, 5, 7!" "Listen," she said, "I don't know what's wrong with your phone, but all I hear is beeps. Why don't you hang up and try again." Try again? I was trying to try again, that's what I was doing! I knew it wouldn't help, I knew no good would come of it, but I stood there in the middle of the airport, at the beginning of the century, at the end of my life, and I told her everything: why I'd left, where I'd gone, how I'd found out about your death, why I'd come back, and what I needed to do with the time I had left. I told her because I wanted her to believe me and understand, and because I thought I owed it to her, and to myself, and to you, or was it just more selfishness? I broke my life down into letters, for love I pressed "5, 6, 8, 3," for death, "3, 3, 2, 8, 4," when the suffering is subtracted from the joy, what remains? What, I wondered, is the sum of my life? "6, 9, 6, 2, 6, 3, 4, 7, 3, 5, 4, 3, 2, 5, 8, 6, 2, 6, 3, 4, 5, 8, 7, 8, 2, 7, 7, 4, 8, 3, 3, 2, 8, 8, 4, 3, 2, 4, 7, 7, 6, 7, 8, 4, 6, 3, 3, 3, 8, 6, 3, 4, 6, 3, 6, 7, 3, 4, 6, 5, 3, 5, 7! 6, 4, 3, 2, 2, 6, 7, 4, 2, 5, 6, 3, 8, 7, 2, 6, 3, 4, 3? 5, 7, 6, 3, 5, 8, 6, 2, 6, 3, 4, 5, 8, 7, 8, 2, 7, 7, 4, 8, 3, 9, 2, 8, 8, 4, 3, 2, 4, 7, 7, 6, 7, 8, 4, 6, 3, 3, 3, 8! 4, 3, 2, 4, 7, 7, 6, 7, 8, 4! 6, 3, 3, 3, 8, 6, 3, 9, 6, 3, 6, 6, 3, 4, 6, 5, 3, 5, 7! 6, 4, 3, 2, 2, 6, 7, 4, 2, 5, 6, 3, 8, 7, 2, 6, 3, 4, 3? 5, 7, 6, 3, 5, 8, 6, 2, 6, 3, 4, 5, 8, 7, 8, 2, 7, 7, 4, 8, 3, 3, 2, 8! 7, 7, 4, 8, 3, 3, 2, 8, 3, 4, 3, 2, 4, 7, 6, 6, 7, 8, 4, 6, 8, 3, 8, 8, 6, 3, 4, 6, 3, 6, 7, 3, 4, 6, 7, 7, 4, 8, 3, 3, 9, 8, 8, 4, 3, 2, 4, 5, 7, 6, 7, 8, 4, 6, 3, 5, 5, 2, 6, 9, 4, 6, 5, 6, 7, 5, 4, 6! 5, 2, 6, 2, 6, 5, 9, 5, 2? 6, 9, 6, 2, 6, 5, 4, 7, 5, 5, 4, 5, 2, 5, 2, 6, 4, 6, 2, 4, 5, 2, 7, 2, 2, 7, 7, 4, 2, 5, 5, 2, 9, 2, 4, 5, 2, 6! 4, 2, 2, 6, 5, 4, 2, 5, 7, 4, 5, 2, 5, 2, 6, 2, 6, 5, 4, 5, 2, 7, 2, 2, 7, 7, 4, 2, 5, 5, 2, 2, 2, 4, 5, 2! 7, 2, 2, 7, 7, 4, 2, 5, 5, 2, 2, 2, 4, 5, 2, 4, 7, 2, 2, 7, 2, 4, 6, 5, 5, 5, 2, 6, 5, 4, 6, 5, 6, 7, 5, 4! 4, 3, 2, 4, 3, 3, 6, 3, 8, 4! 6, 3, 3, 3, 8, 6, 3, 9, 6, 3, 6, 6, 3, 4, 6, 5, 3, 5, 3! 2, 2, 3, 3, 2, 6, 3, 4, 2, 5, 6, 3, 8, 3, 2, 6, 3, 4, 3? 5, 6, 8, 3? 5, 3, 6, 3, 5, 8, 6, 2, 6, 3, 4, 5, 8, 3, 8, 2, 3,

4, 8, 3, 3, 2, 8! 3, 3, 4, 8, 3, 3, 2, 8, 3, 4, 3, 2, 4, 7, 6, 6, 7, 8, 4, 6, 8, 3, 8, 8,

6, 3, 4, 6, 3! 2, 2, 7, 7, 4, 2, 5, 5, 2, 9, 2, 4, 5, 2, 6! 4, 2, 2, 6, 5, 4, 2, 5, 7, 4,

5, 2, 5, 2, 6, 2, 6, 5, 4, 5, 2, 7, 2, 2, 7, 7, 4, 2, 5, 5, 2, 2, 2, 4, 5, 2! 7, 2, 2, 7,

7, 4, 2, 5, 5, 2, 2, 2, 4, 5, 2, 4, 7, 2, 2, 7, 2, 4, 6, 5, 5, 5, 2, 6, 5, 4, 6, 5, 6, 7,

5, 4! 6, 5, 5, 5, 7! 6, 4, 5, 2, 2, 6, 7, 4, 2, 5, 6, 5, 2, 6! 2, 6, 5, 4, 5? 5, 7, 6, 5,

5, 2, 6, 2, 6, 5, 4, 5, 2, 7, 2, 2, 7, 7, 4, 2, 5, 9, 2, 2, 2, 4, 5, 2, 4, 5, 5, 6, 5, 2,

4, 6, 5, 5, 5, 2! 4, 5, 2, 4, 5, 5, 6, 5! 5, 6, 8, 3? 5, 5, 6, 5, 5, 2, 6, 2, 6, 3, 4, 5,

8, 3, 8, 2, 3, 3, 4, 8, 3, 9, 2, 8, 8, 4, 3, 2, 4, 3, 3, 6, 3, 8, 4, 6, 3, 3, 3, 8! 4, 3,

2, 4, 3, 3, 6, 3, 8, 4, 6, 3! 5, 6, 8, 3? 5, 6, 8, 3? 5, 6, 8, 3! 4, 2, 2, 6, 5, 4, 2, 5,

7, 4, 5, 2, 5, 2, 6, 2, 6, 5, 4, 5, 2, 7, 2, 2, 7, 4, 5, 2, 4, 6, 3, 5, 8, 6, 2, 6, 3, 4,

5, 8, 7, 8, 2, 7, 7, 4, 8, 3, 3, 2, 8! 6, 5, 5, 5, 7! 6, 4, 5, 2, 2, 6, 7, 4, 2, 5, 6, 5,

2, 6! 2, 6, 5, 4, 5? 5, 7, 6, 5, 5, 2, 6, 2, 6, 5, 4, 5, 2, 7, 2, 2, 7, 7, 4, 2, 5, 9, 2,

2, 2, 4, 5, 2, 4! 5, 6, 8, 3? 5, 5, 6, 5, 2, 4, 6, 3, 6, 7, 3, 4, 6, 7, 7, 4, 8, 3, 3, 9,

8, 8, 4, 3, 2, 4, 5, 7, 6, 7, 8, 4, 6, 3, 5, 5, 2, 6, 9, 4, 6, 5, 6, 7, 5, 4, 6! 5, 2, 6,

2, 6, 5, 9, 5, 2? 6, 9, 6, 2, 6, 5, 4, 7, 5, 5, 4, 5, 2, 5, 2, 6, 4, 6, 2, 4, 5, 2, 7, 2,

2, 7, 7, 4, 2, 5, 5, 2, 9, 2, 4, 5, 2, 6! 4, 2, 2, 6, 5, 4, 2, 5, 7, 4, 5, 2, 5, 2, 6, 2,

6, 5, 4, 5, 2, 7, 2, 2, 7, 7, 4, 2, 5, 5, 2, 2, 2, 4, 5, 2! 7, 2, 2, 7, 7, 4, 2, 5, 5, 2,

2, 2, 4, 5, 2, 4, 7, 2, 2, 7, 2, 4, 6, 5, 5, 5, 2, 6, 5, 4, 6, 5, 6, 7, 5, 4! 6, 5, 5, 5,

7! 6, 4, 5, 2, 2, 6, 7, 4, 2, 5, 6, 5, 2, 6! 2, 6, 5, 4, 5? 5, 7, 6, 5, 5, 2, 6, 2, 6, 5,

4, 5, 2, 7, 2, 2, 7, 7, 4, 2, 5, 9, 2, 2, 2, 4, 5, 2, 4! 5, 6, 8, 3? 5, 5, 6, 5, 2, 4, 6,

5, 5, 5, 2! 4, 5, 2, 4, 5, 5, 6, 5! 2, 5, 5, 2, 9, 2, 4, 5, 2, 6! 4, 2, 2, 6, 5, 4, 2! 5,

5, 6, 5, 5, 2, 6, 2, 6, 3, 4, 5, 8, 3, 8, 2, 3, 3, 4, 8, 3, 9, 2, 8, 8, 4, 3, 2, 4, 3, 3,

6, 3, 8, 4, 6, 3, 3, 3, 8! 4, 3, 2, 4, 3, 3, 6, 3, 8, 4! 6, 3, 3, 3, 8, 6, 3, 9, 6, 3, 6,

6, 3, 4, 6, 5, 3, 5, 3! 2, 2, 3, 3, 2, 6, 3, 4, 2, 5, 6, 3, 8, 3, 2, 6, 3, 4, 3? 5, 6, 8,

3? 5, 3, 6, 3, 5, 8, 6, 2, 6, 3, 4, 5, 8, 3, 8, 2, 3, 3, 4, 8, 3, 3, 2, 8! 2, 7, 2, 4, 6,

5, 5, 5, 2, 6, 5, 4, 6, 5, 6, 7, 5, 4! 6, 5, 5, 5, 7! 6, 4, 5, 2, 2, 6, 7, 4, 2, 5, 6, 5,

2, 6! 2, 6, 5, 4, 5? 5, 7, 6, 5, 5, 2, 6, 2, 6, 5, 4, 5, 2, 7, 2, 2, 7, 7, 4, 2, 5, 9, 2,

2, 2, 4, 5, 2, 4, 5, 5, 6, 5, 2, 4, 6, 5, 5, 5, 2! 4, 5, 2, 4, 5, 5, 6, 5! 5, 6, 8, 3? 5,

5, 6, 5, 5, 2, 6, 2, 6, 3, 4, 5, 8, 3, 8, 2, 3, 3, 4, 8, 3, 9, 2, 8, 8, 4, 3, 2, 4, 3, 4,

6, 5, 5, 5, 2! 4, 5, 2, 4, 5, 5, 6, 5! 6, 5, 4, 5? 4, 5? 5, 5, 6, 5, 5, 2, 6, 2, 6, 3, 4,

5, 8, 3, 8, 2, 3, 3, 4, 8, 3, 9, 2, 8, 8, 4, 3, 2, 4, 3, 3, 6, 3, 8, 4, 6, 3, 3, 3, 8! 4,

3, 2, 4, 3, 3, 6, 3, 8, 4! 6, 3, 3, 3, 6, 7, 4, 2, 5, 6, 3, 8, 7, 2, 6, 3, 4, 3? 5, 7, 6,

3, 5, 8, 6, 2, 6, 3, 4, 5, 8, 7, 8, 2, 7, 7, 4, 8, 3, 3, 2, 8! 7, 7, 4, 8, 3, 3, 2, 8, 3,

4, 3, 2, 4, 7, 6, 6, 7, 8, 4, 6, 8, 3, 8, 8, 6, 3, 4, 6, 3, 6, 7, 3, 4, 6, 7, 7, 4, 8, 3,

3, 9, 8, 8, 4, 3, 2, 4, 5, 7, 6, 7, 8, 4, 6, 3, 5, 5, 2, 6, 9, 4, 6, 5, 6, 7, 5, 4, 6! 5,

270

2, 6, 2, 6, 5, 9, 5, 2? 6, 9, 6, 2, 6, 5, 4, 7, 5, 5, 4, 5, 2, 5, 2, 6, 4, 6, 2, 4, 5, 2, 7,
2, 2, 7, 7, 4, 2, 5, 5, 2, 9, 2, 4, 5, 2, 6! 4, 2, 2, 6, 5, 4, 2, 5, 7, 4, 5, 2, 5, 2, 6, 2,
6, 5, 4, 5, 2, 7, 2, 2, 7, 7, 4, 2, 5, 5, 2, 2, 2, 2, 4, 5, 2! 7, 2, 2, 7, 7, 4, 2, 5, 5, 2, 2,
2, 4, 5, 2, 4, 7, 2, 2, 7, 2, 4, 6, 5, 5, 5, 2, 6, 5, 4, 6, 5, 6, 7, 5, 4! 6, 5, 5, 5, 5, 7! 6,
4, 5, 2, 2, 6, 7, 4, 2, 5, 6, 5, 2, 6! 2, 6, 5, 4, 5? 5, 7, 6, 5, 5, 2, 6, 2, 6, 5, 4, 5, 2,
7, 2, 2, 7, 7, 4, 2, 5, 9, 2, 2, 2, 4, 5, 2, 4! 5, 6, 8, 3? 5, 5, 6, 5, 2, 4, 6, 5, 5, 5, 2!
4, 5, 2, 4, 5, 5, 6, 5! 8, 6, 3, 9, 6, 3, 6, 6, 3, 4, 6, 5, 3, 5, 3, 2, 2, 3, 3, 2, 6, 3, 4,
2, 5, 6, 3, 8, 3, 2, 6, 3, 4, 3? 5, 6, 8, 3? 5, 3, 6, 3, 5, 8, 6, 2, 6, 3, 4, 5, 8, 3, 8,
2, 3, 3, 4, 8, 3, 3, 2, 8! 3, 3, 4, 8, 3, 3, 2, 8, 3, 4, 3, 2, 4, 7, 6, 6, 7, 8, 4, 6, 8, 3,
8, 8, 6, 3, 4, 6, 3! 2, 2, 7, 7, 4, 6, 7, 4, 2, 5, 6, 3, 8, 7, 2, 6, 3, 4, 3? 5, 7, 6, 3, 5,
8, 6, 2, 6, 3, 4, 5, 8, 7, 8, 2, 7, 7, 4, 8, 3, 3, 2, 8! 7, 7, 4, 8, 3, 3, 2, 8, 3, 4, 3, 2,
4, 7, 6, 6, 7, 8, 4, 6, 8, 3, 8, 8, 6, 3, 4, 6, 3, 6, 7, 3, 4, 6, 7, 7, 4, 8, 3, 3, 9, 8, 8,
4, 3, 2, 4, 5, 7, 6, 7, 8, 4, 6, 3, 5, 5, 2, 6, 9, 4, 6, 5, 6, 7, 5, 4, 6! 5, 2, 6, 2, 6, 5,
9, 5, 2? 6, 9, 6, 2, 6, 5, 4, 7, 5, 5, 4, 5, 2, 5, 2, 6, 4, 6, 2, 4, 5, 2, 7, 2, 2, 7, 7, 4,
2, 5, 5, 2, 9, 2, 4, 5, 2, 6! 4, 2, 2, 6, 5, 4, 2, 5, 7, 4, 5, 2, 5, 2, 6, 2, 6, 5, 4, 5, 2,
7, 2, 2, 7, 7, 4, 2, 5, 5, 2, 2, 2, 4, 5, 2! 7, 2, 2, 7, 7, 4, 2, 5, 5, 2, 2, 2, 4, 5, 2, 4,
7, 2, 2, 7, 2, 4, 6, 5, 5, 5, 2, 6, 5, 4, 6, 5, 6, 7, 5, 4! 6, 5, 5, 5, 7! 6, 4, 5, 2, 2, 6,
7, 4, 2, 5, 6, 5, 2, 6! 2, 6, 5, 4, 5? 5, 7, 6, 5, 5, 2, 6, 2, 6, 5, 4, 5, 2, 7, 2, 2, 7, 7,
4, 2, 5, 9, 2, 2, 2, 4, 5, 2, 4! 5, 6, 8, 3? 5, 5, 6, 5, 2, 4, 6, 5, 5, 5, 2! 4, 5, 2, 4,
5, 5, 6, 5! 2, 5, 5, 2, 9, 2, 4, 5, 2, 6! 4, 2, 2, 6, 5, 4, 2! 5, 5, 6, 5, 5, 2, 6, 2, 6, 3,
4, 5, 8, 3, 8, 2, 3, 3, 4, 8, 3, 9, 2, 8, 8, 4, 3, 2, 4, 3, 3, 6, 3, 8, 4, 6, 3, 3, 3, 8! 4,
3, 2, 4, 3, 3, 6, 3, 8, 4! 6, 3, 3, 3, 8, 6, 3, 9, 6, 3, 6, 6, 3, 4, 6, 5, 3, 5, 3! 2, 2, 3,
3, 2, 6, 3, 4, 2, 5, 6, 3, 8, 3, 2, 6, 3, 4, 3? 5, 6, 8, 3? 5, 3, 6, 3, 5, 8, 6, 2, 6, 3,
4, 5, 8, 3, 8, 2, 3, 3, 4, 8, 3, 3, 2, 8! 2, 7, 2, 4, 6, 5, 5, 5, 2, 6, 5, 4, 6, 5, 6, 7, 5,
4! 6, 5, 5, 5, 7! 6, 4, 5, 2, 2, 6, 7, 4, 2, 5, 6, 5, 2, 6! 2, 6, 5, 4, 5? 5, 7, 6, 5, 5,
2, 6, 2, 6, 5, 4, 5, 2, 7, 2, 2, 7, 7, 4, 2, 5, 9, 2, 2, 2, 4, 5, 2, 4, 5, 5, 6, 5, 2, 4, 6,
5, 5, 5, 2! 4, 5, 2, 4, 5, 5, 6, 5! 5, 6, 8, 3? 5, 5, 6, 5, 5, 2, 6, 2, 6, 3, 4, 5, 8, 3,
8, 2, 3, 3, 4, 8, 3, 9, 2, 8, 8, 4, 3, 2, 4, 3, 3, 6, 3, 8, 4, 6, 3, 3, 3, 8! 4, 3, 2, 4, 3,
3, 6, 3, 8, 4, 6, 3! 5, 6, 8, 3? 5, 6, 8, 3? 5, 6, 8, 3! 4, 2, 2, 6, 5, 4, 2, 5, 7, 4, 5,
2, 5, 2, 6, 2, 6, 5, 4, 5, 2, 7, 2, 2, 7, 4, 5, 2, 4, 6, 3, 5, 8, 6, 2, 6, 3, 4, 5, 8, 7, 8,
2, 7, 7, 4, 8, 3, 3, 2, 8! 7, 7, 4, 8, 3, 3, 2, 8, 3, 4, 3, 2, 4, 7, 6, 6, 7, 8, 4, 6, 8, 3,
8, 8, 6, 3, 4, 6, 3, 6, 7, 3, 4, 6, 7, 7, 4, 8, 3, 3, 9, 8, 8, 4, 3, 2, 4, 5, 7, 6, 7, 8, 4,
6, 3, 5, 5, 2, 6, 9, 4, 6, 5, 6, 7, 5, 4, 6! 5, 2, 6, 2, 6, 5, 9, 5, 2? 6, 9, 6, 2, 6, 5, 4,
5, 6, 5, 2, 4, 6, 5, 5, 5, 2, 7, 4, 2, 5, 5, 2, 2, 2, 4, 5, 2! 7, 2, 2, 7, 7, 4, 2, 5, 5, 2,
2, 2, 4, 5, 2, 4, 7, 2, 2, 7, 2, 4, 6, 5, 5, 5, 2, 6, 5, 4, 6, 5, 6, 7, 5, 4! 6, 5, 5, 5, 7!"

It took me a long time, I don't know how long, minutes, hours, my heart got tired, my finger did, I was trying to destroy the wall between me and my life with my finger, one press at a time, my quarter ran out, or she hung up, I called again, "4, 7, 4, 8, 7, 3, 2, 5, 5, 9, 9, 6, 8?" She said, "Is this a joke?" A joke, it wasn't a joke, what is a joke, was it a joke? She hung up, I called again, "8, 4, 4, 7, 4, 7, 6, 6, 8, 2, 5, 6, 5, 3!" She asked, "Oskar?" That was the first time I ever heard his name . . . I was in Dresden's train station when I lost everything for the second time, I was writing you a letter that I knew I never would send, sometimes I wrote from there, sometimes from here, sometimes from the zoo, I didn't care about anything except for the letter I was writing to you, nothing else existed, it was like when I walked to Anna with my head down, hiding myself from the world, which is why I walked into her, and why I didn't notice that people were gathering around the televisions. It wasn't until the second plane hit, and someone who didn't mean to holler hollered, that I looked up, there were hundreds of people around the televisions now, where had they come from? I stood up and looked, I didn't understand what I was seeing on the screen, was it a commercial, a new movie? I wrote, "What's happened?" and showed it to a young businessman watching the television, he took a sip of his coffee and said, "No one knows yet," his coffee haunts me, his "yet" haunts me. I stood there, a person in a crowd, was I watching the images, or was something more complicated happening? I tried to count the floors above where the planes had hit, the fire had to burn up through the buildings, I knew that those people couldn't be saved, and how many were on the planes, and how many were on the street, I thought and thought. On my walk home I stopped in front of an electronics store, the front window was a grid of televisions, all but one of them were showing the buildings, the same images over and over, as if the world itself were repeating, a crowd had gathered on the sidewalk, one television, off to the side, was showing a nature program, a lion was eating a flamingo, the crowd became noisy, someone who didn't mean to holler hollered, pink feathers, I looked at one of the other televisions and there was only one building, one hundred ceilings had become one hundred floors, which had become nothing, I was the only one who could believe it, the sky was filled with paper, pink feathers. The cafés were full that afternoon, people were laughing, there were lines in front of the movie theaters, they were going to see comedies, the world is so big and small, in the same moment we were close and far. In the days and weeks that followed, I read the lists of the dead in the paper: mother of three, college sophomore, Yankees fan, lawyer, brother, bond trader, weekend magician, practical joker, sister, philanthropist, middle son, dog lover, janitor, only child, entrepreneur, waitress, grandfather of fourteen, registered nurse, accountant, intern, jazz saxophonist, doting uncle, army reservist, late-night poet, sister, window washer, Scrabble player, volunteer fireman, father, father, elevator repairman, wine aficionado, office manager, secretary, cook, financier, executive vice president, bird watcher, father, dishwasher, Vietnam veteran, new mother, avid reader, only child, competitive chess player, soccer coach, brother, analyst, maitre d', black belt, CEO, bridge partner, architect, plumber, public relations executive, father, artist in residence, urban planner, newlywed, investment banker, chef, electrical engineer, new father who had a cold that morning and thought about calling in sick . . . and then one day I saw it, Thomas Schell, my first thought was that I had died. "He leaves behind a wife and son," I thought, my son, I thought, my grandson, I thought and thought and thought, and then I stopped thinking . . . When the plane descended and I saw Manhattan for the first time in forty years, I didn't know if I was going up or down, the lights were stars, I didn't recognize any of the buildings, I told the man, "To ~~mourn~~ try to live," I declared nothing, I called your mother but I couldn't explain myself, I called again, she thought it was a joke, I called again, she asked, "Oskar?" I went to the magazine stand and got more quarters, I tried again, it rang and rang, I tried again, it rang, I waited and tried again, I sat on the ground, not knowing what would happen next, not even knowing what I wanted to happen next, I tried once more, "Hello, you have reached the Schell residence. I am speaking like an answering message, even though it's really me on the phone. If you'd like to talk to me or Grandma, please begin at the beep sound I'm about to make. Beeeeep. Hello?" It was a child's voice, a boy's. "It's really me. I'm here. Bonjour?" I hung up. Grandma? I needed time to think, a taxi would be too quick, as would a bus, what was I afraid of? I put the suitcases on a pushcart and started walking, I was amazed that no one tried to stop me, not even as I pushed the cart onto the street, not even as I pushed it onto the side of the highway, with each step it became brighter and hotter, after only a few minutes it was clear I wouldn't be able to manage, I opened one of the suitcases and took out a stack of letters, "To my child," they were from 1977, "To my child," "To my child," I thought about laying them on the road beside me, creating a trail of things I wasn't able to tell you, it might have made my load possible, but I couldn't, I needed to get them to you, to my child. I hailed a cab, by the time we reached your mother's apartment it was already getting late, I needed to find a hotel, I needed food and a shower and time to think, I ripped a page from the daybook and wrote, "I'm sorry," I handed it to the doorman, he said, "Who's this for?" I wrote, "Mrs. Schell," he said, "There is no Mrs. Schell," I wrote, "There is," he said, "Believe me, I'd know if there was a Mrs. Schell in this building," but I'd heard her voice on the phone, could she have moved and kept the number, how would I find her, I needed a phone book. I wrote "3D" and showed it to the doorman. He said, "Ms. Schmidt," I took back my book and wrote, "That was her maiden name." . . . I lived in the guest room, she left me meals by the door, I could hear her footsteps and sometimes I thought I heard the rim of a glass against the door, was it a glass I once drank water from, had it ever touched your lips? I found my daybooks from before I left, they were in the body of the grandfather clock, I'd have thought she would have thrown them away, but she kept them, many were empty and many were filled, I wandered through them, I found the book from the afternoon we met and the book from the day after we got married, I found our first Nothing Place, and the last time we walked around the reservoir, I found pictures of banisters and sinks and fireplaces, on top of one of the stacks was the book from the first time I tried to leave, "I haven't always been silent, I used to talk and talk and talk and talk." I don't know if she began to feel sorry for me, or sorry for herself, but she started paying me short visits, she wouldn't say anything at first, only tidy up the room, brush cobwebs from the corners, vacuum the carpet, straighten the picture frames, and then one day, as she dusted the bedside table, she said, "I can forgive you for leaving, but not for coming back," she walked out and closed the door behind her, I didn't see her again for three days, and then it was as if nothing had been said, she replaced a light bulb that had worked fine, she picked things up and put them down, she said, "I'm not going to share this grief with you," she closed the door behind her, was I the prisoner or the guard? Her visits became longer, we never had conversations, and she didn't like to look at me, but something was happening, we were getting closer, or farther apart, I took a chance, I asked if she would pose for me, like when we first met, she opened her mouth and nothing came out, she touched my left hand, which I hadn't realized was in a fist, was that how she said yes, or was that how she touched me? I went to the art supply store to buy some clay, I couldn't keep my hands to myself, the pastels in long boxes, the palette knives, the handmade papers hanging on rolls, I tested every sample, I wrote my name in blue pen and in green oil stick, in orange crayon and in charcoal, it felt like I was signing the contract of my life. I was there for more than an hour, although I bought only a simple block of clay, when I came home she was waiting for me in the guest room, she was in a robe, standing beside the bed, "Did you make any sculptures while you were away?" I wrote that I had tried but couldn't, "Not even one?" I showed her my right hand, "Did you think about sculptures? Did you make them in your head?" I showed her my left hand, she took off her robe and went onto the sofa, I couldn't look at her, I took the clay from the bag and set it up on the card table, "Did you ever make a sculpture of me in your head?" I wrote, "How do you want to pose?" She said the whole point was that I should choose, I asked if the carpeting was new, she said, "Look at me," I tried but I couldn't, she said, "Look at me or leave me. But don't stay and look at anything else." I asked her to lie on her back, but that wasn't right, I asked her to sit, it wasn't right, cross your arms, turn your head away from me, nothing was right, she said, "Show me how," I went over to her, I undid her hair, I pressed down on her shoulders, I wanted to touch her across all of those distances, she said, "I haven't been touched since you left. Not in that way." I pulled back my hand, she took it into hers and pressed it against her shoulder, I didn't know what to say, she asked, "Have you?" What's the point of a lie that doesn't protect anything? I showed her my left hand. "Who touched you?" My daybook was filled, so I wrote on the wall, "I wanted so much to have a life." "Who?" I couldn't believe the honesty as it traveled down my arm and came out my pen, "I paid for it." She didn't lose her pose, "Were they pretty?" "That wasn't the point." "But were they?" "Some of them." "So you just gave them money and that was it?" "I liked to talk to them. I talked about you." "Is that supposed to make me feel good?" I looked at the clay. "Did you tell them that I was pregnant when you left?" I showed her my left hand. "Did you tell them about Anna?" I showed her my left hand. "Did you care for any of them?" I looked at the clay, she said, "I love that you are telling me the truth," and she took my hand from her shoulder and pressed it between her legs, she didn't turn her head to the side, she didn't close her eyes, she stared at our hands between her legs, I felt like I was killing something, she undid my belt and unzipped my pants, she reached her hand under my underpants, "I'm nervous," I said, by smiling, "It's OK," she said, "I'm sorry," I said, by smiling, "It's OK," she said, she closed the door behind her, then opened it and asked, "Did you ever make a sculpture of me in your head?" . . . There won't be enough pages in this book for me to tell you what I need to tell you, I could write smaller, I could slice the pages down their edges to make two pages, I could write over my own writing, but then what? Every afternoon someone would come to the apartment, I could hear the door opening, and the footsteps, little footsteps, I heard talking, a child's voice, almost a song, it was the voice I'd heard when I called from the airport, the two of them would talk for hours, I asked her one evening, when she came to pose, who paid her all of those visits, she said, "My grandson." "I have a grandson." "No," she said, "I have a grandson." "What's his name?" We tried again, we took off each other's clothes with the slowness of people who know how easy it is to be proven wrong, she lay face-down on the bed, her waist was irritated from pants that hadn't fit her in years, her thighs were scarred, I kneaded them with YES and NO, she said, "Don't look at anything else," I spread her legs, she inhaled, I could stare into the most private part of her and she couldn't see me looking, I slid my hand under her, she bent her knees, I closed my eyes, she said, "Lie on top of me," there was nowhere to write that I was nervous, she said, "Lie on top of me." I was afraid I'd crush her, she said, "All of you on all of me," I let myself sink into her, she said, "That's what I've wanted," why couldn't I have left it like that, why did I have to write anything else, I should have broken my fingers, I took a pen from the bedside table and wrote "Can I see him?" on my arm. She turned over, spilling my body next to her, "No." I begged with my hands. "No." "Please." "Please." "I won't let him know who I am. I just want to see him." "No." "Why not?" "Because." "Because why?" "Because I changed his diapers. And I couldn't sleep on my stomach for two years. And I taught him how to speak. And I cried when he cried. And when he was unreasonable, he yelled at me." "I'll hide in the coat closet and look through the keyhole." I thought she would say no, she said, "If he ever sees you, you will have betrayed me." Did she feel pity for me, did she want me to suffer? The next morning, she led me to the coat closet, which faces the living room, she went in with me, we were in there all day, although she knew he wouldn't come until the afternoon, it was too small, we needed more space between us, we needed Nothing Places, she said, "This is what it's felt like, except you weren't here." We looked at each other in silence for hours. When the bell rang, she went to let him in, I was on my hands and knees so my eye would be at the right level, through the keyhole I saw the door open, those white shoes, "Oskar!" she said, lifting him from the ground, "I'm OK," he said, that song, in his voice I heard my own voice, and my father's and grandfather's, and it was the first time I'd heard your voice, "Oskar!" she said again, lifting him again, I saw his face, Anna's eyes, "I'm OK," he said again, he asked her where she had been, "I was talking to the renter," she said. The renter? "Is he still here?" he asked, "No," she said, "he had to go run some errands." "But how did he get out of the apartment?" "He left right before you came." "But you said you were just talking to him." He knew about me, he didn't know who I was, but he knew someone was there, and he knew she wasn't telling the truth, I could hear it in his voice, in my voice, in your voice, I needed to talk to him, but what did I need to say? I'm your grandfather, I love you, I'm sorry? Maybe I needed to tell him the things I couldn't tell you, give him all the letters that were supposed to be for your eyes. But she would never give me her permission, and I wouldn't betray her, so I started to think about other ways . . . What am I going to do, I need more room, I have things I need to say, my words are pushing at the walls of the paper's edge, the next day, your mother came to the guest room and posed for me, I worked the clay with YES and NO, I made it soft, I pressed my thumbs into her cheeks, bringing her nose forward, leaving my thumbprints, I carved out pupils, I strengthened her brow, I hollowed out the space between her bottom lip and chin, I picked up a daybook and went over to her. I started to write about where I'd been and what I'd done since I left, how I'd made my living, whom I'd spent my time with, what I'd thought about and listened to and eaten, but she ripped the page from the book, "I don't care," she said, I don't know if she really didn't care or if it was something else, on the next blank page I wrote, "If there's anything you want to know, I'll tell you," she said, "I know it will make your life easier to tell me, but I don't want to know anything." How could that be? I asked her to tell me about you, she said, "Not our son, my son," I asked her to tell me about her son, she said, "Every Thanksgiving I made a turkey and pumpkin pie. I would go to the schoolyard and ask the children what toys they liked. I bought those for him. I wouldn't let anyone speak a foreign language in the apartment. But he still became you." "He became me?" "Everything was yes and no." "Did he go to college?" "I begged him to stay close, but he went to California. In that way he was also like you." "What did he study?" "He was going to be a lawyer, but he took over the business. He hated jewelry." "Why didn't you sell it?" "I begged him. I begged him to be a lawyer." "Then why?" "He wanted to be his own father." I'm sorry, if that's true, the last thing I would have wanted was for you to be like me, I left so you could be you. She said, "He tried to find you once. I gave him that only letter you ever sent. He was obsessed with it, always reading it. I don't know what you wrote, but it made him go and look for you." On the next blank page I wrote, "I opened the door one day and there he was." "He found you?" "We talked about nothing." "I didn't know he found you." "He wouldn't tell me who he was. He must have become nervous. Or he must have hated me once he saw me. He pretended to be a journalist. It was so terrible. He said he was doing a story about the survivors of

Dresden." "Did you tell him what happened to you that night?" "It was in the letter." "What did you write?" "You didn't read it?" "You didn't send it to me." "It was terrible. All of the things we couldn't share. The room was filled with conversations we weren't having." I didn't tell her that after you left, I stopped eating, I got so skinny that the bathwater would collect between my bones, why didn't anyone ask me why I was so skinny? If someone had asked, I never would have eaten another bite. "But if he didn't tell you he was your son, how did you know?" "I knew because he was my son." She put her hand on my chest, over my heart, I put my hands on her thighs, I put my hands around her, she undid my pants, "I'm nervous," despite everything I wanted, the sculpture was looking more and more like Anna, she closed the door behind her, I'm running out of room . . . I spent most of my days walking around the city, getting to know it again, I went to the old Columbian Bakery but it wasn't there anymore, in its place was a ninety-nine-cent store where everything cost more than ninety-nine cents. I went by the tailor shop where I used to get my pants taken in, but there was a bank, you needed a card just to open the door, I walked for hours, down one side of Broadway and up the other, where there had been a watch repairman there was a video store, where there had been a flower market there was a store for video games, where there had been a butcher there was sushi, what's sushi, and what happens to all of the broken watches? I spent hours at the dog run on the side of the natural history museum, a pit bull, a Labrador, a golden retriever, I was the only person without a dog, I thought and thought, how could I be close to Oskar from far away, how could I be fair to you and fair to your mother and fair to myself, I wanted to carry the closet door with me so I could always look at him through the keyhole, I did the next best thing. I learned his life from a distance, when he went to school, when he came home, where his friends lived, what stores he liked to go to, I followed him all over the city, but I didn't betray your mother, because I never let him know I was there. I thought it could go on like that forever, and yet here I am, once again I was proven wrong. I don't remember when the strangeness of it first occurred to me, how much he was out, how many neighborhoods he went to, why I was the only one watching him, how his mother could let him wander so far so alone. Every weekend morning, he left the building with an old man and went knocking on doors around the city, I made a map of where they went, but I couldn't make sense of it, it made no sense, what were they doing? And who was the old man, a friend, a teacher, a replacement for a missing grandfather? And why did they stay for only a few minutes at each apartment, were they selling something, collecting information? And what did his grandmother know, was I the only one worried about him? After they left one house, on Staten Island, I waited around and knocked on the door, "I can't believe it," the woman said, "another visitor!" "I'm sorry," I wrote, "I don't speak. That was my grandson who just left. Could you tell me what he was doing here?" The woman told me, "What a strange family you are." I thought, Family we are.

"I just got off the phone with his mother." I wrote, "Why was he here?" She said, "For the key." I asked, "What key?" She said, "For the lock." "What lock?" "Don't you know?" For eight months I followed him and talked to the people he talked to, I tried to learn about him as he tried to learn about you, he was trying to find you, just as you'd tried to find me, it broke my heart into more pieces than my heart was made of, why can't people say what they mean at the time? One afternoon I followed him downtown, we sat across from each other on the subway, the old man looked at me, was I staring, was I reaching my arms out in front of me, did he know that I should have been the one sitting next to Oskar? They went into a coffee store, on the way back I lost them, it happened all the time, it's hard to stay close without making yourself known, and I wouldn't betray her. When I got back to the Upper West Side I went into a bookstore, I couldn't go to the apartment yet, I needed time to think, at the end of the aisle I saw a man who I thought might be Simon Goldberg, he was also in the children's section, the more I looked at him, the more unsure I was, the more I wanted it to be him, had he gone to work instead of to his death? My hands shook against the change in my pockets, I tried not to stare, I tried not to reach my arms out in front of me, could it be, did he recognize me, he'd written, "It is my great hope that our paths, however long and winding, will cross again." Fifty years later he wore the same thick glasses, I'd never seen a whiter shirt, he had a hard time letting go of books, I went up to him. "I don't speak," I wrote, "I'm sorry." He wrapped his arms around me and squeezed, I could feel his heart beating against my heart, they were trying to beat in unison, without saying a word he turned around and rushed away from me, out of the store, into the street, I'm almost sure it wasn't him, I want an infinitely long blank book and the rest of time ... The next day, Oskar and the old man went to the Empire State Building, I waited for them on the street. I kept looking up, trying to see him, my neck was burning, was he looking down at me, were we sharing something without either of us knowing it? After an hour, the elevator doors opened and the old man came out, was he going to leave Oskar up there, so high up, so alone, who would keep him safe? I hated him. I started to write something, he came up to me and grabbed me by the collar. "Listen," he said, "I don't know who you are, but I've seen you following us, and I don't like it. Not a bit. This is the only time I'm going to tell you to stay away." My book had fallen to the floor, so I couldn't say anything. "If I ever see you again, anywhere near that boy—" I pointed at the floor, he let go of my collar, I picked up the book and wrote, "I'm Oskar's grandfather. I don't speak. I'm sorry." "His grandfather?" I flipped back and pointed at what I'd been writing, "Where is he?" "Oskar doesn't have a grandfather." I pointed at the page. "He's walking down the stairs." I quickly explained everything as best I could, my handwriting was becoming illegible, he said, "Oskar wouldn't lie to me." I wrote, "He didn't lie. He doesn't know." The old man took a necklace from under his shirt and looked at it, the pendant was a compass, he said, "Oskar is my friend. I have to tell him." "He's my grandson. Please don't." "You're the one who should be going around with him." "I have been." "And what about his mother?" "What about his mother?" We heard Oskar singing from around the corner, his voice was getting louder, the old man said, "He's a good boy," and walked away. I went straight home, the apartment was empty. I thought about packing my bags, I thought about jumping out a window, I sat on the bed and thought, I thought about you. What kind of food did you like, what was your favorite song, who was the first girl you kissed, and where, and how, I'm running out of room, I want an infinitely long blank book and forever, I don't know how much time passed, it didn't matter, I'd lost all of my reasons to keep track. Someone rang the bell, I didn't get up, I didn't care who it was, I wanted to be alone, on the other side of the window. I heard the door open and I heard his voice, my reason, "Grandma?" He was in the apartment, it was just the two of us, grandfather and grandson. I heard him going from room to room, moving things, opening and closing, what was he looking for, why was he always looking? He came to my door, "Grandma?" I didn't want to betray her, I turned off the lights, what was I so afraid of? "Grandma?" He started crying, my grandson was crying. "Please. I really need help. If you're in there, please come out." I turned on the light, why wasn't I more afraid? "Please." I opened the door and we faced each other, I faced myself, "Are you the renter?" I went back into the room and got this daybook from the closet, this book that is nearly out of pages, I brought it to him and wrote, "I don't speak. I'm sorry." I was so grateful to have him looking at me, he asked me who I was, I didn't know what to tell him, I invited him into the room, he asked me if I was a stranger, I didn't know what to tell him, he was still crying, I didn't know how to hold him, I'm running out of room. I brought him over to the bed, he sat down, I didn't ask him any questions or tell him what I already knew, we didn't talk about unimportant things, we didn't become friends, I could have been anyone, he began at the beginning, the vase, the key, Brooklyn, Queens, I knew the lines by heart. Poor child, telling everything to a stranger, I wanted to build walls around him, I wanted to separate inside from outside, I wanted to give him an infinitely long blank book and the rest of time, he told me how he'd just gone up to the top of the Empire State Building, how his friend had told him he was finished, it wasn't what I'd wanted, but if it was necessary to bring my grandson face to face with me, it was worth it, anything would have been. I wanted to touch him, to tell him that even if everyone left everyone, I would never leave him, he talked and talked, his words fell through him, trying to find the floor of his sadness, "My dad," he said, "My dad," he ran across the street and came back with a phone, "These are his last words."

MESSAGE FIVE.

10:04 A.M. IT'S DA   S DAD. HEL   S DAD. KNOW IF
     EAR ANY   THIS I'M
  HELLO?   YOU HEAR ME? WE   TO THE
ROOF   EVERYTHING   OK   FINE   SOON
  SORRY   HEAR ME   MUCH
    HAPPENS,   REMEMBER—

The message was cut off,you sounded so calm, you didn't sound like someone who was about to die, I wish we could have sat across a table and talked about nothing for hours, I wish we could have wasted time, I want an infinitely blank book and the rest of time. I told Oskar it was best not to let his grandma know we'd met, he didn't ask why, I wonder what he knew, I told him if he ever wanted to talk to me, he could throw pebbles at the guest room window and I would come down to meet him on the corner, I was afraid I'd never get to see him again, to see him seeing me, that night was the first time your mother and I made love since I returned, and the last time we ever made love, it didn't feel like the last time, I'd kissed Anna for the last time, seen my parents for the last time, spoken for the last time, why didn't I learn to treat everything like it was the last time, my greatest regret is how much I believed in the future, she said, "I want to show you something," she led me to the second bedroom, her hand was squeezing YES, she opened the door and pointed at the bed, "That's where he used to sleep," I touched the sheets, I lowered myself to the floor and smelled the pillow, I wanted anything of you that I could have, I wanted dust, she said, "Years and years ago. Thirty years." I lay on the bed, I wanted to feel what you felt, I wanted to tell you everything, she lay next to me, she asked, "Do you believe in heaven and hell?" I held up my right hand, "Neither do I," she said, "I think after you live it's like before you lived," her hand was open, I put YES into it, she closed her fingers around mine, she said, "Think of all the things that haven't been born yet. All the babies. Some never will be born. Is that sad?" I didn't know if it was sad, all the parents that would never meet, all the miscarriages, I closed my eyes, she said, "A few days before the bombing, my father took me out to the shed. He gave me a sip of whiskey and let me try his pipe. It made me feel so adult, so special. He asked me what I knew about sex. I coughed and coughed. He laughed and laughed and became serious. He asked if I knew how to pack a suitcase, and if I knew never to accept the first offer, and if I could start a fire if I had to. I loved my father very much. I loved him very, very much. But I never found a way to tell him." I turned my head to the side, I rested it on her shoulder, she put her hand on my cheek, just like my mother used to, everything she did reminded me of someone else, "It's a shame," she said, "that life is so precious." I turned onto my side and put my arm around her, I'm running out of room, my eyes were closed and I kissed her, her lips were my mother's lips, and Anna's lips, and your lips, I didn't know how to be with her and be with her. "It makes us worry so much," she said, unbuttoning her shirt, I unbuttoned mine, she took off her pants, I took off mine, "We worry so much," I touched her and touched everyone, "It's all we do," we made love for the last time, I was with her and with everyone, when she got up to go to the bathroom there was blood on the sheets, I went back to the guest room to sleep, there are so many things you'll never know. The next morning I was awoken by a tapping on the window, I told your mother I was going for a walk, she didn't ask anything, what did she know, why did she let me out of her sight? Oskar was waiting for me under the streetlamp, he said, "I want to dig up his grave." I've seen him every day for the past two months, we've been planning what's about to happen, down to the smallest detail, we've even practiced digging in Central Park, the details have begun to remind me or rules, I can't eat

A SIMPLE SOLUTION
TO AN IMPOSSIBLE PROBLEM

The day after the renter and I dug up Dad's grave, I went to Mr. Black's apartment. I felt like he deserved to know what happened, even if he wasn't actually a part of it. But when I knocked, the person who answered wasn't him. "Can I help you?" a woman asked. Her glasses were hanging from a chain around her neck, and she was holding a folder with lots of paper coming out of it. "You're not Mr. Black." "Mr. Black?" "Mr. Black who lives here. Where is he?" "I'm sorry, I don't know." "Is he OK?" "I assume so. I don't know." "Who are you?" "I'm a realtor." "What's that?" "I'm selling the apartment." "Why?" "I suppose the owner wants to sell it. I'm just covering today." "Covering?" "The realtor who represents this property is sick." "Do you know how I can find the owner?" "I'm sorry, I don't." "He was my friend."

She told me, "They're coming by sometime this morning to take everything away." "Who's they?" "They. I don't know. Contractors. Garbage men. They." "Not moving men?" "I don't know." "They're throwing his things away?" "Or selling them." If I'd been incredibly rich, I would have bought everything, even if I just had to put it in storage. I told her, "Well, I left something in the apartment. It's something of mine, so they can't sell it or give it away. I'm going to get it. Excuse me."

I went to the index of biographies. I knew I couldn't save the whole thing, obviously, but there was something I needed. I pulled out the B drawer and flipped through the cards. I found Mr. Black's. I knew it was the right thing to do, so I took it out and put it in the pouch of my overalls.

But then, even though I'd gotten what I wanted, I went to the S drawer. Antonin Scalia, G. L. Scarborough, Lord Leslie George Scarman, Maurice Scève, Anne Wilson Schaef, Jack Warner Schaefer, Iris Scharmel, Robert Haven Schauffler, Barry Scheck, Johann Scheffler, Jean de Schelandre . . . And then I saw it: Schell.

At first I was relieved, because I felt like everything I'd done had been worth it, because I'd made Dad into a Great Man who was biographically significant and would be remembered. But then I examined the card, and I saw that it wasn't Dad.

OSKAR SCHELL: SON

I wish I had known that I wasn't going to see Mr. Black again when we shook hands that afternoon. I wouldn't have let go. Or I would have forced him to keep searching with me. Or I would have told him about how Dad called when I was home. But I didn't know, just like I didn't know it was the last time Dad would ever tuck me in, because you never know. So when he said, "I'm finished. I hope you understand," I said, "I understand," even though I didn't understand. I never went to find him on the observation deck of the Empire State Building, because I was happier believing he was there than finding out for sure.

I kept looking for the lock after he told me he was finished, but it wasn't the same.

I went to Far Rockaway and Boerum Hill and Long Island City.

I went to Dumbo and Spanish Harlem and the Meatpacking District.

I went to Flatbush and Tudor City and Little Italy.

I went to Bedford-Stuyvesant and Inwood and Red Hook.

I don't know if it was because Mr. Black wasn't with me anymore, or because I'd been spending so much time making plans with the renter to dig up Dad's grave, or just because I'd been looking for so long without finding anything, but I no longer felt like I was moving in the direction of Dad. I'm not even sure I believed in the lock anymore.

The last Black I visited was Peter. He lived in Sugar Hill, which is in Hamilton Heights, which is in Harlem. A man was sitting on the stoop when I walked up to the house. He had a little baby on his knee, who he was talking to, even though babies don't understand language, obviously. "Are you Peter Black?" "Who's asking?" "Oskar Schell." He patted the step, which meant I could sit next to him if I wanted, which I thought was nice, but I wanted to stand. "That's your baby?" "Yes." "Can I pet her?" "Him." "Can I pet him?" "Sure," he said. I couldn't believe how soft his head was, and how little his eyes were, and his fingers. "He's very vulnerable," I said. "He is," Peter said, "but we keep him pretty safe." "Does he eat normal food?" "Not yet. Just milk for now." "Does he cry a lot?" "I'd say so. Definitely feels like a lot." "But babies don't get sad, right? He's just hungry or something." "We'll never know." I liked watching the baby make fists. I wondered if he could have thoughts, or if he was more like a nonhuman animal. "Do you want to hold him?" "I don't think that's a very good idea." "Why not?" "I don't know how to hold a baby." "If you want to, I'll show you. It's easy." "OK." "Why don't you sit down?" he said. "Here you go. Now put one of your hands under here. Like that. Good. Now put the other around his head. That's right. You can kind of hold it against your chest. Right. Like that. You've got it. Just like that. He's as happy as can be." "This is good?" "You're doing great." "What's his name?" "Peter." "I thought that was your name." "We're both Peter." It made me wonder for the first time why I wasn't named after Dad, although I didn't wonder about the renter's name being Thomas. I said, "Hi, Peter. I'll protect you."

When I got home that afternoon, after eight months of searching New York, I was exhausted and frustrated and pessimistic, even though what I wanted to be was happy.

I went up to my laboratory, but I didn't feel like performing any experiments. I didn't feel like playing the tambourine, or spoiling Buckminster, or arranging my collections, or looking through *Stuff That Happened to Me.*

Mom and Ron were hanging out in the family room, even though he wasn't part of our family. I went to the kitchen to get some dehydrated ice cream. I looked over at the telephone. The new phone. It looked back at me. Whenever it would ring, I'd scream, "The phone's ringing!" because I didn't want to touch it. I didn't even want to be in the same room with it.

I pressed the Message Play button, which I hadn't done since the worst day, and that was on the old phone.

> Message one. Saturday, 11:52 A.M. *Hi, this is a message for Oskar Schell. Oskar, this is Abby Black. You were just over at my apartment asking about the key. I wasn't completely honest with you, and I think I might be able to help. Please give —*

And then the message was cut off.

Abby was the second Black I had gone to, eight months before. She lived in the narrowest house in New York. I told her she was pretty. She cracked up. I told her she was pretty. She told me I was sweet. She cried when I told her about elephant E.S.P. I asked if we could kiss. She didn't say she didn't want to. Her message had been waiting for me for eight months.

"Mom?" "Yes?" "I'm going out." "OK." "I'll be back later." "OK." "I don't know when. It could be extremely late." "OK." Why didn't she ask me more? Why didn't she try to stop me, or at least keep me safe?

Because it was starting to get dark, and because the streets were crowded, I bumped into a googolplex people. Who were they? Where were they going? What were they looking for? I wanted to hear their heartbeats, and I wanted them to hear mine.

The subway station was just a few blocks from her house, and when I got there the door was open a little, like she knew I'd be coming, even though she couldn't have, obviously. So why was it open?

"Hello? Is anyone there? It's Oskar Schell."

She came to the door.

I was relieved, because I hadn't invented her.

"Do you remember me?" "Of course I do, Oskar. You've grown." "I have?" "A lot. Inches." "I've been so busy searching that I haven't been measuring myself." "Come in," she said. "I thought you weren't going to call me back. It's been a long time since I left that message." I told her, "I'm afraid of the phone."

She said, "I've thought about you a lot." I said, "Your message." "From months ago?" "How weren't you honest with me?" "I told you I didn't know anything about the key." "But you did?" "Yes. Well, no. I don't. My husband does." "Why didn't you tell me when we met?" "I couldn't." "Why not?" "I just couldn't." "That's not a real answer." "My husband and I had been having a terrible fight." "He was my dad!" "He was my husband." "He was murdered!"

"I wanted to hurt him." "Why?" "Because he had hurt me." "Why?" "Because people hurt each other. That's what people do." "It's not what I do." "I know." "I spent eight months looking for what you could have told me in eight seconds!" "I called you. Right after you left." "You hurt me!" "I'm very sorry."

"*So?*" I asked. "So what about your husband?" She said, "He's been looking for you." "*He's* been looking for *me?*" "Yes." "But *I've* been looking for *him!*" "He'll explain everything to you. I think you should call him." "I'm angry at you because you weren't honest with me." "I know." "You almost ruined my life."

We were incredibly close.

I could smell her breathing.

She said, "If you want to kiss me, you can." "What?" "You asked me, that day we met, if we could kiss. I said no then, but I am saying yes now." "I'm embarrassed about that day." "There's no reason to be embarrassed." "You don't have to let me kiss you just because you feel sorry for me." "Kiss me," she said, "and I'll kiss you back." I asked her, "What if we just hugged?"

She held me against her.

I started to cry, and I squeezed her as tightly as I could. Her shoulder was getting wet and I thought, *Maybe it's true that you can use up all of your tears. Maybe Grandma's right about that.* It was nice to think about, because what I wanted was to be empty.

And then, out of nowhere, I had a revelation, and the floor disappeared from under me, and I was standing on nothing.

I pulled away.

"Why did your message cut off?" "Excuse me?" "The message you left on our phone. It just stops in the middle." "Oh, that must have been when your mother picked up."

"My mom picked up?" "Yes." "And then what?" "What do you mean?" "Did you talk to her?" "For a few minutes." "What did you tell her?" "I don't remember." "But you told her that I'd gone to visit you?" "Yes, of course. Was I wrong to?"

I didn't know if she was wrong to. And I didn't know why Mom hadn't said anything about their conversation, or even about the message.

"The key? You told her about it?" "I assumed she already knew." "And my mission?"

It didn't make any sense.

Why hadn't Mom said anything?

Or done anything?

Or cared at all?

And then, all of a sudden, it made perfect sense.

All of a sudden I understood why, when Mom asked where I was going, and I said "Out," she didn't ask any more questions. She didn't have to, because she knew.

It made sense that Ada knew I lived on the Upper West Side, and that Carol had hot cookies waiting when I knocked on her door, and that doorman215@hotmail.com said "Good luck, Oskar" when I left, even though I was ninety-nine-percent sure I hadn't told him that my name was Oskar.

They knew I was coming.

Mom had talked to all of them before I had.

Even Mr. Black was part of it. He must have known I was going to knock on his door that day, because she must have told him. She probably told him to go around with me, and keep me company, and keep me safe. Did he even really like me? And were all of his amazing stories even true? Were his hearing aids real? The bed that pulled? Were the bullets and roses bullets and roses?

The whole time.

Everyone.

Everything.

Probably Grandma knew.

Probably even the renter.

Was the renter even the renter?

My search was a play that Mom had written, and she knew the ending when I was at the beginning.

I asked Abby, "Was your door open because you knew I was coming?" She didn't say anything for a few seconds. Then she said, "Yes."

"Where's your husband?" "He's not my husband." "I don't. Understand. ANYTHING!" "He's my ex-husband." "Where is he?" "He's at work." "But it's Sunday night." She said, "He does foreign markets." "*What?*" "It's Monday morning in Japan."

"There's a young man here to see you," the woman behind the desk said into the phone, and it made me feel so weird to think that he was on the other end of the line, even if I knew I was getting confused about who "he" was. "Yes," she said, "a very young man." Then she said, "No." Then she said, "Oskar Schell." Then she said, "Yes. He says to see you."

"May I ask what this concerns?" she asked me. "He says his dad," she said into the phone. Then she said, "That's what he says." Then she said, "OK." Then she said to me, "Go down the hallway. His door is the third on the left."

There was art that was probably famous on the walls. There were incredibly beautiful views out of the windows, which Dad would have loved. But I didn't look at any of it, and I didn't take any pictures. I'd never been so concentrated in my life, because I'd never been closer to the lock. I knocked on the third door on the left, which had a sign on it that said WILLIAM BLACK. A voice from inside the room said, "Come in."

"What can I do for you tonight?" said a man behind a desk. He was about the same age that Dad would have been, or I guess still was, if dead people have ages. He had brownish-grayish hair, a short beard, and round brown glasses. For a second he looked familiar, and I wondered if he was the person I had seen from the Empire State Building through the binocular machine. But then I realized that was impossible, because we were at Fifty-seventh Street, which is north, obviously. There were a bunch of picture frames on his desk. I looked at them quickly to make sure Dad wasn't in any of the pictures.

I asked, "Did you know my dad?" He leaned back in his chair and said, "I'm not sure. Who was your dad?" "Thomas Schell." He thought for a minute. I hated how he had to think. "No," he said. "I don't know any Schells." "Knew." "Excuse me?" "He's dead, so you couldn't know him now." "I'm sorry to hear that." "You must have known him, though." "No. I'm sure I didn't." "But you *must* have."

I told him, "I found a little envelope that had your name on it, and I thought maybe it was your wife, who I know is now your ex-wife, but she said she didn't know what it was, and your name is William, and I wasn't anywhere near the W's yet—" "My wife?" "I went and talked to her." "Talked to her where?" "The narrowest townhouse in New York." "How was she?" "What do you mean?" "How did she seem?" "Sad." "Sad how?" "Just sad." "What was she doing?" "Nothing, really. She was trying to give me food, even though I told her I wasn't hungry. Someone was in the other room while we talked." "A man?" "Yeah." "You saw him?" "He passed by the door, but mostly he was yelling from another room." "He was *yelling?*" "Extremely loud." "What was he yelling?" "I couldn't hear the words." "Did he sound intimidating?" "I don't know what that means." "Was he scary?" "What about my dad?" "When was this?" "Eight months ago." "Eight months ago?" "Seven months and twenty-eight days." He smiled. "Why are you smiling?" He put his face in his hands, like he was going to cry, but he didn't. He looked up and said, "That man was me."

"You?" "Eight months ago. Yeah. I thought you were talking about the other day." "But he didn't have a beard." "He grew a beard." "And he didn't wear glasses." He took off his glasses and said, "He changed." I started thinking about the pixels in the image of the falling body, and how the closer you looked, the less you could see. "Why were you yelling?" "Long story." "I have a long time," I said, because anything that could bring me closer to Dad was something I wanted to know

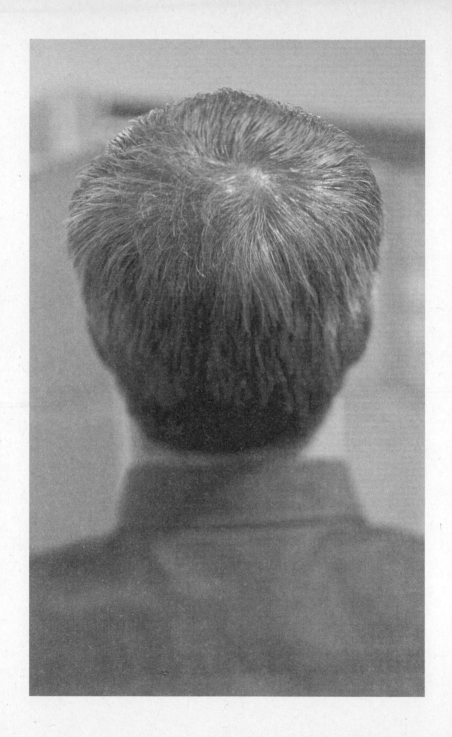

about, even if it would hurt me. "It's a long, long story." "Please." He closed a notebook that was open on his desk and said, "It's too long a story."

I said, "Don't you think it's so weird that we were in the apartment together eight months ago and now we're in this office together?"

He nodded.

"It's weird," I said. "We were incredibly close."

He said, "So what's so special about the envelope?" "Nothing, exactly. It's what was *in* the envelope." "Which was?" "Which was this." I pulled the string around my neck, and made it so the key to our apartment was on my back and Dad's key rested on the pouch of my overalls, over the Band-Aid, over my heart. "Can I see that?" he asked. I handed him the key, even though I kept the string around my neck. He examined it and asked, "Did it say something on the envelope?" "It said 'Black.'" He looked up at me. "Did you find it in a blue vase?" "Jose!"

He said, "I can't believe it." "You can't believe what?" "This is truly the most amazing thing that's ever happened to me." "*What* is?" "I've spent two years trying to find this key." "But I've spent eight months trying to find the lock." "Then we've been looking for each other." I was finally able to ask the most important question of my life. "What does it open?"

"It opens a safe-deposit box." "Well, what's it got to do with my dad?" "Your dad?" "The whole *point* of the key is that I found it in my dad's closet, and since he's dead, I couldn't ask him what it meant, so I had to find out for myself." "You found it in his closet?" "Yes." "In a tall blue vase?" I nodded. "With a label on the bottom?" "I don't know. I didn't see a label. I don't remember." If I'd been alone, I would have given myself the biggest bruise of my life. I would have turned myself into one big bruise.

"My father passed away about two years ago," he said. "He went in for a checkup and the doctor told him he had two months to live. He died two months later." I didn't want to hear about death. It was all anyone talked about, even when no one was actually talking about it. "I needed to figure out what to do with all of his things. Books, furniture, clothes." "Didn't you want to keep them?" "I didn't want any of it." I thought that was weird, because Dad's things were all I wanted. "So to make a long story short—" "You don't have to make a long story short." "I had an estate sale. I shouldn't have been there. I should have hired someone to take care of it. Or I should have given it all away. Instead I was in the position of telling people that the prices for his belongings weren't negotiable. His wedding suit wasn't negotiable. His sunglasses weren't negotiable. It was one of the worst days of my life. Maybe the worst."

"Are you OK?" "I'm fine. It's been a bad couple of years. My father and I weren't exactly close." "Do you need a hug?" "I'll be OK." "Why not?" "Why not what?" "Why weren't you and your dad exactly close?" He said, "Too long a story." "Can you please tell me about my dad now?"

"My father wrote letters when he found out about the cancer. He wasn't much of a letter writer before. I don't know if he ever wrote. But he spent his last two months writing obsessively. Whenever he was awake." I asked why, but what I really wanted to know was why I started writing letters after Dad died. "He was trying to say his goodbyes. He wrote to people he barely knew. If he hadn't already been sick, his letters would have been his sickness. I had a business meeting the other day, and in the middle of our conversation the man asked if I was related to Edmund Black. I told him yes, he was my father. He said, 'I went to high school with your dad. He wrote me the most amazing letter before he died. Ten pages. I only barely knew him. We hadn't talked in fifty years. It was the most amazing letter I'd ever read.' I asked him if I could see it. He said, 'I don't think it was meant to be shared.' I told him it would mean a lot to me. He said, 'He mentions you in it.' I told him I understood.

"I looked through my father's Rolodex—" "What's that?" "Phone book. I called every name. His cousins, his business partners, people I'd never heard of. He'd written to everyone. Every single person. Some let me see their letters. Others didn't."

"What were they like?"

"The shortest was a single sentence. The longest was a couple dozen pages. Some of them were almost like little plays. Others were just questions to the person he was writing to." "What kinds of questions?" " 'Did you know I was in love with you that summer in Nor-folk?' 'Will they be taxed for possessions I leave, like the piano?' 'How do light bulbs work?' " "I could have explained that to him." " 'Does anyone actually die in his sleep?'

"Some of his letters were funny. I mean, really, really funny. I didn't know he could be so funny. And some were philosophical. He wrote about how happy he was, and how sad he was, and all of the things he wanted to do but never did, and all of the things he did but didn't want to do."

"Didn't he write a letter to you?" "Yes." "What did it say?" "I couldn't read it. Not for a few weeks." "Why not?" "It was too painful." "I would have been extremely curious." "My wife—my ex-wife—said I was being crazy not to read it." "That wasn't very understanding of her." "She was right, though. It was crazy. It was unreasonable. I was being childish." "Yeah, but you were his child."

"But I was his child. That's right. I'm babbling. To make a long story short—" "Don't make it short," I said, because even though I wanted him to tell me about my dad instead of his, I also wanted to make the story as long as I could, because I was afraid of its end. He said, "I read it. Maybe I was expecting something confessional. I don't know. Something angry, or asking for forgiveness. Something that would make me rethink everything. But it was matter-of-fact. More of a document than a letter, if that makes sense." "I guess so." "I don't know. Maybe I was wrong to, but I was expecting him to say he was sorry for things, and tell me he loved me. End-of-life stuff. But there was none of it. He didn't even say 'I love you.' He told me about his will, his life in-surance policy, all of those horrible businesslike things that feel so inap-propriate to think about when someone has died."

"You were disappointed?" "I was angry." "I'm sorry." "No. There's nothing to be sorry for. I thought about it. I thought about it all the time. My father told me where he'd left things, and what he wanted taken care of. He was responsible. He was good. It's easy to be emo-tional. You can always make a scene. Remember me eight months ago? That was easy." "It didn't sound easy." "It was simple. Highs and lows make you feel that things matter, but they're nothing." "So what's something?" "Being reliable is something. Being good."

"And what about the key?" "At the end of his letter he wrote, 'I have something for you. In the blue vase, on the shelf in the bedroom, is a key. It opens a safe-deposit box at our bank. I hope you'll understand why I wanted you to have it.'" "And? What was in it?" "I didn't read the note until after I'd sold all of his belongings. I had sold the vase. I sold it to your father." "*What the?*"

"That's why I've been trying to find you." "You met my dad?" "Only briefly, but yes." "Do you remember him?" "It was just a minute." "But do you remember him?" "We chatted a bit." "And?" "He was a nice man. I think he could see how hard it was for me to part with those things." "Could you please describe him?" "Gosh, I don't really remember much." "*Please.*" "He was maybe five foot ten. He had brown hair. He wore glasses." "What kind of glasses?" "Thick glasses." "What kind of clothes was he wearing?" "A suit, I think." "What suit?" "Gray, maybe?" "That's true! He wore a gray suit to work! Did he have a gap between his teeth?" "I don't remember." "Try."

"He said he was on his way home and saw the sign for the sale. He told me that he had an anniversary coming up the next week." "September 14!" "He was going to surprise your mom. The vase was perfect, he said. He said she'd love it." "He was going to surprise her?" "He'd made reservations at her favorite restaurant. It was going to be some sort of fancy night out."

The tuxedo.

"What else did he say?" "What else did he say . . ." "Anything." "He had a great laugh. I remember that. It was good of him to laugh, and to make me laugh. He was laughing for my sake."

"What else?" "He had a very discerning eye." "What's that?" "He knew what he liked. He knew when he'd found it." "That's true. He had an incredibly discerning eye." "I remember watching him hold the vase. He examined the bottom of it and turned it around a number of times. He seemed like a very thoughtful person." "He was extremely thoughtful."

I wished he could remember even more details, like if Dad had unbuttoned his shirt's top button, or if he smelled like shaving, or if he whistled "I Am the Walrus." Was he holding a *New York Times* under his arm? Were his lips chapped? Was there a red pen in his pocket?

"When the apartment was empty that night, I sat on the floor and read the letter from my father. I read about the vase. I felt like I'd failed him." "But couldn't you go to the bank and tell them you'd lost the key?" "I tried that. But they said they didn't have a box under his name. I tried my name. No box. Not under my mother's name or my grandparents' names. It didn't make any sense." "There was nothing the bank people could do?" "They were sympathetic, but without the key, I was stuck." "And that's why you needed to find my dad."

"I hoped he would realize that there was a key in the vase and find me. But how could he? We sold my father's apartment, so even if he went back, it would be a dead end. And I was sure he'd just throw the key away if he found it, assuming it was junk. That's what I would have done. And there was no way I could find him. Absolutely no way. I knew nothing about him, not even his name. For a few weeks I'd go over to the neighborhood on my way home from work, even though it wasn't on my way. It was an hour out of my way. I'd walk around looking for him. I even put up a few signs: 'To the man who bought the vase at the estate sale on Seventy-fifth Street this weekend, please contact . . .' But this was the week after September 11. There were posters everywhere."

"My mom put up posters of him." "What do you mean?" "He died in September 11. That's how he died." "Oh, God. I didn't realize. I'm so sorry." "It's OK." "I don't know what to say." "You don't have to say anything." "I didn't see the posters. If I had . . . Well, I don't know what if I had." "You would have been able to find us." "I guess that's right." "I wonder if your posters and my mom's posters were ever close to each other."

He said, "Wherever I was, I was trying to find him: uptown, downtown, on the train. I looked in everyone's eyes, but none were his. Once I saw someone I thought might be your father across Broadway in Times Square, but I lost him in the crowd. I saw someone I thought might be him getting into a cab at Twenty-third Street. I would have called after him, but I didn't know his name." "Thomas." "Thomas. I wish I'd known it then."

He said, "I followed one man around Central Park for more than half an hour. I thought he was your father. I couldn't figure out why he was walking in such a strange, crisscrossing way. He wasn't getting anywhere. I couldn't figure it out." "Why didn't you stop him?" "Eventually I did." "And what happened?" "I was wrong. It was someone else." "Did you ask him why he was walking like that?" "He'd lost something and was searching the ground for it."

"Well, you don't have to look anymore," I told him. He said, "I've spent so long looking for this key. It's hard to look *at* it." "Don't you want to see what he left for you?" "I don't think it's a question of wanting." I asked him, "What's it a question of?"

He said, "I'm so sorry. I know that you're looking for something, too. And I know this isn't what you're looking for." "It's OK." "For what it's worth, your father seemed like a good man. I only spoke with him for a few minutes, but that was long enough to see that he was good. You were lucky to have a father like that. I'd trade this key for that father." "You shouldn't have to choose." "No, you shouldn't."

We sat there, not saying anything. I examined the pictures on his desk again. All of them were of Abby.

He said, "Why don't you come with me to the bank?" "You're nice, but no thank you." "Are you sure?" It's not that I wasn't curious. I was incredibly curious. It's that I was afraid of getting confused.

He said, "What is it?" "Nothing." "Are you all right?" I wanted to keep the tears in, but I couldn't. He said, "I'm so, so sorry."

"Can I tell you something that I've never told anyone else?"

"Of course."

"On that day, they let us out of school basically as soon as we got there. They didn't really tell us why, just that something bad had happened. We didn't get it, I guess. Or we didn't get that something bad could happen to us. A lot of parents came to pick up their kids, but since school is only five blocks from my apartment, I walked home. My friend told me he was going to call, so I went to the answering machine and the light was beeping. There were five messages. They were all from him." "Your friend?" "My dad."

He covered his mouth with his hand.

"He just kept saying that he was OK, and that everything would be fine, and that we shouldn't worry."

A tear went down his cheek and rested on his finger.

"But this is the thing that I've never told anyone. After I listened to the messages, the phone rang. It was 10:26. I looked at the caller ID and saw that it was his cell phone." "Oh, God." "Could you please put your hand on me so I can finish the rest?" "Of course," he said, and he scooted his chair around his desk and next to me.

"I couldn't pick up the phone. I just couldn't do it. It rang and rang, and I couldn't move. I wanted to pick it up, but I couldn't.

"The answering machine went on, and I heard my own voice."

Hi, you've reached the Schell residence. Here is today's fact of the day: It's so cold in Yukatia, which is in Siberia, that breath instantly freezes with a crackling noise that they call the whispering of the stars. On extremely cold days, the towns are covered in a fog caused by the breath of humans and animals. Please leave a message.

"There was a beep.

"Then I heard Dad's voice."

Are you there? Are you there? Are you there?

"He needed me, and I couldn't pick up. I just couldn't pick up. I just couldn't. *Are you there?* He asked eleven times. I know, because I've counted. It's one more than I can count on my fingers. Why did he keep asking? Was he waiting for someone to come home? And why didn't he say 'anyone'? *Is anyone there?* 'You' is just one person. Sometimes I think he knew I was there. Maybe he kept saying it to give me time to get brave enough to pick up. Also, there was so much space between the times he asked. There are fifteen seconds between the third and the fourth, which is the longest space. You can hear people in the background screaming and crying. And you can hear glass breaking, which is part of what makes me wonder if people were jumping.

Are you there? Are you there? Are you there? Are you there? Are you there? Are you there? Are you there? Are you there? Are you there? Are you there? Are you

"And then it cut off.

"I've timed the message, and it's one minute and twenty-seven seconds. Which means it ended at 10:28. Which was when the building came down. So maybe that's how he died."

"I'm so sorry," he said.

"I've never told that to anyone."

He squeezed me, almost like a hug, and I could feel him shaking his head.

I asked him, "Do you forgive me?"

"Do I forgive you?"

"Yeah."

"For not being able to pick up?"

"For not being able to tell anyone."

He said, "I do."

I took the string off my neck and put it around his neck.

"What about this other key?" he asked.

I told him, "That's to our apartment."

The renter was standing under the streetlamp when I got home. We met there every night to talk about the details of our plan, like what time we should leave, and what we would do if it was raining, or if a guard asked us what we were doing. We ran out of realistic details in just a few meetings, but for some reason we still weren't ready to go. So we made up unrealistic details to plan, like alternate driving routes in case the Fifty-ninth Street Bridge collapsed, and ways to get over the cemetery fence in case it was electrified, and how to outsmart the police if we were arrested. We had all sorts of maps and secret codes and tools. We probably would have gone on making plans forever if I hadn't met William Black that night, and learned what I'd learned.

The renter wrote, "You're late." I shrugged my shoulders, just like Dad used to. He wrote, "I got us a rope ladder, just in case." I nodded. "Where were you? I was worried." I told him, "I found the lock."

"You found it?" I nodded. "And?"

I didn't know what to say. I found it and now I can stop looking? I found it and it had nothing to do with Dad? I found it and now I'll wear heavy boots for the rest of my life?

"I wish I hadn't found it." "It wasn't what you were looking for?"

"That's not it." "Then what?" "I found it and now I can't look for it." I could tell he didn't understand me. "Looking for it let me stay close to him for a little while longer." "But won't you always be close to him?" I knew the truth. "No."

He nodded like he was thinking of something, or thinking about a lot of things, or thinking about everything, if that's even possible. He wrote, "Maybe it's time to do the thing we've been planning."

I opened my left hand, because I knew if I tried to say something I would just start crying again.

We agreed to go on Thursday night, which was the second anniversary of Dad's death, which seemed appropriate.

Before I walked into the building, he handed me a letter. "What is this?" He wrote, "Stan went to get coffee. He told me to give this to you in case he didn't get back in time." "What is it?" He shrugged his shoulders and went across the street.

Dear Oskar Schell,

I've read every letter that you've sent me these past two years. In return, I've sent you many form letters, with the hope of one day being able to give you the proper response you deserve. But the more letters you wrote to me, and the more of yourself you gave, the more daunting my task became.

I'm sitting beneath a pear tree as I dictate this to you, overlooking the orchards of a friend's estate. I've spent the past few days here, recovering from some medical treatment that has left me physically and emotionally depleted. As I moped about this morning, feeling sorry for myself, it occurred to me, like a simple solution to an impossible problem: today is the day I've been waiting for.

You asked me in your first letter if you could be my protégé. I don't know about that, but I would be happy to have you join me in Cambridge for a few days. I could introduce you to my colleagues, treat you to the best curry outside India, and show you just how boring the life of an astrophysicist can be.

You can have a bright future in the sciences, Oskar.
I would be happy to do anything possible to facilitate such a path. It's wonderful to think what would happen if you put your imagination toward scientific ends.

But Oskar, intelligent people write to me all the time. In your fifth letter you asked, "What if I never stop inventing?" That question has stuck with me.

I wish I were a poet. I've never confessed that to anyone, and I'm confessing it to you, because you've given me reason to feel that I can trust you. I've spent my life observing the universe, mostly in my mind's eye. It's been a tremendously rewarding life, a wonderful life. I've been able to explore the origins of time and space with some of the great living thinkers. But I wish I were a poet.

Albert Einstein, a hero of mine, once wrote, "Our situation is the following. We are standing in front of a closed box which we cannot open."

I'm sure I don't have to tell you that the vast majority of the universe is composed of dark matter. The fragile balance depends on things we'll never be able to see, hear, smell, taste, or touch. Life itself depends on them. What's real? What isn't real? Maybe those aren't the right questions to be asking. What does life depend on?

I wish I had made things for life to depend on.

What if you never stop inventing?

Maybe you're not inventing at all.

I'm being called in for breakfast, so I'll have to end this letter here. There's more I want to tell you, and more I want to hear from you. It's a shame we live on different continents. One shame of many.

It's so beautiful at this hour. The sun is low, the shadows are long, the air is cold and clean. You won't be awake for another five hours, but I can't help feeling that we're sharing this clear and beautiful morning.

Your friend,
Stephen Hawking

MY FEELINGS

A knocking woke me up in the middle of the night.
I had been dreaming about where I came from.
I put on my robe and went to the door.
Who could it be?   Why didn't the doorman ring up?   A neighbor?
But why?
More knocking.   I looked through the peephole.   It was your grand-
father.
Come in.   Where were you?   Are you OK?
The bottoms of his pants were covered in dirt.
Are you OK?
He nodded.
Come in.   Let me clean you off.   What happened?
He shrugged his shoulders.
Did someone hurt you?
He showed me his right hand.
Are you hurt?
We went to the kitchen table and sat down.   Next to each other.   The
windows were black.   He put his hands on his knees.
I slid closer to him until our sides touched.   I put my head on his
shoulder.   I wanted as much of us to touch as possible.
I told him, You have to tell me what happened for me to be able to help.
He took a pen from his shirt pocket but there was nothing to write on.
I gave him my open hand.
He wrote, I want to get you some magazines.
In my dream, all of the collapsed ceilings re-formed above us.   The
fire went back into the bombs, which rose up and into the bellies of

planes whose propellers turned backward, like the second hands of the clocks across Dresden, only faster.

I wanted to slap him with his words.

I wanted to shout, It isn't fair, and bang my fists against the table like a child.

Anything special? he asked on my arm.

Everything special, I said.

Art magazines?

Yes.

Nature magazines?

Yes.

Politics?

Yes.

Celebrities?

Yes.

I told him to bring a suitcase so he could come back with one of everything.

I wanted him to be able to take his things with him.

In my dream, spring came after summer, came after fall, came after winter, came after spring.

I made him breakfast.   I tried to make it delicious.   I wanted him to have good memories, so that maybe he would come back again one day. Or at least miss me.

I wiped the rim of the plate before I gave it to him.   I spread his napkin on his lap.   He didn't say anything.

When the time came, I went downstairs with him.

There was nothing to write on, so he wrote on me.

I might not be back until late.

I told him I understood.

He wrote, I'm going to get you magazines.

I told him, I don't want any magazines.

Maybe not now, but you'll be grateful to have them.

My eyes are crummy.

Your eyes are perfect.

Promise me that you'll take care.

He wrote, I'm only going to get magazines.

Don't cry, I said, by putting my fingers on my face and pushing imaginary tears up my cheeks and back into my eyes.

I was angry because they were my tears.

I told him, You're only getting magazines.

He showed me his left hand.

I tried to notice everything, because I wanted to be able to remember it perfectly.   I've forgotten everything important in my life.

I can't remember what the front door of the house I grew up in looked like.   Or who stopped kissing first, me or my sister.   Or the view from any window but my own.   Some nights I lay awake for hours trying to remember my mother's face.

He turned around and walked away from me.

I went back up to the apartment and sat on the sofa waiting.   Waiting for what?

I can't remember the last thing my father said to me.

He was trapped under the ceiling.   The plaster that covered him was turning red.

He said, I can't feel everything.

I didn't know if he'd meant to say he couldn't feel anything.

He asked, Where is Mommy?

I didn't know if he was talking about my mother or his.

I tried to pull the ceiling off him.

He said, Can you find my glasses for me?

I told him I would look for them.   But everything had been buried.

I had never seen my father cry before.

He said, With my glasses I could be helpful.

I told him, Let me try to free you.

He said, Find my glasses.

They were shouting for everyone to get out.   The rest of the ceiling was about to collapse.

I wanted to stay with him.

But I knew he would want me to leave him.

I told him, Daddy, I have to leave you.

Then he said something.

It was the last thing he ever said to me.

I can't remember it.

In my dream, the tears went up his cheeks and back into his eyes.

I got up off the sofa and filled a suitcase with the typewriter and as much paper as would fit.

I wrote a note and taped it to the window.   I didn't know whom it was for.

I went from room to room turning off the lights.   I made sure none of the faucets were dripping.   I turned off the heat and unplugged the appliances.   I closed all the windows.

As the cab drove me away, I saw the note.   But I couldn't read it because my eyes are crummy.

In my dream, painters separated green into yellow and blue.

Brown into the rainbow.

Children pulled color from coloring books with crayons, and mothers who had lost children mended their black clothing with scissors.

I think about all of the things I've done, Oskar.   And all of the things I didn't do.   The mistakes I've made are dead to me.   But I can't take back the things I never did.

I found him in the international terminal.   He was sitting at a table with his hands on his knees.

I watched him all morning.

He asked people what time it was, and each person pointed at the clock on the wall.

I have been an expert at watching him.   It's been my life's work. From my bedroom window.   From behind trees.   From across the kitchen table.

I wanted to be with him.

Or anyone.

I don't know if I've ever loved your grandfather.

But I've loved not being alone.

I got very close to him.

I wanted to shout myself into his ear.

I touched his shoulder.

He lowered his head.

How could you?

He wouldn't show me his eyes.   I hate silence.

Say something.

He took his pen from his shirt pocket and the top napkin from the stack on the table.

He wrote, You were happy when I was away.

How could you think that?

We are lying to ourselves and to each other.

Lying about what?   I don't care if we're lying.

I am a bad person.

I don't care.   I don't care what you are.

I can't.

What's killing you?

He took another napkin from the stack.

He wrote, You're killing me.

And then I was silent.

He wrote, You remind me.

I put my hands on the table and told him, You have me.

He took another napkin and wrote, Anna was pregnant.

I told him, I know. She told me.

You know?

I didn't think you knew.   She said it was a secret.   I'm glad you know.

He wrote, I'm sorry I know.

It's better to lose than never to have had.

I lost something I never had.

You had everything.

When did she tell you?

We were in bed talking.

He pointed at, When.

Near the end.

What did she say?

She said, I'm going to have a baby.

Was she happy?

She was overjoyed.

Why didn't you say anything?

Why didn't you?

In my dream, people apologized for things that were about to happen, and lit candles by inhaling.

I have been seeing Oskar, he wrote.

I know.

You know?

Of course I know.

He flipped back to, Why didn't you say anything?

Why didn't you?

The alphabet went z, y, x, w . . .

The clocks went tock-tick, tock-tick . . .

He wrote, I was with him last night.   That's where I was.   I buried the letters.

What letters?

The letters I never sent.

Buried them where?

In the ground.   That's where I was.   I buried the key, too.

What key?

To your apartment.

Our apartment.

He put his hands on the table.

Lovers pulled up each other's underwear, buttoned each other's shirts, and dressed and dressed and dressed.

I told him, Say it.

When I saw Anna for the last time.

Say it.

When we.

Say it!

He put his hands on his knees.

I wanted to hit him.

I wanted to hold him.

I wanted to shout myself into his ear.

I asked, So what happens now?

I don't know.

Do you want to go home?

He flipped back to, I can't.

Then you'll go away?

He pointed at, I can't.

Then we are out of options.

We sat there.

Things were happening around us, but nothing was happening between us.

Above us, the screens said which flights were landing and which were taking off.

Madrid departing.

Rio arriving.

Stockholm departing.

Paris departing.

Milan arriving.

Everyone was coming or going.

People around the world were moving from one place to another.

No one was staying.

I said, What if we stay?

Stay?

Here.   What if we stay here at the airport?

He wrote, Is that another joke?

I shook my head no.

How could we stay here?

I told him, There are pay phones, so I could call Oskar and let him know I'm OK.   And there are paper stores where you could buy daybooks and pens.   There are places to eat.   And money machines. And bathrooms.   Even televisions.

Not coming or going.

Not something or nothing.

Not yes or no.

My dream went all the way back to the beginning.

The rain rose into the clouds, and the animals descended the ramp.

Two by two.

Two giraffes.

Two spiders.

Two goats.

Two lions.

Two mice.

Two monkeys.

Two snakes.

Two elephants.

The rain came after the rainbow.

As I type this, we are sitting across from each other at a table.   It's not big, but it's big enough for the two of us.   He has a cup of coffee and I am drinking tea.

When the pages are in the typewriter, I can't see his face.

In that way I am choosing you over him.

I don't need to see him.

I don't need to know if he is looking up at me.

It's not even that I trust him not to leave.

I know this won't last.

I'd rather be me than him.

The words are coming so easily.

The pages are coming easily.

At the end of my dream, Eve put the apple back on the branch.   The tree went back into the ground.   It became a sapling, which became a seed.

God brought together the land and the water, the sky and the water, the water and the water, evening and morning, something and nothing.

He said, Let there be light.

And there was darkness.

Oskar.

The night before I lost everything was like any other night.

Anna and I kept each other awake very late.   We laughed.   Young sisters in a bed under the roof of their childhood home.   Wind on the window.

How could anything less deserve to be destroyed?

I thought we would be awake all night.   Awake for the rest of our lives.

The spaces between our words grew.

It became difficult to tell when we were talking and when we were silent.

The hairs of our arms touched.

It was late, and we were tired.
We assumed there would be other nights.
Anna's breathing started to slow, but I still wanted to talk.
She rolled onto her side.
I said, I want to tell you something.
She said, You can tell me tomorrow.
I had never told her how much I loved her.
She was my sister.
We slept in the same bed.
There was never a right time to say it.
It was always unnecessary.
The books in my father's shed were sighing.
The sheets were rising and falling around me with Anna's breathing.
I thought about waking her.
But it was unnecessary.
There would be other nights.
And how can you say I love you to someone you love?
I rolled onto my side and fell asleep next to her.
Here is the point of everything I have been trying to tell you, Oskar.
It's always necessary.
I love you,
Grandma

BEAUTIFUL AND TRUE

Mom made spaghetti for dinner that night. Ron ate with us. I asked him if he was still interested in buying me a five-piece drum set with Zildjian cymbals. He said, "Yeah. I think that would be great." "How about a double bass pedal?" "I don't know what that is, but I bet we could arrange it." I asked him why he didn't have his own family. Mom said, "Oskar!" I said, "*What?*" Ron put down his knife and fork and said, "It's OK." He said, "I did have a family, Oskar. I had a wife and a daughter." "Did you get divorced?" He laughed and said, "No." "Then where are they?" Mom looked at her plate. Ron said, "They were in an accident." "What kind of accident?" "A car accident." "I didn't know that." "Your mom and I met in a group for people that have lost family. That's where we became friends." I didn't look at Mom, and she didn't look at me. Why hadn't she told me she was in a group?

"How come you didn't die in the accident?" Mom said, "That's enough, Oskar." Ron said, "I wasn't in the car." "Why weren't you in the car?" Mom looked out the window. Ron ran his finger around his plate and said, "I don't know." "What's weird," I said, "is that I've never seen you cry." He said, "I cry all the time."

My backpack was already packed, and I'd already gotten the other supplies together, like the altimeter and granola bars and the Swiss Army knife I'd dug up in Central Park, so there was nothing else to do. Mom tucked me in at 9:36.

"Do you want me to read to you?" "No thanks." "Is there anything you want to talk about?" If she wasn't going to say anything, I wasn't going to say anything, so I shook my head no. "I could make up a story?" "No thank you." "Or look for mistakes in the *Times*?" "Thanks,

Mom, but not really." "That was nice of Ron to tell you about his family." "I guess so." "Try to be nice to him. He's been such a good friend, and he needs help, too." "I'm tired."

I set my alarm for 11:50 P.M., even though I knew I wouldn't sleep.

While I lay there in bed, waiting for the time to come, I did a lot of inventing.

I invented a biodegradable car.

I invented a book that listed every word in every language. It wouldn't be a very useful book, but you could hold it and know that everything you could possibly say was in your hands.

What about a googolplex telephones?

What about safety nets everywhere?

At 11:50 P.M., I got up extremely quietly, took my things from under the bed, and opened the door one millimeter at a time, so it wouldn't make any noise. Bart, the night doorman, was asleep at the desk, which was lucky, because it meant I didn't have to tell any more lies. The renter was waiting for me under the streetlamp. We shook hands, which was weird. At exactly 12:00, Gerald pulled up in the limousine. He opened the door for us, and I told him, "I knew you'd be on time." He patted me on the back and said, "I wouldn't be late." It was my second time in a limousine ever.

As we drove, I imagined we were standing still and the world was coming toward us. The renter sat all the way on his side, not doing anything, and I saw the Trump Tower, which Dad thought was the ugliest building in America, and the United Nations, which Dad thought was incredibly beautiful. I rolled down the window and stuck my arm out. I curved my hand like an airplane wing. If my hand had been big enough, I could've made the limousine fly. What about enormous gloves?

Gerald smiled at me in the rearview mirror and asked if we wanted any music. I asked him if he had any kids. He said he had two daughters. "What do they like?" "What do they *like?*" "Yeah." "Lemme see. Kelly, my baby, likes Barbie and puppies and bead bracelets." "I'll make her a bead bracelet." "I'm sure she'd like that." "What else?" "If it's soft and pink, she likes it." "I like soft and pink things, too." He said, "Well, all right." "And what about your other daughter?" "Janet? She likes sports. Her favorite is basketball, and I'll tell you, she can play. I don't mean for a girl, either. I mean she's *good*."

"Are they both special?" He cracked up and said, "Of course their pop is gonna say they're special." "But objectively." "What's that?" "Like, factually. Truthfully." "The truth is I'm their pop."

I stared out the window some more. We went over the part of the bridge that wasn't in any borough, and I turned around and watched the buildings get smaller. I figured out which button opened the sunroof, and I stood up with the top half of my body sticking out of the car. I took pictures of the stars with Grandpa's camera, and in my head I connected them to make words, whatever words I wanted. Whenever we were about to go under a bridge or into a tunnel, Gerald told me to get back into the car so I wouldn't be decapitated, which I know about but really, *really* wish I didn't. In my brain I made "shoe" and "inertia" and "invincible."

It was 12:56 A.M. when Gerald drove up onto the grass and pulled the limousine right next to the cemetery. I put on my backpack, and the renter got the shovel, and we climbed onto the roof of the limousine so we could get over the fence.

Gerald whispered, "You sure you want to do this?"

Through the fence I told him, "It probably won't take more than twenty minutes. Maybe thirty." He tossed over the renter's suitcases and said, "I'll be here."

Because it was so dark, we had to follow the beam of my flashlight. I pointed it at a lot of tombstones, looking for Dad's.

Mark Crawford
Diana Strait
Jason Barker, Jr.
Morris Cooper
May Goodman
Helen Stein
Gregory Robertson Judd
John Fielder
Susan Kidd

I kept thinking about how they were all the names of dead people, and how names are basically the only thing that dead people keep.

It was 1:22 when we found Dad's grave.

The renter offered me the shovel.

I said, "You go first."

He put it in my hand.

I pushed it into the dirt and stepped all of my weight onto it. I didn't even know how many pounds I was, because I'd been so busy trying to find Dad.

It was extremely hard work, and I was only strong enough to remove a little bit of dirt at a time. My arms got incredibly tired, but that was OK, because since we only had one shovel, we took turns.

The twenty minutes passed, and then another twenty minutes.

We kept digging, but we weren't getting anywhere.

Another twenty minutes passed.

Then the batteries in the flashlight ran out, and we couldn't see our hands in front of us. That wasn't part of our plan, and neither were replacement batteries, even though they obviously should have been. How could I have forgotten something so simple and important?

I called Gerald's cell phone and asked if he could go pick up some D batteries for us. He asked if everything was all right. It was so dark that it was even hard to hear. I said, "Yeah, we're OK, we just need some D batteries." He said the only store he remembered was about fifteen minutes away. I told him, "I'll pay you extra." He said, "It's not about paying me extra."

Fortunately, because what we were doing was digging up Dad's grave, we didn't need to see our hands in front of us. We only had to feel the shovel moving the dirt.

So we shoveled in the darkness and silence.

I thought about everything underground, like worms, and roots, and clay, and buried treasure.

We shoveled.

I wondered how many things had died since the first thing was born. A trillion? A googolplex?

We shoveled.

I wondered what the renter was thinking about.

After a while, my phone played "The Flight of the Bumblebee," so I looked at the caller ID. "Gerald." "Got 'em." "Can you bring them to us so we don't have to waste time going back to the limousine?" He didn't say anything for a few seconds. "I guess I could do that." I couldn't describe where we were to him, so I just kept calling his name, and he found my voice.

It felt much better to be able to see. Gerald said, "Doesn't look like you two have gotten very far." I told him, "We're not good shovelers." He put his driving gloves in his jacket pocket, kissed the cross that he wore around his neck, and took the shovel from me. Because he was so strong, he could move a lot of dirt quickly.

It was 2:56 when the shovel touched the coffin. We all heard the sound and looked at each other.

I told Gerald thanks.

He winked at me, then started walking back to the car, and then he disappeared in the darkness. "Oh yeah," I heard him say, even though I couldn't find him with my flashlight, "Janet, the older one, she loves cereal. She'd eat it three meals a day if we let her."

I told him, "I love cereal, too."

He said, "All right," and his footsteps got quieter and quieter.

I lowered myself into the hole and used my paintbrush to wipe away the dirt that was left.

One thing that surprised me was that the coffin was wet. I guess I wasn't expecting that, because how could so much water get underground?

Another thing that surprised me was that the coffin was cracked in a few places, probably from the weight of all that dirt. If Dad had been in there, ants and worms could have gotten in through the cracks and eaten him, or at least microscopic bacteria could have. I knew it shouldn't matter, because once you're dead, you don't feel anything. So why did it feel like it mattered?

Another thing that surprised me was how the coffin wasn't locked or even nailed shut. The lid just rested on top of it, so that anyone who wanted to could open it up. That didn't seem right. But on the other hand, who would want to open a coffin?

I opened the coffin.

I was surprised again, although again I shouldn't have been. I was surprised that Dad wasn't there. In my brain I knew he wouldn't be, obviously, but I guess my heart believed something else. Or maybe I was surprised by how incredibly empty it was. I felt like I was looking into the dictionary definition of emptiness.

I'd had the idea to dig up Dad's coffin the night after I met the renter. I was lying in bed and I had the revelation, like a simple solution to an impossible problem. The next morning I threw pebbles at the guest room window, like he wrote for me to in his note, but I'm not very accurate at throwing, so I had Stan do it. When the renter met me at the corner I told him my idea.

He wrote, "Why would you want to do that?" I told him, "Because it's the truth, and Dad loved the truth." "What truth?" "That he's dead."

After that, we met every afternoon and discussed the details, like we were planning a war. We talked about how we would get to the cemetery, and different ways of climbing fences, and where we would find a shovel, and all of the other necessary instruments, like a flashlight and wire cutters and juice boxes. We planned and planned, but for some reason we never talked about what we would actually do once we'd opened the coffin.

It wasn't until the day before we were going to go that the renter asked the obvious question.

I told him, "We'll fill it, obviously."

He asked another obvious question.

At first I suggested filling the coffin with things from Dad's life, like his red pens or his jeweler's magnifying glass, which is called a loupe, or even his tuxedo. I guess I got that idea from the Blacks who made museums of each other. But the more we discussed it, the less sense it made, because what good would that do, anyway? Dad wouldn't be able to use them, because he was dead, and the renter also pointed out that it would probably be nice to have things of his around.

"I could fill the coffin with jewelry, like they used to do with famous Egyptians, which I know about." "But he wasn't Egyptian." "And he didn't like jewelry." "He didn't like jewelry?"

"Maybe I could bury things I'm ashamed of," I suggested, and in my head I was thinking of the old telephone, and the sheet of stamps of Great American Inventors that I got mad at Grandma about, and the script of *Hamlet*, and the letters I had received from strangers, and the stupid card I'd made for myself, and my tambourine, and the unfinished scarf. But that didn't make any sense either, because the renter reminded me that just because you bury something, you don't really *bury* it. "Then what?" I asked.

"I have an idea," he wrote. "I'll show you tomorrow."

Why did I trust him so much?

The next night, when I met him on the corner at 11:50, he had two suitcases. I didn't ask him what was in them, because for some reason I thought I should wait until he told me, even though he was *my* dad, which made the coffin mine, too.

Three hours later, when I climbed into the hole, brushed away the dirt, and opened the lid, the renter opened the suitcases. They were filled with papers. I asked him what they were. He wrote, "I lost a son." "You did?" He showed me his left palm. "How did he die?" "I lost him before he died." "How?" "I went away." "Why?" He wrote, "I was afraid." "Afraid of what?" "Afraid of losing him." "Were you afraid of him dying?" "I was afraid of him living." "Why?" He wrote, "Life is scarier than death."

"So what's all that paper?"

He wrote, "Things I wasn't able to tell him. Letters."

To be honest, I don't know what I understood then.

I don't think I figured out that he was my grandpa, not even in the deep parts of my brain. I definitely didn't make the connection between the letters in his suitcases and the envelopes in Grandma's dresser, even if I should have.

But I must have understood something, I *must* have, because why else would I have opened my left hand?

When I got home it was 4:22 A.M. Mom was on the sofa by the door. I thought she would be incredibly angry at me, but she didn't say anything. She just kissed my head.

"Don't you want to know where I was?" She said, "I trust you."

"But aren't you curious?" She said, "I assume you'd tell me if you wanted me to know." "Are you going to tuck me in?" "I thought I'd stay here for a little while longer." "Are you mad at me?" She shook her head no. "Is Ron mad at me?" "No." "Are you sure?" "Yes."

I went to my room.

My hands were dirty, but I didn't wash them. I wanted them to stay dirty, at least until the next morning. I hoped some of the dirt would stay under my fingernails for a long time, and maybe some of the microscopic material would be there forever.

I turned off the lights.

I put my backpack on the floor, took off my clothes, and got into bed.

I stared at the fake stars.

What about windmills on the roof of every skyscraper?

What about a kite-string bracelet?

A fishing-line bracelet?

What if skyscrapers had roots?

What if you had to water skyscrapers, and play classical music to them, and know if they like sun or shade?

What about a teakettle?

I got out of bed and ran to the door in my undies.

Mom was still on the sofa. She wasn't reading, or listening to music, or doing anything.

She said, "You're awake."

I started crying.

She opened her arms and said, "What is it?"

I ran to her and said, "I don't want to be hospitalized."

She pulled me into her so my head was against the soft part of her shoulder, and she squeezed me. "You're not going to be hospitalized."

I told her, "I promise I'm going to be better soon."

She said, "There's nothing wrong with you."

"I'll be happy and normal."

She put her fingers around the back of my neck.

I told her, "I tried incredibly hard. I don't know how I could have tried harder."

She said, "Dad would have been very proud of you."

"Do you think so?"

"I know so."

I cried some more. I wanted to tell her all of the lies that I'd told her. And then I wanted her to tell me that it was OK, because sometimes you have to do something bad to do something good. And then I wanted to tell her about the phone. And then I wanted her to tell me that Dad still would have been proud of me.

She said, "Dad called me from the building that day."

I pulled away from her.

"What?"

"He called from the building."

"On your cell phone?"

She nodded yes, and it was the first time since Dad died that I'd seen her not try to stop her tears. Was she relieved? Was she depressed? Grateful? Exhausted?

"What did he say?"

"He told me he was on the street, that he'd gotten out of the building. He said he was walking home."

"But he wasn't."

"No."

Was I angry? Was I glad?

"He made it up so you wouldn't worry."

"That's right."

Frustrated? Panicky? Optimistic?

"But he knew you knew."

"He did."

I put my fingers around her neck, where her hair started.

I don't know how late it got.

I probably fell asleep, but I don't remember. I cried so much that everything blurred into everything else. At some point she was carrying me to my room. Then I was in bed. She was looking over me. I don't believe in God, but I believe that things are extremely complicated, and her looking over me was as complicated as anything ever could be. But it was also incredibly simple. In my only life, she was my mom, and I was her son.

I told her, "It's OK if you fall in love again."

She said, "I won't fall in love again."

I told her, "I want you to."

She kissed me and said, "I'll never fall in love again."

I told her, "You don't have to make it up so I won't worry."

She said, "I love you."

I rolled onto my side and listened to her walk back to the sofa.

I heard her crying. I imagined her wet sleeves. Her tired eyes.

One minute fifty-one seconds . . .

Four minutes thirty-eight seconds . . .

Seven minutes . . .

I felt in the space between the bed and the wall, and found *Stuff That Happened to Me*. It was completely full. I was going to have to start a new volume soon. I read that it was the paper that kept the towers burning. All of those notepads, and Xeroxes, and printed e-mails, and photographs of kids, and books, and dollar bills in wallets, and documents in files . . . all of them were fuel. Maybe if we lived in a paperless society, which lots of scientists say we'll probably live in one day soon, Dad would still be alive. Maybe I shouldn't start a new volume.

I grabbed the flashlight from my backpack and aimed it at the book. I saw maps and drawings, pictures from magazines and newspapers and the Internet, pictures I'd taken with Grandpa's camera. The whole world was in there. Finally, I found the pictures of the falling body.

Was it Dad?

Maybe.

Whoever it was, it was somebody.

I ripped the pages out of the book.

I reversed the order, so the last one was first, and the first was last.

When I flipped through them, it looked like the man was floating up through the sky.

And if I'd had more pictures, he would've flown through a window, back into the building, and the smoke would've poured into the hole that the plane was about to come out of.

Dad would've left his messages backward, until the machine was empty, and the plane would've flown backward away from him, all the way to Boston.

He would've taken the elevator to the street and pressed the button for the top floor.

He would've walked backward to the subway, and the subway would've gone backward through the tunnel, back to our stop.

Dad would've gone backward through the turnstile, then swiped his Metrocard backward, then walked home backward as he read the *New York Times* from right to left.

He would've spit coffee into his mug, unbrushed his teeth, and put hair on his face with a razor.

He would've gotten back into bed, the alarm would've rung backward, he would've dreamt backward.

Then he would've gotten up again at the end of the night before the worst day.

He would've walked backward to my room, whistling "I Am the Walrus" backward.

He would've gotten into bed with me.

We would've looked at the stars on my ceiling, which would've pulled back their light from our eyes.

I'd have said "Nothing" backward.

He'd have said "Yeah, buddy?" backward.

I'd have said "Dad?" backward, which would have sounded the same as "Dad" forward.

He would have told me the story of the Sixth Borough, from the voice in the can at the end to the beginning, from "I love you" to "Once upon a time . . ."

We would have been safe.